Dan Moren

THE ARMAGEDDON PROTOCOL

THE GALACTIC COLD WAR, BOOK IV

ANGRY
ROBOT

ANGRY ROBOT
An imprint of Watkins Media Ltd

Unit 11, Shepperton House
89 Shepperton Road
London N1 3DF
UK

angryrobotbooks.com
twitter.com/angryrobotbooks
This is where things start to get hairy.

An Angry Robot paperback original, 2024

Cover by Karen Smith
Edited by Robin Triggs and Andrew Hook
Set in Meridien

ISBN 978 1 91599 800 2
Ebook ISBN 978 1 91599 801 9

Printed and bound in the United Kingdom by CPI Group (UK) Ltd,
Croydon CR0 4YY.

9 8 7 6 5 4 3 2 1

MIX
Paper | Supporting
responsible forestry
FSC
www.fsc.org   FSC® C171272

For Atlas: Welcome to the family, kid.

CHAPTER 1

Rolling with the punches had always been Simon Kovalic's operating principle. Keeping your cool in the face of adversity was a key trait for any intelligence operative – it was the kind of thing that kept you alive in the field, or even just when dealing with the never-ending bureaucracy.

But in this exact moment, he had to admit to a deep temptation within himself to wipe the smug look off the face of Aidan Kester, newly installed acting director of the Commonwealth Intelligence Directorate.

Instead, Kovalic smoothed down his shirtfront, which Kester had recently gripped in a fit of pique, and attempted to restore his equanimity along with it.

It wasn't every day you got accused of treason.

"I don't know what you think you've accomplished," said Kester, his arch tone back in place as he carefully smoothed his slicked-back hair. He jutted his chin at the wisps of smoke still issuing from a terminal on the desk. Just moments ago, a command had melted the terminal's innards into slag. "I'm sure the Commonwealth Security Bureau's forensics team will have no trouble retrieving any incriminating information."

Behind the desk sat the issuer of said command, Kovalic's boss – and, if Kester was to be believed, co-conspirator – General Hasan al-Adaj. Hands steepled, the characteristic gleam in the general's eye was back in full force after the accusations hurled in his direction. "By all means, Director Kester. They are welcome to it, though I suspect the recyclers might be a more appropriate destination."

Kester flicked his fingers at the man behind him, indicating the terminal.

A pained look flashed across the face of Inspector Rashad Laurent as he stepped forward, ducking his head in the general's direction. "If you'd please move away from the desk, sir."

The impulse rose within Kovalic: move fast and with purpose. It was only Laurent and Kester; the former was the more formidable, but Kovalic suspected the Bureau agent's heart might not be entirely in it. He could probably incapacitate them both in short order, all he had to do was–

But in his peripheral vision he caught sight of two figures standing just outside the door to the general's office: a pair of marines, sidearms at their hips. A formality, perhaps, but not to be trifled with.

Kovalic forced himself to relax, let the tension ebb from his muscles. This wasn't a confrontation that was going to be won by violence – not right now, anyway. They were still deep within the Commonwealth Executive campus, and those marines would just be the first of many lines of defense.

"You said you have evidence that links us to the recent attacks on Commonwealth soil. I'd be *very* interested to see it," said Kovalic, pointedly not looking at the data chip that he himself had tossed on the general's desk not five minutes ago.

The data on that chip had been acquired over the course of several months by Kovalic's former team member Aaron Page: it showed a series of financial transactions originating on the banking hub of Bayern from accounts linked to the general. Those transactions had ultimately led to a domestic terrorist group, the Novan Liberation Front – the very organization that had only this past week bombed a communications hub in the Commonwealth capital and threatened further violence. Ultimately, Kovalic and his team had helped narrowly avert the worst of it, though somehow he didn't think that would do much to assuage Kester's suspicions.

Kovalic didn't believe in coincidences: Page's intelligence had led him to confront the general about the transactions, only to have that discussion cut short by the arrival of Kester and Laurent, who had accused *both* of them of treason against the Commonwealth.

He'd assumed Kester had the same banking records; the question was how the man had gotten ahold of them. Given that Page had at one point been Kester's informant, that might seem like a clear, logical path. But Page had come clean to Kovalic about his betrayal, and they had buried the hatchet. He wasn't the type to make the same mistake twice.

If anything, Kester's allegations only served to cast doubt on the intel. Kovalic had long harbored his own distrust of the new CID director, stemming from Kester's involvement with a mission on Caledonia that had gone south, plus the fact that he had turned Page to his own ends and seemed to have an axe to grind against the general. Much as Kester might seem like just another bureaucrat, he had demonstrated an expertise in twisting situations to his own advantage. So when he suddenly showed up with evidence of treason?

Convenient.

Still, given Kester's recent promotion, the situation didn't bode well for them – which only resurrected the impulse to wipe the smug look off the stuffed shirt's face.

"You'll have plenty of time to see the evidence at your trial," said Kester, his expression just one lip-curl short of a sneer. "We'll be arranging secure transport for you to a detention facility pending formal charges. Your security clearances, freedom to move about the compound, and network access are all hereby revoked. The inspector will check you for weapons."

Laurent's face turned carefully blank, though not fast enough that Kovalic didn't catch a look that said "oh, will I?" But the Bureau officer stepped forward anyway. "Arms out please, major."

Kovalic complied. It's not as if there was anything to find: the Executive compound had probably the highest security of anyplace onworld, and he hardly carried a weapon even when on active duty.

Laurent's frisk was quick and efficient and, once satisfied, he moved onto the general, who rose from behind his desk with the accompaniment of whines from the servos in his artificial legs. If anything, the general seemed amused and even a little bit flattered by the attention.

"They're clean," said Laurent, stepping back.

At a snap of Kester's fingers, the pair of marines filled the doorway: one, a hulking brute with pale skin and a crew cut, the other a woman with sharp eyes, her hair in dark cornrows. Both of them had an air of quiet competency that said they weren't just there for show.

Just beyond the pair Kovalic caught sight of the general's aide, Rance, who was watching the two marines with a contemplative look.

"I suppose we might as well make ourselves comfortable, then," said the general. "Can I offer anybody a coffee? Tea? I'm afraid my bar is not particularly well stocked."

Kovalic wouldn't have thought the proffering of beverages the kind of thing to set one off, but the simmering ire beneath Kester's facade broke through nonetheless. "Sit down, Adaj. We don't want anything from you."

Laurent looked as though he might disagree; the shadows under his eyes said he could use a coffee. But he kept it to himself.

A gentle shrug rippled across the general's shoulders as he lowered himself back into his chair. "Apologies for the hospitality."

"You'll be getting a taste of hospitality soon enough," Kester sneered. "The hole they're going to throw you into is going to be so deep and dark that even you will forget you ever existed. The only question is which one of you will have it worse: the Illyrican defector who turned out to be a double agent..." His eyes lingered on the general before sliding to Kovalic, "...or the war hero who has been providing aid and comfort to the enemy he supposedly swore to fight." His smile turned sharp. "At least you'll have company when we drag in your whole team – unless, of course, they decide to save their own skins by testifying against you. I'm sure at least one of them would like to keep enjoying sunlight and fresh air for the rest of their lives."

For the first time since Kester had stepped into the general's office, Kovalic's spirits rose. From what he knew of the man's dossier, the acting director hadn't spent much time in the field – he'd come up as a desk officer in the intelligence directorate and made his way to the top more through political acumen and connections than personal experience.

It showed.

"What are you grinning at?" Kester snapped at him. "You think this is funny, Kovalic? Treason's a laughing matter?"

He hadn't even been conscious of the smile on his face, but he really poured it on as he took a seat on the edge of the general's desk, arms crossed over his chest. "I get it. As first days on the job go, this is a tough one. By my count, you've already made at least two serious mistakes."

Kester's brow darkened. "What the devil are you talking about?"

"You said '*when* we drag in your whole team'."

"What of it?"

Kovalic spread his hands. "That means you haven't got them yet." He shook his head. "Sloppy. Always make sure your arrests are timed – Inspector Laurent would agree, I'm sure."

The Bureau agent's expression of thinly veiled amusement was quickly wiped away by a look that definitively said "leave me out of this".

Kester gritted his teeth. "You should concern yourself with your own situation. We'll have all your colleagues in custody soon enough."

"Maybe. Anyway, that was just your first mistake – and the less serious one, if I'm going to be honest."

"Oh? Do enlighten me."

"I think you'll find you owe us each a call."

Kester laughed. "Finally, something sensible. I hope you've got a hell of an attorney."

"Oh, I'm not calling my lawyer. I just need to tell my wife that I'm going to be late for lunch."

CHAPTER 2

The formal offer had come through mid-morning. Nat had seen the subject line in her inbox but had read through every other message first, until only the single unwinking eye of a blue unread indicator had remained.

Reading would make it real. Up until then, it was merely a hypothetical, one that she could ponder in an abstract manner – a "what if" that rivaled her occasional dalliances into sketching out plans for a nice retirement cottage outside Nova's capital city. But the second she opened the message, it was a fact. One that meant decisions would have to be made.

After lunch. She wanted to talk with Simon anyway; she still wasn't sure what he'd make of this.

She'd be lying if she said she wasn't conflicted. Like she'd told him a few months back, she missed being out in the field. Her recent trip home to Centauri, complicated as it had been, had only reinforced that feeling. But there was only so far you could go in your career without moving behind a desk.

She was still mulling it over as she swiped her military ID and passed through the checkpoint at the Commonwealth Executive building. Even without her uniform, the armed security guards barely spared her a glance. Not that there was any reason to: they'd see her picture and vitals onscreen – Lieutenant Commander Natalie Taylor, Commonwealth Naval Intelligence Command. She'd spent enough time briefing people in the complex that she'd been given permanent clearance, instead of having to register as a visitor every time she came and went.

The holographic clock hanging in the atrium told her she was half an hour early. With time to kill, she strolled towards the gardens that occupied the central part of the complex. Nova's climate veered towards the sub-tropical and the eco-landscapers had taken advantage of the enormous open space – a quarter-mile in diameter – to cultivate a variety of native flora, providing a shady retreat for those on their breaks or just looking to hold a meeting outdoors.

Plus they had a pretty good coffee stand.

With a latte in hand, she circulated around the perimeter of the gardens, the dirt path scuffing beneath her shoes, little clouds rising in her wake. Well, this was silly. What point was there in waiting, when she knew exactly what the message said anyway? Might as well read it and get it over with.

Settling down on one of the benches next to the path, she took a deep breath and opened her inbox, finger hovering over the unread message. Her eyes ran over the tantalizing preview below the subject: *Lieutenant Commander Taylor, we're pleased to formally offer you the position of chief of staff…*

The smart fabric display of her sleeve blanked suddenly, its haptics squeezing her forearm as the entire display was overwritten by an alert bearing a single word, screaming in all caps.

ESCHATON.

The breath already caught in her chest expelled outwards with such force that it almost sounded like she'd huffed a deep laugh. Blood roared in her ears so ferociously that for a moment she thought the garden had been buzzed by a low flying aircraft.

ESCHATON? Here? Now?

Her head came up, eyes already searching the immediate vicinity, half expecting to see armed security closing in, but there was nobody.

Didn't mean they weren't coming, though.

Nat forced herself into calm, regulating her breathing. Casual. Stay casual.

Getting to her feet as though she'd just noticed the time, she strolled around the perimeter of the garden back towards the main lobby. But she couldn't quiet her mind, which ran through a series of conclusions at speed.

The ESCHATON signal didn't exactly come with details attached, but Simon had briefed her on it as part of her onboarding to the Special Projects Team. In any operational situation, it meant to abort without delay: Break all contact, walk away, ditch any trackable technology, and regroup at a predefined rendezvous point.

It wasn't a signal she'd ever expected to receive on the Commonwealth capital world, which meant that the shit had truly hit the ion engine.

Simon had also explained that it took both him and the general to authorize its use. And they were supposed to be in a meeting right now, just steps away.

She quickened her pace, even as her brain reminded her that throwing herself into harm's way was the exact opposite of the signal's intent.

Circling back through the garden, she returned to the front lobby – and the choice that lay before her. By all rights, following the ESCHATON protocol meant making a beeline right back through the security gates and catching the first transportation option that put as much distance between her and this building as possible.

Or she could turn left, towards the general's office.

Towards Simon.

It ought to be a no-brainer: she couldn't help Simon – or anybody else – if she was compromised too. But somehow those feeble protestations were beside the point; her feet had already sent her veering leftwards.

She collided almost instantly with a marine lieutenant coming in the other direction, the latte Nat had been carrying sloshing all over the decorations and ID badge clipped to the other woman's chest.

"Oh shit," said Nat, "I'm so sorry!"

The lieutenant stared down at the rapidly spreading stain. "Watch where you're going!"

"I'm such a klutz, so sorry. I don't know where my head's at," said Nat, producing a crumpled napkin from one pocket and attempting to dab at the dark patch, flipping up the lieutenant's ID badge to get at the damp shirt beneath. "I just got turned down for a promotion, and I don't know *what* I'm going to tell my husband. We'd really been counting on this job to have enough to start a family and…"

Inwardly, Nat breathed a sigh of relief that she hadn't worn her uniform; otherwise, the lieutenant probably would have bit her tongue and insist that somehow she'd spilled the coffee all over herself rather than blame it on a superior officer. Instead, the woman's expression softened

– still annoyed, mind you, but curtailed with a sigh of resignation. "Look, it's OK. I've got a spare jacket in my office. I'm sure it'll come out in the wash."

Nat's eyes glimmered with unshed tears and she pressed the already sodden napkin into the other woman's hand. "Are you sure? Let me at least pay for the cleaning."

The lieutenant waved a hand. "Don't worry about it. Sounds like you've got enough on your plate already. Just... good luck."

With a sigh, the lieutenant turned down another corridor, blotting at the stain as she went.

Nat watched her go, then clipped the ID she'd lifted to her own jacket. The badges were trackable as long as you were on campus and they were tied to the owner's biometrics. So as soon as the lieutenant tried to swipe into her office, she'd realize that she inexplicably had a stranger's badge clipped to her chest instead.

In other words, Nat didn't have long.

She double-timed it down the hallway and slowly wriggled her sleeve off her left forearm, wadding it up as she went. When a cleaning drone pushing a full wastebasket trundled past, she slipped it into the trash bin and continued on her way.

A couple minutes later, having wound her way through several twists and turns until she found herself well off the main thoroughfare, she rounded a corner to the corridor where the general's office sat.

It took all her presence of mind not to draw up short at the sight of an armed marine posted outside the door, hands clasped in front of him. The door itself was open and she slowed as she walked past, displaying the idle curiosity of the passerby.

She caught a glimpse of Rance, the general's aide, sitting at her desk in a daze. But then the yeoman's eyes met hers and sharpened, like a knife slashing through a curtain, and the other woman gave a barely perceptible shake of her head.

Nat's eyes flicked past, through the open doorway to the general's inner office, hoping for even a sliver of a view of Simon, just to reassure herself that he was all right. But two other armed guards blocked the way.

Then, just as she couldn't linger any further, they parted for the briefest of moments, and she spotted a familiar figure in a very expensive worsted gray suit.

Aidan Kester.

She almost faltered, but managed to catch herself, passing it off as though she'd tripped over her own feet while not watching where she was going. Shaking her head, she continued on her way, not slowing until she'd rounded the next corner.

Stupid. This whole detour had been stupid, and unlike her. Some fanciful part of her mind had envisioned plowing into the office, incapacitating several marines along the way – she could see how it would be done: a punch to an unprotected windpipe here, an elbow to the solar plexus there – and dragging Simon out with her.

But Rance's silent warning had put her straight: that idea was self-indulgent at best and dangerously foolish at worst. At least someone was thinking clearly.

With Simon and the general behind her, she shifted their plight to the back burner. There was nothing to be done for them now. Front sight focus: deal with the problems ahead of her, the ones she could solve.

After all, she wasn't the only one who'd be receiving the ESCHATON signal, and the rest of them were going to need all the help they could get.

CHAPTER 3

The sun beamed lazily through the waving branches of the tree and in through the windows of the loft, directly into Adelaide Sayers's eyes.

Oh come on. What goddamn time is it?

After the events of the past day – space walks, zero-g combat, bomb disposal – she could have slept for a million years, a fact her body was quick to remind her as she rolled over in bed and all her muscles issued a unified chorus of complaints.

At least Kovalic had put them all on leave for the week. She was lucky that none of her injuries were worse than a few bruises and pulled muscles. Nothing that some stretching, a hot shower, and some breakfast wouldn't cure.

Even as the thought of the last percolated through her mind she caught a whiff of something cooking downstairs, accompanied by the sizzle of fat on a skillet.

One arm flailed out, patting the spot in the bed where there should have been a warm body but finding only a molehill of rumpled covers. Not that long ago, that would have spiked her pulse, spun her out: abandoned, on her own again.

But she was pleasantly surprised to find something else

in her chest that wasn't a knot of icy fear. Instead, it was… peaceful contentment? Maybe it was because she could hear – and smell – him puttering downstairs in the kitchen, sense that he hadn't left her. Instead, he'd let her sleep in while he made breakfast.

Wait… does he know how to make breakfast?

Addy stifled a laugh and rolled over to plant her face in the pillow, enjoying the brief smothering of warmth. A toasty bed, breakfast cooking, the luxurious anticipation of a day with nothing to do; it shouldn't be this mind-blowing, but it kind of was. What more could she ask–

A sharp buzz rattled her bedside table and she sighed and rolled over, hand grasping for the spot where she'd shed her sleeve last night. Her hand hit the pile of smart fabric but it slithered from her grasp onto the floor.

With a roll of her eyes, she leaned over the edge of the bed. The sleeve was puddled on the carpet, an alert splashed across it in large letters, unreadable in its crumpled-up state. She smoothed it out, not quite ready to face the intrusion of the real world yet.

The light glinting from outside caught her in the eyes again and she put up a hand to block it, frowning. *Geez, how sunny is it today?* She peered through the window. It was almost like it was reflecting off something, but there shouldn't be anything out there…

Deep within her, some animal instinct flared and she was already rolling off the bed as the window on the other side shattered into a million fragments.

It was followed almost immediately by an individual in black tactical gear, swinging in through the now gaping opening.

What the fuck?!

Her brain was still processing exactly what it was seeing, but that didn't matter, because her body had gone into autopilot.

There was a knockout gun in the nightstand, but it would take too much time to open the drawer and pull it out, and the trooper who had burst in was already detaching their repelling line and reaching for a lancer carbine hanging from a strap across their shoulders.

So instead, Addy picked herself up off the floor and launched herself across the bed, using the mattress's bounce to propel her straight into the torso of the figure, who didn't seem to be expecting much resistance from someone in pajamas.

The loft was narrow – there were only a couple of feet of clearance around the bed – so the two of them slammed into the wall with some force, knocking them both into a heap on the floor.

Close quarters. Minimize the advantage of body armor and neutralize an unwieldy weapon. Addy's combat training had fully taken over and, as the trooper struggled against her, she dug a forearm into their unarmored throat, pressing their own helmet strap back against their windpipe. She couldn't see their face, hidden behind a black balaclava and goggles, but she recognized the gear well enough – it was the same worn by the security officers she'd tangled with on two separate rooftops in the past few days.

CID's joint task force goons? I thought we were done with this!

There wasn't time to worry about that, though, as a second crash came from behind her and another trooper swung through the window on the side of the bed she'd recently vacated.

Shit shit shit.

She wrestled the carbine from the grasp of the trooper she had pinned, who was flailing at her with the urgency of someone who couldn't breathe, and drove the butt of the gun into their face. There was a thud as their head rebounded inside their helmet, and if they weren't unconscious they were at least reeling from the hit.

Addy rolled to one side, trying to bring the carbine to bear on the new assailant, but it was still attached to the trooper on the floor and the strap snapped taut before she could aim it in the right direction.

Which wasn't great, because the second goon had skipped their bigger weapon in favor of going for a KO gun at their waist, clearly opting to incapacitate both her and their colleague and let god sort it out later.

Addy flopped onto her back and kicked out with both legs at the bed frame, knocking it into the other trooper's legs. They issued a muffle curse of pain and Addy, who had banged her own shins on it more times than she could count, spared all of a nanosecond of sympathy before pressing her advantage, vaulting back over the bed and trying to kick them in the stomach.

Unfortunately for her, the body armor over the abdomen meant it was much better protected. It took the force of her kick in stride and, honestly, hurt her foot a bit. The trooper took a step backward, slightly off balance, but seemed otherwise no worse for wear.

Guess I should have slept in my boots.

Scrambling backwards on the bed, Addy pushed the blankets aside, looking for something harder than a pillow to chuck at the trooper.

Finding nothing, she went for the pillow.

It bought her a second, just enough time to see the first trooper getting to their feet, coughing and wheezing from her ministrations as they stumbled towards the foot of the bed.

And right at the top of the stairs.

Sorry about this – well, not really. Even as the trooper she'd thrown the pillow at batted it aside, she was leaping off the bed, knees pointed right at the chest of the first trooper, who probably looked pretty surprised under their balaclava.

She hit them with a solid thud, tipping them backwards onto the floor and sliding them to the top of the stairs. They flailed for a fraction of a moment, and then they were going backwards down the stairs, Addy atop their chest like they were a sled careening down a snowy hill.

The trooper's helmet *thump thump thumped* against the wooden stairs, and Addy leaned backwards, shifting her center of balance to prevent herself from flying off, head over heels. They rattled downward at a surprisingly speedy pace, jarring Addy's teeth so hard that she thought she might have bitten her tongue, but the pain didn't register through the adrenaline haze.

Hitting the bottom with a muted groan from the trooper, Addy pitched out across their full length. She lay still for a second, catching her breath.

I could stay here. This would be fine.

No such luck. Behind her she heard the telltale whine of a KO gun charging – the trooper's partner was still at the top of the stairs, and they were already in position, lining up a shot at Addy's back.

Never a dull moment. With a grunt, she rolled over, using all of her leverage to put her trooper/makeshift sled between her and the incoming shot.

The other goon had already pulled the trigger, and a stun field washed over the two of them, mostly absorbed by the mass of the trooper atop her – she could tell because she was suddenly trapped under two-hundred-some pounds of dead weight that was slowly compressing the air out of her lungs. The edge of the field nicked her too, her vision swimming slightly as though she'd had too much to drink.

Oh, fuck. Good plan, Addy.

Her breath wheezed as she pawed at the trooper, trying to shove him off. She could deadlift two hundred pounds, but she generally didn't try it after several bourbons. Gasping for air, she tried to stave off the black creeping in around the edges of her vision.

Where the fuck is Brody? The thought suddenly popped into her head just as the smell of bacon reached her nostrils.

But she had more pressing concerns. Through the haze she could see the second trooper coming down the stairs, weapon still leveled at her.

The carbine from the goon atop her was jammed in between them, the strap snug around the trooper's chest. Addy fought with it, but there was no way she'd be able to get it loose, much less aimed anywhere useful.

As she wrestled with it, her hand brushed something else on the trooper's belt: a small, squat cylinder.

A feral grin crossed Addy's face as she unclipped it from the belt. She knew the shape well enough by feel, her thumb sliding across the ridges to find the activation stud, which she held for the requisite three seconds as a muffled beep sounded.

The other trooper, seeing her already trapped beneath their unconscious colleague, had apparently decided not to try stunning her again. She had to time this just right or she'd probably be waking up in a cell somewhere, and once this week had been enough for her.

When the trooper was about halfway down the stairs, she moved. Using all her strength, she rolled the goon off far enough to free her right arm and lobbed the cylinder towards their partner.

They seemed startled to see the projectile describing a pleasant arc toward them, and some weird innate response kicked in as they caught it in their free hand, then stared at it blankly for a second before realizing that holding a live concussion grenade was not recommended procedure.

Addy, for her part, curled up beneath the goon, who'd already proved an adequate shield once. At least if they were already unconscious, the grenade probably wouldn't do them any more damage.

The *whump* of the explosion was loud, even from beneath the body, and what little air she had left in her lungs was squeezed out as the concussion wave pressed the dead weight down on her even further.

But it was all over a moment later, except for the slow bumping of the trooper on the stairs, sliding down the rest of the flight to puddle in a heap next to their colleague.

Addy rocked back and forth and pushed with all her might, rolling the body off of her. Blessed air rushed into her lungs. Dragging herself to her feet, she was still gathering her wits when, behind her, the front door splintered with the loud bang of a battering ram.

Come the fuck on.

She spun around even as a third black-suited trooper stormed in the door, carbine pointed in her direction. They had her dead to rights. Her hands went up, even as her mind raced, looking for some way out.

"Get on the fucking grou – urgh." A sound like a gong cut their command short as they crumpled to the floor atop the blue-and-white throw rug that she hated.

Where they'd been standing a moment earlier was a bizarre, but Addy had to admit, oddly attractive, sight: Eli Brody, clad only in boxer shorts and a grungy shirt, stood holding a frying pan. He was looking at the floor, his expression surprisingly forlorn.

"Aw, man. My bacon!"

Addy's breath heaved and she stared at him. "Where the fuck have you been?"

He jerked a thumb over his shoulder at the kitchenette. "I was cooking breakfast."

"Did you not hear the pitched combat going on above your head?"

Abashed, he raised his other hand, which held a small white pebble. "Uh, so, it turns out these noise-canceling earbuds work way better than I thought." He nudged the unconscious trooper in front of him with a bare foot. "Who the hell are these guys?"

Addy reached down and unclipped the carbine from their chest, checked its loadout: shock gel rounds. So at least they hadn't been aiming to kill them. "I don't know, but they sure look like Kester's task force goons."

"Again? I thought that all got cleared up."

"Apparently not," said Addy. As the blood rushing in

her ears subsided, she suddenly heard an insistent buzzing from the direction of the kitchen counter. "What's that?"

"Huh? Oh, I think it's my sleeve," said Brody. "I don't wear it when I'm cooking – you know how hard it is to get bacon grease out of smart fabric?"

Addy rolled her eyes and walked over to the counter, grabbing the pile of cloth that, despite Brody's protestations, was still a bit slick. Unease settled in her gut as she spread it out on the countertop, remembering the message she hadn't had time to read on her own sleeve upstairs, right before everything had gone to shit.

"Eschaton," said Addy, her mouth dry. "Fuck."

"Eska–wha?" Brody repeated before his eyes widened in recognition. "Come on, that's got to be a mistake, right?"

Addy jutted her chin at the unconscious trio of goons. "Sure feels like the end of the fucking world." She balled up the smart fabric in one hand. "We need to go."

"Go? Right now? I mean… I did cook breakfast… "

But Addy was already moving, tearing the pilot's sleeve into shreds over his protestations. She jogged over to the stairs, ignoring the pile of unconscious troopers, and grabbed the third step from the bottom, then yanked upwards.

"What are you –" Brody blinked as the stair came up in her hands. "Well, so much for my security deposit."

Addy ignored him, pulling out two small duffel bags. Unzipping one, she removed a KO gun and checked the charge. *Eighty percent. It'll have to do*. She slung it over her shoulder and then tossed the other duffel to Brody, who caught it with a confused expression.

"What's this?"

"It's your go bag."

"Uhh... my what? And how long has it been in my stairs?"

Crossing to the troopers, Addy pulled a pair of quick cuffs off one of their belts and looped one around each of their wrists. Then she thought for a second and, with a shrug, took the pair off the other's belt and attached their other wrists. That'll keep them busy.

"Kovalic asked me to prep it for you – he didn't want to worry you."

"Worry me? About what?"

Addy stared him and then gestured around her at the trio of unconscious figures.

"Fair point," said Brody.

"Now, come on, flyboy – we don't have all day. There's no way these guys don't have backup."

Brody looked down at his skinny, pale legs. "I don't suppose there's pants in here?" he asked hopefully, raising the go bag. "Or, I dunno, maybe that guy's my size..." He eyed the trooper Addy had just cuffed.

Collecting the carbines and KO guns from the trio of troopers, Addy tested the triggers, but they all appeared to be biometrically locked to their owners. She slid them across the floor into the kitchenette. Won't stop them, but it'll slow them down.

"Never mind the pants," said Addy, regretting it immediately. "Does your skimmer have a full charge?"

"Sure."

"Good. Then get your butt to the garage and let's get moving. Unless you want to end up in another windowless room?"

"Right," said Brody. He started towards the garage, still holding the duffel bag between his hands. "Uh, where are we going?"

"There's a rendezvous point," said Addy. "We'll meet the rest of the team there and figure out what the fuck is happening."

Brody's eyes darted to the heap of troopers and Addy found, to her mild dismay, she could tell exactly what he was thinking. "Don't worry, Brody. Kovalic, Taylor, Tapper... they know what they're doing. They'll be fine."

I hope.

CHAPTER 4

Fighting off armed interlopers was not how Eli Brody had seen his morning going. He'd been looking forward to a nice leisurely breakfast with his – girlfriend? lady friend? special friend? *Ugh, those are all terrible* – and then maybe vegging out on the couch with the latest season of that baking show. After the week they'd just had – dealing with Page's reappearance, Nova Front's bombings, and stopping an ex-CID operative from completely destabilizing the Commonwealth – he was aiming for something that didn't require a lot of thought. And if they found themselves back in bed at some point, well, there was nothing wrong with that.

The wind whipped past Eli as he wove the skimmer through Salaam's early morning traffic.

Should he be shivering? He felt like he should be shivering. His t-shirt was full of holes, and the hair on his bare legs was standing up, but if anything he still felt vaguely flushed.

Hello adrenaline, my old friend. The let-down was going to suck, but for the moment, his heart was still pumping double time, his perception widening to encompass all the obstacles around them. Sparing a glance for the rearview camera hovering on the inside of his helmet, he checked to see if there was anyone following them, but if they were, it wasn't with lights and sirens blaring.

Behind him, Addy leaned forward, consolidating their weight to help Eli lean into the turns as the skimmer zipped between a pair of hovertrucks. Her warmth bled through the pajamas they were both still wearing. The go bags – now strapped to the skimmer's rear rack – hadn't contained a change of clothes, so they were going to stick out like a sore thumb until they found something less, well, bedroom to wear.

But given that the priorities had been survival and freedom, Eli was OK with that for the moment.

A blip appeared on his heads-up, followed by a series of blinking arrows telling him to take the next exit. To where, he still wasn't sure, but Addy had provided coordinates for the rendezvous point.

Which nobody bothered to tell me *about.* He couldn't summon much anger about it; this was last-ditch emergency stuff. The kind of thing that everybody hoped they'd never have to use, especially on their own home planet. Besides, he hardly had the same combat training as the rest of the team. If Addy hadn't been there this morning, he hesitated to think where he'd have ended up. Probably with yet another bag over his head. That was a streak he was pretty happy to break.

He followed the exit ramp up and around the cloverleaf and on to the surface streets. Eli hadn't been to this particular part of suburban Salaam before, but at first glance it seemed like one of the more upscale neighborhoods. Verdant streets were shaded in bowers of trees, forming a canopy high above. Stately homes stood on impressive lots, most behind walls and security gates.

"Nice digs," he said over the local comm link.

Addy's voice crackled back into his ears. "Yeah. When I was a kid we avoided Friede; it's the kind of place where the cops show up if you even look like you might be thinking about how much money is behind those doors."

"I'll tell my imagination to take five, then."

Following the map on his HUD took them down a long boulevard, then through a traffic circle and into a large park. The signs by the entrance mentioned a number of attractions, including sporting fields, a golf course, and a zoo. *We have a zoo? Who knew?*

But the map instead led him to a long, impressive building made mostly of glass, with a central dome and wings extending to either side. He pulled into an open parking spot and powered down the skimmer, then pulled off his helmet.

"Ismail Park Conservatory," Eli said, reading the sign by the entrance. He looked down at his boxer shorts. "I hope they don't have a dress code."

"You're wearing a shirt and shoes," said Addy, stowing her helmet in the skimmer's storage compartment. "They can't complain."

Eli looked down at the ratty shoes that he'd grabbed on their way out the door. He'd been meaning to get rid of them, but at least they were worn-in and comfortable. Not as much so as the beloved boots that he'd had for ten years, but close. He tugged his shirt down in a pathetic attempt to hide the most egregious holes and tried to walk into the place like he belonged there, exuding the air that a tattered shirt and boxer shorts was just the latest style. Maybe it was. Who was he to judge?

The gray-haired man behind the welcome desk gave him

a hard look, but Addy waved over a generous amount that was roughly four times the voluntary admission fee and he seemed to rethink his stance, pointing them in the direction of the self-guided tour's start.

The first room featured enormous tropical plants native to Nova, some of them with thick green, glossy leaves the size of Eli's torso. A fresh, sharp vegetative scent pervaded the whole area, reminding him of a cross between pine and eucalyptus. At this hour, it was otherwise pretty empty, with only one other figure, wearing a brimmed cap pulled low, peering at the plaques next to the flora with an interest that bordered on the prurient.

"Look, these are... impressive. But is this really the best time to be looking at plants?" whispered Eli.

"Just keeping walking," said Addy, taking his arm. "Pretend you're interested."

"Well, I am interested. Who wouldn't be?" said Eli. "Just, you know, not my highest priority at this exact moment. Sorry, plants."

They stepped into the next room, which was overflowing with ferns. Eli had to brush through the fronds to walk down the aisle, and they practically blocked the light coming in from the glass roof overhead.

The hair on the back of Eli's neck went up as he sensed the person from the first room trailing them. *Oh shit.* His muscles tensed, ready to run, when a familiar voice, pitched at a low murmur, reached him.

"Anyone follow you?" asked Natalie Taylor.

Addy, for her part, seemed utterly unsurprised; clearly she'd already recognized the commander on the way in. In Eli's defense, he hadn't even gotten to eat his breakfast.

"We're clean."

Taylor didn't reply, just stepped up to a plant and leaned over to smell it.

"Is anybody going to explain what's happening?" asked Eli, looking back and forth between the two women. "Why are those goons breaking into our home? And at such an unreasonable hour?"

"I don't know all the details," said Taylor. "But I trust Simon not to invoke ESCHATON protocol without a hell of a good reason."

"Speaking of which," said Eli, craning his neck. "Where is Kovalic? Looking at hothouse orchids?" The conservatory was still empty, save for the three of them. "And Tapper for that matter? He loves a good clandestine meeting." *Although he really prefers it if he can blow them up.*

Taylor stiffened, then made an effort to visibly relax her shoulders. "I don't know the sergeant's whereabouts, but Simon..." She took a breath. "Kester already has him. And the general."

Eli stopped short.

"*What?*" His voice reverberated off the glass, echoing back at him. "What the hell are we doing wandering through the jungle then? We need to go get them."

He turned on his heel, towards the entrance, but Addy grabbed his arm.

"That's a negative," said Taylor quietly, but her eyes didn't meet his. "ESCHATON protocol is to rendezvous and then exfil as soon as possible."

"Exfil? But this is Nova, not some backwater moon. We live here."

"Those are our orders, lieutenant."

"Fuck that. Kovalic wouldn't leave us behind."

Taylor's exhalation was sharp, her jaw tight. "Don't you think I know that? You think I don't want to go in and extract him?" Another indrawn breath and her characteristic calm settled over her once again. "We can't help him if they arrest us too. So we follow protocol, get offworld, and regroup. Understood?"

Addy's hand tightened around his arm and Eli spared a glance to see her shake her head. In that moment, the impulse ebbed out of him. Jesus, Taylor's his wife. If she can control her emotions, so can you.

"OK. What's our next move?"

"Transport," said Taylor, and Eli could see her relief that they were all on the same page.

"Commercial spaceports are going to be under close surveillance," said Addy, releasing Eli's arm. "Cargo lines too, probably. We could take a gravtrain out of the city... maybe even to the southern continent. Probably lower security there? Or lay low for a few days and then try to get out."

"They'll be locking everything down," said Taylor. "We stay put, we're mice in the trap."

Eli cleared his throat. "This might be a dumb idea, but what about the *Cavalier*?"

Two pairs of eyes turned on him, both incredulous.

"You mean our ship? The one in a hangar on a military base?" said Addy.

"I said it might be dumb! Look, the way I see it, it's the last thing they'll be expecting. If they're focused on locking down commercial and cargo spaceports, then military bases might not be high priority. Plus, we have a way better chance of getting out on our own ship then trying to navigate spaceport security with whatever un-compromised IDs we have."

Addy sighed. "Brody, you've had a lot of stupid ideas –"

"Actually, I don't hate it," said Taylor. "He's right that walking into any spaceport will leave us boxed in. But we'll need to move fast."

"What about Tapper?" said Eli.

The commander shook her head. "We can't afford to wait. The sergeant's been doing this a long time. Either he'll catch up or…"

"Or he's already been arrested," Eli finished her thought. *Although if they only send three guys for him, I wish them luck.*

They wound their way to the nearest exit, passing through a room of transplanted Earth flora and even a couple plants native to Eli's home of Caledonia, then back out to the parking lot. Eli headed towards his skimmer, but Taylor instead waved him towards a hovercar parked nearby.

"Better if we all stick together," she said, then looked both of them up and down. "Also you'll stand out a little bit less in a car. Sayers, I think I've got a jacket that will fit you. Brody… uh… just put a blanket over your legs maybe?"

"Oh yeah, that will look totally normal."

I knew I should have taken those pants off that guy.

Addy retrieved their go bags from the skimmer, at which Eli cast one last longing glance before piling into the car. *I know, I know – I just got you all tuned up! I'll come back for you, I promise.*

Tactical driving was no doubt something they taught in special ops training, but Taylor did something far more impressive on their way to Yamanaka Base: she drove perfectly normally. No speeding, no running lights, nothing that would garner any attention. If anything, it made Eli even tenser than being in a high-speed chase; his hands started twitching like they wanted to be on a steering yoke.

Fifteen minutes later, they were swinging around the perimeter of the airfield to the direct-access gate that the team habitually used. It was smaller and lower-traffic than the main entrance to the base, but still had a guard booth and a heavy-duty boom barrier.

This is where things start to get hairy.

They'd discussed their options on the ride over and come up with a plan and a contingency. First, they'd just attempt to bluff their way in with their usual military IDs. That was banking on traditional military inefficiency; hopefully the gate guards wouldn't have gotten the memo about their credentials being revoked yet. Those kinds of things took a while to wend their way through the bureaucracy; plus, civilian intelligence and the military had plenty of internecine squabbles that slowed down the free flow of information.

The backup plan was a KO gun at close range and running like hell.

Eli's blood started pumping overtime as they pulled up towards the gate, then spiked as he saw that there were two figures in the security booth instead of the usual one. "Uhhh... do we abort?"

"Too late," said Taylor as one of them looked up and waved them forward. "Everybody get ready."

There was a whine as Taylor charged the knockout gun and held it low, behind the car door. In the passenger seat, Addy did her best to look as relaxed as someone wearing a borrowed jacket over pajamas could.

And here I am, sitting in the backseat with a blanket over my lap like an eighteenth century invalid.

The sentry at the booth, who Eli recognized as one of the usuals on rotation, put up a hand for them to stop. Behind him, the second figure was fiddling with a piece of equipment, their back to them.

"Afternoon, commander," said the guard, leaning down. "How are you today?"

Taylor's smile seemed genuine, not an ounce of insincerity behind it. "Morning, Jasper. Doing just fine. How about yourself?"

Jasper sighed, throwing up his hands and producing a tablet. "Oh, comms are on the fritz. So we're doing things the old fashioned way today." He jerked a thumb over his shoulder at the other figure. "Your man's been trying to give me a hand. Any luck, sarge?"

There was the hissing spit of an electrical circuit and the figure jerked, shaking out their hand. "Bloody hell." A familiar weathered face glanced over his shoulder, grimacing, and Eli's heart almost stopped in his chest. "Oh, hey, commander. Nah, Jas, I think this thing's dead. You're going to have to get a tech out to look at it. I'll catch a ride in with them and call it in when I get to the hangar."

Jasper sighed. "Just my luck. Well, thanks for trying, Tap. Here, let me just sign you all in."

Eli held his breath as the sentry slowly and methodically

took all their military IDs and copied the information down on the tablet.

Tapper, meanwhile, dusted off his hands, clapped Jasper on the shoulder, and squeezed out of the booth. He hopped into the backseat alongside Eli, his brows knitting at the red plaid blanket. "It's like 24 degrees, Brody. You cold?"

"…Yes?"

The sergeant shook his head. "Sure, whatever."

As Jasper finally returned their IDs and waved them on base, Eli let out a long breath.

Taylor fixed a glance on Tapper via the rearview, raising an eyebrow. "Communications problem, sergeant?"

"Oh, yeah. Problem is I unplugged the transceiver. Then it was just a matter of making sure he was distracted – and trust me, that's no hard sell where Jasper's concerned. Get him started on the Dynamos' season and he'll take care of the rest himself."

"How'd you know even know we'd be here?" said Addy.

"I didn't," said Tapper with a shrug. "I was already on base when I saw the ESCHATON signal and figured you'd be trying to get out in a hurry. Seemed like the least I could do. Another twenty minutes and I would have bailed." His eyes gleamed. "Probably."

He glanced around. "Where's the boss?"

Eli's breath caught in his throat and he met Taylor's eyes in the rearview. *Tapper's worked with Kovalic for a long time – if anybody's going to insist we go after the major, it'll be him.*

"Taken," said Taylor, her voice clipped. "By Kester and his goons."

Tapper's mouth settled into a hard line. "We getting him back?"

"After we get offworld. We'll figure it out."

The atmosphere in the car felt like it was filled with explosive gas, just waiting for a spark. But after a moment, Tapper let out a long breath and it depressurized. "Right, then. Let's hop to it. Sooner we're gone, sooner we're back."

CHAPTER 5

The good news was that there was only so long that even Aidan Kester could extend his gloating. After half an hour of concentrated pomposity and grandstanding he seemed to run out of steam. Or maybe he just realized that he had other actual responsibilities to take care of now that he ran the Commonwealth's foremost intelligence agency.

That point was drilled home when his sleeve chimed and he answered it with sharp irritation. "Yes, Lawson, what is it?"

"Sorry to bother you, depu – er, acting director," came the voice of, presumably, his assistant. "You've got a meeting in ten minutes with the deputy directors. Er, the other ones, that is."

Kester's irritation was wiped away with a heady dose of self-importance, and Kovalic could see his spine straightening. "Right. I'll be there shortly." He disconnected mid-way through the response. "Well, I'm off. And you two have a prison transport to catch." His teeth gleamed. "I'll leave you in the capable hands of Inspector Laurent."

Straightening his tie, he was about to nod in acknowledgement to them, then apparently decided they weren't worth the respect and ended up with an odd sort of head bob before turning on his heel and stalking out.

Kovalic heaved a sigh of relief without thinking and caught Laurent's sympathetic expression before the Bureau agent could hide it.

"Well," said the general, steepling his fingers. "Now, Inspector, perhaps you could provide us with some further information about the charges against us?"

The inspector looked conflicted, torn between the rigors of duty and his personal sympathies. "I'm afraid there isn't much I can share. Director Kester probably revealed too much already." Here Laurent didn't quite manage to avoid rolling his eyes, his opinion of the spy chief clearly apparent. "But as he's already said it, I'm free to repeat that new evidence suggests a connection between the two of you and the Novan Liberation Front, possibly facilitating their bombing on the ConComm hub in Salaam, as well as their assault on Station Zero."

Even from Kovalic's limited acquaintance with Laurent, he could detect the Bureau agent's skepticism in the charges. Kovalic and Laurent had met some days prior while investigating the bombing, which had revealed the existence of a covert CID program to monitor communications within the capital city; a similar operation on the space station in orbit would have expanded that capability throughout the Commonwealth – if Kovalic and his team hadn't intervened, anyway.

"Very interesting," said the general. "And I don't suppose you can detail that evidence, or how it was provided."

"I can't disclose how we gather our intelligence, you know that – sources and methods. As for the evidence, it will be provided at your hearing."

"And when will that be?" Kovalic asked, crossing his arms.

Laurent glanced at him. "The matter is... pending. There are issues of jurisdiction that still need to be resolved."

The general made an "ah" sound. "Whether to try us in a civilian or military court, I'm assuming, given that Major Kovalic is an active duty member of the Commonwealth Marine Corps and I am *technically–*" the old man's trademark twinkle gleamed in his eye "–a civilian consultant."

"Quite," said Laurent.

"Then I suppose we may be here for some time," said the general, reclining in his chair. "Given the speed at which bureaucracy normally progresses. Perhaps we could get some lunch? While we await our eventual... disposition." A beatific smile of pure innocence crossed his lips and Kovalic tried to keep a straight look on his own face.

Laurent considered them both, as if looking for a reason to turn them down flat, but he came up empty. "Yeah, sure. I'll have someone get you some sandwiches from the cafeteria."

"And I'm sure you have more important demands on your time, inspector. So don't feel you need to keep us company. We're not going anywhere, after all."

Brow knitting, the inspector muttered something under his breath. He stepped through the outer office into the corridor, dispatching the guard standing there, then disappeared himself, leaving them under the capable watch of the remaining pair of marines.

"Interesting morning so far," said Kovalic dryly.

"Indeed." The general picked up his cane and passed it from hand to hand thoughtfully. "I admit, these events have taken me by surprise."

"You have any theory about where Kester got this 'evidence'?"

"I'm not sure precisely, but I assume it's connected to our..." the general's blue eyes darted to the pair of marines, "...feathered friend."

Kovalic bit his lip. The information Aaron Page had found on Bayern had shown the funds originating from the general's accounts that had eventually ended up in the hands of Nova Front had, en route, been laundered through a shell company called Tanager Holdings.

Which, the general had pointed out, was a species of bird that happened to be closely related to another with particular resonance: CARDINAL was the code name for the general's most secretive source, highly placed in the Illyrican establishment. Over the past years, it had provided a slew of difficult to obtain intelligence, even as the general had kept their identity a secret from everyone else. Had the name of the company been a message for the general? That perhaps whoever had arranged all of this had compromised his asset? Perhaps even captured or killed them?

"That doesn't seem to bode well for us," said Kovalic.

"No." The twinkle in the general's eye had hardened into a glint. "No, it does not."

The deck was stacked against them, that much was certain. Kovalic wasn't sure what had become of the rest of the Special Projects Team, but he hoped that most of them had gotten the ESCHATON signal and made themselves scarce before Kester's goons had come for them.

But even if they were still at liberty and had discovered Kovalic and the general's predicament – and he knew them well enough to conclude that they would make it their top priority once their own situation was secure – they were lacking some crucial details. None of them, for example, even knew about the existence of CARDINAL.

Which led to one inescapable conclusion: the best chance to clear their names of these charges lay with themselves. And step one would be getting out of this office.

Almost lazily, Kovalic let his eyes drift towards the two marines in the doorway. Security at the Commonwealth Executive complex might seem like a cushy gig, but it was one that you got as a reward for being damn good at your job. Here that was borne out by the ramrod straight posture and eyes-front bearing of their two guards. The bottom of the barrel they were not.

Kovalic felt relatively certain that he could hold his own against them, but it wouldn't be easy and, more to the point, it wouldn't be quiet. And the louder it was, the more likely he'd soon be facing even more overwhelming odds.

There was a quiet clearing of the throat at the doorway, and a tremulous voice spoke up. "Sorry to interrupt, but since they won't let me go yet, I figured I would just make some coffee for everyone."

Rance, the general's assistant, stood in the door, holding a tray with four steaming cups on it. Her usually confident demeanor was decidedly uncertain, as though she wasn't sure exactly what she was supposed to be doing right now.

The two marines exchanged a stoic glance, but the man's face softened as he looked down at the decidedly shorter aide. "Not while we're on duty, I'm afraid. And we can't let you through."

"Oh," said Rance, crestfallen. "Right, of course." She made to go, but the female guard held out a hand.

"It's fine," she said curtly. "We can take them in."

"Thanks! Here you g – oh *no*." Rance fumbled the tray, the mugs rattling as she tried to right it.

The female guard bent down to try and steady them from tipping, and in that moment, Rance's gaze went straight to Kovalic, her eyes hard.

There was no need to tell him twice. He launched himself out of the chair towards the guards, even as a small cylinder slid out of Rance's sleeve and into her hand. Kovalic had just enough time to register it as contact stunner before she pressed it against the thigh of the male marine behind her.

The guard spasmed, eyes wide. He half-stumbled, half-fell back against the doorframe. His partner reached for the knockout gun at her waist, but her hands were still in position to catch Rance's tipping tray, which fell towards her, sloshing hot coffee across her uniform. To her credit, she didn't yell, just gritted her teeth and tried to reverse her momentum.

But Kovalic had gotten there first, plucking the KO gun from the holster and stepping out of reach even before the tray hit the ground with a clatter of mugs.

"Sorry about this, corporal," said Kovalic. "Nothing personal."

She started towards him determinedly, but didn't make it a step before Kovalic pulled the trigger, knocking her senseless.

He glanced down. "Shame about the coffee. Smelled good."

Stepping into the room, Rance grabbed the male marine under the arms and dragged him into the general's inner office. "Laurent stepped out, but he'll be back any minute. If we're going, we need to go now."

From behind the desk, the general rose, leaning on his stick. "I find myself in full agreement with you, Yeoman Rance. After you."

"One second," said Kovalic. He grabbed the data chip with Page's files from the desk and tucked it in his jacket. They needed to start somewhere; lucky for them, Page had already done the heavy lifting.

The three of them stepped back into the outer office, closing the door behind them, even as the door to the hallway slid open, admitting a startled Inspector Laurent carrying a couple boxed sandwiches.

"What are you d–" His eyes jumped to the closed door behind them and then instinct took over and he dropped the sandwiches, reaching into his coat.

Before Kovalic could even raise the KO gun in his hand there was a high-pitched whine and a blur lunged past him, closing the distance faster than a championship long jumper. A flash of metal and Laurent suddenly had a three-foot blade pointed directly at his chest.

"I'd advise you to put up your hands slowly, inspector," said the general, not even remotely winded. "I respect you immensely and would hate to have to skewer you."

Laurent's eyes had practically crossed as they focused on the sharp point in front of him and, taking the general's instructions to heart, he removed his hand from his coat at a snail's pace, then raised both into the air.

"This is a bad idea," said the inspector. His eyes went to Kovalic. "You know this. Running just makes you look guilty. Stick around and at least you've got a shot at exonerating yourselves."

In normal circumstances, he wouldn't be wrong. But

they had left normal far, far behind. Kovalic stepped forward and removed the sidearm from inside Laurent's coat. The general lowered his sword, re-sheathing it inside his walking stick, which locked with a click. Had he been carrying that around all this time? And how had he moved so fast?

Kovalic shook his head. "You're a good agent, Laurent, and an honorable man. But Kester? He's a political creature and to him this is a gold-plated opportunity to consolidate even more of what he wants: power."

In the end, if the evidence was the same information Page had given him about Tanager Holdings and money from the general's accounts then it would come down to Kester's word against the general's. And who was more likely to get the benefit of the doubt: the acting head of the Commonwealth's intelligence agency, or an Illyrican defector with a past full of secrets and duplicity?

"I will bring you in," said Laurent, his dark eyes serious. "Just so we're clear. No matter how much I might like you personally."

"I'd expect nothing less," said Kovalic. "Now, I'm afraid I'm going to have to ask you to sit down so we can tie you up. It's that or…" He raised the KO gun. "The less voluntary option."

The inspector sighed. "We've all got to do what we've got to do." And with that he grabbed at Kovalic's outstretched hand, trying to knock the weapon aside.

But nobody was outrunning a stun field at point blank range. The inspector collapsed to the floor, where Kovalic rolled him over and made sure he was unconscious but stable.

"All right," he said, having satisfied himself that Laurent would wake with nothing more than a headache. He stowed the KO gun in the back of his waistband. "Now what?"

"I can get us out of the building," said Rance, moving towards the door. "I've got egress routes all planned out. And I... borrowed... codes for a groundcar in the motor pool from a friend over in Logistics. It's not untraceable, but it'll get us clear of the complex."

Kovalic's eyebrows went up at that, and his gaze went to the general.

The older man shrugged. "Preparation is my watchword, Simon. You know that."

"Hm." Kovalic added it to the list of things that the general hadn't told him, along with the sword cane, the real story behind his legs, and CARDINAL's identity. It was getting to be a lengthy list. Not for the first time he was reminded that Page had told him, way back on Bayern, to look into a project called LOOKING GLASS with which the general was involved – a project about which Kovalic had been able to discover vanishingly little, other than that it was part of the Commonwealth's Research & Development arm and was extremely secret. He'd planned on asking the general about it at their meeting, but that was for another moment – one when they weren't running for their lives.

"We don't have a lot of allies left in Salaam," said Kovalic, "especially if the rest of the team's gotten safely offworld. I'd like to follow suit, but without a pilot, that's going to be tricky."

"No," said the general, shaking his head. "It's too risky.

Besides, I have a suspicion that the answers we need are on Nova somewhere. We need to find a place to lay low." His head cocked to one side, thoughtful. "And I think I know someone who can help us out."

CHAPTER 6

Nat had half-expected the *Cavalier*'s hangar to at least be cordoned off, if not secretly filled with tactical personnel just waiting for them to be foolish enough to walk right in.

But it proved deserted except for the small patrol ship itself, sitting in the middle of the cavernous space. No alarms went off when they swiped themselves in; the heavy end of the hammer had yet to come down, it seemed.

Tapper and Sayers made a beeline for the team's storage lockers while Brody followed Taylor up onto the *Cavalier* to get the preflight checklist started.

"Damn it," said the pilot as they climbed the ramp into the ship's main hold. He'd cocked an ear to one side, listening for something, and after a moment Nat understood what he was hearing: nothing. No engine hum or the faint chirp of the ship's electronics. "Ship's on battery power, so it's going to be a cold start for the engines. Cassie and Mal must have powered the main systems down while they did repairs."

Nat raised an eyebrow. "And the state of those repairs?"

Brody scratched the back of his head. "Re… paired? It's been a busy week."

That was an understatement. "Best get started then. How long?"

"Fifteen minutes?"

"You've got ten."

Opening his mouth, Brody seemed to think better about whatever quip he'd been about to deliver; he just nodded, dropped his go bag on the nearest seat, and disappeared towards the ship's cockpit.

Nat, meanwhile, headed aft towards the ship's bunk rooms to stow her own bag and do a quick check of the onboard inventory.

She tapped the access panel for the nearer of the two berths and the door slid aside, the lights blinking on in harsh blue-white tones.

A figure sat bolt upright in the lower bunk, their movement arrested by a sudden *clang* as their forehead rebounded off the support strut for the upper berth. That was followed by a groan as they collapsed back into the mattress, rubbing at their forehead. "Owwwwwww."

Nat, for her part, had taken a step back, and instinctively drawn her knockout gun, pointing it at the bunk. "… Maldonado?" She sighed and lowered the weapon. "Why are you sleeping on the *Cavalier*?"

Cary Maldonado gingerly raised themselves up on their elbows, then swung their legs out of the bunk, casting a careful eye upward. "Uh… yeah, sorry." They pressed two tentative fingers at the red spot blooming on their forehead and winced. "I was working late last night, patching the firmware on the *Cav*'s main computer and, you know, it just seemed like going home and coming all the way back in the morning – oh geez, what time is it?"

"Time for you to go home," said Nat, tucking the KO gun away.

Mal stuffed their feet into a pair of shoes on the deck and pulled themselves to their feet. "Yes, ma'am. Wait, is the team getting spun up?"

Nat hesitated. Mal was their technical expert, but like Cassie Engel, the team's mechanic, they occupied an awkward position: as support staff, they were civilian contractors attached to Yamanaka base and assigned to the Special Projects Team. Neither of them would have received the ESCHATON protocol, so the less they knew, the better. "Something like that. I need you to clear the ship immediately."

"Oh, man, I just need like *five seconds* up front," said Mal. "I can't let you go out into the field without one last systems check."

Beneath Nat's feet, the deck started to vibrate and a deep bass tone rumbled through the bulkhead as the *Cavalier*'s main reactor came online. "I'm afraid there's no time."

But Mal was already slipping past her and trotting towards the front of the ship, leaving Nat to toss her bag on the empty bunk and then follow suit. Simon had remarked that dealing with the team and its attendant personnel was like herding cats that were technically supposed to be herding sheep. Just a bad idea all around.

She heard Brody's surprise before she even reached the cockpit. "Mal? What are you doing here?"

"Oh, hey, Brody. Just finishing up some of that repair work."

By the time she stepped into the doorway, Mal already had one of the console panels flipped up, their hands buried in the wiring beneath.

"It'll only take a sec," said Mal, eyes rolling up as they rooted around for something.

Brody shook his head and turned back to the pilot's console, flipping switches and checking readouts as the various displays lit up. "Reactor temp steady," said the pilot, more to himself than to Nat or Mal. "Fuel levels nominal. Control surfaces pass all checks. Repulsors coming online now."

Nat dropped into the co-pilot's seat, running an eye over the information on the monitors in front of her. She could fly the *Cavalier* just fine, if need be, though without Brody's signature… flair, for lack of a better word, and it never hurt to have a second pair of eyes on things. Behind her, Mal was still digging through the console. Her gaze slipped to the chronometer on the ship's dashboard: it had been an hour since the ESCHATON signal had gone out; their window of opportunity was rapidly dwindling.

The clomp of boots sounded from the main hold and, sparing a last look at Mal and Brody, both of whom were in their element, she left them to it.

"…the heaviest one you could find?" Sayers was saying. They were halfway up the ramp, and she was straining as she held up one end of a large trunk.

"I'm prioritizing," said Tapper.

"Next time prioritize a box with its own repulsor field. Or one full of pillows."

"Can't blow anything up with pillows," Tapper grumbled.

Nat was about to offer a hand when a loud klaxon sounded. For a moment, she thought it was coming from the cockpit and that Mal had accidentally triggered a reactor overload, but both Tapper and Sayers had paused what they were doing and looked out into the hangar.

"Well, that can't be good," said the sergeant.

Nat pushed her way back into the cockpit where Brody and Mal were staring out the front canopy. Red emergency lights flashed from the hangar's ceiling, and the klaxon blared again, loud even within the confines of the ship. It was followed this time by what seemed to be an announcement, though the words were muffled. She reached over and flipped on the external pickups.

"...perimeter breach. Lockdown protocols in place. Quick response force, mobilize immediately."

So much for their time running out. "Brody?"

"Already on it," said the pilot. "What about...?" he jerked his head at Mal, who had frozen, wide-eyed.

Nat gently nudged the tech. "Mal, close it up and get going."

"Huh? Oh, yes, ma'am. Right away." They turned back to the console they'd been working on and pulled down the cover, locking it into place. "Should be good to go. What do you think that's all about? Drill of some kind?" They nodded to the klaxons as they brushed their hands off on their trousers.

"Couldn't say." Out in the hold, she heard another thump and a muted exchange between Sayers and Tapper. "But it's time to clear out."

Mal nodded and let Nat usher them out into the cargo hold, where the other two members of the team were locking the trunk into place against a bulkhead with a pair of heavy duty ratchet straps. "That's all we've got time for," she said, nodding at the trunk. "Get yourselves strapped in. We're lifting off."

The tech looked back at her as they were poised at the top of the ramp. "Commander..."

"Not now, Mal. Get moving."

"No, it's just that –"

Brody's voice echoed down the corridor from the cockpit. "We've got company!"

Tapper pulled the cargo strap tight, then stepped over to one of the wall consoles and tapped a few commands, bringing up a holoscreen of the hangar's external cameras. A military truck had pulled up on the tarmac, disgorging half a dozen uniformed marines, all carrying rifles.

"Looks like two breach teams," said Tapper.

"Good thing we're leaving," said Sayers as she headed towards the cockpit.

Nat's fingers curled into fists. They were sitting ducks here. "Mal. Off, now."

"Wait," said the tech, eyes darting back and forth between her and Tapper. "Are you all in some kind of trouble? I can help!"

With a sigh, Nat turned them by the shoulders and sent them down the ramp. "You can help by getting yourself clear. And don't do anything risky – these people aren't playing around."

"But –"

"Take care of yourself, Mal," she said with a wan smile. She reached over and palmed the ramp control and the hydraulics groaned as it rose into place. The hatch in front of her slid down and she let out a breath, pressing her head against the metal for a second before making her way to the cockpit.

Tapper and Sayers were already fastening their harness restraints and Brody was leaning over the console in front of him. He glanced up as she came in. "Board's green. We're good to go."

"Then get us the hell out of here," she said, dropping into the co-pilot seat.

Brody reached over and was about to pull a lever when he froze. "Oh, shit. Shit shit shit."

"What's wrong?"

"Several tons of reinforced steel," he said, pointing out the canopy at the hangar doors, which were still closed in front of them. "Lockdown protocol's frozen remote control of the doors. The *Cav*'s tough, but we're not going through a half-foot of metal without some serious damage."

Blood pounded in Nat's chest. God damn it, they were so close. She spun to the terminal to her right and flicked up a holoscreen. "I'm going to try to override. Standby." Her fingers danced over the keys, probing the remote system for loopholes she could exploit. There was bound to be one, if she just had the time to find it – but that was the one resource they were precious short on.

"Can we slow them down?" she asked without looking up.

There was a hesitation from behind her, a pause pregnant with possibility, and Tapper finally let out a sigh. "Yeah, we can."

She heard the click of restraints being released, and the sergeant was up out of his seat and vanishing back towards the cargo hold.

"Shit," said Nat, as yet another probe was rejected. "The door systems are hardened. They're not even accepting a remote connection."

"There is a manual override," said Brody. "But it's all the way over th –"

An alert chime sounded from the console, and Nat didn't have to look over to know that the cargo hatch had been opened. Her breath caught – she didn't have time to think through whatever Tapper was doing: the lines of code scrolling across her display were blurring in her vision as she tried an oblique route into the door systems via the hangar's somewhat more vulnerable power system.

"Oh, fuck it, Mal," said Brody suddenly.

Nat looked up sharply, following the pilot's gaze out the transparisteel viewport. And then, to one side, where the slim figure of the technician was standing next to a large junction box. As she watched, they pulled it open and started fiddling with something inside.

Mal had realized they'd be locked in – that's what the tech had been trying to tell her, but she hadn't listened. If she had, would she even have asked them to do it? Put themselves at risk to help the rest of them?

She could feel Simon's presence hovering over her shoulder. *That's the burden of command*, she could almost hear him saying.

Tapper's voice crackled over the ship's intercom suddenly. "They're breaching!"

Flicking up the holoscreens from the hangar's internal cameras, she watched as the doors on either side slid open and teams of three marines, rifles at the ready, moved in swiftly and silently. They had the *Cavalier* in a pincer, with no way out except the still-sealed hangar doors in front of them.

Reaching over, Nat toggled the intercom. "Sergeant, I need you to buy as much time as possible."

"Already on it, commander," he grunted. "Just prepping a special delivery for them right now."

"Brody," she said. "The second you can get through those doors…"

"Full speed ahead," he confirmed. "You're all going to want to strap in tight."

"Package away," reported Tapper. "Deployed in three… two…"

Even from the cockpit they could hear the rapid series of bangs and pops, like a whole fireworks display going off at once. Which proved not far off the mark: the trunk she'd seen Tapper and Addy loading earlier had been slid to the bottom of the *Cavalier*'s ramp, and the sergeant had apparently rigged several concussion and smoke grenades to fire in series. A blanket of thick gray smoke billowed around them, and she could smell it wafting back up through the hatch and into the cockpit.

So thorough was the distraction that she almost missed the groan of the hangar doors cracking open. But a vertical slit of sunlight knifed down through the cockpit canopy, the blue sky of the Novan afternoon tantalizingly framed just out of reach.

"Nice one, Mal," murmured Brody.

Tapper barged back into the cockpit, fanning at his face and coughing. "I hope that worked because it was my whole goddamn reserve." He dropped into his seat and clicked his harness into place. "Let's get the hell out of here."

The hangar doors were inching apart at a glacial pace, tendrils of smoke snaking through the opening. Nat leaned forward against her own safety webbing, just able to make out Mal through the clouds, still working feverishly at the junction panel.

But she wasn't the only one who'd spotted them. "Shit."

The lead of one of the teams of marines was pointing in the tech's direction, and as Nat watched, they peeled off and headed towards the junction box. Mal still had their head buried in the wiring, back to the incoming troops. There had to be a way to keep them off the tech, just for a few more moments.

"Thirty seconds," said Brody. "Retracting landing struts, switching to repulsors." He reached over and tapped a control. The ship bounced slightly, buoyed on its antigravity field.

Nat blinked, then leaned forward and grabbed the yoke in front of her. "Brody, I've got the stick."

To his credit the pilot didn't protest, just slid back from the controls and put his hands up. "All yours."

Gently, she nudged the ship forward on its repulsors, sliding towards the hangar doors. A series of shots pinged off the exterior as the team not heading towards Mal opened fire on the *Cavalier*, but what the ship lacked in weaponry it made up for in concealed armor plating.

Just a few more meters and the opening in the hangar doors would be wide enough for the ship to get through. They had to buy Mal more time.

Nat pushed the yoke to portside and the ship rolled on its axis. The wash from the starboard repulsors, no longer pointed at the ground, bled out over the side, sending the team of marines skittering across the hangar floor.

Leveling the ship off, she glanced out the cockpit to see Mal looking up at them, flashing a thumbs up and grinning. An expression that melted off their face as a knockout gun's stun field caught them full on, and they crumpled to the ground.

"Mal!" cried Brody, seizing the yoke.

"Brody," said Nat sharply. "We can't help them. We need to go."

The pilot's hands white-knuckled the controls. Nat had seen that look on his face before – the one that suggested he was about a hair's breadth away from saying "fuck orders" and doing whatever the hell he wanted.

But he'd come a long way in the time she'd known him. An icy calm descended over his face, belied only by a twitch of his lips.

The hangar doors were still grinding open, even as the two squads of marines converged on the junction box, waving at one another. More shots pinged off the *Cav*'s armored hull, to no effect.

"Just a little more," muttered Brody, eyes on the doors and the slowly widening gap between them. Beneath them, the ship fidgeted like a horse champing at the bit.

And then the doors clanged to a stop.

Nat's hands gripped the console in front of her. No. They were so close. Just a little farther.

"Oh, fuck this," said Brody. "Hold on!" He slammed the throttle forward and the ship jumped like it had been scalded, right towards the too narrow gap.

"Brody!" She squeezed her eyes tightly shut and braced for the impact.

Then she was flung sideways as the whole ship shifted beneath her, rolling hard to port. There was a scraping sound and a few stomach-churning crunches as the edge of the hull dragged along the permacrete of the tarmac, but the ship squeezed through the hangar door gap with inches to spare. Then her stomach was left far behind her as they rapidly climbed, the g-forces pressing her back into the seat.

"Holy shit," Addy gasped from behind her. "I can't believe that worked."

"Don't celebrate yet," said Brody, his expression grim. "This is where things get interesting."

CHAPTER 7

Following Rance's surefooted lead, Kovalic and the general made their way through the corridors of the Commonwealth Executive campus. Glancing sideways at his boss, Kovalic noticed he'd foregone any pretense of leaning on his walking stick, carrying it in one hand like the sheathed weapon it was and easily keeping pace with them.

He shook his head. Even after all this time, the things he didn't know about Hasan al-Adaj surprised him – and worried him, too.

The general caught his gaze and offered a tight smile. "Come now, Simon. You didn't think I would spring for anything less than the top of the line." He rapped the end of the stick against his lower leg with the clank of wood against metal. "It always pays to be prepared."

"That was a bit of fancy footwork," said Kovalic.

"Three-time epee champion at the Illyrican War College," said the general modestly. "I've tried to keep up in recent years, but it's so hard to find a sparring partner who can be discreet. Other than Rance, of course," he said, nodding to the young woman in front of them.

Kovalic couldn't help but wonder which of her boss's other secrets the yeoman was privy to. Her unhesitating willingness to take out a pair of marines and an inspector for the Commonwealth Security Bureau suggested more loyalty to the general than to her own government.

Which, to be fair, was the same argument Kester had made about Kovalic himself. Not for the first time, Kovalic started to wonder if he was making the right decision, hitching his wagon to the general's fortunes. The man had done plenty that could be seen as suspicious… but they'd worked together for a long time; that had to count for something. And despite the circumstances, there was still something in Kovalic's gut that was telling him he'd rather be on the run with the general than at Kester's mercies.

He'd lost track of exactly where in the compound they were, but Rance strode straight ahead and pushed open a heavy security door, letting them out into the warm breeze of a Novan afternoon. They were in one of the campus's modest parking structures and the young woman made a beeline for a sleek black groundcar parked in the row across from the door. Raising her sleeve, she tapped in a sequence and the car's locks clicked open.

Kovalic cast a last look over his shoulder as the door behind them swung closed and, with it, their last hope of pleading that this was anything but a mistake. They'd incapacitated several official personnel and were about to become fugitives. Coming back from that was going to be a hard sell.

But somewhere out there the rest of his team had presumably already made that same choice, on his say so. He couldn't hang them out to dry any more than he could leave the general twisting in the wind.

With a sigh, he slid into the front passenger seat, next to Rance, who had already powered up the car. With the general in the back, Rance pulled out of the space and down the ramp towards the exit.

"Now what?" Kovalic asked. "Another one of your secret offices?" The general had at least a half-dozen locations that he rotated through, and Kovalic had always assumed that there were a few that even he didn't know about.

"While I have nothing but faith in Rance's security precautions, that seems unwise. We have to assume all of them have been compromised."

Rance glanced back at the general as she pulled the car up to the exit gate, which opened obligingly for them. "Even Thursday?"

"I'm afraid so."

Sunlight glinted through the windshield as they turned onto the long drive that led out of the campus. As far as Kovalic could tell, it looked like any other day. People walking around the campus, clear skies overhead, the blue Commonwealth flag flapping in the breeze. Not a hint that anything was amiss.

"We probably don't have too long before they find Laurent and those marines and put the campus on lockdown," said Kovalic. His heart was thumping in his chest as he looked down the road, which seemed impossibly long at their current pace. But rushing would just make them that much more conspicuous.

He held his breath all the way to the exit checkpoint, but the marines there waved them on without a second look. After all, their primary job was keeping people *out*, not keeping them in.

Even so, he didn't let the air out of his lungs until they were back on the highway, the skyscrapers of downtown Salaam fading into the distance behind them.

"So," he said, glancing back at the general. "This person you said could help us... who are they?"

He'd already mentally flipped through his own contacts, but the ones he trusted the most – the ones who wouldn't blink even at a treason accusation – were few and far between. Most of his old friends from his time in the service had retired. Besides, they were exactly who Laurent and Kester would expect him to turn to; asking them for help would just be putting them in the crosshairs. Meanwhile, his colleagues in the intelligence community might not like Kester any more than he did, but it wasn't exactly politically expedient to take on the newly installed head of CID, even if his title was still prefaced with "acting."

That left his many and varied contacts offworld but, as the general had pointed out, getting off Nova would be difficult and potentially counterproductive to finding evidence that would clear them.

Behind him, the general's lips thinned. "There's an old friend... well, perhaps that is generous. Once upon a time we were friends, though circumstances have become complicated. But I don't think he will turn us away. He runs a tea shop in Tokai, down by the coast."

Kovalic raised an eyebrow. "That's the better part of a day."

"Staying in Salaam doesn't seem the wisest course of action at present."

It was hard to disagree with that. Tokai was a small town, though. If CID or Laurent followed them there, they wouldn't have many places to run.

"Rance," said the general, "Zuljanah contingency, I should think."

"Got it," said the young woman before checking the rearview displays and pulling off at the next exit ramp. She started following a convoluted series of turns through the surface streets that was no doubt intended to reveal any pursuit, as well as evade tracking by surveillance.

"Do I want to know how many of these contingencies you have?" Kovalic asked after what seemed like the sixth turn in two minutes.

The general's shoulders went up. "Fewer than I'd like and hopefully more than I'll need."

After another few minutes Rance pulled the car over in front of a small bank of shops and the three of them got out. The aide placed a small black puck on the center console and pressed the single glowing blue button atop it.

Upon their exit, she pressed a button on her sleeve and there was a brief squeal and crackling. "Focused EMP charge," she explained. "It'll wipe the car's internal systems and logs, just in case."

The general, leading the way, stepped into what turned out to be a small gourmet grocery store, aisles lined with delicacies from across the known galaxy: truffles from Earth, single-malt Caledonian whisky, even smoked Illyrican hazardfish – all at exorbitant prices. They passed a cheese counter replete with orange-rinded wheels and thick white cakes with a heady aroma of sharp funkiness. Then through a narrow corridor created by shelves of wine, piled high with vintages from seemingly every inhabited system – rare was the human settlement where they hadn't at least attempted the tradition – and out the back of the shop into a small lot with three cars in it.

Rance headed for one, a discreet late-model silver vehicle that you could all too easily lose in a shopping center parking lot, and it opened at a wave from her sleeve. Within moments they were out on the road again, heading in an entirely different direction.

"Well," said the general after a few moments. "That may not totally shake CID from our trail, but I daresay we've bought ourselves some time to reach Tokai without any interference."

Kovalic rubbed a hand over his mouth. "And then what? Your friend helps us hide? Sets up new identities for us? What's the endgame here – and don't tell me you don't have one. It's pretty clear that you were prepared for this eventuality."

Blue eyes glinted as they met Kovalic's in the mirror. "Of course. I came to this planet as a defector, Simon. It seemed more than plausible that at some point I might wear out my welcome. Though, admittedly, this was not the fashion I deemed most likely." He stroked the pointed tip of his beard. "All things being equal, I would prefer to clear our names. Whatever else I may have done, Kester's allegations of treason are soundly false – just as yours were." There was a note of recrimination in his voice, reminding Kovalic that moments before Kester had stormed into the general's office, it had been him leveling the same accusations.

"Given what Kester said about having evidence connecting you to the attacks by the Novan Liberation Front, I assume we both believe he has the same information I do: transactions from your accounts on Bayern to Nova Front, via the Tanager Holdings shell company."

The general winced visibly at the name, and Kovalic turned in his seat to face the man head on. "You said you'd made a terrible mistake. When I said that name for the first time, right before Kester came in."

"Did I?" the general mused, his eyes drifting to the window.

"Now's not the time to play coy," Kovalic said, his tone harsher than intended. His mouth snapped shut; he'd always held the general in high regard, ever since their first meeting back on Illyrica, eight years ago. Even though the man held no real rank in the Commonwealth military, he'd always been accorded the honors of his Illyrican position. Some, like Kester, used it as an ironic cudgel with which to bludgeon the man who had spent most of his career fighting against the very people he now sought to help. But for Kovalic, it was about respect for the man's service, even if it had been on the other side.

That generosity was starting to wear thin. Even if the old man hadn't betrayed the Commonwealth, Kovalic had long since realized that the general could no more stop planning and harboring hidden agendas than he could stop breathing.

That had served Kovalic and his team well over the years, helping them work outside of the framework of bureaucracy and organization that too often seemed to view the conflict between Commonwealth and Imperium as one that could be waged only as war. But the bill had now come due, and the blade that had sliced through the red tape was now at their own throats.

Kovalic fixed the general with the same gray-eyed stare that he usually saved for junior officers. "I think it's time to put all your cards on the table. Sir. Somehow the evidence against us is connected to CARDINAL. What's your exposure? Who exactly *are* they?"

The general didn't respond at first, just kept staring out the window as the buildings blurred by. But at last, he drew a deep breath, then exhaled as though blowing out a candle. "Leaving the Imperium was very difficult for me. I left behind someone who I held very dear, and I was worried about how they would fare in my absence – without my influence to shield them. So I arranged a regular supply of funds for them, in order that they might have an independent source of financial stability. Though I asked for nothing in exchange, they volunteered information from time to time and, given their access, it seemed foolhardy not to accept."

"So," said Kovalic slowly, "this was all to protect an asset. You think whoever took over your old job as director of Imperial Intelligence found out somehow? Used that connection to their advantage?"

A wry twist curled the general's lip. "In a manner of speaking."

Kovalic massaged the spot between his eyes. "Enough with the cryptic hints. Just come out with it."

"Fair enough." The general drew a deep breath. "No, I do not think my replacement at the Imperial Intelligence Service compromised CARDINAL – but only because they had already been compromised, right from the very beginning." His eyes hardened. "I believe our nameless adversary at IIS and CARDINAL are one and the same: Emperor Alaric's daughter, the Princess Isabella."

CHAPTER 8

The yoke bucked in Eli's hands as he pushed the *Cav*'s throttle to its limit. The whole ship was vibrating like a washing machine with an uneven load, rocking from side to side. Nova's thermal layers could be murder if you took them too fast. But right now, there were only two options: fast or dead.

Beside him, Taylor had opened her eyes again and turned, businesslike as ever, to the consoles in front of her.

The speakers squawked to life suddenly. "ST321, this is Yamanaka Tower. You have not been cleared for liftoff and are in violation of Commonwealth airspace regulations. Set down immediately."

"Not bloody likely," said Eli through gritted teeth, eyes on the altimeter. They'd already passed five thousand feet, but breaking atmo would take another several minutes, even at maximum speed. *Too much time. They can have a missile lock on us or scramble interceptors before we even hit the stratosphere. And there's nowhere to hide.*

Taylor glanced over, as if reading his mind. "What's the status of countermeasures?"

"Should be ready to go... assuming Mal got them back online after the other day." *No wonder this all feels so familiar.*

They'd almost been shot out of the sky by their own people after Mal's new transponder spoofing system had fried half the *Cav*'s systems.

Eli's mind spun suddenly at the thought. "Wait – we might have something better. Commander, point me towards the nearest commercial shipping vector."

The commander, to her credit, didn't ask why, just brought up a holoscreen and panned around. "Heading 130, mark 57, distance about twenty klicks."

Eli adjusted course, swinging the ship in the direction she'd given.

"ST321," said the voice over the speaker, "your course change is unauthorized and presents a collision risk with commercial traffic. Spinnaker 1 and 2 are inbound to escort you to a landing."

"I'm guessing they're not going to be offering us their arm," said Tapper.

"Oh, they're going to be arming something."

"Really? Now?"

"Sorry. OK, Addy, on the flight engineer console there should be an interface for Mal's spoofing program." User-friendliness had probably not been high on the list of the tech's priorities, but hopefully it wasn't an inscrutable mess.

Addy spun to her left, tapping the controls. "Got it. Wow, there's a whole database of codes in here. Commonwealth passenger ships… Hanif couriers…" He could hear her eyebrows rising. "Illyrican dreadnoughts? Who's going to believe this ship is a dreadnought?"

"Hopefully, the Illyricans," said Tapper.

"Traffic control still has our position," said Taylor, shaking her head. "Even if we change transponder codes, they'll still know it's us broadcasting a different signal. It doesn't stop them from shooting us out of the sky."

"That's just part one," said Eli, more assuredly than he felt. "Next, we have to find the nearest ship in this vector."

Taylor opened her mouth, then paused. "I think I see where this is going."

"And?"

"I don't love it." But she turned back to her display anyway. "There's a cargo hauler at point three-five. ID Bravo One-Nine." She slid the information across to Eli's own display: a *Niguruma* class Mark Seven bulk freighter.

Just what we need: big and slow. "Copy, matching course."

A rapid set of beeping alerts came from a station behind Eli, and he didn't have to look to know what it meant: nothing good.

"We've got those interceptors inbound," said Tapper, pulling up a sensor display. "Closing fast. Maybe a minute before we're in their weapons range."

Eli glanced at his own HUD; they'd reach the bulk freighter a hair before that, which meant they had no time to lose. "Commander, send the freighter's transponder code to the flight engineer console – Addy, there should be an option to clone and broadcast."

Silence fell over the cockpit, leaving just the thrumming of the engine and the beeps of the various stations. "We're going to pretend to be a commercial cargo ship?" said Addy, a note of disbelief in her voice.

"That's part two of the plan."

"How many parts does this plan have?"

"I'll let you know as soon as I do."

Addy didn't respond. Just as well: Eli was running out of answers. "Transponder code is cloned," she said. "Ready to broadcast."

Eli leaned forward. "OK," he said under his breath, "this next part gets a little tricky." Waving a hand at the HUD, it isolated and magnified the commercial ship, which otherwise would have been little more than a shiny dot streaking contrails behind it. Zoomed in, it proved to be a much larger shiny dot: a long cylinder with cargo pods hanging off it like feet off a centipede. Ungainly, to say the least. A tag in his heads-up display showed the transponder ID and a few other relevant details, like course, speed, and – most crucially – distance.

"Ten klicks away," said Taylor, looking at the same readout. "Thirty seconds."

"Those fighters are about forty-five seconds out," Tapper added.

Sucking in a lungful of air, Eli grasped the throttle and eased up just slightly. Out of the corner of his eye, he watched the speed tick down until it was just the same as the cargo hauler.

"Uh, that ship's getting pretty close," said Addy.

Indeed, the hauler had suddenly filled the cockpit window, a whale of battleship gray, as much larger than the *Cavalier* as an Illyrican dreadnought was to a starfighter. It hung eerily still, given that their relative speeds were almost the same.

"Matching course and speed," said Eli, maneuvering the *Cavalier* even closer. A series of alarms started chiming with increasing frequency as he closed. A dialog reading COLLISION ALERT popped up on the HUD and he waved it away. The hauler, clearly getting the same alert that Eli had, attempted to drift away, but it was far bigger and less agile than the *Cavalier* and Eli had little trouble adjusting course to match.

"Jesus, kid," said Tapper, gripping the back of Eli's seat, "is your escape plan to crash us into another ship? Because that's a little more final than I'm looking for."

Just a little closer.

"OK, Addy... broadcast now."

There was a series of beeps and Eli held his breath, waiting for the entire cockpit to go dark, but whatever work Mal had done had apparently paid off. He expelled the air from his lungs.

"Did it work?" said Addy.

"We're not dead," Tapper pointed out.

"The sensors on the ground aren't fine-grained enough to separate the *Cav*'s small mass from the hauler's shadow," Eli explained, pointing at the heads-up display. "So all Yamanaka Tower can see is two identical transponder signals coming from the same location – it doesn't know which one's real."

"What about those incoming fighters?" said Addy. "Can't the pilots just look out their canopies and see us?"

"Nobody's ever satisfied with what they have," Eli muttered.

"*Brody.*"

"I'm working on it!"

Tapper took that moment to helpfully chime in. "Ten seconds."

Eli nudged the yoke up until there was nothing to see through the cockpit viewport but the cargo ship. He gingerly twitched the controls, keeping the ship level with the hauler, even as he could feel the vibrations from the ship's wake making the *Cav* buck and shudder.

"Interceptors are in weapons range," said Tapper.

As one, all four of them held their breath. *If I'm wrong about the capabilities of those fighters… or we're not quite close enough…*

"No contact," said Tapper. "Looks like they're closing to visual range, but that's going to take a couple minutes."

"We'll break atmosphere in less than that," said Eli. "Which raises the question: where exactly are we going, commander?"

Taylor sat back in her chair and rubbed a hand over her mouth. "We need to get out of the system." She grimaced. "Preferably out of Commonwealth space entirely. Can you make it to the Badr gate?"

The wormhole to the Badr sector was halfway across the system – getting there would take a few hours, and it was unlikely they could shadow the cargo ship the whole way there – if that was even where it was bound. "And here I was hoping you'd ask for something easy, like taking down those interceptors in a dogfight." Eli rubbed at his eyes, which suddenly felt gummy, like he hadn't blinked in several minutes. "There's a whole lot of empty space between here and the gate. Plus, even if we get through, it's nothing more than a head start – they'll be able to track us on the traffic network."

"I've got an idea about that," said Taylor. "But one thing at a time. Look," she craned her neck, taking in Addy and Tapper as well as Eli. "I realize these are extreme circumstances, so if anybody's got any objections, now's the time."

Nobody said anything for a moment, then Tapper cleared his throat. "I can't speak for anybody else, but I just want to point out that we've already made the choice to run, and everybody back on Nova, they're going to be assuming we're guilty of... well, of whatever bullshit they're accusing us of. We're not going to be able to clear our names – or the boss's – if we're looking over our shoulder for the bullseye on our back."

"I mean, I think sarge overloaded his metaphor at the end there, but he's right," said Eli. "After what we saw with Page and Alys Costa, I can't say I trust the system to find the truth."

As Kovalic had relayed it after their confrontation on Station Zero, Costa – Nova Front's leader and a former CID operative – claimed she'd been hung out to dry after a particularly shady black ops mission. More to the point, she'd decided to frame Page for the bombing of a ConComm communications hub.

Addy snorted. "You're just figuring that out now, huh? Yeah, I'm in. Sticking around for rendition to a black site seems like a bad deal. Let's get gone."

"All right, then," said Taylor, nodding and turning back to her console. "Lieutenant, set your course."

"That still leaves the problem of how we get there," said Tapper. "The second we leave the cargo ship's mass shadow, they're going to be over us like ants on honey."

Eli rubbed his chin, the bristles stiff against his fingers. He hadn't gotten to shave in a few days, what with all the running around and trying not to die, and he was getting perilously close to a beard. Or whatever he could grow that passed for one.

What we need is just a way for them to not pay attention to us. They could shut off the transponder entirely, but that would just flag them as an unidentified ship to all parties, which would be like politely asking to be shot down. Switching up the transponder code to clone another ship could work, but they'd still only be prolonging the inevitable – the Commonwealth navy was more than capable of interdicting two vessels and sorting it out afterwards.

An alarm beeped on the console. *More unwelcome news.*

Tapper had already picked up on it. "The cargo ship's reducing speed. Changing course, too."

"Yeah," said Eli. "I'm guessing Yamanaka Tower directed them to heave to." But something Mal had said the other day was niggling at his brain, worming its way in there. Something important about what their system upgrade could do...

"So, now you can broadcast a clone of any transponder the Cav *has seen," they'd said. "I could make it look like the secretary-general of the Commonwealth's personal transport. I'm telling you: nobody would know the difference."*

He almost whirled around to look at Addy before remembering that he was keeping the ship from crashing into a gigantic cargo hauler just meters away. "Addy, there should be a catalog of transponders in the system... see if you can find one with the call sign CSG1."

There was a sharply indrawn breath from Taylor. "Brody, that *cannot* be a good idea."

"No, no, trust me! I know what I'm doing."

"First time for everything I suppose," muttered Tapper from behind him.

"It's here," said Addy. She paused. "Uh. You want me to turn this on?"

The rumbling from the *Cav* started to die out, and ahead of them through the cockpit, Eli watched the blue sky darken to the black of space, pinpricks of stars flitting into existence like holes in the firmament itself. "Yeah. Yeah, I do."

"OK, here goes nothing." There was a click as Addy hit the broadcast switch, and then… nothing.

Eli heaved a sigh of relief. "There's a target lockout on official government transponders. You can override, but it's a lot of paperwork because who wants to be the one to order shooting down the leader of their own government? Anyway, right now, there are a lot of people down there yelling at each other and by the time they've cleared it all up, we should be long gone."

There was a brief sensation of settling in Eli's stomach as they hit space proper and the ship's systems began their switchover process: flying through vacuum wasn't quite like flying through atmosphere – for one thing, there was effectively no drag – and though the controls did their best to abstract the difference, a good pilot could always tell.

Eli reached out and brought up a navigation holoscreen, outlining their course in dotted green lines towards a point near the edge of the system. "Once we're clear of Nova's defense perimeter, our best option is to switch off the transponder and do a hard burn towards the gate, then kill most of the ship systems."

Taylor's eyebrows went up. "That'll essentially turn the ship into an asteroid. We'll be flying blind."

"True, but it goes both ways. Any sentry ships near the gate won't be able to see us either. Just in case they do manage to sort out the paperwork."

The commander nodded. "Do it. ETA to the gate?"

Eli's fingers danced over the navigation computer. "Two hours. With a two-hour gate transit to the Badr system, that gives us four hours to figure out where the hell we're going and how we're going to cover our tracks."

CHAPTER 9

Simon Kovalic had been dropped from the upper atmosphere into a combat zone, boarded an enemy vessel through the empty void of space, and even once hung onto the keel of a fast boat navigating a mine-laden bay. Through all of that he'd never gotten so much as a twinge of motion sickness.

Right now, he felt like he was going to throw up.

"The *princess* of the Illyrican Empire. That was your high-level source?" His head spun and he had to fight off the urge to put it between his knees. How much of what they'd been doing had been unwittingly playing into an agenda orchestrated by the very person they'd thought they'd been fighting against?

"Indeed," said the general. "Her identity was known only to me."

Kovalic's eyes flicked to Rance, sitting in the driver's seat, but a subtle raise of the yeoman's eyebrows suggested that the general's confidante had been none the wiser about CARDINAL's identity either.

"And what makes you think that she's taken over your old job?"

"We were close, once upon a time." A wistful note crept into his voice. "Alaric's focus was always on his sons,

Hadrian and Matthias, but Isabella never seemed to hold much interest for him. He'd made me her godfather – I believe he'd intended it as a slight, that he didn't consider me in that role for either of his male heirs, but he misjudged that, for she was easily the smartest and most driven of them. With her father's eye fixed elsewhere, I took it upon myself to ensure that she received a thorough education."

"In other words, you taught her everything she knows."

"Hardly. I taught her everything *I* knew, certainly, but I have no doubt she has long since surpassed me. I taught her chess from an early age, but by the time she had reached her teenage years she would regularly emerge triumphant from our matches. This strategy of hers, carefully feeding us information over the course of years, is just her style."

Kovalic's mind rifled through the little the general had revealed to him of his secretive source. "To what end? The information CARDINAL has provided has been, frankly, not just accurate but helpful. The Bayern operation, for example – she provided the information that Prince Hadrian would be serving as the Imperium's envoy to the planet."

"Indeed," said the general, nodding. "And what was the end result of our intervention there?"

"We stopped Prince Hadrian from providing a pretext for the Imperium to invade Bayern." Kovalic's brow furrowed. "Surely the increase in capital it would have provided – especially given that we know the Imperium has been on shaky financial ground – would have been to her benefit."

"Ah." The general raised one gnarled finger. "But that was not the only result. The deal we struck with Colonel Frayn also limited Prince Hadrian's influence. The heir apparent was effectively taken out of the line of succession."

Kovalic felt his stomach sinking even further. "I'm guessing Isabella didn't see eye to eye with her brother."

The older man spread his hands, as if demonstrating facts in evidence.

"So she used us to do her dirty work," said Kovalic. "To neutralize her biggest rival." He shook his head. "I'd be impressed if I didn't feel like passing out." Outplaying the general at the long game, now that was quite the accomplishment. But something still nagged at him. "Why do all this? Why *you*? You said you were close once, but it sure seems like she's throwing you under the gravbus."

With a sigh, the general leaned back in his seat. "A combination of things, I think. Some of them eminently rational. If I may be permitted to indulge in some light egotism, Isabella knows that I am the biggest impediment to carrying out whatever her agenda is. So concocting this evidence of treason effectively takes me out of the picture. But..." and here his eyes drifted out the window at the scenery zipping past, "...I also believe there is some degree of emotion at play. She's angry at me."

Kovalic raised an eyebrow. "For what?"

The general clutched his stick tightly. "Oh, the list of reasons could be quite long, I'm afraid. Chief among them my failure to prevent her mother's death."

News from within the Imperium had often been spotty, especially in the early days of the war, but that was a story that even the emperor had not been able to contain. "The assassination attempt," said Kovalic. "Right after the invasion of Earth. As I recall, there was a faction who believed that Alaric's war would destroy the

Imperium. Some sort of toxin, right? It didn't kill him, but that's why his health has been slowly failing for the last two decades."

"Indeed," said the general. "Unfortunately, the empress happened to be present as well, and took a much stronger dose." A shadow flitted over the man's face, a cloud of darkness that Kovalic had rarely seen there. It was a reminder that these figures, larger than life, the stuff of history books and galaxy-shaking events, had at one point been just *people* to the older man.

"So why does Isabella blame you for her death? Shouldn't that responsibility lie with the people that actually killed her?"

"I was a colonel at that point," said the general, his shoulders slumping. "Head of IIS's internal security and counterintelligence division. The attack was on my watch, and I should have stopped it, but we didn't find out until it was already underway. Alaric was too focused on his war to even stop and mourn, and the boys were offworld, with the fleets. That left not only all the arrangements for her state funeral – but also all the grieving – to Isabella alone. Our relationship was never quite the same after that."

"And yet she agreed to feed you information, at least nominally betraying her own people. What changed?"

"She came to me, six years ago, with concerns about her father. This was when his declining health had started to become more apparent. That provided a… thawing of the bond between us, one that I was all too eager to embrace. It led, in a roundabout fashion, to my defection, and our arrangement: she would share intelligence from within the Imperium, I would work to combat Alaric's worst impulses from without." At this, the general allowed himself a rueful chuckle. "I have to admit, it was masterfully done. In other circumstances, I would be proud of her – I've been beaten at my own game."

Kovalic rubbed his chin. "But this can't all simply be about revenge. If she's as smart as you say, she must have some goal in mind."

"On that we agree. If she views me as a potential threat that must be removed, then it is because I am an obstacle *to* something else. Whatever that is, we cannot allow her to ride roughshod over us. It may be that we're the only ones who *can* stand in her way. Which we must. Even if Isabella does not have her father's desire for conquest, the Commonwealth will not survive her agenda. It would be the difference between the firing squad and slow strangulation."

"Which means," said Kovalic, "that we need to figure out how to clear our names."

"It's easier said than done, I'm afraid. The evidence that Kester has is *technically* accurate. Money from my accounts on Bayern were sent to Isabella as part of our arrangement – but she then turned around and used that to fund Alys Costa and the Novan Liberation Front."

"You can't be responsible for something you didn't know," Kovalic objected. "You were supporting her in good faith; what she does with that money isn't on you."

The general gave a small smile. "Ah. Then I look merely obtuse and ineffectual rather than scheming and duplicitous. I'm not convinced that's going to be an improvement in the eyes of the Commonwealth government or, in particular, Aidan Kester."

Kovalic had to admit he wasn't wrong. Kester seemed to have it out for the two of them and, one way or another, Kovalic and the general had neatly coiled up the rope for their own hanging and handed it over with a bow on top. "Let's set that aside at present. I'm more concerned with how Kester got his hands on that intelligence. From what you've said, Isabella seems far too methodical to simply wait for CID or someone to stumble upon this clever evidence trail. Not only did she want it found, but wanted it found at a specific *time*. Doesn't seem like she'd want to leave that to chance."

A bit of the old spark had returned to the general's eyes, crowding out the melancholy that had set in during their conversation. "Agreed. And if she wanted it delivered at a specific time, then she must have a mechanism for doing so – an asset of some kind positioned to provide that information right when it would do the most damage."

Kovalic met the old man's gaze. "A mole. Somewhere within Commonwealth intelligence. And if we find them, we can clear our names – and maybe throw a wrench in whatever Isabella is planning."

Still, one thing was bothering him, as it had been since the general had begun his revelations; it itched like a tag on the back of a new shirt.

"Why do you think Isabella called the company Tanager Holdings? Surely she would have known that you'd figure it out, connect it to her."

The general's head cocked to one side. "Agreed. I have landed upon two mutually possible conclusions: First, that she wanted me to know. None of us are immune from gloating." A faint note of disappointment crept into his voice. "Second, and more pressingly, she believes it doesn't matter. Likely because I wouldn't be in a position to do anything about it. About which," he sighed and gestured to their surroundings, "she was not wrong. I can only conclude that such confidence means Isabella is in her endgame. But what it is, I fear I have no idea." His gaze drifted out the window and in it was something that Kovalic had never seen in all the years they'd known each other.

Worry.

CHAPTER 10

The *Cavalier* was uncharacteristically quiet with the engines powered down. After Brody had finished the initial burn they'd been able to unstrap from their seats and Addy had wandered back into the main hold.

It had always felt cozy and comfortable before, but the compartment suddenly seemed cold and too small. *Maybe it's just knowing that we're trapped here – there's nowhere else to go.* She was used to the wide-open spaces of a planet, sky stretching overhead. Instead she felt all too aware of the thin skin of the ship's hull that was all that separated them from the gaping expanse of space.

The adrenaline's wearing off, she reminded herself, even as she felt her forehead turn clammy. Just a few hours ago, she'd been fighting off armed intruders in her bedroom. Now she didn't even know when she'd get to go home again.

Home. When had she started thinking of it as home, and not just a place that she was staying?

She shook off the maudlin thoughts and stepped into the galley, pulling a drinking bulb of water. At least the ship had been restocked with the essentials in its downtime; they'd be fine for provisions until they got where they were going.

Wherever that was. Right now they were just running to get *away* – a feeling Addy knew all too well. No destination, no plan other than survival. But that wasn't going to be enough.

That wouldn't get them back home.

Boots clomped down the passage from the cockpit and Tapper stepped into the compartment. The weathered sergeant's eyes moved to her and gave a wry crinkle, as though he knew exactly what she was thinking.

"Come on," he said with no preamble. "The commander wants an inventory of our resources."

Addy nodded to the empty space where the trunk had been. "I think you blew up all our resources back in the hangar."

Tapper shrugged. "Like the old saying goes, easy come, easy go up in flames."

"I don't think I've ever heard that one before."

"Kids today," said the sergeant with a mock grumble. "Grab the go bags."

They'd each brought one. Addy retrieved the ones for herself and Brody and found Taylor's in the bunk room she and the commander were sharing. Tapper's was larger and he'd dropped it onto the table in one corner of the cargo compartment, then unzipped it and unceremoniously dumped its contents into a pile on the table: two knockout guns, three burner sleeves, a concussion grenade, a pair of false IDs, and a not insignificant pile of credit chips.

Addy and Brody's bags were somewhat more meager, but she'd packed each of them with a fake ID and a decent handful of credits – her own had an old but reliable Marks & Gray slug-thrower in there as well, and she saw Tapper cast an appraising eye in its direction.

Taylor's was perhaps the best stocked of them all, a fact that didn't remotely surprise Addy. *There's nothing she doesn't think through.* Five fake IDs, including Illyrican citizenship papers that looked totally genuine; four unactivated sleeves; a portable terminal; a KO gun, and enough credits to probably buy a brand new ship if they needed to. It was more than Addy's official pay for a year.

"I guess she was saving them for a rainy day," said Addy, as she let them sift through her fingers.

"Good," said Tapper, "because it's fucking pouring."

So we're not exactly going to have to look through the sofa cushions for spare change.

"Well, this seems fairly promising," said Tapper. The sergeant still had a hint of the morose about him, which Addy could only attribute to a decided lack of high explosives amongst their little collection.

There were more footsteps from the ship's fore, presaging Brody and Taylor's arrival; the other two members of the team joined them to survey the haul. Brody's eyes widened at the pile of money.

"Whoa. Are we buying a moon?" He reached out and poked them, as if he wasn't sure they were real.

"Uh, shouldn't someone be watching things up front?" said Addy.

"Not much flying required right now," said Brody, with a shrug. "At this point, we're basically just a rock somebody's thrown."

"I've been arguing for years that we don't even need a pilot," said Tapper. "Nobody ever listens."

"I mean, it's not intellectually challenging like setting off explosives or anything."

"Try it and see how many fingers *you* have left."

"Listen up," said Taylor sharply, cutting through the repartee. "We've got a limited amount of time before we have to make some decisions. I know this," she gestured at the pile of credits and fake IDs, "seems like a lot, but you'll be amazed at how fast we can burn through it, especially without a plan. Those papers won't raise questions at a glance, but they're quick jobs, not backstopped by extensive legends like the ones we're used to. If anybody starts digging into them, they'll fall apart fast."

"Come on, commander. We're used to working without a net," said Brody.

Tapper snorted. "There's working without a net, kid, and then there's working over a pit of spikes. One will get you killed a lot faster."

Addy rolled her eyes. *Without Kovalic to keep a lid on them, this is going to get old in a hurry.* "Will you two shut up? The commander's got the floor."

They both had the decency to look abashed at the reprimand.

"Sorry, commander," said Brody.

Taylor sent a curt nod in Addy's direction. "Look, I know all of this is overwhelming, and it's hard to even know where to start. So let's take it step by step: We can't stay in Commonwealth space."

Leaning against one of the bulkheads, Tapper gave a wry grin. "I'm guessing Illyrican territory is right out."

Brody coughed. "Yeah, one of us is still technically a deserter from the Illyrican military, so I'm going to give that a hard pass."

As Commonwealth operatives, none of them were

going to be particularly safe in the Imperium, but Brody had served as an Illyrican fighter pilot before Kovalic had recruited him, which made it even riskier for him.

"Hanif space is right off the Badr sector," Addy suggested. "The Ring's big – we could easily disappear in there."

Taylor seemed to weigh the option for a second, then shook her head. "The clans tightly police entry, and, more importantly, Aidan Kester came up on the Hanif desk at CID. We can't risk that he still has connections there. We need someplace off the beaten path."

"We're running low on options, then," said Brody, eyes rolling upward as he consulted the pilot's charts that Addy knew were seared into his brain. "Haran's too small... Anselm doesn't have any habitable planets... hmm, there are a few moons in Juarez. I think one has a palladium mining operation."

"Perfect. Just the kind of place where we can disappear. Any objections?" asked Taylor, looking around.

Addy had never set foot in the Juarez system, couldn't even remember having heard much about it, which hopefully boded well. There was the pesky matter of what they could actually *do* from a remote mining colony, but that was a problem for later.

"It'll take us around fourteen hours once we're out of the system," said Brody. "Commander, if you've got an idea about how to hide our course from the comm buoy on the other end of the gate, now would be a good time to share."

"Oh, no, lieutenant," said Taylor, and the smile that crossed her face was genuine and, Addy thought, a little unnerving in its enthusiasm. "Transparency's important: I plan on telling them exactly where we're going."

Brody's course setting was on the money; the *Cav* hit the bullseye from half a system away, sailing right past a small handful of Commonwealth naval ships that were clearly doing their best to patrol the huge swath of empty space before the immense whirlpool of blue and purple that was the Badr wormhole.

Hell of a darts throw.

They used the transit time to get all their gear stowed safely and securely in the ship. After disbursing the credits among the team, the rest had been stashed in a variety of secret compartments throughout the *Cavalier*. Likewise with the weapons and extra fake IDs.

Tapper, over Brody's protestations, even secured one of their pistols with a magnetic holster on the underside of the pilot's console in the cockpit.

"Sarge, I don't really *do* guns," said Brody.

The old man snorted. "That's only because the rest of us have been here to cover your ass." He sighed and put up a hand to forestall Brody's argument. "Look, *I'll* feel better if I know you've got it. Just in case."

Addy watched Brody's dubious expression turn to one of resignation, shot through with sympathy. *The old man knows exactly what buttons to press.*

Each of them also chose one of their identities to carry, because the only thing more suspicious than no papers were too many papers. Addy's proclaimed her as Sabaean native Regina Allingham, though she'd privately already decided that she went by "Reggie". It also listed her occupation as a freelance journalist, which hopefully provided adequate cover for asking a bunch of nosy questions, should the need arise. She'd even invented a dog named Ginger, because why not? *Fictitious pets are way easier to clean up after, although definitely less cuddly.*

All of that busywork filled the two-hour trip through the wormhole surprisingly easily, and in no time they'd reconvened in the cockpit as they prepared to exit the gate back into normal space.

"OK, here we go," said Brody, grasping the *Cavalier*'s yoke.

Outside the canopy, the blue-purple mottling of the wormhole flashed white, leaving a bright corona in Addy's eyes, and then they were looking out once again into empty space as they emerged into the uninhabited Badr sector.

"Re-entry complete. Commander, it's your show."

Seated at the co-pilot's console, Taylor reached out and tapped a control on the holoscreen in front of her, lines of code unspooling at a breakneck pace. "Deploying the countermeasures now."

Tapper leaned forward, staring at the lines as if he could unpack their meaning just by looking, then shook his head. "So this virus…"

"Worm, technically," said Taylor. "It doesn't require any further human intervention once it's infiltrated the comm network. From there, it'll self-propagate across the system, making it look like several thousand ships with several thousand different transponder signals exited at this precise time and plotted a thousand courses to every corner of the sector. Even if someone combs through all that data, it's going to be nearly impossible to figure out which signal was real."

"Why not just delete our log entry?" the sergeant asked. "Surely that would be easier."

"Redundancy and backups. There are a lot more protections against removing data than inserting extra data."

"I don't suppose this would work with my pension?"

"Worm deployed," said Taylor. "Lieutenant, the helm is yours. Plot a course for the Juarez gate."

"Copy that. We're going to take a nice, long comfortable trip across the system. So I hope you all like sixth wave instrumental techno-pop, because that's the only playlist I have loaded."

Tapper groaned. "I'm going to go put a pillow over my head and try to get some rack time."

Grinning to himself, Brody leaned back and put his feet up on the console, still wearing the dingy shoes that he'd grabbed from the apartment. *We're all going to need to buy some new clothes, I'm guessing.* Addy started mentally spending the credits in her head, watching them drain away. *The commander was right – it seems like a lot until you start using it.*

Taylor stood and jerked her head at Addy, gesturing towards the cargo hold. Leaving Brody to start bopping his head to a particularly aggressive synth track, she followed the other woman out, making sure to close to cockpit door behind them. *Like any virus, that music needs to be contained or it's going to embed itself in my brain.*

In the hold, Taylor turned and cleared her throat, shifting her weight back and forth between her legs in a decidedly un-Taylor-like pose. *She's...* Addy blinked. *Nervous?*

"I just wanted to say, I know you and I haven't always seen eye to eye... but I appreciate your support back there. This is going to be an adjustment for all of us. Not having Simon here, I mean. It's not a position I thought I'd find myself in. Especially under these circumstances."

Oh god, she's trying to bond. Uhhhh... how do I.... "Sure," she said after a slightly too long pause. "I get it. But like you said, we're all in this, so we'd better stick together. Otherwise we're not going to last long."

"Right." Taylor offered up a wan smile. "Anyway, thanks." She nodded her head, as if satisfied she'd gotten her point across. "I'm going to check our medical supplies."

And with that, she headed across the cargo hold, leaving Addy shaking her head. *Never thought I'd see the day when* Taylor *feels out of her element.* A cold tendril snaked its way into her gut, sitting heavy, like a meal of fried food.

I think we might really be in trouble this time.

CHAPTER 11

It was nearly evening when Rance pulled them off the highway and down a lengthy set of cliffside switchbacks to the picturesque town nestled on a crescent-shaped beach. Despite the two decades that Kovalic had spent on Nova, his ventures outside of Salaam had largely been limited to the cabin he'd built on a lake several hours away. Unless you counted trips to military bases, which one probably shouldn't.

Maybe he should have taken more vacation days.

Frustrating as their circumstances were, it was difficult to see the sinking sun reflected off the waves crashing into the sand and not be at least a little bit heartened. The car wound into town on narrow streets, passing colorful low-slung shops and a number of people clearly on holiday.

When they eventually pulled to a stop in the municipal lot on the edge of town – which itself was cordoned off from the predominantly pedestrian village – Kovalic stepped out to find the sharp tang of saltwater in his nose and a warm ocean breeze ruffling his hair. It felt weirdly idyllic and surreal for a trio of fugitives on the run.

"So," he said, looking over the top of the car at the general, who had gotten out the other side. "Who's this old friend we're meeting?"

From somewhere the general produced a white broad-brimmed hat and seated it atop his bald head. It was joined by a pair of sunglasses and, though that might not have seemed like an effective disguise, it did give him the air of a grandfather on vacation, especially when he swung his walking stick in a jaunty fashion.

Rance had shucked her uniform's tunic; her sleeveless undershirt, decidedly out of place in a military setting, fit in perfectly in the beachside village. Kovalic tugged at his own coat, which was definitely on the warm side for the weather, and settled for taking it off and slinging it over one shoulder. That was how a relaxed person looked, right?

"Calling him a friend might be overselling it," said the general as the three of them fell into step, walking towards the bustling center of town. "We haven't seen each other in seven years, and we did not part on the best of terms."

"Seven years?" Kovalic echoed. "That's… a specific number. Right about the time you defected." Slowing to a stop, he gave the general a hard stare. "He's Illyrican, isn't he? Another of your 'undisclosed' contacts."

The general, who had continued on for a few steps after Kovalic halted, waved his stick. "Come now, Simon, you're blocking the street."

With a sigh, Kovalic pressed two fingers to his forehead. "I can't believe this. Again. How many other things are you not telling me?"

Strolling back, the general planted both his hands atop the stick's pommel and let out a long breath. "You're right, of course. For so long, secrets were the currency of my life, and I became all too accustomed to hoarding them. It's a hard habit to break, but I will endeavor to do better."

It hit all the right notes. The older man even looked regretful. But a knot still burned in Kovalic's chest, reminding him that it was the general playing his cards close to his vest that had landed them in this rapidly boiling water. "Who is he?"

The general waved a conciliatory hand towards Kovalic and started walking again. Rance had taken up a position on point, a few yards ahead, looking for all the world as though she just happened to be strolling through town, with no connection to the two men behind her.

Reluctantly, Kovalic fell into step with the general as they crossed over a stone bridge and into Tokai proper.

"Yevgeniy Esterhaus." The name fell from the general's lips like lead weights. "You know him?"

"No. Should I?"

"He was a high-ranking Imperial Intelligence officer. Seven years ago he left the Imperium and came here under an assumed identity."

Kovalic's eyebrows rose. "Another defector?"

Here the general's mouth pulled back in a tight smile that didn't reach his eyes. "Not as such. Yevgeniy's departure was not as... voluntary as mine."

"Exiled?"

"Let us say he managed to get out one step before the firing squad."

"And he fled here, to Nova. Did CID know about him?" Surely he would have been debriefed by the Commonwealth's intelligence agencies, pumped for every last bit of intel. But even as Kovalic asked, he already knew the answer: had Esterhaus been a known defector, Kovalic would have heard of him.

"No," said the general. "The circumstances of his departure were so deeply upsetting that he decided to leave all vestiges of that life behind him. Hence, opening a tea shop in these lovely surroundings."

"Wait," said Kovalic, putting up his hands. "You want us to put our lives in the hands of a former Illyrican spy? What makes you think he won't just turn around and sell us out to the Imperium to get back in their good graces?"

They walked in silence for a moment, passing a low stone wall that looked out over the beach. Novan gulls wheeled and cried overhead, their screeches echoing through the narrow streets. "Yevgeniy was one of my top lieutenants at IIS," said the general at last. "Deeply loyal to the Imperium. Losing him was a devastating blow to IIS and to me personally."

"Why'd he leave?"

A wince shot through the general, and he paused and raised a shaky hand. "Must we dredge all this up? It's ancient history."

"You *just* told me you were trying to do better. What aren't you telling me?"

The general sighed and looked out over the beach, his eyes invisible behind the dark lenses of the sunglasses. "I was the one who burned him. Forced him to flee and leave his life behind." He glanced up at the falling sun, then nodded. "It's getting late. I'd like to get to the tea shop before it closes, if you don't mind."

Kovalic had a litany of other questions and, as tempted as he was to demand answers, a public street didn't seem like the place to do it. It wasn't as if they had a lot of other recourse at this point: they were here, for better or worse.

But it didn't mean he was going in blind. He still had the KO gun he'd taken off the marine that morning tucked within his folded jacket, concealed but within easy reach.

They trailed Rance, who was herself following a route through the winding streets of Tokai that she had apparently memorized. At one point they were up on a flyover, pedestrians milling below, then later they walked under a bridge on a street where restaurants were dragging tables out onto patios and sidewalks in anticipation of the upcoming dinner crowd.

After a ten-minute walk – longer than Kovalic had figured, given the town's small size, but all the twists and turns made it larger than it looked from the outside – they turned down a side street towards a yellow building, outside of which hung a filigreed sign with elegant cursive lettering.

"'Tea for Two'," Kovalic read. "Cute."

The sign on the door still said "Open," so the general pushed his way in, leaving Kovalic and Rance in his wake. Kovalic caught the yeoman's arm before she could follow her boss, and she shot him a questioning look.

"How much of that did you know?"

She leveled him with a calculating look that sent a pang through him, it so reminded him of Nat. "I knew what I needed to know, major."

"And you still trust him? After everything you just learned?"

"It doesn't change what he's done – or what we've accomplished together. He's more than earned my trust. Hasn't he earned yours?" Gently, she disengaged his hand; a chime sounded gently from within as the door closed behind her.

Kovalic stood on the sidewalk, feeling the paths branching out before him. What was the alternative? Sacrifice the general to save his own skin? Despite all his misgivings, the best chance of uncovering Isabella's mole person was here, working with the general – not in a prison cell. So, really, there was no decision at all.

He stepped up and pushed open the tea shop door, another jingle sounding above his head.

A cool blast of air hit him, respite from the warmth of the day. The shop's interior was simple but elegant: half a dozen bamboo-topped tables with wrought iron feet, each surrounded by high-backed chairs with comfortable cushions. Most of the tables were occupied by small groups of customers, and a low murmur of polite conversation percolated through the space. There was a small counter at the back, fronted by display cases of confections, some of which were being carefully laden onto tiered trays ferried to the tables by smiling servers.

Rance was already in conversation with the host, a small man with dark brown skin and a pencil mustache, who was smiling and gesturing her and the general to one of the few free tables, next to the front window. Kovalic followed them and took the seat against the wall, draping his jacket over the back of the chair and using the opportunity to surreptitiously slide the knockout gun into his pocket.

The maître d' handed them hardbound menus, elegantly embossed with the shop's name in gold. Anachronistic, but it fit the decor and atmosphere. And, after all, wasn't that what you were paying for in a place like this? The experience?

Looking up from his perusal of the menu, the general peered around the shop. "Is the proprietor about, by any chance? He's an old friend."

The maître d' couldn't have been more surprised if someone had told him that their tea was cold. "You know Monsieur Giroux? I must admit, that is a first. But yes, he's in the back. I'll tell him you're here – what was the name?"

"We haven't seen each other for some years," said the general, adopting a conspiratorial tone. "The name's McCrae."

Kovalic froze, his fingers tightening on the menu. The general never did anything by accident, or left it to chance. If he was dredging that name from their shared past – the night when they'd first met, no less – it was to send a message.

With a nod, the host disappeared towards the back of the room. Without explicitly meeting Kovalic's gaze, the general acknowledged him with a dip of his chin. "I'll explain later," he murmured.

That didn't reassure Kovalic. His hand dipped towards the weapon in his pocket, every instinct flaring into high alert. All of this was increasingly feeling like a bad idea, and he was on the verge of suggesting they should go when a slightly accented voice boomed out from the rear of the shop. "Hamish McCrae, my god."

Its owner proved to be a rotund man in a well-cut seersucker suit, with a brilliant red flower in his lapel. Everything about the man was expansive, from his broad, friendly face to his meaty hands. He crossed the shop, arms wide open as though greeting a long-lost friend. The rest of the patrons – and the staff for that matter – looked surprised at the display.

He crossed to the table, still smiling, and took the general's hand, pumping it enthusiastically. The general, for his part, covered a rare bout of discomfiture by summoning a veneer of politesse no doubt ingrained from his upbringing. "Hello, Jean, it has been too long."

The big man leaned closer, and Kovalic caught his grip tightening around the general's. His smile held, but the eyes – dark, wide set – were steel. His voice lowered, pitched for the three of them alone as he spoke through gritted teeth. "Not long enough for me, Hasan al-Adaj. You have one minute to get the fuck out of here before I kill you with my bare hands."

CHAPTER 12

"Oh, I think I'll have the Darjeeling," said the general, tapping the menu. "Is it first flush or second?"

The man now known as Jean Giroux froze, his face in an almost comic rictus. For a moment, Kovalic wasn't sure which way it would go – it didn't seem out of the question that the big man would attempt to throttle the general, who was calmly sitting as though his life hadn't just been threatened. But Giroux's lips merely pressed into a thin line. "Still the same old stubborn pain in the ass, I see."

"I'm far too old to change my ways."

"I don't know why you thought coming here was a good idea and," Giroux put up a hand to forestall an explanation, "I don't really care. Have a cup of tea, if you must – it's on the house – but then go and leave me alone." He'd already snapped his fingers for the server and turned to go when the general spoke quietly.

"Yevgeniy, I am sorry. And I need your help."

For the second time in as many minutes, Giroux stopped, as if tugged by some invisible thread stringing back years into his past. He sighed and his shoulders slumped.

The server, who had appeared beside them ready to take their order, gave them all a perplexed look until her boss waved a hand towards the back of the tea shop. "This party will be joining me in the private room, Della. Have two pots of Darjeeling sent in. Thank you."

She nodded in response and hurried off, while the general, Kovalic, and Rance rose to follow Giroux through the main dining room to the door at the rear.

The back room proved to be mostly storage but with a small private dining area, not nearly as elegant as the front of house had been, but somewhat cozier. Instead of high-backed chairs, there were a few plush armchairs and a sofa around a low coffee table. Stacks of supplies were lined against one wall, stenciled with the names of teas. A terminal sat on a desk in one corner.

"Sit," said Giroux. As invitations went, it sounded grudging to Kovalic's ears, but the general wasted no time in taking one of the armchairs, his walking stick held loosely in one hand. Rance and Kovalic seated themselves on the sofa, and Giroux dragged over the wooden desk chair, perching atop as one accustomed to having spent long hours in it. He rubbed his face with both hands, as if removing a layer of makeup, and when he looked up again, he seemed almost a different person altogether.

Not through any trick of cosmetics or prosthetics, or even advanced technology like a holoprojector mask, Kovalic realized. No, it was more intrinsic than that: something in the way he held himself, the way his features were composed, had shifted. This was no longer the ebullient, extravagant tea house owner, but someone harder, a piece of stone polished after years of having tumbled against the rougher edges of life.

Yevgeniy Esterhaus. Hiding in plain sight.

"What, exactly, is it you want from me, Hasan?" His voice was flat now, devoid of the resonance he'd displayed in the shop; it had become something rougher, meaner. Kovalic could hear an accent straining to push free – not the indistinct one that he'd used in his Giroux persona, the one that could have belonged to an expatriate from a dozen different worlds, but neither the cultivated tones of Illyrican nobility that still tinged the general's voice, though it shared similar notes.

"As I said, we need your help," said the general, his head tilt encompassing Rance and Kovalic. "There is a well-placed Illyrican mole within the Commonwealth intelligence community, and, thanks to some conveniently planted evidence, we've been accused of treason. I want your help clearing our names."

The ensuing silence was so completely quiet that Kovalic was sure you could hear electrons buzzing in the terminal. Esterhaus was staring at the general with a look of bald-faced astonishment.

It was a chuckle that broke the spell, a sharp punctuating laugh. It grew until Esterhaus was clutching his stomach, his head thrown back as he wiped the tears from his eyes. "*You*. You want *me* to help clear you of *treason*?" That set off a new chain reaction of laughter, his whole body shaking with mirth.

"I don't see what's so funny," said the general stiffly.

"Of course you don't. Of *course* you don't. And that, Hasan, was always your problem. You thought your situation so different from everybody else, but despite all your brilliance, you were never able to put yourself in anybody's shoes." The chortles had died away now, Esterhaus's solemnity firmly back in place. "Someone is running your own playbook against you, old friend. Or have you conveniently forgotten what you did to me?"

A solitary crack shot through the general's veneer, and some of the tension went out of his shoulders. "No. I haven't. And, as I said, I am sorry for it. I had no other choice."

"Bullshit. You threw me to the wolves on trumped-up treason charges to cover your own betrayal, and now it's your turn." He shifted in the chair, and his attention swung to Kovalic and Rance. "He hasn't told you that story, has he?"

Kovalic shot a sidelong look at the general, but Esterhaus's words had clearly struck close to the mark. The old man's hand clutched at his walking stick, and, for a moment, Kovalic had the absurd image of him drawing his blade and lunging at Esterhaus.

"No," said Kovalic, though he was starting to piece it together.

"Ah," said Esterhaus, spreading his hands, "then let me paint a picture for you of the *noble* Hasan al-Adaj. A man I once called friend. I worked by his side for a decade, and I would gladly have given my life in his service – but that is something quite different when the choice is made for you. I thought our common purpose was clear: to protect the Imperium. Together we concocted what seemed to be a brilliant plan, to insert a double agent into the Commonwealth intelligence apparatus. We spent months creating this person from whole cloth, fleshing out his background, establishing his bona fides, carefully leaking information to the Commonwealth to prove his willingness to defect."

The hairs on Kovalic's arms had gone up, and he remembered the name that the general had given in the tea shop. "McCrae."

Esterhaus's eyebrows were perhaps the only slight thing about him, slender and dark. They rose at the name. "Indeed. How did you –" Realization broke across his face, followed by something very much like sadness. "Of course. You were the Commonwealth officer he approached – the military attaché at the Illyrican Embassy. Kovalic, yes?"

There was no point in denying it so he just nodded. It had been him on Illyrica, seven years ago on a snowy night, thinking he was off to meet a high-ranking Imperial defector. Which he had – just not the one he'd expected.

"Hasan had been very careful, very precise," Esterhaus continued. "And it wasn't until the night your meet was supposed to happen that I realized that something was off."

Here the general broke in, genuinely curious. "And how exactly did that come to pass? I never got a chance to ask you."

Esterhaus leveled an icy stare in his direction, then ignored the question, turning back to Kovalic. "I was in charge of the surveillance division at IIS – the Bootblacks, as we were familiarly known, though the sobriquet predates my time there. Keeping tabs on enemy operatives on our soil, internal security risks, that kind of thing. The night of the meet, Hasan and I had agreed to pull back surveillance around the location; he didn't want to spook the target. You. But shortly before the meet, I got a high-level order to reinstate my people. Only it was late, and I didn't have time to brief and dispatch a team.

"So I went myself. Imagine my surprise when, instead of our carefully prepared impostor, it was Hasan himself who met with you. *That* had not been the plan. Still, I gave him the benefit of the doubt; I assumed something had gone wrong, and rather than squander the opportunity by calling off the meet, he'd elected to handle it personally. My remit was not to interfere but to observe, which I did. It wasn't until afterwards that I pressed him about it.

"He had an excuse, of course. The weather, I believe. He always did have a way of making things sound eminently reasonable. But a sliver of doubt was lodged so deeply in my mind that I could not excise it – and you knew that too, didn't you, Hasan?"

The general shifted uncomfortably in his seat, as though it had grown suddenly coarse and prickly beneath him.

"Things moved quickly after that," said Esterhaus. "Too quickly for me to get a handle on. Before I knew what was happening, *I* was being accused of treason, of leaking the very information on the upcoming Sabaean invasion that Hasan himself had given you. I wanted to stay and defend myself, but the deck had been clearly stacked against me, and I had no choice but to flee Illyrica before a Special Operations Executive team could bring me in."

Kovalic swallowed, his throat dry. It sounded uncomfortably familiar, and not for the first time he wondered how the rest of his team was faring. If they'd been apprehended, surely he would have heard by now.

Esterhaus folded his hands and continued his story. "I managed to secure a berth on a freighter heading through the bottleneck at Jericho – the Commonwealth wasn't my first choice, but it seemed the only place far enough from IIS's influence to guarantee my safety. And by the time I realized that they had bigger fish to fry," he shot a meaningful glance at the general, "I had already established my life here. There was no going back."

Silence fell once again over the room, and Kovalic glanced over at the couch, where the general wore a slightly dyspeptic expression. Rance, for her part, seemed as unflappable as ever, absorbing the story like a sponge.

"So," Esterhaus said. "You can understand why I'm not *eager* to render you any further service. Especially since the irony of your situation is so particularly delightful."

There was a knock at the door and the server appeared, bearing a tray with a pot of tea and four mugs. She deposited them on the coffee table and, at a nod from Esterhaus – who had briefly donned his beneficent Giroux persona once again – departed.

"And now, let us all enjoy a cup of this excellent tea, and then part ways, never to see one another again." He poured the steaming liquid into the mugs.

The general cleared his throat, and leaned forward to take one of the cups. "Yevgeniy, I am truly sorry. But I'm afraid I do need to ask you one more question about your story. That high-level order, the one that told you to reinstate surveillance. Where did it come from?"

Esterhaus picked up his own mug, blowing to cool it, then tilted his head to one side, regarding the general with a neutral look. "You were the director of Eyes. There was only one authority that could supersede yours."

"The palace."

The big man nodded. "The order itself was unsigned, but it bore the Imperial seal."

With a sigh, the general clutched his tea in both hands. "Then, while I cannot absolve myself of my responsibility for what happened to you, it would seem that we were *both* played, old friend."

"The princess was a step ahead of you even then," said Kovalic. He wouldn't have believed there was anybody who thought more moves in advance than the general.

At that, Esterhaus blinked. "Princess? You mean little Isabella? What does she have to do with any of this?"

The general grimaced. "She appears to have taken up my role as director of IIS and this – all of this – has been part of her plan. I believe she tipped you off in order to force my hand, to make sure that I would have no choice but to ultimately flee the Imperium. I knew even sacrificing you to cover my tracks was only a temporary reprieve."

"Princess Isabella," mused the big man. He shook his head in disbelief. "I remember you used to bring her to the office, sit her up on your desk, and let her play with the holoscreens. In between lectures about soft power and the importance of intelligence gathering, of course." Esterhaus snorted. "It seems perhaps you taught her too well."

"Indeed."

"So you want me to help you out of… what? Some old misplaced sense of friendship? Camaraderie amongst expatriates?"

"Yevgeniy, I've done much that I cannot atone for, though I've tried. I made sure you stayed off the Commonwealth's radar and thus off the Imperium's."

"Ah, it's to be blackmail, then," said Esterhaus, his voice weary.

With a sharp shake of his head, the general raised his hand.

"No. I intend to keep your secret whether you help us or not. That is the least I can do after how I used you. But there are larger stakes here. Whatever Isabella has in mind, I have no doubt it means instability for the Commonwealth, and you know as well as I that will lead to chaos for everybody." He raised a finger and pointed to the door they'd entered through. "I think you've come to value your life here, Yevgeniy. The people out there are lucky enough to go about their lives without having to worry about open war raining down on them. The citizens of the Illyrican Empire, they deserve a future beyond the conflict waged by their leaders. If we don't stop whatever Isabella has planned…" he spread his hands wide, "…that is all they will have. The Yevgeniy Esterhaus I knew did his job to protect people from threats they would never know about. The years change us all, but I don't believe they can truly change our hearts."

Kovalic had heard a lot of arguments from his boss over the last several years, but he could tell that something in this one ran deeper, a vein of emotion straight to the core of why Hasan al-Adaj had actually believed that the only way to save the empire that he loved was to betray it.

Yevgeniy Esterhaus said nothing for a moment, just raised his cup of tea to his mouth, and held it there, staring contemplatively into the middle distance. Beside him, Kovalic could feel Rance holding her breath, while keeping her stoic demeanor in place.

At long last, Esterhaus sighed. "Damn you, Hasan. You always did know exactly which strings to pull to get your way. And damn me for still believing in a greater good, after all these years." He drained the cup in one gulp and got to his feet. "Follow me."

CHAPTER 13

Despite his lingering animosity toward the general, Esterhaus proved to be a generous host. After the tea shop closed for the evening, he dug an assortment of food and drinks from the refrigerator in the small apartment he kept upstairs, the spread being all the more impressive given the lack of time in which he threw it together.

"This aperitif is a tradition of mine," said the big man as he laid an assortment of cheeses and charcuterie down on a wood board, along with a bowl of olives and salted nuts. "It is perhaps the thing I miss the most from Illyrica."

The general's eyebrow flickered at this, but Kovalic noticed he didn't hesitate to accept an old-fashioned from the man. Rance demurred, sticking with a sparkling water, and Kovalic contented himself with a glass of excellent red wine.

"So," said Esterhaus, seating himself in a well-worn leather armchair. The last vestiges of the setting sun, sinking over the horizon, painted the room in reds and golds, even through the automatically tinting windows. "This mole of yours – have you any leads?"

Kovalic exchanged a look with the general, who gestured at him to proceed. "Nothing concrete, but we do have a person of interest. Aidan Kester."

"I don't know the name," said Esterhaus, brows knitting, "but you'll have to forgive me: my memory isn't what it once was."

A slightly skeptical expression played over the general's face, but he covered it with a sip of his drink.

"Deputy Director for Operations of the Commonwealth Intelligence Directorate," Kovalic supplied. "And, thanks to the recent resignation of the two top-ranking CID officials, now its current acting director."

"I see. What makes you think Acting Director Kester is involved?"

"His promotion was a direct result of the same operation being used to cast suspicion upon General Adaj, myself, and the rest of our team," said Kovalic. It had been Nova Front's revelation of CID's AUGUR program, which would have given the agency unchecked ability to spy on Commonwealth citizens, that had forced the CID director and deputy director for intelligence to step down.

"Hm," said Esterhaus, helping himself to a square of hard cheese. "Circumstantial evidence at best. You don't rise that far through the ranks of an intelligence agency without being adept at playing politics – perhaps he was simply in the right place at the right time to capitalize on the misfortune of others."

"Deputy Director Kester has been on our radar for some time," the general broke in, his tone grave. "He was particularly well informed about an operation we conducted on Bayern nine months ago; at the time I chalked it up to his connections – he's married to the son of a high-ranking civil servant – but it ultimately proved to be because he had compromised one of our own team members."

Kovalic's mouth set, his fingers tightening on his wine glass. He had resolved matters with Aaron Page, but both the betrayal and the fact that Kester had wormed his way into his team – and, more to the point, that Kovalic hadn't caught it – still stung.

"My concerns have stretched even further back," the general continued. "There was a CID mission on Caledonia around a year and a half ago that Kester oversaw which resulted in the death of a veteran operative and had some… other significant ramifications."

"Ah," said Esterhaus, raising his own glass, "but I seem to recall you always advising me not to overestimate my adversaries' capabilities, Hasan. What was it you used to say? 'When you posit the existence of a bogeyman, you start to see their hand in everything'."

The general let out a harrumph. "I'm sure I said nothing of the sort."

Esterhaus laughed, a big genial guffaw that filled the room as much as he did, then glanced over at Kovalic and Rance. "He fancies himself very quotable, even if he would never admit it. Very well, Acting Director Kester is a person of interest at the very least. I presume that to clear yourself requires proving someone else's guilt."

"Ideally," said the general.

"And if you were desperate enough to turn to me, then I assume it's because of my own particular skills and specialties. So you want surveillance on Acting Director Kester: video, sound, drone, tails? And for resources you have…" Here he paused, his dark eyes going to Rance and Kovalic. "These two. I assume you yourself will not be heading into the field." A note of irony underscored the non-question.

"I think perhaps I might be more useful elsewhere," said the general dryly.

"Of course, of course." Esterhaus's mouth quivered in a barely contained smile. "It's a tall order, given the resources at hand. There was a time where I could have snapped my fingers and had Acting Director Kester's entire life laid out before us, but these days my capabilities are a bit more modest." At this, he rose from his seat, carefully setting his glass down on a coaster, and walked over to a door that Kovalic had taken for a closet. The big man pressed his finger to the access panel and it blinked green, the lights in the room beyond coming on with a bright snap as the door slid open.

Even from the mere sliver Kovalic could see through the doorway, he was relatively certain this was more than just a place to keep coats. He caught sight of an impressive set of displays, each showing a camera feed from around the tea shop, including even an overhead view that had to be supplied by a drone hovering above them – there was no way Esterhaus could have access to a satellite... right?

"I see old habits do indeed die hard," said the general.

"You know how it is. Once you've been privy to all the details, it's hard to ignore them."

"I'm guessing you don't get a lot of crime here," said Kovalic.

"It is perhaps overkill," Esterhaus acknowledged with a self-deprecating smile. "But I sleep better at night knowing that if Eyes does decide it finally needs to tie up loose ends, I will at least be apprised of their coming."

"Luckily for you, I think they've got more pressing matters to attend to," said Kovalic. He'd met Lakshmi, the putative head of IIS's Nova station, just a few days ago, and she'd struck him as an immensely capable woman who didn't miss a trick. If she'd been ordered to take Esterhaus off the board, he would have been long gone by now.

"But as I said," Esterhaus reiterated, "this will be difficult. The acting director of CID is a hard target – well protected, with a security detail and no doubt myriad anti-surveillance measures in place."

The general spread his hands and grinned with the air of a mischievous schoolboy. "My dear Yevgeniy – I would hardly have come to you if it were going to be *easy*."

Esterhaus gave him a hard look for a moment, then wheezed a rueful chuckle. "I've forgotten how much I did enjoy your flattery." He wagged his head, like a great horse shaking its mane. "Very well, then. Since we cannot hope to overwhelm their technology, our best bet is something low tech: eyes-on surveillance from our younger, sprightlier pair," he said, waving a hand at Kovalic and Rance, "while Hasan and I dig up what we can about Kester's movements from other sources."

Kovalic looked over to Rance, who had taken this with her usual equanimity, and then back at Esterhaus. "So in other words, we're the ones doing all the work, while you two sit here and enjoy appetizers and drinks?"

"Delegation, my friend," said Esterhaus. "Plus, the perks of age. We can't be sitting in a groundcar on a stakeout, leaving every twenty minutes to use the bathroom."

"My legs get very cramped in those vehicles," the general added, his eye twinkling.

"Your legs are *robotic*."

But the older man ignored the comment and turned to Rance. "Is our vehicle still clean, or had we better swap it with another, do you think?"

Rance waggled her hand. "I'd rather not bring it back into Salaam, just in case it's been flagged. They'll have a harder time tracking us down here."

"Yevgeniy," said the general. "I don't suppose you have a car you'd like to lend us?"

"I'm afraid I don't have much need for one in town – I walk most everywhere. But I can borrow one." He raised a finger. "I will, however, need it back in one piece, if you please."

Kovalic was about to open his mouth to point out that it was just surveillance, but given that the number of high-speed chases he'd been in over the past week was more than zero, he decided it was best not trying to score that particular point. "Understood."

The big man clapped his hands, rubbing them together. "Well, then, let's see about getting you outfitted, shall we?"

It turned out that Esterhaus's command center – and Kovalic couldn't come up with a better word for the room – also boasted a sizable storage locker. He opened it up for Rance and Kovalic to peruse, though the general demurred with a wave.

"Just because I'm out of the game doesn't mean I'm going to be caught unprepared," said Esterhaus by way of explanation. The cabinet contained a collection of carefully maintained – if somewhat worn – weaponry and surveillance equipment. "I keep my ear to the ground, as it were, and there's plenty of military surplus on sale if you know where to look."

"Is that a nanoweave pickup?" said Rance, her interest piqued as she peered at a swatch of fabric on one shelf.

"Ah, I see you know your surveillance equipment. Yes – an older model, but perfectly functional. Ideal for passive monitoring, but difficult to use without direct access to your target." He pursed his lips in thought. "This job is going to be tricky. I'd assume that the Acting Director of CID's home, office, and vehicle are swept daily, which makes planted listening devices a bad idea. Compromising his sleeve would obviously be ideal but requires close contact, which could be risky if he knows your faces."

"Yeah, that's not going to fly," said Kovalic. "What we need is some place outside of his control."

Esterhaus's eyes lit up. "Exactly. When the circumstances aren't conducive, change the parameters – another of your little aphorisms, Hasan," he said, raising his voice so the general could hear him, "though, really," he added in a quieter voice, "it's not particularly catchy."

"We force him to break his routine," said Rance. "Move him to an environment where he won't be as well protected."

"Precisely," said Esterhaus. "Even better if you can nudge him in a specific direction, since that allows you to be there ahead of him – then you have the home-field advantage."

Kovalic rubbed his chin, mind already reviewing the possibilities. They'd need to establish a pattern first, before they could figure out the best opportunity, and that was going to require eyes-on. "We'll need some binocs – compact, unobtrusive, with good magnification."

"Here," said Esterhaus, pulling open the drawer and handing a black case to Kovalic. "These are my best set."

Kovalic popped the lid; the grips were worn but still intact, and the lenses were clearly well cleaned. "Analog," he noted approvingly.

Esterhaus gave a *tch* of disgust. "Electronic surveillance has its place, but it can be jammed or scrambled. These won't help you much at night, but they're absolutely reliable."

Personally, Kovalic had to agree. Sometimes the old ways were the best, as a certain sergeant had once taught him. A pang needled his gut at the thought of Tapper; he couldn't remember the last time he'd gone on an op without the old man in the field with him. Had to be years.

He shook his head. "All right, then. Looks like we're headed back to Salaam – after a good night's sleep, anyway." The adrenaline rush that he'd been riding since Kester had stormed into the general's office that morning was ebbing, and his energy along with it. He was left with an almost vertiginous feeling of not quite knowing which way was up, as though the gravity had suddenly shifted.

But maybe tomorrow they could start to set it right.

CHAPTER 14

Juarez 7A was, politely speaking, a shithole. Palladium mining wasn't exactly a pleasant occupation, and even though a lot of the actual digging and refining work was done by machines, people were still required to oversee them. The company that ran the operation, Horvat Heavy Industries, didn't seem to be too concerned with ensuring their personnel had a pleasant stay: the residence buildings were cold slabs of prefab quickcrete, with all the charm of a drafty prison.

The weather's not much to write home about either, thought Eli as his shoes squelched in the mud track that passed for a main drag. Gray skies poured a cold, hard rain that made him long for a head-to-toe poncho. But all he'd been able to find in the *Cav*'s lockers had been a dingy knit hat that he vaguely remembered Kovalic wearing on a mission at some point. There was a stain on it that might have been blood, but also might have been chocolate. He was trying very hard to pretend it was chocolate.

A small settlement had sprung up around the Horvat operations center: some shops and a few eating establishments. Several bars. Enough that Eli found himself wondering about the ratio of inhabitants to watering holes.

Even the businesses not devoted to the serving of alcohol seemed to sell it as well.

Give the people what they want, I guess. And apparently what they want is booze, and lots of it.

They'd landed late last night at what passed for the settlement's spaceport; the dockmaster hadn't blinked at the hour and professed, after the application of a significant number of their credit chips, that he had been sound asleep and never even seen them.

"Remember," Taylor had said, before they all bunked in for the night. "Our goal is to keep a low profile. We'll figure out our next move, and how we can best help Simon, in the morning."

Eli, perpetually the early riser, had taken it upon himself to make the short walk into the settlement and see what could be had in the way of provisions. They had food on the ship, but there was only so much one could eat in the way of prepackaged rations. Literally: you might tear your teeth out. Kovalic tended to stock the kitchen before a mission, and sometimes even found an opportunity to cook during downtime, but with the *Cav* in for maintenance all the fresh produce had been offloaded.

So far, though, the pickings on Juarez 7A had been slim.

The mud sucked at his left shoe, leaving it mired in his wake as he stumbled forward and almost face-planted into the street. Hopping backwards, he reclaimed it – much worse for wear – and wrestled it back on again, managing to coat his hands in the process. *This is stickier than normal mud, right?* He brushed his fingers against his coat, but that just seemed to spread it around.

With a sigh, he made for the most central building on the street, a long low-slung affair that he'd identified as the combination general store and, surprise surprise, bar.

Pushing his way in, he was hit by a blast of warm air that at least dried him off. He stomped his muddy shoes against the floor, little pieces caking off, and tried to stroll as nonchalantly as possible, given that he was leaving brown footprints in his wake. Given the state of the floor, he wasn't the only culprit.

Bustling the store wasn't, but it did have the highest concentration of people he'd seen since coming into the settlement. A handful of customers were perusing the shelves, doing their shopping, and four or five had gathered over near what seemed to be the coffee machine. There were even a couple sitting at the long plastiform bar that occupied one half of the room. Eli checked the local time on his sleeve and confirmed his instinct that it was way too early – or too late – to be drinking.

Picking up a wire basket, he started working his way down the aisles, choosing food that, while it might not have been organically grown or freshly picked, was at least not protein and vitamins molded into bar form. A box of cereal there, some flash-dried greens here; he even found a couple jars of tomato sauce that hadn't yet passed their expiration date.

As he passed by the klatsch around the coffee machine he couldn't help but overhear snatches of conversation, intermingled with the smell of burnt coffee. Much of it was local slang, no doubt related to the mining operation, but one thread happened to grab the attention of the part of his brain that wasn't looking at food packages.

"...can't afford it. But they also can't afford to *not* have it," said one of the locals, a white-bearded man with pale skin and a brass ring through one ear.

"You're full of it, Berrit," another chided him. A large woman, with a red scarf wrapped around her neck and welding goggles up on her forehead. "How would you know what the Emperor, in his good name, can or can't afford?"

"I hear things!" the man insisted.

"Everybody knows the emperor's not even in charge anymore," said a woman with dark skin, her black hair streaked with gray. "He might as well be dead. Hell, maybe he is and they're keeping it to themselves."

One of the participants threw up their hands, another rolled their eyes.

"You got no proof!" said the woman with the red scarf, her tone indignant.

Illyrican politics. Same as they've ever been. Rumors of the emperor's illness and demise had been circulating for as long as Eli could remember – back even before his academy days – but nothing ever seemed to come of it. Still, he wouldn't have figured a mining operation out in the middle of nowhere would care much about what was going on back on the Imperium's homeworld.

"Hey," said a voice. "You're new."

It took a moment for Eli to realize that this was directed at him, and when he looked up, still holding a package of frozen sausages of uncertain provenance, it was to find the entire political debate team staring in his direction.

Eli swallowed. "Uh... yeah. Hi?"

"What do you think?" said Berrit, eyes narrowed.

Eli looked down at the package, then back up at the half-dozen pairs of eyes that had turned in his direction. "I was just buying sausages?" he said uncertainly.

"Come off," said the woman in the scarf. "If you're here, you must have heard."

"Heard what?"

The dark-haired woman interjected. "Keep up, lad. That the crims – sorry, Fiona, the *Illyrican Empire*, holy be its name – are paying top price for palladium. Even though the Imperial mark is barely worth the plastic it's printed on and Berrit here claims that they're up to their ears in debt."

The palladium sales was news to Eli, much less the idea that he should care at all, but apparently the hottest topic in a town full of palladium miners. The Imperium's financial situation, on the other hand, he was well aware of – the team had discovered back during the Bayern operation that the Illyricans were essentially broke, though that wasn't public knowledge and Eli wasn't about to spread it around. "Well, I mean, that is… huh."

His opinion clearly disappointed them, with one faint groan even issuing from the back corner. But the dark-haired woman was not to be deterred. "This is the caliber of people we get now. Look, you have to keep up with what's going on. You can't just spend all day…" She looked him up and down, taking in every detail and apparently synthesizing it into a conclusion about his occupation, "… sitting in an office behind a terminal."

"Oh," said Eli. "No, I'm just passing through."

"That's what they all say," muttered Berrit. "I said that myself back in '05, and here I am."

"No, really," Eli insisted. "I'm a pilot. My ship's just docked at the spaceport." He jerked a thumb outside, only belatedly realizing that this was probably oversharing. *But what else am I supposed to tell them?*

Scarf lady – Fiona, the other woman had called her – frowned. "Ship? You a cargo hauler?"

He could hear Taylor's voice in his head, reminding him that they didn't have any legends backing their fake identities… but that also meant that it would be harder to *disprove* anything they said. Besides, he did his best thinking by the seat of his pants.

"Small loads only," he said. "We're an independent shipping company. Paravaci." He rapidly juggled the sausages into his basket, then stuck out a hand. "Ezekiel Bryce." He hadn't picked out the name on the one fake ID he had – and wasn't sure whether it had been Kovalic or Addy who did – but it wasn't terrible. He could work with it. Although he wasn't sure that he really looked like an Ezekiel, but that was simple enough to fix. "Folks call me 'Easy', cause, well I'm easy," he said, injecting a slight drawl into his voice. *Well, it's probably good that Addy isn't here, because her eyes might have just rolled right out of her head.*

The dark-haired woman eyed his hand, then reluctantly shook it. Her grip was warm and dry. "Vi. Dembélé. I'm construction supervisor on the Bravo 2 shaft. Fiona's a machinist, and Berrit is – what do you do again Berrit, aside from make yourself a pain in my ass?"

"Ha ha," said the white-haired man sourly. "Don't listen to her. I'm the surveyor for this whole mudball. They wouldn't be digging shit without me."

"And yet we're still digging shit," said Vi. "So, Easy, what brings your independent operation to the splendid surroundings of Juarez 7A? Don't tell me: it was our unparalleled vistas."

Eli grinned. "Got it in one. They said a picture couldn't capture them, and they had that right."

There was a guffaw from somewhere back in the crowd, and in that moment, Eli knew he had them. There was a sensation of being lighter than air, floating above it all as the lies rolled off his tongue and buoyed him upwards. *Problem with that is there's nothing to break your fall. Keep it simple.* That last part was, unnervingly enough, in Kovalic's voice.

"Ah, no, just here to deliver some mail, really. We do a lot of courier work, and the relay system out here can be a bit spotty for sensitive materials." Remote systems like this one – especially given Juarez 7A's proximity to a nearby gas giant – often had communications challenges, and couriers were hardly uncommon.

"You got anything for me?" piped up a man from the back of the group. "My husband said he'd send me a care package."

"It's been two years, Franz," said another. "I don't think he cares anymore." Chuckles ran through the group, even from Franz, over what was apparently a running joke.

"I'll have to check," said Eli. "Right now, just doing a little provisioning."

Vi glanced into his basket and sniffed. "You'll be lucky if you find anything that's not been recycled half a dozen times. We don't get a lot of fresh groceries out here, but if it's good food you're after, then it's Carina's place you want.

It's just off the main, a block up. It doesn't have a name because you can't miss it. Only place around here worth eating at." There were murmurs of agreement throughout the crowd.

"Roger that," said Eli. "Thanks!"

Vi nodded. "Maybe we'll see you around. Right now, us working stiffs gotta get back to it. Morning shift's about to start." As if on cue, a whistle shriek pierced the air.

With an assorted chorus of goodbyes, the group dispersed. Eli was about to put the questionable sausages back on the shelf when he felt an uncomfortable itching sensation between his shoulder blades.

Calmly, he turned towards the front of the store, giving him a clear vantage on the direction from which he'd felt the attention, just in time to catch a man standing up from the bar – tall and gaunt, his features shadowed in a raincoat hood that he'd just pulled over his head – turn and leave.

But Eli noticed two things before he did: first, a pair of sharp brown eyes that quickly darted to him and then just as quickly looked away. Whoever this guy was, Eli had piqued his interest.

The second, and far more worrying, was the holstered slug-thrower slung low on the man's thigh, beside a gleam on his belt that could have been a badge.

Well, shit. So much for flying under the radar.

CHAPTER 15

"Brody, what part of 'keep a low profile' did you not understand?" Nat rubbed at her temples. She'd gotten up to check on the network requests that she'd put in before sacking out last night, and found on the main compartment's table a cheery note from the pilot about going into the settlement for supplies. Tempted as she had been to go after him, she'd decided to drink some coffee instead. In the end, it had just made her frustration build, to the point that when the pilot finally returned, groceries in tow, she'd been sitting in the cargo hold, tapping one foot on the floor like a parent waiting up for a teenager.

"Yeah, I know," he said, having the decency to look abashed, and Nat's frustration ebbed out of her as she reminded herself for what felt like the millionth time that, despite a certain amount of instinct and luck, Eli Brody was not a trained covert operative. "I didn't think it would be that big a deal."

Nat took a sip of her rapidly cooling coffee and let out a breath, trying to expel the last remnants of her annoyance. What was done was done. "The man who was watching you. Describe him."

Brody squeezed his eyes closed and ran down the details for her. "I'm not sure it was a badge on his belt, but it could have been." He let one blue eye crack open. "What *is* the law enforcement situation out here anyway?"

"Even calling it 'law enforcement' is giving it too much credit," said Nat, leaning over and flicking a holoscreen into existence from the tablet in front of her. "It's basically Horvat corporate security. They don't enforce the law so much as company policy. Nominally they need to comply with the laws of the governments they do business with – which includes both the Commonwealth and the Imperium – or face sanctions, but there is unsurprisingly a lot of willingness on the parts of politicians to look the other way, especially when they're providing valuable resources."

With an uncharacteristically moody sigh, Brody opened his eyes and flopped into the chair across from her. "My homeworld was strip-mined by the Imperium for every piece of ore and rare metal they could find. Sometimes feels like the whole galaxy has just become a machine for moving resources from one place to another – and wealth along with it."

Nat's eyebrows rose. She hadn't taken the brash young pilot for a deep thinker, but apparently he had hidden depths. Come to think of it, Simon had said as much after he'd first recruited Brody; there was a reason he was still part of the crew, after all.

Drumming her fingers on the table, she considered the rest of what he'd told her. "The news about the Illyricans buying up palladium is curious."

"What do you think they're using it for?"

She shook her head slowly. "I don't know. It's got any number of applications in electronics, manufacturing, fuel storage. Any large industrial project would need it. I'd be tempted to think warships, but we haven't heard any reports of the Imperium spinning up its shipyards recently."

"So they're working on something else."

"Maybe," she said. "Honestly, I'm more curious about how they're affording it; their financial circumstances are shaky to say the least. Last chatter I heard even fueling their fleet seemed like a dicey proposition." Maybe they'd sourced some alternative currency through a third-party, Nat mused. Not that they were widely regarded as a good investment, especially after their botched attempt to annex Bayern. Still… she shook her head to clear it: this wasn't relevant. "Doesn't matter, lieutenant; this isn't our business right now. We've got more urgent problems, as you might recall."

"Right. Well, I mean, we're out in the middle of nowhere. Chances that some rent-a-cop is going to figure out that we're on the Commonwealth's most wanted list seems kind of slim."

He wasn't wrong. Corporate security's job was to prevent things from blowing back on the company, and much as Horvat Heavy Industries valued doing business with the Commonwealth, if they spent all their time checking on whether everybody who showed up on Juarez 7A was wanted in this jurisdiction or that, they'd do little else. Not to mention it would put a bit of a crimp in their hiring practices – most people didn't come here when they had other options.

"Probably not," Nat agreed. "But we should be careful anyway. I don't want anybody going out on their own."

"What happened?" A bleary-eyed Tapper stepped into the hold, stretching. "Brody, did you accidentally kick the mayor's dog or something?"

"I was just making friendly conversation!"

"That's always how it starts. But somehow it always ends with a dog getting kicked."

Brody shot him a look, then dragged his bag of provisions off the table and into the galley to start unpacking.

Meanwhile Tapper pulled himself a cup of coffee and sat down opposite Nat, his levity evaporated. "Anything we need to worry about?" he asked quietly.

"Unclear," said Nat. "We may have attracted some local security attention. Hard to tell if it's just cursory or something more, but it can't hurt to be cautious. Are you armed?"

The sergeant took a sip, but didn't bat so much as an eyelash. "I can be. But as the boss always says –"

"Oh, I know. 'Carrying a weapon is the fastest way to get shot'."

A slight smile crossed the old man's weathered face, but it faded as he put the mug down on the table, cupping it in both hands. "Commander, how long are we going to be out here?"

"I wish I knew." Her gaze drifted to Brody, prodding a bruised tomato and looking disappointed. "How do you think they're doing, sergeant?"

"In what way?"

"This is more than we've ever asked of them." Her chest tightened and she tried to force the knot there to unravel. "It's one thing being on an operation when we're running towards the danger. It's a little different when we're running for our lives."

Tapper snorted. "Tough."

"Good pep talk."

"No, I mean it." He leaned back and held up the mug, steam rising from wisps that made her think of watching the fog rise over the lake from the cabin Simon had built. "Sayers and Brody will follow your lead. But they need you *to* lead."

She pressed her lips together. "I'm not even sure where to start."

Tapper's eyes sharpened, reminding her that the man had been a drill sergeant for a reason. "Don't ask me. I'm just a simple grunt. You, though, you're one of Naval Intelligence's sharpest minds. There's a reason you got that chief of staff job with Admiral Chatterjee."

"I suppose – wait, how did you know? I only found out…yesterday?" Had it just been yesterday? It seemed like a week since she'd been headed into the Commonwealth Executive compound to meet Simon for lunch and break the news.

He sipped his coffee and shrugged with more than a hint of false modesty. "I hear things."

That was Tapper for you: somehow he seemed to know everyone and everything worth knowing – even when that shouldn't be possible. "I hadn't said yes yet."

"Yeahhhh, well, I wouldn't put that high on your priority list right now anyway." Tapper gestured at their surroundings. "It's going to be tough to explain this on your résumé."

Nat leaned back in her chair, staring glumly at her coffee going cold. Everything that she'd worked for her entire career, potentially up in smoke.

Technically, she was only on secondment to the Special Projects Team from Naval Intelligence Command, though that was pretty much academic since she'd chosen to help the team in their flight from the authorities.

But she wasn't about to go sit in a cushy office while Brody, Tapper, and Sayers were all disappeared to a CID black site. For now, she was still the team's executive officer.

And, as Tapper said, she had to set the direction and the tone. The sergeant, you could point him at a problem and he'd solve it – probably with the liberal application of explosives – but he wasn't the ranking officer. Which left Brody who, while capable of incredible feats from behind the controls of a ship, wasn't trained for anything like this. And Sayers, well, there was no question that she was a force to be reckoned with, and Nat saw a lot of promise in her – if she could just get that temper under control.

No, the sergeant was right. This situation they found themselves in required a sharp analytical mind, and she wasn't flattering herself to say that was her wheelhouse.

Pulling out her tablet, she flipped through the newsfeeds that had made their way to Juarez 7A. "There's nothing in any of the Commonwealth sources that mentions anything about arrests on the Executive campus."

"I'm sure they're keeping it quiet," said Tapper. "Military's good at that."

"We don't even know what they were accused of."

"Well, when the acting director of CID shows up at your door with marines, it probably ain't unpaid parking tickets."

Fair point. Aidan Kester wasn't going to waste time on trumped-up charges; if he was there, then the allegations were not only serious, but he had proof to back them up. His presence at the general's office suggested that Adaj was his primary target, which wasn't surprising; there was no love lost between the two.

But if Kester believed he had some sort of smoking gun, they needed to know what it was.

A day ago, Nat would have had access to every database in the Commonwealth, not to mention the technology necessary to analyze all that information. But now here they were, exiled to the far end of nowhere.

"It's an awful coincidence," said Tapper, his fingers drumming across the cup of coffee. "Just a few days back, Page was telling us that he found evidence that the general had been funneling money to those Nova Front loons... and now Aidan Kester shows up to arrest them?" He raised his eyebrows significantly.

Simon had filled her in on what Page had been up to over the last nine months and what he'd found on Bayern. Was it possible that Kester had the same information?

The idea sat uneasy in her stomach. "You know as well as I do, sergeant, that in espionage there are no coincidences."

Tapper lifted a finger. "The operative's creed: never attribute to happenstance that which can be explained by enemy action."

Nat tilted her head towards him. "You think the Illyricans are involved somehow."

"Maybe I'm just taking a river cruise in Egypt, but it's a sight more palatable that the old man is being set up for a fall than that we've been working for a traitor all that time."

It bore investigating, that much was for certain. "I've got some sources I can reach out to. Might take a while to get a response – the net here is spotty at best – but at least it's *something* to do."

Tapper nodded, then stretched as he got up. "And I'll re-check our inventory. Don't want to be caught flat-footed when we do need to move."

Nat turned and made her way to the *Cavalier*'s cockpit, trying to stave off the foreboding feeling that had come with the rain and the sergeant's hypothesis. And Brody's earlier report continued to linger in the back of her mind.

Somebody on this rock had taken an interest in them. Maybe the far end of nowhere wasn't far enough.

CHAPTER 16

The weather on Juarez 7A didn't improve throughout the day. The cold spitting rain pinged off the hull of the *Cavalier* like small arms fire, and Addy considered it a great leap in her personal development that this didn't leave her riding a constant adrenaline high.

Not that she was enjoying being cooped up inside the ship. Taylor's edict about not going out alone meant she'd ended up walking laps around the cargo hold.

How the hell are we supposed to clear our names if we can't go anywhere?

Addy was clearly not the only one frustrated. Brody had been banging around in the galley all morning under the cover of trying to make lunch, but the constant swearing and clattering of pans suggested that it wasn't going well. They'd be lucky to end up with cold cheese sandwiches.

Taylor had closeted herself in the *Cav*'s cockpit while Tapper bustled around, checking and re-checking all of their gear in a seemingly endless loop. None of which was helping Addy's disposition.

This is pointless. We're just hiding. Her fingers twitched into fists at her side, and her chest tightened. If she stayed stuck inside this ship for another minute, she might just explode.

Stalking across the cargo hold, she slapped the release button for the main hatch. As it rolled open and the entry ramp descended, the cold, damp air whistled through the narrow hatchway and into her face with all the force of a wind tunnel. She zipped up her jacket, jamming her hands in her pockets as she strode down onto the permacrete.

Juarez 7A's spaceport was a barren stretch of land, dotted with ships hooked up to umbilicals that snaked over to refueling and power stations. No individual hangars here, just a wide-open field that had been paved over at some point. No windbreaks either, as the stinging rain whipping across her face reminded her.

She tucked herself in the ship's lee, wrapping her arms around herself to try and stay warm.

Maybe this isn't better than staying inside. Fresh air is overrated anyway.

But she didn't move to go back into the ship. Something about being outside clarified matters, cutting through all the bullshit.

Simply put, she felt useless. The situation they found themselves in wasn't one she could punch or shoot her way out of, and she was painfully aware of how limited her skillset was. Fighting off Kester's goons at the apartment, she'd been in her element. Helping exonerate Kovalic? Above her pay grade.

"Addy?" Brody's voice echoed down the ramp. "What are you doing out there?" A sandy-haired head poked down. "I mean, besides getting soaked."

"Just… thinking," she said. She wasn't sure she wanted to admit to anybody, even herself, the thought that had been needling her ever since they left Nova behind.

What if they were on the wrong side?

Ever since she'd learned that the general was Illyrican – and the former head of the Imperial Intelligence Service to boot – she'd had an uneasy feeling in her stomach about the team's mission. The general had proved to Addy that he was more than capable of harboring an ulterior motive. Hell, he'd almost convinced *her* to kill Aaron Page when it had looked like the former SPT member had been responsible for the Nova Front bombings.

Kovalic had made it clear that he trusted the general, asked them to put their faith in *him*, but it sure didn't look good from where she was standing. As much as she didn't trust the system – she'd seen the way it treated way too many of the people she'd grown up with, more often than not for reasons that were at the very least mistaken, if not out-and-out prejudiced – she had to wonder if maybe they *should* all get hauled in.

She let out a long breath – not a sigh so much as a slow exhalation of disbelief – and shook her head. "I don't know how we're going to get out of this one, Brody."

The pilot came the rest of the way down the ramp, pulling his own coat tight. He was still wearing those threadbare shoes, now caked with dried mud that had been flaking off around the cargo hold. "Yeah, I don't know. Normally I'd trust Kovalic to have a plan, but…" he scratched the back of his head, "… even if he does, we're kind of on our own out here."

"Ugh," said Addy. "And *here*, of all places, isn't where I would choose to be. What a dump."

Brody glanced back up into the ship, then shrugged. "Sounds like there's at least one decent restaurant in town. Why don't we go get some lunch?"

She raised an eyebrow. "I thought you were cooking."

He linked his arm through hers jovially. "You know, it's probably best we don't give that any further thought."

"That good, huh?"

"I'll clean it up when I get back."

With a laugh, Addy gave up. Brody's charm could be buoyant at times. "So where's this place? And I thought we weren't supposed to go into the settlement?"

"All the commander said was don't go in alone. Besides, it's like a five-minute walk. What could possibly go wrong?"

"You just had to say it, huh."

With a roll of his eyes, Brody ducked out from under the ship, squinting into the hard-driving rain. "Come on, already."

Even a five-minute walk proved unpleasant under the current conditions, so by the time they found their way along what passed for the mining town's central thoroughfare and then down a side street, they were soaked and considerably worse for wear.

The establishment to which Brody led them was indistinguishable from the rest of the prefab structures: two low-slung stories, same quickcrete exterior covered in mud and grunge. The only concession to its purpose was a faded sign in the window that said "Open".

Addy eyed it dubiously. "You're sure about this?"

"I'm told it's good," said Brody. "Plus, it has the added benefit of being indoors, where it's unlikely to be raining."

It was impossible to argue the point, so when he pulled the door open for her, she stepped inside.

A bell tinkled over her head and a blast of warm air from

an overhead heater wrapped her in a fluffy bubble that let her close her and eyes and pretend, just for a moment, that she was sitting on the beach. Friendly chatter echoed throughout the space, interspersed with a clatter of utensils against plates, but all of it came to a sudden stop as they entered.

Addy's eyes cracked open to find the entire room, maybe twenty-five patrons and another half-dozen staff, staring at the two of them.

"Uhhhh, hi," she said. "You all still open for lunch?"

The silence continued a beat longer, until one of the waitstaff – short, plump, with a name tag that said Flynn and specified they/them pronouns – waved her towards a lone vacant table. "Take a seat, honey. I'll be right with you."

Conversational chatter picked up again as Addy and Brody sat down at the table. It was a bit wobbly, despite having been shimmed with several folded up pieces of cardboard, and the silverware was 3D-printed, but none of that mattered because the smell wafting out from the kitchen at the back was enough to set Addy's stomach rumbling.

Flynn reappeared, bearing a carafe of coffee, the aroma of which was likewise far more appealing than the likes of what the *Cavalier* had on offer. They poured two mugs and then doled out a pair of flimsies that looked like they had been printed out this morning.

There was nothing elegant about the menus: just a list of the dozen dishes on offer. Pancakes, waffles, French toast, eggs for the breakfast crowd, and then a few different sandwiches for those with more of a lunch bent.

"A reuben?" said Brody, looking up, his expression dubious. "You get good sauerkraut all the way out here?"

"Sure do. Make it ourselves," said Flynn.

"I could barely find frozen sausages that weren't expired!"

The server shrugged and grinned. "We've got our ways. Speaking of which, I hear you do a bit of shipping. Might be some business for you."

Addy glanced up at Brody. He'd mentioned the cover that he'd come up with on the fly, and it seemed news traveled fast in the mining settlement, though that wasn't exactly surprising given the small size.

"Uh, that's right," said Brody, brushing a lock of sandy hair out of his eyes. "Well, we're always on the lookout for new business opportunities, isn't that right, Reggie?"

It took Addy a moment to remember her cover identity, a fact she tried to conceal with a hard look at Brody that could be interpreted as something more recriminating. "That's true," she said slowly. "Maybe let's see how the food is first."

"Can't argue with that," said Brody. "Oh well, let's give that reuben a whirl then."

He ordered a side of fries as well, while Addy went for the turkey club that had been calling to her. Flynn flashed them both another smile, collected the flimsies, and disappeared into the kitchen.

As they waited for their food, Addy let her gaze drift around the room. The rest of the clientele were clearly locals; she didn't imagine there were too many offworld visitors dropping in to Juarez 7A – the tourist scene wasn't much to write home about. All had mud-caked shoes like Brody's, though most of them were better equipped, with rain covers or ponchos thrown over the back of their chairs. Conversation was at a low buzz, though punctuated occasionally with short, barked laughs or wet-sounding coughs.

Feels like the kind of place where you perpetually have a cold.

She opened her mouth to turn back to Brody when there was another jingle from the bell at the entrance and a newcomer stepped in. Tall, thin, with glittering eyes beneath a hood. Rain sloughed off as they threw it back, revealing a brown, hawk-nosed face that had seen its fair share of punch-ups and maybe worse.

Across from her, she sensed more than saw Brody freeze.

He wasn't the only one, either. The rest of the room had gone quiet once again, though not with unfamiliarity this time – on the contrary, it seemed clear they knew him too well.

Flynn bustled through the crowd, greeting the man with the same smile they'd offered the other customers. "Morning, chief. Your usual?"

The man tipped his head to one side in acknowledgment, even as his eyes took in the rest of the room, before finally alighting on Addy and Brody with substantial, perhaps even unhealthy, interest.

Oh, I do not *like this.* Taylor's concerns about going into town suddenly felt all too well-founded, and Addy was conspicuously aware of the holstered KO gun that she'd been keeping tucked in the small of her back since they'd landed.

Slowly, the man walked over to their table, peeling off his black gloves, until he towered above them, his shadow blocking out the overhead light.

"Afternoon," he said, his voice a throaty rasp. "I'm Security Chief Patel."

Brody swallowed and nodded. "Hello. What can we do for you?"

Patel slapped his gloves on the table with a wet, ringing smack, then smiled. Unpleasantly. "I'm afraid I need to take a look at your docking permits."

"Permits?" Brody echoed.

"Permits," said the man again, enunciating as if Brody were speaking a different language. "You are the owners of the ship on pad Delta-3, correct?"

"Uh, yes. That's us. But we filed all the necessary paperwork with the dockmaster last night. So you should probably take it up with him."

Patel's lip twitched. "I'm taking it up with you." Almost too casually, he pushed his coat aside, draping his hand over the weapon at his hip.

Slug-thrower, Addy's brain identified it instantly. Rakunas GL-17. An older make, but a reliable one. You'd need special papers to carry one anywhere inside the Commonwealth, even for law enforcement or military.

Juarez 7A didn't seem to hold to the same standards.

"I'm going to need to ask the two of you to come with me," said Patel. "We'll sort this out down at the security office."

Shit. Best case scenario, Patel was bent and looking for his own cut on top of what they'd paid the dockmaster. Addy had only brought a few credit chips from the ship, but there were plenty more onboard, so if he was just looking for a payday, they could handle it.

But a knot in her gut reminded her that the best-case scenario was not the way their luck had been going of late.

"We were just waiting for our lunch. I don't suppose we could come down right after?" said Brody, a note of hope injected into his voice.

"Your lunch can wait," said the security chief, stepping back and gesturing. "After you."

"But my reuben," said the pilot mournfully.

Flynn appeared and patted Brody on the shoulder. "Don't worry, hon, I'll pack it up for you." They bustled off and returned in a moment with a couple foil-wrapped slabs, which they popped into a paper bag, along with a packet of fries. The smell drifted to Addy's nose, and she regretted not backing up Brody on waiting for their food.

Addy reached into her pocket and saw Patel tense, his hand tightening on the butt of his Rakunas, but he was savvy enough to realize that she wasn't reaching for a weapon. She tossed a handful of credit chips onto the table. "Sorry we can't stay."

With that, she rose, making sure to keep her hands well clear of anything that might give Patel an excuse. The adrenaline was ramping up, but she'd managed to keep it at bay so far. "After you."

"Oh no, I insist," said Patel, sweeping out of the way.

There didn't seem to be any other option, so she let Patel usher her and Brody back out into the gloomy rainy day, and direct them down the street in the opposite direction from the spaceport. *Great. Just great.*

She was starting to wish she'd just stayed in the ship.

CHAPTER 17

Surveillance was, as a rule, not the most interesting part of any job. Kovalic glumly tore off a chunk of the compacted fruit bar and set to work chewing it. At least his jaw was getting a good workout.

They'd driven the groundcar that Esterhaus had "acquired" for them back into Salaam early the following morning, leaving before it was even light out, and deposited the general and his former subordinate in a safe house that the latter had likewise arranged.

Neither Rance nor Kovalic had been happy about leaving the general alone with the spy that he'd once burned. While Esterhaus was occupied accessing the apartment, they'd had a hurried discussion.

"I appreciate your concern," the general had said, "but I will be fine with Yevgeniy."

"How can you be sure he's not another of Isabella's contingencies?" Kovalic asked. "She seems to have tied you up into a pretty neat bow – what if that was to force you into going to him for help?"

The general stroked his beard. "I think not. Her objective was to get me out of the way, and she's accomplished that adroitly. Besides, her strength lies in predicting my most likely behavior; I don't think even she would predict I would turn to the very man I once betrayed." He drew himself up slightly, eyes glittering. "I do have *some* surprises left in me."

Rance hadn't looked convinced but, at the general's urging, the two of them had taken the groundcar to the side street in the Vrede neighborhood where Aidan Kester's swanky brownstone stood.

They'd parked about halfway down the street, with a clear view of Kester's front door, waiting for the man himself to make an appearance.

Rance poured a cup of coffee from a thermos and offered it to Kovalic, who accepted it gladly. He was probably mostly coffee at this point, maybe 70 percent. The other 30 percent was terrible processed food.

Ah, stakeouts.

"If Kester is the mole," said Rance, "it doesn't seem likely that he's just going to lead us to his handler. He's gotten this far undetected; why would he slip up now?"

"Agreed," said Kovalic. Something about all of this still didn't sit right with him, though. He'd met Kester enough times to know the man was smart, yes, and ambitious, no question. But treason? Treason was harder to square.

Then again, if he was a mole that had risen this far, then maybe he was just very very good at what he did. And there was no denying that Kester had benefited from the painstaking plan that Isabella had put into motion: the princess had funded Nova Front out of the general's pockets, using Alys Costa and her malcontents to reveal the covert spying program that had catapulted Kester into the director's chair, whilst simultaneously sidelining his most significant rival. The question was why? Why had she gone through all this trouble to take the general – and, by extension, the rest of the SPT – out of the equation? To what end?

That was what they had to figure out. And, no matter how Kovalic's gut felt about it, Kester remained their prime suspect. They needed to do their diligence on the man, even if just to rule him out. That meant first establishing his routine and then figuring out how to break it – forcing him to do something that he normally wouldn't.

About an hour after they'd arrived, a large black groundcar with tinted windows pulled up in front of Kester's residence; it was bulkier than a standard model, a clear sign of a reinforced chassis, and the sheen off the windows told Kovalic that they'd ably resist anything short of artillery.

Beside him, Rance had raised a telescopic lens. Normally they would have used a constellation of micro-drones for this kind of surveillance, but there was too big a chance that Kester's security detail would detect them. So, the old-fashioned method it was.

A live video feed appeared on the car's holoscreen, springing to life between the two of them; it showed a magnified view of the people exiting the car. There were a pair of them, wearing the trademark ill-fitting suits of bodyguards everywhere, heads on a swivel as they surveyed the immediate vicinity for threats.

CID's in-house personal security division. Mostly former operatives from the Activities group who had decided they wanted something a little less exciting, or who had been forced to drop their covert status. Kovalic had worked with plenty of Activities personnel over the years, and they weren't people he wanted to face off against if he could help it. Rance had parked the car a good distance down the street, and fortunately, their groundcar's windows could auto-tint for privacy, otherwise they might be having an unpleasant chat.

The bodyguards were followed by another man: pale complexion, wispy blond hair, nervous energy.

"That's Kester's executive assistant," said Rance. "Lawson. I've dealt with him a lot, seen him around the campus cafeteria." She wagged her head back and forth, appraising. "He's nice enough. Asked me out once."

Kovalic raised an eyebrow.

Rance shrugged. "Turned him down. He's not really my type."

He suppressed a laugh. It was hard to tell much about the man from a distance; he had an unremarkable face that looked vaguely familiar, which was probably a desirable quality in an assistant, but Kovalic had a hard time picturing him keeping up with the exceedingly competent Rance.

Then a third figure exited the car, and Kovalic sucked in a breath. Dark-skinned, with a well-kept beard, he was also wearing a serious-looking suit, but had forgone the formality of a tie. He glanced at his sleeve impatiently, then up at the door to Kester's building, still closed.

"Shit," commented Kovalic.

"Inspector Laurent," said Rance. "What's he doing here?"

"Probably briefing Kester on the search for *us*."

"Well, he's a lot closer than he thinks."

Kovalic gave the woman a sidelong glance, then chuckled despite himself. "Fair point." But he sobered quickly. Laurent was sharp, and Kovalic didn't love the idea that they'd dropped themselves right back in the man's path.

That said, his gut told him that the man was honest, too. Frankly, his gut seeming to trust everyone was starting to make him wonder how reliable an indicator it was.

Still, if they could find evidence that cast doubt upon the treason accusations, Kovalic was confident Laurent would give them a fair shake.

"Movement," said Rance, and Kovalic put his attention back on the holoscreen. The heavy wood door to the apartment had opened and Aidan Kester, impeccably coiffed as always, stepped out onto the stoop. He had his sleeve up and was speaking into it, but without audio surveillance, they couldn't hear him.

"We're going to have to use the lip-reading algorithm," said Rance. "There's no angle with the parabolic mic where we're not going to stick out like a flamingo in the swan pond." She keyed something in on her sleeve, and captions began scrolling across the screen, attempting to reconstruct what Kester was saying.

"…set for 11:30…lunch…with sheaf…"

The two of them exchanged a glance.

"He keeps turning away," said Rance, shrugging. "I'll run a trace, see if I can figure out who he's talking to, but the channel is almost certainly encrypted."

The old ways might be the best, but everything had limitations. You worked with what you had. Another figure stepped into the doorway: a lanky brown-haired man with a square jaw and a fashionable amount of stubble. He smiled at Kester – genuinely, it seemed to Kovalic – and drew him in for an embrace. Kester paused his conversation and returned the gesture with equally authentic affection, squeezing the other man's arm before heading down the stairs towards the car.

"That's the husband," said Rance. "Tomas Akingbola."

Kovalic nodded. And, as it happened, the son of the Commonwealth's Undersecretary for Foreign Affairs. By all accounts, it was a happy marriage, even if it was also politically expedient for a rising star of the intelligence community.

Or an Illyrican mole.

Rance was chewing on her bottom lip. Her eyes slid to Kovalic. "We were looking for a way to get Kester off schedule. He could be leverage," she said, her voice carefully neutral.

Kovalic shifted uncomfortably in his seat. It wasn't as if he'd never involved civilians in this kind of operation before – even politically sensitive ones. But this was a Commonwealth citizen, and it felt like crossing a significant line; not to mention digging them even deeper into this treason charge.

Then again, the line got blurrier when you were talking about a possible enemy agent with the potential to wreak untold havoc. "Let's keep that in our back pocket."

Kester and Laurent were exchanging words now, while the assistant hovered nearby, but there was no clear angle on their mouths for the lip-reading software and, after a moment, they all got into the car.

Rance waited a few beats for Kester's vehicle to get underway, then slowly pulled away from the curb and followed after.

Kovalic spared an approving glance at Rance's technique; she kept a couple car lengths behind the target vehicle, maintaining her speed and calmly allowing other vehicles to get in between them while still keeping sight of Kester's car. That was helped along by the bulky vehicle being tall enough that it was kind of hard to lose, even in heavy traffic.

"Where'd you learn all of this?" said Kovalic. "Last I heard surveillance training wasn't a requirement for yeomen."

Rance smiled, not taking her eyes off the road. "The general's called in some favors over the years and gotten me some crash courses: surveillance from the Bureau, computer security at NICOM, hand-to-hand combat at the School. He thought it was important, in my role, that I have a… well-rounded skillset."

"Impressive. That's above and beyond."

"Well, now I'm a kick-ass assistant in every sense of the word."

Kovalic laughed. "Touché."

Up ahead, Kester's car took a sudden right turn down a side street and Kovalic glanced at the map on the holoscreen. "Well, that's interesting. Up until now, he's been following the most logical route between his home and CID headquarters. Any chance they've spotted us?"

Rance frowned. "It's possible, but I don't think so. Could be just standard countermeasures, checking for tails."

"Let's take it nice and slow then."

They eased around the corner, and Kovalic pushed down a sudden irrational fear that Laurent would be standing in the middle of the road, waiting to arrest them. But no, Kester's car had stopped a few buildings down, and the man himself was getting out. He gestured at his bodyguard and his aide, the pale blond man, to wait for him as disappeared into one of the storefronts that lined the street.

"Should we stop?" asked Rance.

It was a damned if they did, damned if they didn't situation. The street was only sparsely trafficked, and pulling over might be conspicuous – but if they had to pass them and circle back to pick up the tail again, that might draw attention as well.

"Keep going," said Kovalic. Might be the wrong decision, but hesitating wasn't going to improve matters. He reached over and hit the control to tint the windows, just in case Laurent happened to be looking out of the car at the wrong moment. "Let's see where he stopped."

Under Rance's careful driving they rolled past at a respectable speed – not too fast and not too slow. As they went by, Kovalic peered at the building Kester had entered; what was important enough to merit a detour from work? Was the acting director of CID a secret devotee of pastry? Did he simply stop to pick up some groceries? Was his happy marriage an illusion and he was conducting a secret affair... that he didn't mind his bodyguards, assistant, and a Bureau agent knowing about?

Block gilt letters arced across the shop window: "M. Habib." Unspecific, perhaps, but more than compensated for by the understated display in the window, which showed several half-mannequins clad in elegant suits and dress shirts.

Of course.

Kovalic had never seen Aidan Kester anything less than well turned-out, so if there was one place that merited a diversion on his way to the office, it would be his tailor.

In the rearview display, Kovalic just caught sight of Kester exiting, turning back to say something. The lip-reading software caught him full-on for a fleeting second.

"...back when... ready... call me..."

And then Rance was turning onto the next street, and Kester and his detail were out of sight. Kovalic kept his eyes glued to the rearview display, but the vehicle hadn't raced around the corner after them, and there was no sign that Laurent had spotted them.

"Now what?" said Rance, her eyes still on the road. "Do we try to pick them up again?"

Kovalic shook his head. "I think we need to consider this car burned. Let's head back to the safe house. We'll find another vehicle tomorrow." He was sure Esterhaus would be glad to have his loaner back in one piece.

With a curt nod, the ever-capable yeoman started in on a complicated and labyrinthine route designed to shake any pursuers and make sure that anybody tracking the car would be utterly baffled. It was the kind of thing that would take a while, which was just fine by Kovalic, because he needed time to think.

A tailor making custom suits. It could just be an affectation of a man who took the maxim of "dressing for the job you want" to heart. But he couldn't help but note that Kester had left both his aide and his security behind. Which also made it the perfect place for a dead drop, or a meeting with his handler. Kovalic made a note to look into it when they were back at the safe house.

One thing was clear: Aidan Kester was still at the top of their suspects list.

CHAPTER 18

The security office proved to be a short walk away, not that anything seemed particularly far in the tiny mining settlement. As they stepped out into the rainy afternoon, Eli heard a distant *fwump* overhead and looked up in time to see the small, sleek shape of a fast courier break through the clouds that hung like a quilt above them.

Can't imagine anyone wanting to get to this rock in a hurry.

From his spot behind them, Patel issued curt directions, which basically amounted to "walk across the street and open the gray door". It was the first floor of a building that looked more or less identical to the others that lined the thoroughfare, with the exception of a faded and scratched Horvat logo on the outside, overlaid with a shape clearly designed to evoke a sheriff's star.

Inside wasn't any better. There was a metal desk with a terminal and a holding cell in one corner that smelled suspiciously of vomit and stale beer.

Well, with that many bars, stands to reason they'd need a drunk tank.

"Sit," said Patel, pointing to a pair of uncomfortable metal chairs. He peeled off his raincoat, slung it over a hook in the bare permacrete wall, and sat down behind the desk – but not before removing his slug-thrower from its holster and placing it next to the terminal, barrel pointed in their direction.

The chairs he'd indicated were a couple of feet away, so if somebody was dumb enough to make a leap for the gun, it wouldn't end well for them.

Eli mentally sent that thought toward Addy, but glancing over at her stolid expression it was impossible to tell what was going through her head.

"IDs," said Patel, squinting at a holoscreen that he'd summoned. He put out one hand without taking his attention from the display.

Eli leaned forward, putting his most charming smile on. "Look, this is just a case of crossed wires. See it all the time. If you check with the dockmast –"

"IDs. Now."

Mental note: Horvat Heavy Industries does not hire based on friendliness. He sighed and raised his sleeve, flicking over his digital ID docs. Beside him, Addy did the same. She hadn't batted an eyelid from the grim expression that she'd been wearing since the security chief had walked in the restaurant.

"Regina Allingham and Ezekiel Bryce," said Patel.

"Yep, but everybody calls me Eas –"

"Landing permit and customs declarations."

"Yeah, sure." Eli brought up the relevant documents and sent them over to Patel's terminal. "Everything should be in order."

Patel gave something between a sneer and a laugh. *A snaugh?* "I'll be the judge of that."

Should we offer him a bribe? Eli didn't know how many

credit chips Addy had, but he'd only grabbed enough for incidentals, and offering him the assorted contents of his pockets might just end up insulting the man.

"It doesn't list your employer here," said Patel, looking up and down the screen before turning to them. "Word is you're in shipping?" His tone sounded as though he would have just as soon believed they were a traveling circus.

"That's right," said Eli, feeling on steadier ground. "The Paravaci Shipping Company, out of Jericho Station." Sitting as it did in the single system bridging the Illyrican Empire and the Commonwealth, Jericho was a popular incorporation place for companies that did business with both governments – he'd wager all that pocket change that Horvat Heavy Industries itself had been set up in a similar fashion. Plus, it didn't hurt that Jericho's tax and data laws were incredibly favorable towards corporations.

"Never heard of it before," said Patel, waving the screen away and scrutinizing the two of them.

"No reason you should have," said Eli smoothly. "We're a small operation and this is our first trip to Juarez 7A, which, may I say, is absolutely *lovely* this time of year."

"You don't talk much," Patel interrupted, his eyes fixed on Addy.

Addy didn't blink, just held his gaze, as if waiting to see which of them would flinch first. "Trust me, when I have something worth saying, you'll be the first to know."

Patel didn't say anything for moment, then gave another barking laugh. "Tough, huh? What are you, the muscle?"

She cocked her head to one side, but didn't answer the question.

"That's fine, you don't have to say anything," said Patel. "I'm afraid I'm going to need you two to stay put while I send a dispatch to corporate headquarters to double check the validity of your paperwork. Should only take, oh, a few hours." He smiled in self-satisfaction and leaned back to wait for their inevitable indignation.

Which is exactly what he wants. Anything for an excuse to detain them further. Maybe even throw them in that holding cell. But why? Eli's mind was spinning as he considered the options, and to buy time he said the first thing that came to mind.

"Can I eat my sandwich, then?"

Patel's eyebrow twitched. "Yeah, fine, whatever." He turned back to his holoscreen and started typing away.

Eli unwrapped the reuben slowly; the bread had gotten soggy from the moisture but it still smelled amazing, and his mouth began watering almost immediately. He glanced sidelong at Addy, who finally took her eyes off Patel long enough to meet his gaze. Subtly she tapped her left wrist with her right forefinger, then nodded at Patel.

Time? Eli's brow furrowed even as he took a bite of the sandwich, and the mix of flavors melted on his tongue. Where had they found Swiss cheese this good? And real Russian dressing? He chewed thoughtfully, trying to savor everything about it as he parsed Addy's meaning. And then, as he swallowed, it hit home.

Stalling. Patel was stalling.

But for what? Or for… whom?

The sandwich, so delicious a moment ago, turned to lead in his stomach. For someone else to get here. Someone who had a decided interest in four fugitives.

The kind of someone who might just send a fast courier with a small contingent of shock troops to pick up a couple of sitting ducks in the local security office.

He looked down at the rest of the sandwich, resenting that Patel had robbed him of even that modicum of joy, then carefully sealed up the foil. Maybe he could reheat it later, on the *Cav* – if they could get back there in one piece.

"So," said Eli. "Look. Let's cut to the chase here. Did we take some… shortcuts in our paperwork? Yes, we did. But I'm sure we can remedy that. Perhaps a generous contribution to the Horvat Heavy Industries' security officers' pension fund?"

Patel swiped the holoscreen off to one side, then leaned his elbows on the desk. "Are you trying to bribe me, Mr Bryce?"

Eli grinned. "Absolutely. Is it working?"

"Not in the least."

"Shame. Can't blame a guy for trying."

"Actually, I can," said Patel, a nasty smile on his face. "Bribing a security officer is a serious violation of Horvat's corporate policies. I'm afraid I have no choice but to take you into custody." He pulled open a drawer in the desk and pulled out a pair of plasticuffs, dangling them from one finger.

When Addy did move, it was faster than Eli expected. She took advantage of the security chief's distracted attention and lashed out with one booted foot at the metal desk, kicking the whole thing back into Patel.

The security chief grunted and his slug-thrower teetered on the edge of desk before toppling onto the floor.

Addy's hand was already reaching for the KO gun in the small of her back. But while the security chief might be corrupt, he wasn't complacent. He'd already ducked behind the desk; the stun field dissipated harmlessly off it as he dove for his weapon.

"Down," Addy snapped in Eli's direction, and he didn't hesitate to comply, sliding out of the chair and crouching in the meager cover provided by desk, all too aware that there was an armed and unhappy Patel just on the other side.

This place really isn't built for a firefight.

Addy swung to the left of the desk, KO gun leveled, and was met by Patel's swivel chair, kicked in that direction. It hit her in the mid-section, sending her next shot into the ceiling.

From the other side of the desk came the whine of a slug-thrower's magnetic projectile field spinning up and projectiles spat out in white-hot succession. Addy hit the deck to her right, putting the desk in between them again. The slugs peppered the wall of the office with polka dot holes, each about the diameter of a writing stylus – not particularly impressive when seen in a permacrete wall, but much larger than you'd want in your torso.

Eli's breath sounded way too loud in his ears, his heart beating against his ribcage. *We should be able to take him; there's two of us.* Of course, between them they only had one weapon, which leveled the playing field considerably. All Eli had was a sandwich.

Then again…

Both he and Addy had put their backs against the long edge of the desk; it wasn't hard to imagine Patel on the other side doing the same thing. Just a single piece of furniture in between them.

Eli glanced sidelong at Addy, who was gripping the KO gun in both hands. He nodded his head towards the corner of the desk on his side and raised his sandwich, but she frowned and shook her head.

Come on, I can do this. All he needed was to get her a clear shot.

He hefted the packed sandwich in one hand, casting it a last longing glance. *'Tis a far far better thing you do…* And with that, he hurled it towards the other side of the room. It didn't even hit the floor before a slug lanced through it, punching a hole directly through the center.

But something about the sound of it was wrong in Eli's ears. The pitch was off, compared to the shots from earlier; it was higher, slower. Like it was from a different gun…

His breath caught in his chest, but Addy was already going over the top of the desk, her weapon outstretched.

Without a second thought, Eli pushed off the floor and hit Addy in a tackle, even as the deeper *thwip* of Patel's slug-thrower rang out and the shots tore through the space she'd been occupying a second ago.

They hit the floor in a heap, Eli atop Addy, panting hard. "Two guns," he managed. Where the second one had come from, he didn't know, but Patel seemed like the kind of guy who believed in redundancies.

"Yeah," Addy wheezed from beneath him. "I got that."

Meanwhile, Patel rounded the corner of the desk, his smile vicious as he lined up the shot.

As one, Eli and Addy rolled to the left – well, Eli's left, Addy's right – and more slugs traced an ellipsis through the spot they'd just vacated. With the momentum, Eli kept rolling, off of Addy and onto the cold permacrete floor, feeling his elbows and knees complain.

But it left Addy a clear line of fire and she wasn't one to miss an opening. This time, the KO gun shot took Patel directly in the torso, and the security chief's face had just enough time to register a look of surprise before he slumped to the floor, like a bird flash-frozen in mid-flight.

The room was still for a moment, no sound but ragged breaths coming from Eli and Addy. Eli pressed his hand against a tender spot in his side. *Must have bruised it.*

Addy got up first, casting a disgusted look at Patel, then fired one more stun shot into the already limp security chief. She offered a hand to Eli.

Letting himself be pulled to his feet, Eli winced. "We should get moving."

Nodding in agreement, Addy started to make for the door when she stopped. "Brody... you're bleeding."

"Huh?" He looked down at the hand that he'd been pressing against his side. It was red and sticky with something that looked a lot like the blood that should, by all rights, be inside him. "Well. That sucks."

There was a rushing in his ears and everything was suddenly too loud and too bright and would it kill them to have not turned on the disco ball? Then Addy was above him, being yanked upwards by some sort of antigravity field except no, it was him, and he was falling back to the floor and then everything was white.

CHAPTER 19

For the first time in what felt like hours, Kovalic remembered to blink and immediately regretted it. His eyes seared as he pressed the palms of his hands against them, lights scintillating and pulsing.

That's what you got for staring at screens all day, he reminded himself as he resisted the urge to put his head down on the desk.

He'd been searching through every databank he could access or, with his limited technical prowess, hack into – financial ledgers, transit records, communication logs – for any crumb or thread that linked Aidan Kester to the Illyricans. He'd taken a fine-toothed comb through the records for the man's tailor too, Eldon Habib, checking rent payments, any connections to the Imperium, work history, the whole – he snorted at the expression – nine yards.

All he'd gotten was a headache.

He wasn't surprised to find nothing in Kester's background: the vetting the man would have received, given his security clearance, was sure to have been far more thorough than what Kovalic could dig up in a few hours. Habib likewise had no obvious red flags. Both were upstanding citizens with impeccable resumes, plenty of ties to the local community, and not so much as a stain on their records. Either they were very *very* good, or Kovalic was barking up the wrong tree. Perhaps sometimes, a tailor was just that: a tailor.

Leaning back in the chair, he gave his eyes a final rub, then reached for the glass of water he'd poured. Dehydration certainly wouldn't help matters.

There was a creak of floorboards and Kovalic looked up to find the general had joined him in the living area of the small apartment that Esterhaus had arranged for them. For someone who'd supposedly been out of the intelligence game for years, the former agent had proved remarkably resourceful.

"Anything?" the general asked.

Kovalic exhaled. "Too much. And not enough."

"Ah, the classic dilemma." The general settled into a chair, stroking his neat, pointed beard. "In situations like this, I've always found it instructive to start with the facts."

Kovalic shifted in his seat, like he'd found a burr in his trousers. "That's what I've been doing," he said shortly, gesturing to the terminal. "Poring over every piece of information I can find."

"No," said the general, shaking his head. "You've been looking at data, yes, but that's not quite the same thing. There's too much there to find the signal amongst the noise. We need to start with what we know: Those events that we are relatively certain had Isabella's fingerprints on them. Perhaps then we can find someplace where she utilized the services of her mole."

It was, Kovalic had to admit, a good idea. And it would certainly narrow the field. "Fair enough. What have you got?"

The general ticked the items off on his fingers. "Your mission to Sevastapol, last year, to make contact with the defector Albert Bleiden: he was already compromised before you arrived, though it's difficult to say if that was from IIS surveillance or from our side. I suspect Isabella let him get the message to you, ensuring that you would investigate Prince Hadrian's plan for Bayern – which she reinforced by directly communicating to me his presence there. The end result of which was to remove her elder brother from contention for the throne."

"Consolidating her power base," said Kovalic.

"Indeed," said the general, a flicker of worry crossing his face.

"Kester knew about both of those operations, too."

"Yes, I recall. But I believe we also concluded that it was Lieutenant Page who provided him with that information."

"True, but it doesn't eliminate Kester from suspicion. He may have recruited Page as his own asset to help him carry out Isabella's agenda; he certainly preyed upon Page's worries about you."

"Fair enough," the general conceded.

"What about the job aboard the *Queen Amina*? You said Emperor Alaric had been after the Aleph Tablet for some time, so it stands to reason Isabella would know that – and Commander Mirza's Special Operations Executive team would have been working on her orders."

The general nodded his head. "I would add that to our known operations column, certainly. We're just fortunate that the tablet was taken out of play before she could get her hands on it."

Kovalic shifted in his seat, that burr back again. He hadn't shared his suspicions with the general, reinforced only the other day in his conversation with Lakshmi, Eyes's head of station on Nova, that the tablet that had been destroyed aboard the *Queen Amina* had been a forgery. Where the real tablet was, he wasn't sure, but he was sure that the Imperium was at least aware that the genuine article was still out there.

"And then," the general continued, seemingly oblivious to Kovalic's hesitation, "there was the matter of the Novan Liberation Front. We've been so distracted with the fact that the money could be traced back to my accounts that we've ignored the larger picture: that Isabella appears to have been using the organization, and its leader Alys Costa, as cat's-paws to expose corruption and internal strife within the Commonwealth. On a galactic stage, that helps weaken the Imperium's only significant opposition."

Hard as it was to believe, it had been just a couple days ago that Kovalic had tangled with Costa aboard Station Zero; somebody had clearly fed her information about the deployment of CID's AUGUR surveillance program, as well as the schedule of the previous CID director, whom she'd nearly assassinated. All of which Aidan Kester would have been in a position to know, but so far he'd escaped any implication.

"None of this eliminates Kester as our prime suspect," said Kovalic.

"No," agreed the general, "but the evidence remains circumstantial. We have no smoking gun tying him to any of the events in question, and trying to find facts that fit our theory is a dangerous proposition."

"OK," said Kovalic, bringing up the holoscreen again. He tapped a finger against his lips. "Let's take another angle: Can we draw a line between any of those events? Something that they had in common?"

"Beyond the fact that almost all of them directly targeted me – and, by extension, the Special Projects Team?" said the general dryly. "Not upon first glance. Different methodologies, different vectors." He pursed his lips in thought. "But the most interesting, to me, is providing the information about my bank accounts – and not simply because it has put us in our current predicament."

"Why, then?"

"Because Kester wasn't the only one to receive that evidence," said the general, cocking his head. "Where did you say you got it again?"

"I didn't know fishing was one of your pastimes."

"Come come, Simon," the older man said, leveling him with a look. "I think we can dispose with the pretense. Unless you'd like to tell me it *wasn't* the recently resurrected Aaron Page."

Kovalic's lips thinned. He'd tried to leave Page out of it, but that had become impossible. Still, it did open the door to one particular conversation he'd been meaning to have. "Is that why you told Addy to take him out?"

The general did him the courtesy of not denying that he'd given the order. "My suggestion to Specialist Sayers was based purely on my concern for the team. At the time, we believed that Lieutenant Page had aligned himself with Nova Front. I was worried that, as his former colleagues, your objectivity might be compromised." One white eyebrow raised, inviting Kovalic to challenge the assumption.

Once upon a time, he might have taken the general's words at face value, but it had become clear just how much the man had concealed. "You have to admit it doesn't look good that you targeted the person who brought to light compromising information about you."

"I'm not *omniscient*, Simon," said the general, his tone waspish. "Until the Nova Front attacks, I wasn't even aware that Page was still alive... or that you had asked him to look into me."

Kovalic spread his hands. "You can't blame me when it's the very image you've cultivated."

For a moment, the older man seemed poised to issue a sharp rejoinder, his whole body straightened like the very picture of the nobility he'd once been, but the energy drained out of him, his shoulders slumping. "A fair point. I concede that I might have been... overzealous in giving those instructions. But it was not myself I was trying to protect."

It was as close as Kovalic was likely to get to an apology. He could have pressed the point further, but what was there to gain? Page had vanished again after the confrontation with Alys Costa, with no means to contact him.

"So, even if those transactions were left for *someone* to find, I'm guessing you don't think the princess was specifically targeting Page."

After a moment, the general tipped his head to Kovalic, in acknowledgement of the topic they'd abandoned. "Good as Isabella has proven to be, she isn't all-seeing either. I don't think Page's particular circumstances were ideal for her needs, especially since his supposed demise gave him no official channel to report said information. Which is why she moved to her contingency plan."

"Her mole."

"Quite. All things being equal, if they are as valuable as I would assume, she'd prefer not to risk them. But it seems some part of her agenda dictated the timing. And that impatience is sure to leave a trail." One corner of his mouth curved into a faint smile. "Ah, impatience. A cardinal sin, if you'll excuse the expression."

Kovalic rolled his eyes. "Sounds like Brody's been rubbing off on you."

The general sniffed. "I'll have you know that I've dabbled in wordplay longer than young Mr Brody has been alive."

"So," said Kovalic, trying to get the gravtrain back on track. "This makes it more important than ever that we find out how this evidence got into Kester's hands."

"Indeed," said the general. "But again, we must eliminate the alternatives. Let's assume, for a moment, that the information made its way to Kester through legitimate channels. There are a limited number of places that he would be likely to have come across it, the most likely being a Commonwealth counterintelligence operation."

A frown creased Kovalic's brow. "Which narrows it down, but only a little bit. Everybody and their dog has a counterintelligence department: CID, the Commonwealth military, the Bureau. Thanks to the intelligence sharing protocols, a report from any of them would have crossed his desk in his capacity as deputy director for operations."

"Quite. I myself have been included on more than a few reports of that ilk, and if I had to surmise, I would say it would have come to light as a result of Nova Front being surveilled as a domestic terrorist organization."

"Which would put it in the Commonwealth Security Bureau's purview." The Commonwealth's largest law-enforcement agency was tasked with protecting the citizenry of Nova and the rest of the Commonwealth worlds from internal threats. "So we need to talk to someone inside the Bureau who can tell us if the information originated there."

"And we need to be careful," the general added, "because they themselves would be a candidate for Isabella's mole. How would you rate the trustworthiness of Inspector Laurent?"

Kovalic's headache was back, and it had brought reinforcements. He took another sip of the water. "If you'd asked me two days ago, I would have said he was unimpeachable. But from a purely factual standpoint, I don't have any way to rule him out." His gut still told him that Rashad Laurent wasn't the kind of person who would smile to your face, then stab you in the back, but that was a risk they couldn't trust to his digestive system.

"Which presents a conundrum indeed," said the general. "Somehow, we need to locate someone who not only has access to those files, but who also had no means, motive, or opportunity to provide them to Aidan Kester."

Something sparked in Kovalic's brain. "Hard as it may be to believe, I actually think I have just the person."

CHAPTER 20

"Brody. Brody. *Eli.*" Addy was kneeling by the pilot, shaking his shoulder even as a sick feeling settled into her stomach. He must have taken a round from Patel's slug-thrower – probably when he'd tackled her to get her out of the line of fire. *Idiot.*

She pulled open his jacket; the stain was spreading outwards from the right side of his torso, where a small neat hole was punched through the formerly white shirt, rapidly turning pink.

Damn it, no. Stay with me. Her hand went to the boot where she kept her knife, unfolding it with a flick and quickly cutting through the shirt so she could gently peel it back and take a closer look at the wound.

It was still bleeding, but not too badly. Addy tried to summon her rudimentary field medic training, but it kept slipping away like she was trying to grab a fish with her bare hands.

Stop the bleeding.

Her head went on a swivel, checking the room. This was a security office – there had to be a first-aid kit somewhere, unless Patel had added incompetency to malice and corruption.

She pulled off her own jacket, folding it into a makeshift pillow to get Brody's head off the cold, hard floor, then went to Patel's desk, systematically rifling the drawers to find a bottle of cheap no-name whisky, a few reams of flimsies that looked like unfiled paperwork, and a half-eaten box of pretzels.

Finally, in the back of the bottom left drawer she hit the jackpot: a blue standard issue medkit, still in its original packaging. The date stamped on the side said it should have been refreshed two years ago, but she wasn't about to quibble with overcautious regulations while her partner was bleeding out.

She ripped it open as she dropped back onto her knees next to Brody, then pulled out a gauze pad and pressed it hard to the hole in his side. He winced and flailed, still unconscious, as the pad started to turn red.

Keeping pressure on the wound, she gently rolled him onto his uninjured side and heaved a sigh of relief at the sight of a matching exit wound on the back. At least he didn't have a goddamned slug inside his abdomen.

Rummaging in the medkit, she pulled out a canister of pressurized sealant and a tube of antibiotic gel. She waited for the bleeding to ebb, then squirted a big chunk of the gel directly onto the wound, slapped the sealant dispenser over it, and pulled the activation tab. With a hissing sound, the sealant plugged the hole and hardened almost instantaneously. She repeated the procedure on Brody's back, covering both holes with self-adhering gauze pads for good measure, then sat back on her heels to check her handiwork.

Not too bad if I do say so myself. It would hold until they got back to the *Cavalier*'s med bay and Taylor could take a look at him.

Then she looked down at her hands, stained red from Brody's blood, and her vision wavered. *Oh my god.* Her breath started coming in short, ragged gasps, and she lurched to her feet, her hands seizing the edge of Patel's desk where they left stark red handprints. *Fuck fuck fuck.*

The floor started to shift beneath her feet like the deck of a ship, and it was only her grip on the desk that kept her from falling onto the floor. She tried to control her breath and focus. *He's OK. You're OK. Everything's OK.*

Except everything definitely *wasn't* OK. She glanced down at the unconscious security chief, who had taken enough KO shots to incapacitate an elephant for a couple hours. Patel had kept them here for a reason. He'd been stalling them, and to Addy's mind, none of the implications of that were good.

Sticking around seemed like a bad idea.

With a plan in mind, her vision seemed to stabilize. She managed to get her hands mostly clean with a sterilizing pad from the medkit, the alcohol smell sharp in her nose, then patted the pilot's cheek. "Brody. Wake up. Come on." Her heartbeat was still elevated, but she pushed back against it, not willing to let it dictate her behavior.

Brody's expression was still slack, his head on her jacket. Sweat beaded on his forehead, and his face – pale at the best of times – had taken on an ashen tone.

Reaching back for the medkit, she rooted through it until she found a hypo and a med dispenser. *One of these damn things is a stimshot.* The display on the dispenser blurred in her vision and she rubbed the back of her hand across her eyes as she thumbed through the options. *There. Epinephrine.* Toggling the selector, she pressed the hypo to the dispenser's port and watched the progress bar as it dispensed a dose.

OK, here goes nothing. Flipping open the hypo cap, she pressed it against Brody's neck and pressed the activation stud. There was a click and a hiss as the medicine flooded out.

For a moment nothing happened and Addy sat back, a cold grip seizing her heart. Had she used the wrong meds? The wrong dose? Maybe it should have gone in his thigh–

Brody's eyes shot open as he gasped and sat bolt upright.

Addy tumbled backwards onto her butt, one hand clutching her chest. Suddenly she started laughing, but it sounded too high and too loud to her ears. *You're losing it.* She clapped a hand over her mouth as her eyes met Brody's.

"What the hell just happened?" His voice was pitched an octave above its usual timbre, thready with shock. "Did I get shot?"

"Only a little bit."

"A *little* bit?"

"Now isn't the time, Brody. We've got bigger problems. Can you get up?"

"I don't know, Addy. I was *shot.*"

That sounds like the Brody I know. Some of Addy's composure finally returned and she rolled her eyes. "Don't be so dramatic. It was a through-and-through and I patched you up. Come on, we need to go now." She got to her own feet, then offered him a hand.

Gingerly, the pilot took it and let her help him up. He glanced down at his ruined shirt and the gauze pad underneath, then prodded it experimentally. "Huh. How come it doesn't hurt?"

"Antibiotic gel's numbing it. And you're full of adrenaline."

"Oh. Great. Maybe I should always live this way." His smile was wan, but it was there.

Addy drew in a breath through her nose and clamped down hard on her shakiness. Like she'd told Brody, they had bigger problems. Namely, whoever was coming for them. *And I don't think they're delivering us fresh sandwiches.* She scooped up the two slugthrowers that had dropped by Patel's feet – the second proved to be a compact model that would fit in an ankle holster, which explained where he'd come up with it. *Would have hurt just as much.* She owed Brody that much at least, even if he was still an idiot.

"We should call Taylor," said Brody, one hand still on his mid-section, though more out of instinct than what seemed like actual pain.

"You handle that. I'm going to make sure that our exit is clear." The front door was the obvious way out, but it also might drop them right in the path of whoever Patel had been waiting for. She scouted out the rear exit near the holding cell while Brody tried to raise the *Cavalier* on his sleeve.

The back door let out into a narrow alley lined with refuse bins. It seemed to lead to another street, though perhaps calling it that was generous.

Of course, they could be waiting for us there too. But sitting in here with analysis paralysis wasn't going to help anything. Better they choose a course of action and go for it. "Come on," she called over her shoulder. "This way."

Brody came up behind her, his brow creased. "I can't get anyone on comms."

"Jammed?"

He shook his head. "There's no static or feedback... the line's just dead. Like my calls are going into a black hole."

Addy's lips compressed. She didn't like the sound of that, but there was nothing she could do about it from here. "I'm sure they're fine. But the faster we get back to the ship, the sooner we can get out of here." She proffered her KO gun to Brody, who eyed it like she'd was handing him a live viper. He took it with great reluctance, holding it limply at one side.

Rain cascaded off the eaves as they threaded their way through the alley. The smell of trash mingled with the sulfur-like scent that seemed to be everywhere on Juarez 7A; probably a side effect of the mining process.

At the end of the passage, Addy poked her head out. The street wasn't totally empty, with a handful of people coming and going, but neither was it bustling enough to provide cover. They'd have to brazen it out, make a beeline for the spaceport, and hope that luck was with them.

Trusting luck. Who have I become?

She tucked the small holdout pistol in her boot; it was awkward without a holster there, but better to have it and not need it. Patel's full-size slug-thrower she held under her other arm, beneath her coat. At a nod from her, Brody shoved the KO gun into his pocket, though the bulge was so painfully obvious that he might as well have carried it outright.

Steeling herself, she rounded the corner, doing her best attempt at a casual stroll, and started towards the spaceport. Behind her, she could hear the squelch of Brody's shoes as he followed a few steps behind her.

None of the settlement's denizens spared them a second look, all intent on getting wherever they were going – presumably out of the never-ending rain. Eyes down, shoulders hunched, they hurried past, keeping themselves to themselves.

Fine by me. Nobody bothered them as they reached the end of the street, and Addy let her hopes rise as they turned the corner that would lead them back to the spaceport.

And then she froze as she caught sight of a pair of figures in body armor, carrying lancer rifles. They were a block away, at the intersection with the settlement's main street, talking to a couple of the local denizens. One of the armored individuals was holding up their sleeve with a holoscreen floating over it, showing what looked like a pair of pictures.

She might be too far away to tell for sure, but she had no doubt who they were pictures of. *Shit.* They must have already been to the security office and found Patel unconscious.

Brody had come up behind her, slowing to a stop as he took in the scene. "Well, that's not good. Can we go around?"

Addy had already started to survey the surroundings, but the longer they stood here, the more likely they were to attract attention. Her eyes darted across the buildings opposite, looking for something – an open door, alley access – but the structures here were all abutting, with no space in between them, and the doors, as far as she could tell without conspicuously trying each one, sealed tight.

She started inching forward, walking at the slowest pace she could manage, even as her eyes kept flicking from side to side. Could they go up and over the buildings? *No stairs or ladders. Seems like a fire hazard.* With each step, it brought them closer to the pair of armored security, who were still flagging down the inhabitants and pointing at the holoscreen. Most shook their head and trudged on without a second look. So far, the efforts had been focused on the main street, but if they just turned ninety degrees, the jig was up.

Clutching her weapon tighter, Addy continued edging up the street towards the intersection. *There's only two of them.* The best option was a stun-and-run with the KO gun; the body armor would be more effective against her slug-thrower, and the last thing she wanted was to start a firefight in the middle of a population of innocent civilians.

She was about to turn and get Brody to give her the knockout gun – the chances of him being willing to take a preemptive shot seemed low – when a woman with dark brown skin and a long braid of gray-streaked dark hair approached the armored pair, staring at the pictures with a furrowed brow. Beside her, she heard sharp indrawn breath from Brody.

"What?"

"I... met her this morning, at the general store," murmured Brody.

As if on cue, the woman's gaze drifted over the shoulders of the people with guns and landed directly on them. Addy turned towards the building and made as if she were checking her sleeve, but Brody seemed to be frozen, stock still, one hand still holding the KO gun in his pocket, another pressed over the spot where he'd been shot.

"*Brody,*" she hissed.

But it was too late; the woman had clearly made eye contact with him, and with it went any chance that they were going to get out of here without a fight. Addy had started to pull the slug-thrower out from under her jacket when a hand touched her upper arm gently; Brody was looking at her and shaking his head. He jutted his chin back towards the woman.

She was still talking to the pair, but pointing over... down the main drag, away from them.

Addy's breath caught in her throat. Sure enough, after a moment's more discussion, the two armed figures started off in a trot down the street, leaving a nice big gap for them to slip through. This was one gift horse into whose mouth Addy wasn't about to look. Without a hesitation, she quickened her pace, cutting across the intersection towards the spaceport, Brody's arm slung over her shoulder.

The woman didn't come any closer to them, just offered a short, sharp nod in the pilot's direction, which he returned. And then she was gone, back about her daily business, and Addy and Brody were within steps of the spaceport.

"Why didn't she turn us in?" Addy asked, resisting the urge to glance over her shoulder.

Brody shrugged. "I dunno. But why would she, I guess? We always assume the worst of people."

Addy bit her tongue, staving off the response that, in her experience, most people lived up to that expectation. Despite everything Brody had been through, he'd still maintained an optimistic streak, lodged like shrapnel in his heart. It was what made Brody... Brody. And, much as Addy might want to deny it, that was part of what she liked about him.

She breathed more easily when the spaceport came into sight, the *Cavalier* safe on its pad. *Get onboard, get out of here.* If there were more people looking for them – and she felt confident that those two goons hadn't been alone – they were probably spread out searching the settlement.

Still, even as they climbed the ramp to the hatch, Brody's arm still over her shoulder, something sat uneasy in her stomach. They hadn't been able to raise Tapper and Taylor; she only hoped they'd taken the sensible course of action and stayed put, rather than going out looking for them.

So when she palmed open the hatch and saw the commander and the sergeant sitting at the table in the cargo hold, she almost heaved an audible sigh of relief.

It took another moment for her to register the fact that both of them had their hands flat on the table, and that the look on their faces was, in the case of Taylor, a hair too stoic and, for Tapper, far too annoyed.

The sound of weapons being readied came from both sides of Addy, even as she was unlimbering the slug-thrower.

"Well," said a familiar voice that immediately sent ice pouring through her veins. "Here are our errant pair. Glad you could join us."

From the other side of the cargo hold stepped a lithe woman with a midnight complexion and a sharp smile. She was dressed more practically and less elegantly than the last time they'd met, but she moved with the same fluid and dangerous grace that had drawn Addy to her in the first place. Addy's heart thumped hard in her chest as the woman crossed the distance between them and stood before her, then reached out one finger to lift her chin so their gazes could meet. Her eyes were dark violet pools that seemed to go on forever, inviting you to drown in them.

"It's *so* good to see you again, Adelaide," said Ofeibia Xi. "We have some unfinished business, you and I."

CHAPTER 21

I must be hallucinating. From the blood loss. Eli resisted the urge to slap himself in the face with the hand that wasn't slung over Addy's shoulders.

But he could feel her muscles tense and, from the looks on Taylor's and Tapper's faces, he wasn't the only one seeing the head of the White Star Syndicate and one of the galaxy's most ruthless crime lords – a crime lord from under whose nose they'd very nearly stolen a treasured artifact just six months ago – standing in the cargo hold of their ship.

"Is this all of you?" Xi asked, looking around. Her eyelids, painted a startling electric blue, batted once. "I had been looking forward to my next encounter with your boss. Major Kovalic."

"He's not available right now," said Tapper. "But we can take a message."

A flash of annoyance crossed her features and she snapped her fingers in the direction of one of the armed goons, who stepped forward and casually punched Tapper in the face. The sergeant let out a muffled *oof*, then cracked his neck and favored the man who'd hit him with a grin streaked with a fine thread of blood. "Not bad, but keep working on it," he advised, "someday maybe you'll make it to the big leagues."

The goon pulled back his fist for a second go, but Xi sighed and waved a hand in his direction, and he straightened and stepped back. "I do so detest violence, of course. Well, if Kovalic isn't here, which one of you is in charge?" Her dark eyes took them each in turn. "Adelaide, not you, I think. And not the mouthy one... I believe you went by Trevelyan on the *Queen Amina*, though I'm sure that's not your real name."

Unconsciously, Eli tried to make himself small, hunching over, but he still couldn't escape the woman's gaze. "You're the one who broke into my vault." Anger flared in her eyes before she could tamp it down. "The buffoon." She flicked her fingers at him, as if trying to dislodge a leftover piece of food.

"Hey!" Eli protested weakly. *OK, I did shoot out of a gravtube like an uncorked bottle of champagne, so I guess that's fair.*

But Xi had already moved on, turning to look down at Taylor, who was sitting quietly at the table. "That leaves you. I don't know you." Her head cocked to one side. "That in itself tells me that you're a professional. So let's assume you are in charge of this... operation. What's your name?"

Taylor's chin came up, her eyes hard. "Radha Vinson."

Xi looked skeptical. "I'm sure it isn't, but I'll let you have that one. So, then... Major Vinson, is it? I'm delighted to make your acquaintance. I'm sorry that you'll have to preside over the loss of your team; I'm sure that will ruffle some feathers back in the Commonwealth. I wish I could say it's nothing personal..." Her expression hardened. "But it is. It's very personal. You stole from me. I can't have people steal from me and walk away – it's bad for business." She stalked over towards Addy, and, if anything, she looked even angrier. "An example needs to be made."

Addy was just barely holding herself in check, Eli could tell. Every muscle in her neck was taut, standing out like cords. He leaned more heavily on her, which he told himself was to remind her that she wasn't on her own, but also because the adrenaline was starting to wear off and he actually needed the support.

Getting shot really hurts – who knew?

"You're not going to kill us," said Taylor.

Xi didn't turn, still holding Addy's gaze. "No?" she said. "What makes you think that?"

Taylor gestured to their current predicament. "You've got half a dozen people with guns pointed at us, Madam Xi. If you were going to kill us, they'd have done it already. We're alive and talking, which means you want something."

Xi's eyes sparkled. "I'm never wrong about people – though they sometimes *disappoint*." Her glance flicked to Addy, and then away again as though she might be contagious. Lowering herself into an empty seat at the table as gracefully as if she were arranging an elegant gown, Xi folded her hands. "So, what is it I want?"

Eli looked rapidly back and forth between the two women and Tapper, on whose cheek a red spot was rapidly blooming. *Well, I don't think that's a table I'd want a seat at. Unstoppable force, meet immovable object.*

For her part, Taylor was assessing the other woman with her usual piercing gaze. "I'm not usually one to lay a wager, but I know you're a woman who doesn't capriciously discard something that might be useful. My team and I are an asset – and you know this because we were able to compromise *your* security."

A flash of anger crossed Xi's face, but she ironed it out like a wrinkled shirt. "Quite so. You and your team proved most resourceful in breaking into my vault and stealing my property. Amongst *other* betrayals." This time she pointedly did not look in Addy's direction, though Eli could feel that it was taking everything the younger woman had not to spring across the hold. "That's no small feat. And though there's a part of me that would take great pleasure in having you dragged across the surface of this moon while dangling from a low-flying ship... well, I haven't gotten where I am in life by giving in to those baser impulses. At least, not all the time."

I actually might take her up on the low-flying ship offer; if the gravity's just right you might even be able to sell tickets. Eli's vision swam suddenly, his knees wavering.

Half a dozen weapons snapped towards him at the movement and, if it weren't for Addy, he probably would have collapsed onto the deck in a boneless jelly. But she grunted and tightened the arm around his waist, keeping him just barely upright.

"Uh, sorry about that," Eli managed. "Anybody mind if I sit down?"

Taylor's focus on Xi momentarily broken, she glanced sharply in his direction. "Everything all right?"

"We had a run-in with the local security dipshit," said Addy, gritting her teeth. "Who I'm assuming was on your payroll?" She jerked her head in Xi's direction, without favoring the woman with a look.

Xi, for her part, merely shrugged. "I'm sure you're aware that I placed bounties on you after our encounter on the *Queen Amina*. I got a message from Security Chief... what was his name? Patel, yes. He sent word as soon as you landed last night. Fortunately, I was already in the vicinity, so I took my fastest ship and here we are. But if you killed him, then you saved me some money."

Addy's nose wrinkled. *So much for bribing the dockmaster. He must have passed all our IDs along to Patel anyway – I guess he knows where his bread is buttered.* "Patel will live. But he was the trigger-happy sort and..." she hesitated, then sighed, "...*Easy* here took a round. He should be OK, but he could probably use more attention than I was able to give him with a field medkit."

The weapons of Xi's goons shifted suddenly as Taylor started to get to her feet; she put her hands up, palms out.

"Where do you think you're going?" said Xi.

"One of my team needs medical attention, and I'm the best trained."

Xi raised an eyebrow. "Really? Him? How important could he be?"

Hey. Eli opened his mouth to protest, but his knees went wobbly again, and he thought better of it.

"Every member of my team is important," said Taylor. One slim eyebrow went up. "But perhaps you wouldn't do the same for one of your people."

A roll of the eyes signified what Xi thought of that particular gambit. "Very well." She beckoned to one of her goons and gave him a murmured instruction; the man slung his weapon behind his back, then walked over to Addy and Eli. He was built like a small tank, all muscle, with a blunt nose and eyes that were too close together. As though he were handling a baby bird, he took Eli's arm from around

Addy's shoulders and put it over his own. "Andres will see to him while we get down to brass tacks. Where's your medbay?"

Taylor hesitated, clearly torn between trusting Xi or using her minuscule amounts of leverage to insist on treating Eli herself. *It's not worth it, commander,* Eli thought, giving her a short shake of the head. She'd need all her wits about her to deal with Xi, and he didn't want to be a distraction. "Down the corridor," she said, nodding to a hatchway across the cargo hold. "Second right."

Addy released her grip on Eli's waist only reluctantly, shifting her weight to the balls of her feet. "You OK?"

"Oh, yeah, peachy," Eli said. There was a deep ache in his side that had been slowly spreading and intensifying over the last few minutes. "I think I need a nap."

"I'll check on you in a little bit," she promised.

And with that, Andres ushered Eli out of the cargo hold, and towards the medbay. *Hope they can manage without me.* He stifled a laugh, and was pretty sure he caught the goon giving him a weird look.

But he proved, to Eli's surprise, to be an incredibly competent and – perhaps more shockingly – gentle medic. With Eli up on the gurney, Andres donned a pair of blue gloves from one of the compartments in the bay, then carefully and methodically removed the patch that Addy had applied and checked the sealant. Nodding his approval of the work, he added some more antibiotic gel via a syringe inserted in the plug, and neatened the edges, then put on new bandages, front and back.

All his ministrations lulled Eli into a state of complacency, drifting off as his wound was tended to. So much so, that he didn't notice the hypo until it was being pressed against his neck, the soft hiss sending him jerking up on his elbows.

"What the fuck was that?!" But the room was already blurring and spinning around him.

Guess I'm getting that nap after al–

CHAPTER 22

The woman who finally answered the door on the third ring of the buzzer was dressed in a fuzzy blue bathrobe and pajama pants, her brown-blond hair pulled up into a messy bun. She held a baby on one hip. "One minute, one minute, for heaven's sa – Kaplan?" She did a double take at the sight of Kovalic and the general standing on the walkway outside. "What the devil are you doing here?"

"Inspector Fayerweather. Good to see you again. Can we come in?" He gestured to the apartment beyond her.

Veronica Fayerweather gaped, as if still trying to process exactly what was going on. The baby took this opportunity to start wailing, and her eyes took on a glazed expression. "Look, now's not a good time."

The general doffed the snap-brim cap he was wearing and smiled genially. "We're very sorry to bother you at home, inspector, but I'm afraid this matter simply cannot wait. And who is this charmer?" He leaned in close to the baby who suddenly went quiet, large blue eyes studying this new and different face.

Kovalic tried his best not to goggle as the general, the former head of Illyrican intelligence, the most formidable opponent the Commonwealth had faced during its long war with the Imperium, stuck his tongue out at a baby. Of all the things he'd seen in the past week – terrorists threatening to blow up a space station, accusations of treason being flung like so much confetti, conspiracies galore – this might be the most unbelievable.

Fayerweather, for her part, softened as the baby stared at the newcomer. "This is Marcus." She hitched the baby up on her hip, sighed, and stepped aside. "Fine, come in."

The apartment looked like a tornado had hit it, followed in rapid succession by an earthquake and a hurricane. The detritus of an infant was everywhere, from a half-used box of diapers to a playmat on the floor, over which dangled a purple monkey clutching a pair of cymbals.

"I'd say sorry about the mess, but I'm going to be honest: I'm too tired to care," said Fayerweather, dropping back down on the couch with a groan. She cradled the baby against her, but its eyes still went to the general's bearded face.

"I'm given to understand the first few months are the hardest," said the general, who had not banished the kind note from his voice. "But they say it does get easier."

Kovalic stared at him. Who the hell was this, and what had they done with Hasan al-Adaj?

"Couldn't get much harder," said Fayerweather, with a bleak smile. But it brightened as her eyes slid to the baby, and Kovalic saw her relax as the infant rotated inward and snuggled up against her. "I'd offer you something to eat or drink, but..." She waved a hand at the kitchenette off to one side, stacked high with dirty plates and dishes.

"Oh, don't worry about it," said Kovalic. "We're fine."

Fayerweather nodded, a movement which went on a bit too long and looked as though her chin might suddenly slump to her chest. She suddenly snapped back, her eyes widening. "Sorry, what are you doing here again? I haven't seen you since that murder case, when was it… three years ago?" She blinked. "Was it that long? I have to be honest: I've lost all sense of time."

"Yeah," said Kovalic, "about three years ago." A civilian had gotten themselves mistaken for an Illyrican agent at a dead drop, with unfortunate consequences, and Kovalic and Fayerweather had each held a piece of a puzzle that had made little sense until they'd been able to combine them.

Her eyes sharpened. "And Rashad called me about you just the other day – said he ran into you poking around his crime scene. Causing trouble, as usual."

"Was I causing trouble?" said Kovalic. "Or was I doing my civic duty by assisting the authorities in an important investigation?"

"Hmm," said Fayerweather.

Gently setting aside a surfeit of pillows and burp cloths, the general sat down on a nearby armchair. "Again, we are terribly sorry to disturb you while you're on leave, but I'm afraid we are in dire need of your help, inspector."

Fayerweather eyed the general, then turned to Kovalic. "I don't know who he is, but you should always bring him along. Really softens your rough edges."

"I'll keep that in mind." Kovalic spared a glance at the general, who was still making faces at the baby. "We're trying to track down some documents that might have originated in the counterintelligence division of the Bureau and made their way to CID."

She blinked, as if trying to square the request with her current circumstances. "And you came to me." Suspicion had filtered into her voice. She shifted the baby to her knee, bouncing him up and down as he continued to stare wide-eyed at the general. "Why not call Rashad? Or CID? I mean, I have no idea who you actually work for, but I'm guessing you've got contacts there."

"And miss out on this wonderful opportunity to catch up?" said Kovalic.

"Uh huh. Look, it's not that I haven't kept an ear to the ground – there are really only so many hours a day you can spend talking to a baby before you go mad – but I've hardly been what you might call 'in the loop' for the last few months." She nodded to the baby, who burped, as if on cue.

Kovalic exchanged a look with the general, who dipped his head, signaling him to proceed. "We believe there's an Illyrican mole embedded within the Commonwealth intelligence community. Probably highly placed, but we're not sure where. Finding these documents is the best lead we have to track them down."

A gleam of understanding sparked in the inspector's eyes. "And because I've been on leave, you've ruled me out as a suspect."

"That and your charming personality."

"Because double agents can't be charming?"

"Just the opposite," said Kovalic.

Fayerweather gave him a sour look.

"Yes, exactly like that."

The inspector sighed. "So what exactly are these documents? Counterintel files a lot of reports, and our information sharing agreements mean anything above a certain grade is automatically CC'd to all the other relevant agencies."

"This would have been a report on financial activity relating to the Novan Liberation Front," said Kovalic. "In particular, tracking courier movements between Bayern and Nova."

"Nova Front?" said Fayerweather. "The ones who blew up the ConComm hub? Jesus, Kaplan, you don't ask much, do you?"

"I don't call in favors for the small stuff, inspector."

"No shit." She shook her head. "OK, let me see if I've got this straight: you want me to use my clearance to poke around and see if I can find this report and who had access to it."

"Indeed," said the general. "And, it should go without saying, quietly. We can't have anybody else getting wind of it."

For the first time, a troubled expression crossed the woman's face. "Even Rashad."

Kovalic's smile was tight and without mirth. "Much as I'd like to eliminate Inspector Laurent from consideration, he certainly would have had access. We can't discount him yet."

"Very troubling," she muttered. Her gaze alit upon the baby, hands tightening around his mid-section. "How worried should I be that this is going to blow back on me?"

It was a good question, and Kovalic found his eyes drawn to the baby as well. Was it fair to put the inspector – and her family – in harm's way? He let out a long breath. "I don't know," he said honestly. "It's not without risk. I'm sorry. We wouldn't ask if it wasn't important."

The inspector raked her bottom lip with her teeth. "OK." She bounced the baby again and he cooed, or gave at least a reasonable facsimile of happiness. "Can I think about it?"

Kovalic opened his mouth, but the general beat him to it, smiling again. "Of course. We can't ask more than that." The old man got to his feet, with that creaking of joints and servos that Kovalic now knew to be more theater than fact. "And with that, we'll leave you in peace."

Fayerweather snorted. "'Peace' tells me that, for all your airs, you've definitely never raised a kid."

"You're not wrong," the general admitted. "Not without a lot of help, anyway." He gave her a slight bow again and donned his hat.

"Thanks for seeing us," said Kovalic. He raised his sleeve and flicked his contact information towards her. "You can reach me here."

There was a buzz from Fayerweather's own arm as she accepted the transfer. "You'll excuse me if I don't get up."

"Of course," said Kovalic. "We can see ourselves out." He gave her a nod, then picked his way through the minefield back towards the front door.

"Oh, and Kaplan?" the inspector called after him.

"Yes?"

"Stay out of trouble."

Kovalic gave her a rueful look. "Too late for that. Way too late."

They let themselves out and stood on the breezeway, a warm wind whipping around them. Fayerweather's apartment was several stories up a high-rise, and the afternoon light bathed the building in rich hues of orange and pink as they looked out at the skyscrapers of Salaam.

"I suppose that went as well as could be expected," said the general. He peered out over the railing. "Rance ought to be coming around with the car shortly."

Kovalic joined him, his hands curling around the railing. "I can't help worrying that we've just put a target on her back."

The general tilted his head to one side. "She's a veteran field agent at the Bureau, Simon. I imagine she can hold her own."

"Doesn't mean we need to throw her into the frying pan."

"Oh come now, that's a bit dramatic."

Kovalic's hands tightened, the railing the only thing preventing them from becoming fists. "Dramatic? Look at us – accused of treason, on the run from the law, one step from being thrown in prison or worse. That can't happen to her; she has a family."

"We're all taking risks," said the general shortly. "That's what war is."

"But she didn't sign up for it."

"Didn't she?" asked the general, raising one eyebrow. "I think we should be more concerned that she might call Inspector Laurent anyway. I'll notice you didn't bother telling her that we're fugitives and that her partner is the one hunting us."

The thought had crossed his mind, but it had very conveniently not come up. Was he afraid that she wouldn't help them if she knew the truth? Convenient for Kovalic, then, but not for Veronica Fayerweather.

Some habits were so deeply ingrained that they were tough to excise and, as a rule, intelligence agents didn't give away any more than they had to. Not without getting something in return anyway. But at the end of the day, the general wasn't wrong: Kovalic was just as culpable for whatever came next.

Here's hoping it wasn't the worst, for her sake *and* for theirs. They were precious short on friends of any stripe at present, and going to Fayerweather was a calculated risk. If this ended up blowing one of their few allies, then going back to square one wouldn't be their biggest problem.

It took a moment for Kovalic to let go of the railing; he shook out his hands, cold from the metal. "Never mind. Let's just go."

The wind blew back his hair as he stalked down the breezeway, the general silently following. Still, the guilt sat heavy in his stomach, its tendrils snaking their way up and outward. At least he felt *bad* about it; the general seemed to take it as the cost of doing business.

And Kovalic was starting to realize that when it came to that cost, the two of them weren't necessarily in perfect alignment. The general had been willing to let Sayers kill Page. He'd burned Yevgeniy Esterhaus, one of – nominally – his closest friends.

Kovalic's priority had always been the safety of his people; he worried that the general's was preserving his agenda.

Even if it meant casualties.

CHAPTER 23

Nat hadn't crossed paths with Xi during the operation on the *Queen Amina*, but she'd read the after-action reports. The syndicate leader was sharp and not to be trifled with. Kind of like handling a live grenade: safe so long as you were careful.

"So," she said, studying the other woman. "You want us to steal something."

Xi leaned back. "You've proved yourself able thieves. And I have a feeling that you're going to be more than willing to help."

At that, Nat raised an eyebrow. "Oh?"

"I have to admit: at first, I was quite cross with you all for stealing my property only to get it destroyed. Hence the placing of certain bounties that made it unwise for you to set foot outside the Commonwealth." Xi unclasped one of the bangles around her wrist, silver with an etched pattern weaving around it, and placed the piece on the table. "However, the more time I spent considering our encounter, the more suspicious I became of the outcome. The Aleph Tablet has, after all, been through many different hands in its time, and has been thought lost more than once. So I decided to do a bit of digging."

"Oh, Christ," said Sayers, rolling her eyes. "You think it's still out there? Don't tell me you want us to steal it *again*."

"Not quite what I had in mind. But I thought you might be interested to know the results of my investigations." At a tap of her forefinger, the bangle started to glow and a holoscreen sprang into existence, showing the image of a man standing at what looked to be a spaceport. A vertiginous sensation struck Nat as she took in his face, which looked both familiar and unfamiliar at the same time. It wasn't just the features – the snub nose, dark hair, and wide-set eyes – but elements that seemed like they should be there, but weren't – a trim goatee, wrinkles, an ounce of kindness in his gaze. Behind her, she felt both Sayers and Tapper go still as well.

"I take it you recognize this man," Xi continued. "I believe you knew him as Dr Seku al-Kitab, an expert in ancient history and archaeology."

On that score, she was right: al-Kitab had been the scholar who Xi had brought in to authenticate the Aleph Tablet, and who Nat and Kovalic had subsequently convinced to help them. But the man they'd known had been a meek, anxious academic – a demeanor clearly not shared by the person in the picture.

"I still have not managed to determine his real name," said Xi. "But at the time this was taken, he was going by the alias of Sadiq."

Nat felt as though she'd been hit by a knockout gun, but she struggled to maintain her composure. "You're saying he was a thief?" She tried to reconcile that with the nebbish professor she'd known – *thought* she'd known – and boggled all over again. Whoever this man was, he was *good*.

"Thief… impostor… occasional assassin," said Xi. "Frankly, I'm surprised we hadn't crossed paths before."

Tapper clucked his tongue. "I *thought* that tablet was too easily destroyed," he grumbled. "So this Sadiq guy made off with the real one, huh?"

"It would seem likely," said Xi.

Sayers jumped in, unable to keep a note of smugness from her voice. "I guess that means we're off the hook."

Xi's violet eyes seized on her, glittering like opals. "You still *tried* to steal from me, Adelaide, and I can't let that go unpunished… but instead of killing you outright, I'm going to generously allow you to repay your debt with this job."

Nat shifted in her chair, tamping down her frustration. They were meant to be out here figuring out a way to help clear Simon and the general – not to mention giving the team a path home – and now they were being dragooned into a heist? They didn't have time for this.

Then again, you didn't exactly have the luxury of choice when the guns were pointed at you.

"I hate to disappoint you, Madam Xi, but we aren't thieves."

Xi clucked her tongue. "Don't sell yourself short, major." She raised a finger. "Besides, I haven't even gotten to the best part." And at that, she touched another control on the holoprojector and the image shifted.

This time, it was from an overhead angle of what looked to be a private residence, glass and steel set amongst a thriving garden. Sadiq had just exited a car, and another figure stood outside the house, waiting for him, though the angle made their features hard to discern.

"Sadiq is merely a criminal for hire. Ultimately, my dispute is not with him, but with his employer. I pride myself on knowing people…" her eyes darted to Sayers again, sparking, "…so when I give you an opportunity to deal a significant blow to an enemy of the Commonwealth, I think you'll take it." With that, she pressed the holoprojector control and the image shifted again. The angle had changed as the drone had maneuvered, and this time the shot had been taken from a better angle that clearly showed the features of the person Sadiq was meeting with.

For all of that, it still took a moment for Nat to recognize them. But as it clicked into place, Tapper and Sayers were only a step behind her.

"Holy shit," said Tapper, leaning forward, "is that…?"

"Her Royal Highness, Duchess of König Satrapy, Princess of the House of Malik, Isabella Valeria Josephine," said Xi in a tone that dripped like velvet whispering off satin sheets.

Nat sat back as though a gravball had smacked her directly in the gut. Princess Isabella had orchestrated the Aleph Tablet theft? That made about as much sense as all of them being fugitives from the Commonwealth.

The smile on Ofeibia Xi's face only broadened. "I see I've piqued your interest, major."

Interest was one word for it. Befuddlement was perhaps more accurate. What the Emperor's daughter – a woman known for her charity causes and ceremonial duties – was doing mixed up in the theft of antiquities, well, that was something that Nat would really like to know more about. Was it a point of vulnerability for the princess; perhaps one that Commonwealth Intelligence could exploit? "Say more about this job. How exactly does it concern her?"

"All in good time," said Xi. "But our timetable is somewhat strict, so first things first: I'd like to depart this barren rock immediately."

"It would help if I knew where we were headed," said Nat. "And I'll need my pilot, once he's patched up."

"Oh, that won't be necessary," said Xi. "Yancy here is a more than capable of flying your ship." She gestured to one of her armed goons – a short woman with a buzzed scalp. "And I'll share the details of this particular undertaking en route to our destination. As for your pilot?" Raising a hand, she waved toward the corridor that led to the medbay, and the man she'd sent to see to Brody's wounds appeared. The gurney floated along on its repulsor field, and atop it lay an unconscious Eli Brody, his sandy hair plastered to his forehead with sweat. "I've decided he'll be accompanying my people for the duration of the job. Just to incentivize your good behavior."

Nat's breath caught, and Sayers surged forward, making it halfway to Xi before the woman's security detail trained their weapons on her. "What did you do to him?"

Xi's musical laugh rippled through the hold, though Nat could see that there was something nastier underpinning it; she'd aimed this directly at Sayers. "A mild sedative, my dear, nothing more. I assure you he will be perfectly fine."

The man led the gurney down the ramp as Sayers watched with gritted teeth. A pair of Xi's goons followed suit, leaving three still in the hold with them.

Nat's stomach sank in sympathy. Everything was slipping out of her grasp: she couldn't help Simon, the whole team had been dragged into Xi's orbit, and now Brody was a hostage against their good behavior. It was increasingly looking like the only way out of this mess was through this job.

"I'll hold you to that," was all she said. "If any harm comes to him, we'll be having a very different conversation."

"That does sound… interesting," said Xi, regarding her through half-lidded eyes. You didn't rise to the head of one of the galaxy's biggest crime syndicates without a certain degree of unflappability. "Now, if you don't mind taking your seats, we'll get underway." She waved a hand at the woman Yancy, who nodded and stowed her rifle, then headed towards the cockpit.

At another signal from Xi, the other two goons relaxed their stances; with Brody as insurance, they were redundant. One of them palmed the controls for the hatch, and it rolled down and sealed as the ramp outside rose with a whine of hydraulics.

Moments later, the ship's engine thrummed to life and the *Cavalier* rose on its repulsors and made its way skyward, leaving Juarez 7A in their wake – along with any easy opportunity to retrieve the pilot. Nat let the cold anger simmering beneath the surface fade into the background. This was a long game now: strategy, not tactics.

"So," she said, leaning forward on the table as the rumble of the ship's engines faded with their transition from atmosphere to vacuum. "Seems like you should at least tell us where we're going."

Xi tapped one lacquered fingernail against her lips, then dipped her head in acknowledgment. Reaching down to her bangle, she tapped a control and another holoscreen flared into existence above the table, showing a mottled brown world, broken only occasionally by patches of blue. Xi's eyes turned to the rest of them. "How familiar are you with the Illyrican colony of Caledonia?"

CHAPTER 24

Addy had taken some rough flights, but she'd have gladly swapped any of them for the transit from Juarez to Caledonia. It was the better part of a day to get between the two, and Ofeibia Xi wasn't about to let them have free rein on their own ship; even Addy's trip to the head meant having one of the goons in the corridor outside, with the door open.

It's enough to make me miss flying commercial.

The worst part was that she had to look at Xi's stupid gleeful face and *not* punch her in the mouth.

The syndicate leader had promised more details on the job to come, but suggested that they use the next few hours to rest up, as they'd have to hit the ground running when they reached Caledonia.

Restful was the last thing Addy was feeling.

The revelation of the princess's role in the Aleph Tablet's theft had taken them all by surprise, but Addy was content to let Taylor and Tapper worry about the big picture: she had more immediate concerns.

Without access to the *Cavalier*'s communication systems or sensors, there was no way of knowing where Brody had been taken, but the few calls that Xi did retreat to the cockpit to take suggested that the rest of her people were within real-time comms range. Probably the fast courier in which Xi had arrived on Juarez 7A.

That was good – at least Brody hadn't been left back on the mining colony – but it didn't solve the problem. Addy would have unhesitatingly banked all her money on herself, Taylor, and Tapper over Xi and her goons, but all it took was one signal to the other ship – or, given how thorough the crime boss was, one *missed* signal – and the pilot's life was forfeit. That only fed back into her pissed-off mood like a perpetual rage machine.

Taylor had, to her credit, taken on the primary role of dealing with Xi, insulating Addy and Tapper from having to interact with her directly. The sergeant, for his part, had apparently decided to take the crime lord's suggestion, and spent most of the journey napping in his seat, arms crossed over his chest.

How the hell can he sleep right now? Addy was far too amped; even when she managed to doze, she woke with a start almost immediately. It left her feeling frayed at the edges, her eyes watering and blurring.

Even if you got a chance at Xi, you'd probably just end up punching yourself in the face. Great, now she was trash-talking herself.

Stretching, she stood and stalked to the galley, all too cognizant of Xi's goons watching her every move. What was she going to try to do, stab them with a fork?

Although, come to think of it... She eyed the silverware, then sighed and pulled another cup of coffee, letting the steam drift into her nostrils. At least they still had plenty of food and drink, even with the extra crew load.

They hadn't been formally introduced to Xi's people, but Addy had picked up what she could. Besides Yancy, the pilot – her hand tightened on the mug – there was Stack, the bigger of the two, who wore his brown hair pulled back in a tight ponytail that seemed to also stretch his face muscles taut, rendering him incapable of any facial expression; and Deng, the smaller and wirier one, who had a perpetually amused look in his hazel eyes that Addy trusted even less. Despite having Brody as their hostage, neither of them ever let their fingers stray too far from the triggers of their weapons, and definitely never at the same time.

We can't take them in a fair fight, and there's definitely no way we can pay better than Xi, even if we offer them all of the credits we've squirreled away. We're walking examples of what happens if you get on her bad side. Nor was intimidation likely to gain much traction; after all, they were the ones with the guns.

Addy plopped herself back down in her seat. Despite being threatened with bodily harm and having one of their number kidnapped, this was somehow still the dullest trip ever. She pressed her hands to her face, rubbing at her eyes. It was taking a lot of restraint to avoid a plaintive whine of "Are we there yet?" *Damn it, I think Brody's rubbing off on me.*

"Ah, glad you're all still here," said Xi, walking in from the cockpit.

"Where the fuck else would we be?" snapped Addy before she could stop herself.

The syndicate boss just smiled even wider in response, and Addy mentally fired off a string of curses for giving Xi exactly what she wanted.

"Something we can help you with?" asked Taylor calmly, ignoring the outburst.

"We'll be exiting the wormhole into the Caledonia system shortly," said Xi, taking a graceful seat at the table. "I thought I might lay out some details for you. If you're not too…" Her gaze slid to the sleeping Tapper, "…busy."

Addy never thought she'd be this glad to get a mission briefing – especially from Ofeibia Xi, of all people – but at least it was something to do.

Taylor elbowed Tapper in the ribs, and the sergeant snuffled and blinked his eyes open. Had he really been asleep, or just cleverly biding his time? Addy realized she had no idea. "Did I miss the in-flight meal?" he asked with a convincing yawn.

Xi paid little attention to the older man, just brought up the holoscreen once again. This time it showed a picture clearly taken from a distance in a crowded marketplace. A man with dark, thinning hair and an expensive-looking suit stood behind a phalanx of security.

"Roche Flores. He's the head of the Coire Ansic, currently the largest criminal organization in Illyrican space, but I've heard he's looking to expand his business beyond the Imperium into unaligned territory – *my* territory." Xi's fingers fanned, dagger sharp tips cutting through the screen. "Naturally, I can't have that."

Both the name and the organization were unfamiliar to Addy, but she wasn't exactly tapped in to the Caledonian crime scene; her criminal past had been petty and decidedly Nova-bound.

The screen blinked to a new image, once again showing Caledonia hanging in space. Xi zoomed in on a continent in the southern hemisphere that seemed to be mostly barren desert, with a single finger of land crooked into the dusky blue of an ocean.

"The port city of Tralee. Home to the Coire Ansic's nominal base of operations on the planet, though they do most of their business in Stranraer." Panning across the map, through the desert, she stopped at a sprawling settlement that seemed to be in the midst of nowhere. "At one time it was the largest mining settlement in the known galaxy. After the Imperium occupied Caledonia, they depleted its significant reserves of natural resources – iron, palladium, titanium, and so on – in order to build up the Illyrican navy. But Stranraer still remains the onworld hub for shipbuilding and repair. Most of the work is done in the orbital shipyards, but materials need to be ferried in from the planet itself, so it's also home to one of the biggest industrial spaceports in the Imperium. Consequently, there's a big market for illicit goods of all kinds, from smuggling to weapons to drugs."

Taylor's cool blue gaze swept over the city. "A lot of opportunity, but also a lot of risk. There's bound to be high law enforcement presence."

Xi dipped her head. "Quite so. In addition to the Imperial Intelligence Service, both Imperial Fleet Security *and* the local Caledonian Security Agency have a strong presence there. The Coire Ansic does most of its business in untraceable hard currency, but Flores has chosen not to keep the vast majority of his capital within Stranraer itself, instead sending it north to Tralee. Except Flores is both paranoid and stingy: he doesn't want to fly it back and forth because Illyrican security is tight at Stranraer, and bribing multiple officials would cut into his profits."

"So if he's not flying it," said Tapper, his brow furrowed, "how's he moving all that cash?"

"There's an old gravtrain line that runs between Stranraer and Tralee," said Xi. "It dates back to the original colonization, when sending all of the mined ore up to orbit was cost prohibitive, and even point-to-point flights were limited. The planetary government keeps it maintained for the transportation of goods and materials that aren't worth being loaded up on a ship."

"He's sending it on a *train*?" said Addy. *What year is it again?*

Taylor was eyeing the screen, tapping a finger against her lips. "What's in between the two cities?"

"Ah," said Xi. "So glad you asked." Zooming out, the holoscreen once again showed the large barren stretch of brown in between the two cities. "The Burns Expanse. Ten million square kilometers of desert, almost totally uninhabited, with no accessible water. And if that's not enough, the entire region is frequently engulfed in massive sandstorms. Ships don't even bother flying through the atmosphere anywhere near it; it's far too risky."

"But the train still runs?" said Taylor, arching an eyebrow.

"Indeed. I hear it's become quite the attraction for local thrill seekers."

"Through sandstorms? That's the stupidest thing I've ever heard..." muttered Tapper, though Addy thought he looked a little bit impressed. "I guess it does explain a few things about Caledonians." He glanced around, almost like he expected a rejoinder but was disappointed when it didn't come. His brow darkened as he gave Xi a sidelong look, but Addy was pretty sure the woman didn't catch it.

"That brings us to our opportunity," said Xi. "Once a month, the Coire Ansic loads up all of its proceeds from its business in Stranraer and buys out two entire train cars – one to transport the currency, and another for its coterie of armed guards. It's roughly two-thousand kilometers from Stranraer Terminal to Tralee, which takes about four hours at the gravtrain's maximum speed. The next of these shipments leaves…" she glanced at her sleeve, then flicked a glowing timer to the holoscreen, "…roughly eighteen hours from now, and I intend for us to be on it."

"I presume the train doesn't stop along the way," said Taylor, eyeing the screen.

Xi zoomed out and gestured at the blankness of the expanse. "There's no reason *to* stop. There was a settlement on a short spur line once – Fort Mull – but it was abandoned when the local mine dried up. People don't live in the Burns Expanse. For obvious reasons."

After a moment of thinking, Taylor leaned back, her eyes resting on Xi. Addy knew the commander well enough to know when she was thinking through all the angles.

"Why not just take the train on your own? You've clearly got people at your disposal." Taylor nodded to the armed guards.

Xi uncurled her fingers like a fan; her nails glittered, pearlescent in the light. "I admit, that was my plan until you conveniently fell into my lap. But why risk my own people when I can have you do it for free? Besides, as I said, you've demonstrated an *aptitude* for this kind of thing. I might as well put it to use."

Addy's lips pressed into a thin line. In other words, Xi had them over a barrel. *I don't know exactly how, but I'm going to make sure she's not smiling at the end of this.*

For her part, Taylor kept to her usual cool demeanor. "You suggested this would be to our benefit too, and I've yet to see how."

"Ah," said Xi, leaning back in her chair. "Yes. After Sadiq led us to her highness, I was intrigued. I kept our surveillance of the location – it's a compound in Mexico City on Earth – in place for several days, curious to see what else I might be able to find. This is three days after that meeting." At the press of a control, the image on the holoprojector flickered and was replaced with the same overhead drone view of the house, the same black car in the drive.

Three people were in evidence, two having clearly just stepped out of the car, and one waiting for them outside the house. Even from the overhead angle, the latter was clearly not the princess. Xi held up a finger for patience, then flicked to another image showing the pair's faces more clearly. Two men: one out of focus in the background, pale complexion and light-colored hair, but in the foreground a familiar face with sparse hair and a blunt nose.

"Roche Flores," said Taylor, her eyes meeting Xi's.

"Yes."

"Wait a second," Addy interjected. "First you tell us she hired al-Kitab – Sadiq... whatever his name is – to steal the Aleph Tablet, and now she's meeting with the very same criminal boss you're asking us to rob? Convenient."

"Perhaps, but not in the way you mean," said Xi. "It's precisely this connection that I intend to exploit. Her highness arranged to have something stolen from me, and I'd like to return the favor." One eyebrow arched upward. "I presumed you wouldn't have any objection to doing some damage to a member of the Imperium's ruling family."

Taylor tapped a finger against her lips, eyes still on the image. "I still don't understand the connection here. Why is the princess even involved with Flores or Sadiq?"

"Yeah," said Tapper, "art thieving of the rich and famous, that I get – who hasn't wanted a Renoir for the living rooms of each of their seventeen houses. But running drugs and smuggling? Bit outside a princess's remit."

"Indeed." Xi held out her hand, studying her fingernails with faux fascination. "However, it's my understanding that the princess has taken up a sideline career – one perhaps more fulfilling than acting as a goodwill ambassador for the crown. Director of Imperial Intelligence."

The silence at that announcement was somehow more deafening than if Addy had been standing next to a spacecraft's engine at full speed. Her jaw dropped as she tried to process everything that Xi had just said. Across the table, Taylor's eyes had widened in shock, and she seemed to be having trouble finding the right words.

Tapper, with his usual eloquence, obliged. "You're fucking *kidding*."

"Pull the other one," said Addy, crossing her arms. "Everybody knows she's just a pretty face for all the shit her dad's too sick to do: charitable causes and cutting ribbons at ceremonial openings and waving to her adoring public from the back of a hovercar."

One of Xi's eyebrows rose. "I would have thought you, Adelaide, of all people, would know not to underestimate a pretty face."

Addy scowled at the table, keeping her gaze well clear of the syndicate leader's.

Taylor drummed her fingers on the table, and Addy could see the commander's mind whirring away. "How much more surveillance do you have of the compound?"

Xi tilted her head to one side. "A few weeks' worth. Comings, goings – the very sort of thing the Commonwealth might be interested to know about the head of the Imperium's intelligence apparatus, no?" She bared her teeth, the confident smile of someone who knows they have their opponent over a barrel. "The point, major, is that we both have a vested interest in this job. You can either join me in the endeavor or…" She left the alternative unsaid, but Addy doubted that it was "walk away unscathed".

At the best we'll be looking over our shoulders for the rest of our lives. At worst we won't have to worry because we'll be dead.

The commander spent a few moments eyeing the image, but Addy could see her mind working overtime as she ran the numbers. "Eighteen hours isn't a lot of time to prepare for a job with this many moving parts – literally. We'd be going in short on resources and intel."

"Whatever I have is at your disposal," said Xi with an expansive gesture around the compartment, as if generously offering them the run of their own ship. "Anything else?"

"One more thing," Tapper interjected. He jutted his chin in Xi's direction. "I'm guessing neither you nor your *employees* have spent a lot of time on Caledonia."

Eyes narrowing, Xi tilted her head to one side. "Go on."

"We're working on the fly here, which means no time for recon. So we need someone who knows all the players, is tapped into local resources, saves us from having to waste precious time figuring out who to buy our supplies from or who to bribe to get us on that train."

"Let me guess: you have someone in mind."

The sergeant broke into a craggy smile. "As it happens, I surely do."

CHAPTER 25

Eli spent a brief moment wondering why the room was upside down before it spun vertiginously back into the correct orientation, almost taking his lunch with it. *I bet that reuben is not nearly as good coming up as it was going down.*

The disorientation didn't stop there. *I'm definitely not on the* Cav. He knew every inch of that ship, unless he'd been unconscious so long that they'd redecorated to a – he glanced around at the small room woozily – really utilitarian look.

Slowly he levered himself up on his elbows, his head still on a carousel, and did a quick survey. It was a small bunk room, with six berths stacked in two sets of three. He was retroactively glad he'd moved slowly, because the top of this bunk was only a couple inches from his head; any higher and he'd have had another reason to be discombobulated.

Carefully, he swung his legs out, glad to see that he was still wearing all the same clothes with the exception of his shoes, which were sitting on the floor – deck, he corrected himself; he could feel the telltale hum of an engine. Someone had even knocked most of the caked mud off them, which was oddly kind. Or maybe just self-serving if they were also the ones who had to keep the place clean.

Pulling the shoes on, he got to his feet, keeping one hand braced against the frame until he felt steady enough. Aside from the bunks, the room was almost featureless, with the exception of a half dozen lockers embedded in one bulkhead and a doorway opposite.

All expenses spared. He tried the door release, but unsurprisingly the panel blinked red at his touch. Memories started assembling in his head: Xi's goon – Andres? – seeing to him in the medbay, then knocking him out with a hypo. He pressed a hand against his abdomen where Patel had shot him, preemptively wincing. But it didn't actually hurt, even when he prodded it experimentally. Lifting his shirt, he craned his neck and saw that there were fresh dressings in place since the ones Andres had applied back on the *Cav*.

Which meant he'd been out for a while.

So, a ship, but not our *ship. Probably one of Xi's, then – I'm guessing that fast courier.* It fit with the compact nature of the room and the pitch of the engine; this thing was tuned for speed, and he could hear it.

But it didn't make him feel any better. *Maybe I can override the door panel.* Mal had started teaching him some tricks for circumventing systems, which he'd taken to like a fish to air. It just wasn't his thing. Plus he didn't even have anything he could use to lever the panel off, much less strip wires–

There was a click from the hatch and it slid open.

Holy shit, did I just do that with my mind?

Andres filled the doorway, looking him up and down as if assessing his condition, then grunted and nodded at Eli to follow him down the corridor.

Oh good, trapped on a tiny ship with a master conversationalist.

Then again, it wasn't like he had a lot of options, and being locked in a windowless bunk was surely the worse of the two.

Andres had gone toward what Eli sensed was the ship's fore, not that there was much else. He glanced in the other direction; the corridor terminated in an airlock hatch, and he saw only one other door on the opposite wall – the head, he presumed, unless this ship was *really* bare bones. Walking forward, he passed a compact engineering station, beyond which was a second hatchway that Andres palmed open.

Eli's assessment that it was the ship's cockpit proved correct. It was cramped, with just two stations; the pilot's seat, front and center, and behind it, a second station that handled seemingly everything else: communications, navigation, co-piloting, and so on. Only the pilot's station was currently occupied, by a woman so pale and blonde that it looked like all the color had been leached out of her.

Beyond them, through the canopy, was a broad canvas of stars, in the midst of which hung a single planet: a wash of brown continents and blue oceans.

As though they'd started a sudden plummeting descent, his stomach dropped out from under him. *Oh no. It can't be.*

He steadied himself on the back of the co-pilot's seat, but it swiveled away from him and he almost stumbled to the deck.

Andres shot him a look, and even the blonde woman glanced over her shoulder with a sneer. "I thought this guy was a pilot. Barely got his space legs."

No no no no. Maybe I'm still sedated and this is all a dream. He pinched a big chunk of his forearm between two fingers. *Ow!*

His throat was dry and creaky when he finally managed to get the words out. "Why the fuck are we going to *Caledonia*?"

"We go where the boss tells us to," said Andres. His voice sounded like what a mountain's would if it could talk. "Sit down." He punctuated the command with a hand on Eli's shoulder, pressing him down into the co-pilot seat, leaving Eli little option but to stare out of the canopy in dismay.

Caledonia, his homeworld. The one that he'd abandoned at age eighteen to join the Illyrican navy, over the objections of, well, everybody in his life. The one he'd come back to almost two years ago on his first mission with Kovalic and the team, to track down his brother, who had turned out to be the leader of a terrorist group.

There were a *lot* of emotions to process.

"Soooo, this is just a flyby, right?" said Eli hopefully. "We're not actually landing or anything?"

Andres and the pilot shared a look that said they were wondering whether or not Eli had all his brain cells. Neither of them bothered to respond, but as the pilot turned back Eli could see her locking in an approach vector. He glanced down at the station in front of him but the controls had all been preemptively locked out, leaving only one sensor display showing local traffic.

One blip jumped out at him, marked as a friendly green, and his heartbeat quickened. The transponder – a light freighter out of Jericho – was the same he'd set before they'd landed on Juarez 7A. Even if it hadn't been, the ship's drive profile was a fingerprint that he'd recognize anywhere: the *Cavalier*, on the same vector as them.

His shoulders slumped in relief. Part of him had worried that Xi had figured out who he was and dispatched him back to Caledonia to sell him to the Imperium. Or, maybe worse, to whatever remained of his brother's cadre of self-styled freedom fighters. But presumably the rest of the team was still on the *Cav* with Xi and more of her goons. So, whatever they were doing here, it wasn't about Eli.

Which made him... what? Insurance? *Christ am I sick of being taken captive.*

But at least he was all still alive, so he had that going for him.

Andres leaned against the bulkhead until it was time for them to strap in for descent, at which point he disappeared back to the engineering station, though he left the hatch open to keep one eye on Eli.

The pilot's landing was aggressively fine – Eli noticed she wasn't quite ready for Caledonia's hot air pockets, which generated some bumps and shimmies on the descent. He was surprised to notice that they hadn't headed towards the capital, Raleigh City, but rather toward the less populated southern continent and the large mining settlement of Stranraer.

A memory floated to the surface of his mind, from just before he'd been dragged off to the medbay on the *Cavalier*: Xi had wanted them to do a job for her. *But what the hell down here is worth stealing?* Even by the time he'd left to join the Illyrican navy, Stranraer's heyday had been long past.

After the courier settled down on the tarmac and the pilot powered down the engines, it was eerily quiet in the cockpit. The only sound came from the faint hum of the ship's electronics and the wind whistling outside.

It was a bright mid-day here, with the hot Caledonian sun blaring down on the flat expanse that was the spaceport. In the distance rose brown hills covered with scrub vegetation, but the landscape was otherwise unbroken.

Oh good. Home.

At the rear of the ship, the hatch slid open and a small ramp descended to the tarmac. A wave of hot air writhed inside, its dry heat ruffling Eli's hair.

And the smell. Even here, thousands of miles from where he'd grown up, he got the same tang of metallic dirt in his nose and mouth. He hacked a cough, earning a look from Andres and the pilot – Prentiss, he'd heard Andres call her – though neither of them spared him a word as they walked down the ramp.

Terminal security here was tighter than what he'd seen in Raleigh City two years ago. A flash of fear ran down his spine as they queued: these weren't local customs officials but the crimson-clad members of Imperial Fleet Security.

Xi's people had, at least, let him retain the Ezekiel Bryce identity that he'd been using on Juarez 7A, so there was no risk that he'd pop up as Elijah Brody, deserter from the Illyrican Navy. *Thank god for small favors.*

Which made it an unpleasant surprise when the Illyrican officer at the gate lazily waved him aside into a separate line from Andres and Prentiss. Both of them cast him suspicious looks as Eli, befuddled, found himself being patted down by a security officer.

"Something the matter?" he asked, under the officer's businesslike ministrations.

"Random check," he said brusquely. "Need to swab you for explosives. Where's your luggage?"

"Uhh, I'm traveling light." All he had was what was on him, which wasn't much. Andres had given him a new sleeve, because not having one looked even more suspicious, but it had been locked down to prevent him contacting anybody that wasn't pre-approved.

The officer gave him a hard look, then touched his own sleeve and murmured something into it.

Eli offered a hapless shrug in the direction of Andres and Prentiss, who had lingered as long as they could in the main security line without looking conspicuous.

"Come with me," said the officer abruptly.

Sweat beaded on Eli's forehead, his heart starting to pound in his chest as he followed the security officer to a small windowless room with a metal table and two chairs. *Shit.* He tried to tell himself there was nothing to worry about: as far as the Imperial Navy was concerned, Eli Brody had died in the invasion on Sabaea seven years ago and the SPT had previously hacked his Illyrican records to replace his biometric data.

So I guess I'm just lucky?

The officer closed the door behind him, leaving him to stew in the spartan room, under the watchful eyes of security cameras. Was it just his imagination, or had they cranked up the heat too? He plucked at his collar.

This is just what they want. Calm down. Nothing you haven't dealt with before. Plus, was he really in such a hurry to get back to Xi's goons?

He'd started to regain his equilibrium when a few minutes later the door opened to admit a woman in a dark suit, her hair pulled back into a severe bun. The chair legs scraped against the floor as she sat down, consulting a tablet without looking up at Eli's face.

She placed a small black ovoid on the table and pressed a control on it, and Eli felt his ears pop as though the pressure in the room had changed. *A baffle?* His eyebrows went up and he resisted the powerful urge to back into a corner and take up a defensive posture. An anti-eavesdropping device sure felt like the kind of thing the authorities used when they didn't want anybody to know what they were going to do to you.

"Now," said the woman, looking up. "That's better. I'm Special Agent Liang, and I've got something for you."

Eli blinked. "Huh?"

She reached into a pocket and pulled out an object the size of a tiny pebble, then slid it across the table to him.

He stared at it for a moment before his brain caught up: it was an earbud. Hesitantly, he glanced back up at the woman, but she seemed to be absorbed in whatever she was looking at on the tablet and paid him no mind.

With a shrug, he reached out and took it: it was a standard issue model with adaptive chromatics and, as he touched it, it mimicked his skin tone; when he put it in his ear, it'd be all but invisible. He could tell from the rustling as he inserted it that there was already a live connection. His throat dry, he swallowed down the lump there.

"Uh...hello?"

"Hello yourself, Eli Brody," said a familiar voice with a thick Caledonian brogue. "About time you took me up on that dinner offer."

CHAPTER 26

Yevgeniy was hunched over a terminal when Kovalic, the general, and Rance returned to the safe house. Night had fallen and, lit only by the amber glow of the holoscreen, the older man looked weary, the lines in his face valleys cut into a stark relief map. He leaned back as they tromped in, then raised an eyebrow at their expressions.

"That bad?"

"It went fine," said Kovalic shortly.

Rance perched on a stool at the kitchenette's counter and the general sat down heavily in an armchair. Being on the run was taking a toll on the old man, too – or was that just pretense, like the whole charade with his legs? Kovalic resisted the urge to press the palms of his hands against his eyes. They were all starting to get a little fried here.

His stomach rumbled, but he'd already made the mistake of checking the kitchenette upon their arrival and found it disappointingly devoid of anything worth the description of "food".

But he had seen a small neighborhood grocery store nearby, and it wouldn't take many ingredients to throw something together. Omelets maybe. The gnawing feeling got stronger at the idea of something that wasn't a ready-to-eat meal bar.

"I'm going to go around the corner and get us some real food," he said.

Yevgeniy looked up. "I'm not sure that's wise. The Bureau will surely be analyzing feeds from surveillance cameras around Salaam. Facial, auditory, even gait analysis could all pick you out of a crowd."

"I know how to avoid a camera."

"But do you know how to avoid all of them?"

Kovalic opened his mouth to snap back a reply about not relying on a washed-up Illyrican spy to tell him how to do his job and, at that point, realized how really and truly his own nerves had frayed. "We can't sit here and starve. And I need some air. I'll be careful." He grabbed a brimmed hat from the shelf.

The man cast a glance at his former boss, who put up a reassuring hand, which only really served to needle Kovalic further. He stalked back towards the door and climbed down the two flights of stairs to find a rear exit onto the alleyway behind the building.

Stepping out into the narrow passage, he relished the sharp, fresh night air as it filled his lungs. Was it the same air being recycled into the apartment upstairs? Sure. But there was something soothing about getting it in its *pre*cycled state.

Sliding his hands into the pockets of his coat, he started down the alley in the direction of the store. It felt good to stretch his legs and move at his own pace; he hadn't realized just how constrained he'd felt with the general in tow. It was like sitting in the cramped seat of a spaceliner for an intersystem trip.

The alley let him out just a few storefronts down from

the market. He gave a surreptitious glance about before stepping onto the street, but there were no obvious cameras pointed in that direction. Keeping his head down anyway, he strolled casually to the store.

Neither the street nor the market were busy at this early evening hour; only a few other customers wandered the aisles. A teenager with a spotty complexion leaned on their elbows behind the counter, looking bored as they watched a holoscreen currently showing an alcohol commercial.

Kovalic made his way up and down the brightly lit aisles, picking up a few simple items off the shelves: a loaf of bread, a carton of eggs, feta cheese, and a container of spinach. It wasn't a gourmet meal, but at least it'd be hot and filling.

He wasn't sure at what point the sound from the holoscreen reached him; he'd only registered it as background noise until his brain processed exactly what he was hearing.

"...continue their search for three individuals who reportedly escaped custody of the Commonwealth Security Bureau some thirty-six hours ago."

Kovalic's hand was in the midst of closing on a container of milk and he squeezed it in surprise, even as his heartbeat paused to jump over a chasm.

Shit.

He forced himself to put the milk into the shopping basket he was carrying and continue his perusal of the shelves as if nothing had happened. But he moved towards the front of the store, trying to get a better view of the holoscreen.

The teenager behind the front desk didn't seem particularly interested in the news report, staring at it with the same vacant disinterest as the commercial that had preceded it.

"The three were last seen leaving the Commonwealth Executive compound mid-day yesterday in a groundcar," continued the voiceover. The image shifted to a security video of the garage from which they'd taken the car: three figures were caught mid-step, their backs to the camera.

From bad to worse. Rance had been so careful with her escape plan, but had somehow missed a security camera? It seemed only dumb luck that the angle didn't give a clear view of any of their faces.

"Our sources confirm that car was later found abandoned in a south Salaam neighborhood. The Bureau has so far refused to confirm the identity of the fugitives, other than to say that they are all persons of interest in an ongoing case. However, they did provide these images. Those with any information about the individuals are advised to contact the authorities."

Kovalic's stomach dropped like he'd fallen off a trapeze as a trio of pictures appeared on the screen: clear head-on shots of the general, Rance, and himself, and, below them, a contact code for submitting tips.

The Bureau hadn't distributed their official Commonwealth file photos, since that would no doubt have raised a few questions about why they had such pristine, clear pictures. Instead, they seemed to be images from other security cameras around the Commonwealth Executive buildings.

But it didn't really matter, because as imperfect as the pictures might be, they were all still unmistakably identifiable.

Had it been just a few days prior that Kovalic had seen Aaron Page's picture plastered across the nets and news media and wondered how a covert operative came back from that? Well, he didn't have to wonder anymore, because he was about to live it.

Despite feeling like he'd rather do anything other than eat, Kovalic paid for his purchases at the automated terminal, gathering them in a provided compostable bag and trying not to look like he was deliberately avoiding dealing with the teenager or keeping his head down to avoid the terminal's camera, then stepped back onto the street.

He stood for a moment, as if unsure which way to go. Did it really matter? His face was out there now – and yes, the general's and Rance's too, but neither of them spent their time out in the field, where anonymity could be the difference between life and death. This was it for him. The long path of the career in front of him, everything he and the SPT had yet to accomplish – that future was, if not obliterated, then severely damaged.

As if dealt a physical blow, he felt himself slump back against the wall. Roll with the punches, he'd always said, but there were some blows from which you just didn't – couldn't – get back up.

He pushed himself off the wall and trudged back towards the alley, carrying his almost forgotten bag of groceries loosely in one hand. At the rear of the safe house he stopped and stared dully at the metal fire door.

And then, at a sudden impulse, he put down his groceries, raised his sleeve, and fired up a communications obfuscation program that would bounce his signal through multiple different relays, off a satellite or two, and then through a private network interface. Tracing it wasn't impossible, but it would be considerably harder – at the very least it ought to buy him a couple minutes. He started a timer and tapped in an address that he'd committed to memory only a few days back.

The connection was picked up almost immediately, a familiar deep voice on the other end. "Laurent."

Kovalic felt almost like his head was floating off his shoulders, but he tried to imbue his voice with a light tone. "You could have at least shown my good side, inspector."

There was a pause, only the smallest fraction of a moment, but Kovalic could picture the bearded CSB officer snapping at one of the junior agents in his department. No doubt he'd gotten quite a few assigned to him, given the importance of this case.

"Kovalic," said the inspector, his tone carefully neutral. "I have to admit, I didn't expect to be hearing from you."

Glancing down at his sleeve, Kovalic watched the timer ticking down. "I'm well aware you're tracing this call, so I'll keep it short."

"Fine by me," said Laurent. "Tell me where you are and I'll come down there personally."

Kovalic laughed. "I admire your confidence. But no, I'm not coming in. I just wanted to ask you a question."

"Fire away."

"Who do you trust, inspector?"

Another pause, and Kovalic glanced at the timer. A minute left.

"Who *should* I trust?"

"Answering a question with a question – solid technique. But I meant it more as a thought exercise. Think about this case. Ask yourself *why*."

"We can hash out the whys and wherefores when you come in, major."

Thirty seconds.

"Look, we can make a deal," Laurent continued, his words rushed now. He knew the trace was getting close. "You, Hayley Rance... you're just accessories. Hasan al-Adaj, he's the big fish. You two, the rest of your team – wherever they are – I'm not saying you can walk, but we can work something out."

Kovalic's heart rate picked up speed like a gravtrain leaving the station. "You want me to throw the general under the bus."

"You're a loyal man, Kovalic. I'd admire that. Let me ask *you* a question. Who deserves your loyalty: the people above you, or the people who look up to you?"

Ten seconds. "Good luck, inspector."

"Kova –"

But he'd broken the connection and whatever else Laurent had been about to say was lost, echoing into the ether. Kovalic heaved a breath and braced a hand against the wall.

The whole exercise had been stupid, indulgent. He'd wanted to put a bug in the inspector's ear, maybe force him to look elsewhere – specifying Kester would have been too much, but maybe he could pique his curiosity. But he should have known that the man was steadfast in his dedication to the job. Too much to lose, not enough to gain.

Other than that one glimmer of opportunity: Laurent would deal. And all it would cost was giving up the general... plus his own sense of honor, and maybe his self-worth along with it. But with his picture out there, his future already looked like a dead-end – were his ideals worth potentially staying out of prison? Or, more to the point, to get his people home? Laurent had seemed to confirm they weren't in custody: An olive branch to show he was operating in good faith? Or an appeal to Kovalic's guilt? If they were still out there, exiles facing armageddon, then it was within Kovalic's power to make sure they were safe. What *wouldn't* he give for that chance?

And weighed against that, the increasingly tenuous goal of finding a mole burrowed deep within the Commonwealth, for which they had no real leads, no evidence, and perhaps even no real hope.

It was a lot to turn over. Especially on an empty stomach.

He reached down and picked up the bag of groceries, then let himself back into the building and started slowly climbing the stairs to the apartment.

CHAPTER 27

Nat couldn't remember the last time she'd set foot on Caledonia. A school trip, maybe, before the war? It had been hot and dusty, decidedly unlike the climate-controlled domes on her homeworld of Centauri, but at the time there had been something decidedly thrilling about being out there, exposed to the elements.

Her first impression, as they crossed the tarmac to the security and customs lines, was that it hadn't changed much in the intervening years. She shaded her eyes against the harsh sun, watching the heat rise in waves from the permacrete. There hadn't been many reasons to come back; despite the planet's internal conflicts, its strategic position in the Imperium had been moderate at best, though NICOM had paid close attention to activity at the Illyrican shipyards in orbit. There was a Commonwealth intelligence presence based out of the capital Raleigh City, though last she'd heard the station-chief post had been vacant for more than a year. Since then CID had been running its Caledonian operations out of Earth, a wormhole jump away.

So at least the chances of getting spotted by Commonwealth personnel in Stranraer seemed low – all they had to worry about was the Illyricans.

And the murderous crime boss at their heels.

Despite Nat's concerns, they all sailed through customs without a second look, their fresh identities raising no flags, and in no time found themselves in the cool air of a hovercar that Xi had summoned. Tapper prodded the cushy faux leather seats and nodded approvingly, while Addy contented herself with glowering in silence at their captor turned partner.

Nat had more practical concerns. She'd spent the trip studying what information she could get off the nets, including schematics for the gravtrain model used and the scant reports about the Coire Ansic that she still had access to. In a perfect world, she'd have more time to vet the plan before executing it, but time was limited. "We'll need some place to stage this operation."

"I've arranged for a property within the city," said the syndicate leader. "The train departs first thing tomorrow morning, so that's your timeline for any preparation you need to make."

"And our local contact?"

Xi's fingers danced across the armrest. She hadn't exactly been thrilled by Tapper's request for them to bring in outside help, but even she had grudgingly admitted that it would have its utility. She'd carefully vetted the sergeant's message, which had been short, but to the point:

Job on. Flight inbound, next day. Entrance location in Stranraer.

"No response to your communique," said Xi, "but it was delivered. Tell me more about this contact."

"Caledonian born and bred," said Tapper. "Mostly works as a fixer these days – making connections, locating people the things they need. Used to be with a local group that... fell apart a couple years back."

Xi's carefully sculpted eyebrows rose. "The Black Watch?"

The Black Watch had been a terrorist organization – though they'd dubbed themselves freedom fighters – of native-born Caledonians who had decided to take the fight to their Illyrican oppressors. They'd done some damage over the course of the Imperium's occupation – even once bombed an Illyrican dreadnought being retrofitted in orbit – but almost two years ago they had collapsed into disarray after the death of their leader.

Right around the time Kovalic and the SPT had been on Caledonia, Nat had noted, though those files were classified and she knew better than to pry.

"Neither confirm nor deny," said the sergeant with an insouciant shrug. "You know how it goes."

"What if told my men to drag you along behind this car? Would that loosen your tongue?"

Tapper grinned. "Don't threaten me with a good time."

The split-second silence had Nat holding her breath, and she could see out of the corner of her eye Addy tensing, but then Xi let out a melodious chuckle. "I do appreciate a man who knows what he's about."

Nat barely managed to restrain herself from shaking her head in disbelief. It sometimes felt like you could toss Tapper into a lion's den only to come back later and find them all enjoying a nice game of poker. "What about resources?"

Xi's glance in her direction was decidedly cooler. "We'll pull together what we can, major, but you'll have to make do."

She couldn't deny the twinge every time Xi referenced her assumed rank; it made her wonder how Simon was faring back on Nova. By now, she assumed that he and the general had been transferred to some sort of secure facility – an aboveboard one, if they were lucky, though she would have placed her bet on a CID black site. Her mind had already started spinning through what it would take to break them out, but she forced herself to put it aside and concentrate on the task at hand. Rescuing them from a government installation would just solidify their status as fugitives; what she needed was the evidence to clear their names.

To that end, Nat badly wanted to see the rest of the surveillance footage that Xi had collected of the princess's compound. The identity of the director of Imperial Intelligence had been a well-kept secret and Nat had to concede that Isabella had never even made it onto the list of suspects.

The princess's name had, of course, been bandied about in intelligence reports forever, but every single assessment Nat had ever seen had deemed the woman a minor player in the Imperium's future – her father's least favorite child, a figurehead used by the palace for pomp and circumstance with no power base of her own.

All of which Nat had now hastily swept into the dustbin. If Isabella truly was running IIS, then this job wasn't just in Xi's interest – it was in the Commonwealth's. And, potentially, theirs: as Tapper had pointed out, Simon and the general's current predicament certainly felt like it owed something to the Illyricans.

Now they were just feet away from several days of raw surveillance footage of the princess and everybody she'd met with during that time. Who knew what information they might be able to uncover? Nothing made Nat itchy like data that needed analyzing. She just needed to find a way to get her hands on it. Wriggling out of this job had already seemed a tall order, what with Brody being Xi's hostage; now the question was whether they could afford *not* to see it through.

And if that meant going along with Xi's demands, so be it. At least for the moment.

After a fifteen-minute drive, the car pulled up to a low-rise block on an otherwise sleepy street. A reinforced shutter door that looked like it could hold off a tank slid upwards and the car drove into an unlit garage on the first level. They climbed a flight of metal stairs, against which their steps rang like church bells, and walked through a security door at the top.

Nat hadn't expected much, but when the door opened onto a luxurious apartment with wraparound windows looking out over the city, she chided herself. Ofeibia Xi wasn't about to hole up in some ratty den, eating ready-made rations. Though Nat did wonder how she'd found the place – was there some sort of service that catered to wealthy crime lords on the move? She had little doubt that the windows, expansive as they were, would turn back anything short of aerial bombardment, and that garage door had clearly not been just for show.

"Make yourselves at home," said Xi, waving a hand. "I've taken the liberty of providing some fresh clothes, and there is what I'm told is a particularly comfortable shower. Food and drink has been provided, but I'll ask you to refrain from alcohol, since we *are* here on business."

Tapper, who'd let out a low whistle as he turned to survey the place, wrinkled his nose at the last. "How am I supposed to get anything done without a proper pint?"

Sayers, meanwhile, was looking decidedly uncomfortable with both their surroundings and their host. Nat didn't know all the details of what had passed between the two on the *Queen Amina*, but she could read between the lines enough to know that there was more tension there than a steel cable. It'd be best to keep them separated – and, most importantly, not leave them alone together.

"Why don't we get settled in and then regroup?" she suggested.

Scrubbed up in the refresher unit's sink – under the watchful eyes of Xi's goons, naturally – and dressed in the new attire, they made their way back downstairs to join the syndicate boss around the large dining table in one corner of the apartment's main floor. A small spread of cheese, fruit, and crackers had been laid out, and much as Nat didn't want to admit it, her stomach rumbled at the sight; the trip on the *Cavalier* had left her a little sick of ship food.

"Please, help yourselves," said Xi, waving a hand. "Never let it be said that I don't offer the finest in hospitality."

Sayers's mouth set in a flat line, but the sergeant wasn't one to pass up food when it was on offer, and he dug in with gusto.

Nat helped herself to some water and a handful of fruit. Taking a seat, she drummed her fingers atop the table. "If you don't mind, I'd like to discuss the matter of my pilot." Brody's absence had gnawed a hole in her gut, a constant reminder that he was her responsibility. And, much as she hated to admit it, she'd missed the buoyancy his carefree attitude had brought to the team.

"I gave you my word that he would be unharmed, and he has been," said Xi.

"And I appreciate that," said Nat, trying to keep her tone cool and matter of fact. "But I'm going to need him for this job."

Xi sniffed. "What for? My people are perfectly capable of providing any needed air support."

Nat shook her head. "No. You wanted my team; he's part of it. This job is going to be hard enough as it is – I'm not doing it with one hand tied behind my back. I don't know what we might run into, but I know I need the best pilot I can get. And that's ours."

Steel flashed in Xi's expression; leaders of crime empires weren't exactly known for letting others dictate terms. The kind of people who didn't understand that were usually the same ones who found themselves on the wrong side of an airlock.

But the expected explosion never came. Xi merely gave a curt nod in return. "Very well. I'll have him returned to your ship. But he'll be there to *advise*, nothing more."

For her part, Nat tried not to make her relief obvious. She could feel the tension radiating off Sayers from the other side of the room, but there was no point in pressing for more – even getting Xi to give up that much felt like a win. At least she'd insured Brody's safety for a little while longer. "That's acceptable."

"Good," said Xi. Raising her bangled wrist, she tapped out a message and sent it with a flick of her wrist. "With that settled, let us get down to brass tacks. I'd like to know –"

The larger of Xi's bodyguards, Stack, appeared suddenly, holding a tablet, and bent over to whisper something into his boss's ear. Xi's comfortable expression melted away as he spoke, and she glanced down at whatever he was showing her on the screen. Presently, she waved him away, and turned her attention to the rest of them.

"It seems we have company," she said, her voice hard. Flicking on the tablet, a screen appeared floating over the holotable, showing what appeared to be a live video feed of the building's exterior; Nat recognized the street that they'd turned down to enter the garage.

Standing outside the door next to the garage was a single figure, arms crossed, staring up at the camera with an impatient look on her face. Red, curly hair was pulled back into a ponytail at the nape of her neck, and even through the video feed, her brown eyes burned intently.

"This was supposed to be a secure location," said Xi, irritation creeping into her voice. But she quickly smoothed it out. "The timeline is too short to move the operation, so we'll have to question this interloper and then... deal with them appropriately." As if to punctuate her sentiment, Stack appeared in the video feed, seizing the woman by her arm and pulling her inside.

Nat tensed. It was one thing for them to help Xi take down another criminal organization, but random civilian casualties? Not acceptable. Could they talk Xi into just holding the woman prisoner? Maybe, but Nat wasn't prepared to bet the stranger's life on it. Her eyes slid to Sayers and the younger woman gave her an almost imperceptible duck of the head, signaling her readiness. Tapper, for his part, was eyeing the screen with a mildly amused expression.

A loud voice echoed up from below. " – your hands off me, before you're one mitt short."

Up the stairs came the pair, Stack behind the woman with one hand still on her shoulder. He was fully a foot taller than her, which made it look a little like he was dealing with a recalcitrant child. Suddenly spotting the rest of them, she fell silent.

In her head, Nat was already executing the move: she'd take down Stack, dropping him with a punch to the neck. That ought to be enough cue for Tapper to make his move to keep the crime boss's other two goons busy while Sayers went for Xi herself. It was long odds, seeing as they were outnumbered and outgunned, but if the alternative was an innocent person's death on her conscience, then it was no choice at all.

Xi stood and stalked over to the redhead, her slim height towering over the other woman. "I'm only prepared to ask this once: who are you and what are you doing here?"

"I was bleeding *invited*." She shrugged off the heavy hand on her shoulder, shooting a glare behind her. "This isn't exactly the hospitality I was expecting."

"Invited? By whom?"

Tapper cleared his throat. "Oh sorry, did I forget to mention? That's our local contact that your man's pawing."

Nat swore she could hear the muscles in Xi's neck twanging like taut bowstrings as the syndicate leader slowly turned to regard the sergeant, who was leaning back in his chair with a grin on his face. Well, if Xi was going to force them into helping her, then at least she was definitely getting the full Tapper experience.

"Oh, is it," said Xi, her voice dripping. "And how exactly did she come by our location? Your message didn't specify."

The redhead huffed, crossing her hands over her chest. "You hired me for my local expertise. How good would I be if I couldn't find a bunch of out-of-towners dropping hefty cash on secure transport and lodgings in my own backyard?"

Xi's glittering nails rustled against the light fabric of her trousers. Finally she seemed to reel in a sneer and replace it with a tight smile. "Of course. Welcome, Ms…?"

"Collins. Gwen Collins, at your service," she said, giving a mock bow. "Now, are we here to chitchat or shall we get to work?"

CHAPTER 28

By the time Eli walked out into the spaceport baggage claim, he was starting to wonder if maybe he should have just taken the opportunity to disappear. But going missing would have set off alarm bells for Xi and her goons, and maybe even put the rest of the team in danger.

They're probably OK for the moment.

And now they had Gwen.

His heart had skipped a beat when Gwendolyn Rhys's voice had come over the earbud. He'd met the Caledonian Security Agency officer – at the time deep undercover with the Black Watch – when Kovalic had first recruited him almost two years ago to help locate his brother, Eamon. She'd proved tenacious and resourceful and Eli had thought they'd also had... a connection? Maybe? It hadn't turned into anything, though, probably in large part because Eli hadn't been back to Caledonia since.

A fact that Gwen hadn't let him forget.

"At least Tapper writes," she'd needled him after he'd gotten over the shock of hearing her voice. "What's the matter, Brody, can't send a girl a message?"

"Uh, well, that is, I *meant* to, but life's been... complicated."

"And here I've been, sitting by the comm unit just pining away *waiting* for your call."

"I'm… sorry?"

He could picture her eyes rolling. "I'm kidding, dummy. Anyway, we're not here to discuss missed dinners. Though, to clarify, you will definitely owe me an entire bottle of whisky for this. Ofeibia Xi? How the devil did you get mixed up with her?"

"Long story," said Eli. "But she's almost as pissed at me as you are."

Gwen laughed. "I'm not even going to ask what you forgot to do for her. I did a little digging and found where your mates are holed up; I'm on my way there now."

"Any idea why we're here?"

"If she's in Stranraer then I'd bet my last mark that it's something to do with the Coire Ansic."

Eli blinked. The name was in the old tongue, but that was about all he knew. "The who?"

"These are the things you'd know if you bothered to write. Local muscle; they've gone big time since the Black Watch shut down. Control pretty much every illicit operation around these parts. CalSec's been trying to get inside, but our undercover agents keep getting caught." Her voice turned hard. "The results haven't been pretty."

"Oh. Sorry," said Eli awkwardly. "I did overhear Xi saying something about a job. Any ideas?"

"Hm," said Gwen, and Eli could picture her twisting a strand of red hair around one finger in thought. "Could be a turf war… or a strategic partnership. Even odds. I'll give the situation a recce and be in touch. For the moment, you just stay on course. Keep the earbud on receive but don't

transmit unless it's an emergency – we don't know if they'll
be scanning. Copy?"

"Copy that… and Gwen?"

"Yeah?"

"It's good to hear your voice."

There was a snort on the other end of the line, but her
tone softened. "You too, Eli. Take care of yourself." And
with that, she'd signed off, leaving Eli alone with Agent
Liang, who had been studiously poring over her tablet and
doing her best to ignore the one-sided conversation.

Liang had cut him loose, giving him a line to feed Xi's
people about random search and bureaucratic paperwork, and
within fifteen minutes of being dragged in, he was walking
out into the cavernous interior to find a stolid, if slightly more
displeased looking Andres, and an antsy, pacing Prentiss.

"Where the fuck have you been?" snapped the blonde
pilot. "What did they want with you?"

Eli gave his best long-suffering sigh. "Nothing, far as I can
tell. Just asked me questions about where I was from, where
I was going, what my business was on Caledonia – the usual."

Andres eyed him. "What'd you tell them?"

"Nothing! Well, I mean, I had to tell them *something*, so I
gave them the most boring story I could think of. We came
in from Jericho, we're doing a consulting gig, and we'll only
be here a few days. I think they were a little sketched out
by the lack of baggage, but I told them it was a sudden trip."

The two goons exchanged glances, and Eli could almost
read the thoughts passing between them. Xi might have
once boasted that her people loved her, but it was impossible
to deny that they were also scared of her – and it was clear
that neither Andres or Prentiss wanted to call this one in,

especially since their charge was here, standing right in front of them. He resisted the powerful urge to tap at his ear and make sure the earbud was still in place.

"So," he said, "should we get going, or what?"

Grudgingly, Andres led them out of the baggage claim and across an open-air breezeway to the adjacent garage. The hot Caledonian wind ruffled Eli's hair as they stepped outside, and he couldn't help his thoughts drifting north to his hometown of Raleigh City.

Guilt clenched his gut; his younger sister Meghann lived a few hours south of there, in a care home; he hadn't seen her since his last trip to Caledonia either. He did his best to keep in touch, sending messages every week; as a Commonwealth military officer, traveling to an Illyrican-controlled world was a complex process. Not to mention the concern that her connections to both Eli and their late brother Eamon might have encouraged the Imperial Intelligence Service to keep an eye on her. Still, he owed her a visit – and more, probably. *Maybe when we get clear of the crime lord who wants to use us as her personal marionettes.*

Andres acquired a big black hovercar from the rental agency and they piled into its lush air-conditioned interior, rife with the smell of whatever industrial cleaning products they used to wipe it down between drivers. Then it was off, down the highway, into Stranraer proper.

If Raleigh City were a vertical city, tall buildings and reaching spires, Stranraer was like somebody had repeatedly mashed it with a tenderizer: flat sprawl that went on for kilometer after kilometer. It was almost hard for Eli to believe this was the same planet he'd grown up on; it seemed almost alien to him now. There had been a time – the first eighteen years of his life – that he'd literally been nowhere else. But over just the last few years, he'd been to a slew of worlds; if not more than he could count, then at least enough that he sometimes had trouble remembering them all. And when he thought of home, he realized that it was no longer his family's dusty apartment in the dry heat of a Caledonian summer, or his bunk in the Illyrican naval academy, or the cramped bedroom on a Sabaean arctic base that he pictured.

It was his little loft in a Novan suburb, with Addy curled up in the bed, dozing.

He flushed even in the cool of the car, though his chaperones weren't paying close enough attention to him to notice. Or care.

Glad Tapper isn't here. He'd never let me hear the end of it. Even as the thought passed through his mind, he felt a pang in his stomach that wasn't from his healing gunshot wound. No, strike that, he *wished* Tapper was here. And Addy. And Taylor. Mal. Kovalic. Somehow, not for the first or even third time, he'd found himself on his own, separated from the rest of his team.

Guess I'm just going to have to save the rest of them. Again. The laughter bubbled up inside of him and escaped in the form of an undignified snort, earning him a sharp look from Prentiss in the front seat.

After twenty minutes of driving, the car pulled off the highway and meandered through a warren-like maze of city streets – no sensible grid here, like in Raleigh City – and pulled up to a squat two-story building. Andres parked and he and Prentiss ushered Eli out and up a short staircase into a tiny one-room apartment that made his berth on an Illyrican carrier look well-appointed: a compact galley kitchen with a single burner, a sofa that looked like it folded out into a bed, and a bathroom that was just big enough to hold a toilet and sink.

"What," said Eli, looking around, "no mini bar?"

That earned a grunt from Andres and a sour look from Prentiss, neither of whom bothered to actually voice a response.

Great, what the hell am I supposed to do now? Gwen's instructions had been to play this out, but the idea of sitting on his hands while the rest of the team was in the thick of it made him antsy. Downtime had never been his specialty.

What would Kovalic do? It had been a while since he'd summoned that particular mantra, but it had served him... OK, maybe not *well* in the past, but at least it had usually gotten him somewhere.

Find a small task to accomplish.

He glanced around again, taking in his surroundings. One thing was clear: wherever Xi had taken the rest of the team, it wasn't here. He still didn't know exactly what the syndicate boss wanted from them, beyond doing a job for her. But evidently he wasn't needed for whatever the gig was – or at least, this part of it.

Xi was holding him as leverage over the rest of the team, but, as he'd already decided, running for it wasn't an option. Which meant his main job was trusting the team and waiting for the right moment.

In the meantime, maybe he could turn to more pressing matters, like food. His stomach had started rumbling and he tried to remember when he'd last eaten. It might have been that reuben back on Juarez 7A, which was way too long ago. His watchers didn't seem too concerned, so he wandered over to the compact kitchen and poked around the refrigerator, which contained a half empty bottle of mayonnaise, some sriracha, and a can of beer.

Clearly some bachelor's apartment. All too familiar. As tempting as a meal consisting purely of a spicy aioli was, he was going to need something more than that.

"Soooo," he said, turning back to the room, where Andres and Prentiss had taken up spots on the sofa. Prentiss was eyeing something on her sleeve, while Andres had brought up the wall screen and was watching sports highlights on mute. "Lunch anyone? Or… an early dinner?" Wormhole lag was real; he had to glance at his sleeve to see that it was late afternoon local time.

Both of the goons looked at him, then at each other. Silently they held out fists and quickly shook them; Andres put out two fingers, while Prentiss held her hand flat.

"Damn it," said the blonde pilot. "Two out of three?"

"Nah," said Andres. "This one's yours."

With a sigh, Prentiss rocked forward on the couch and leveled Eli with a glare. "I think there's a noodle place around the corner."

Eli gave a helpful shrug. "I mean, *I* could go, if you want…"

"Right," she said. "And why don't you just take my sleeve too? Charge it to the boss, I'm sure she'll understand." She glanced over at Andres. "What do you want?"

"Don't care," said the big man. "Tonkotsu if they got it, but I'm easy."

"Fine," said Prentiss. "Three ramens. I'll be back in twenty minutes."

"Make mine spicy!" Eli called after her as she headed out the door, but got only a single raised finger in response. Politeness apparently was not his captors' strong suit.

He plopped down onto the couch in Prentiss's recently vacated seat; it was still warm. "Just us guys, eh? Anything good on vids?" He looked up at the silent highlights reel cycling through the various results of last night's matches. "How are the Griffins doing this season, anyway?"

Not that he'd expected Andres to open up to him; the man had all the personality of a sidewalk, except if you tried to draw on him with chalk he'd probably break your hand. But if Eli had learned anything from his prior captivities, it was that you could wear people down with good old-fashioned friendliness and charm. Eventually, either they'd open up to you or they'd stick a bag over your head. It was about fifty-fifty.

Andres didn't have a bag handy, so Eli at least had that going for him. But neither did the man seem like he was open to bonding over gravball highlights. *Just as well. I think the last time I knew the Griffins' starting lineup I was fourteen.*

Eli sat quietly, watching the sports highlights, for as short a time as he reasonably could without looking weird, then got up, went into the refresher, and sat on the closed toilet, mulling.

He rubbed at his face. *I really am on my own here.* Not even a weapon he could stash about himself for later; he'd considered rifling the drawers in the kitchenette for a knife or even a frying pan – he'd proved handy with one of those – but that would be conspicuous as hell.

He flushed the toilet without using it, washed his hands anyway, and stepped out of the bathroom. Andres barely spared him a glance from the sofa.

So, what, I'm going to just sit around here with this brick wall all day? Part of him wondered if he should make a run for it, just for believability's sake. Trying to escape was *logical*, right? Wasn't it more suspicious if he didn't? They probably wouldn't kill him outright, especially if he really was insurance for the rest of the team doing this job.

Then again, there were a lot of things that weren't "being killed outright" that would still hurt a whole lot.

A chime broke the silence, the suddenness startling Eli so that he almost tripped over his own feet without even moving. He managed to catch himself, though he still earned a strange look from Andres.

The big man shook his head, then turned to his sleeve, reading a message there. After a moment, he grunted. "Looks like we're on for tomorrow. The boss wants us on your ship."

"*Our* ship?" Eli repeated dumbly.

"That's what it says." Andres didn't offer any more than that, just turned back to watching the holoscreen, leaving Eli to process the news.

Down below, there was a click and a creak as Prentiss climbed back up the stairs, returning with the food.

Even the sour disposition of his babysitters couldn't dent the relief he'd felt from Xi's message. They were going to put him on the *Cavalier*. If there was any chance at all that he'd be able to help the rest of the team, then it would be from behind the stick.

Buoyed by the news, he didn't even balk at the idea of spending the next few hours in the company of two of the least charismatic people he'd ever met.

And at least there was ramen.

CHAPTER 29

Gwen was not what Addy had expected at all when Tapper had volunteered his local contact. She'd assumed it would be another one of the sergeant's grizzled war buddies, not a woman young enough to be his granddaughter.

After a moment, Xi waved off her thugs and the awkward house party vibe returned in full force.

Tapper squeezed the younger woman's shoulder. "Always good to see you, lass. Glad you got my message." Addy raised an eyebrow. The sergeant's tone had gone up at the end, almost questioningly.

"Loud and clear," said Gwen, slapping the man on the back with a grin.

"Great. Let me introduce you."

"No need," she said, her gaze taking in the room's other occupants. "You must be Addy." She extended her hand. "The old man says you're a mean shot with a sniper rifle and you don't take any bullshit."

I think that might be the nicest thing he's ever said about me?

"Uh, hi," said Addy, shaking the other woman's warm hand. "Yeah. Nice to meet you. Wait, when did he…?"

"Oh, we're pen pals," said Gwen brightly. She lowered her voice to a conspiratorial level, glancing over her shoulder at

Tapper, who now seemed to be engaged in a staring contest with Stack. "I don't know many people who write letters, but he's surprisingly good at it."

"How did you two meet?"

"Oh, we helped each other out on a job a couple years ago." Her eyes caught on Xi. "Best not to go into the details here and now, but let's just say it was a mutually beneficial situation."

Addy faintly recalled hearing Brody mention meeting Kovalic and the rest of the team on a job on Caledonia, but more than that she couldn't recall.

Still, she wasn't about to turn down more backup.

A sharp cough came from across the room, and Ofeibia Xi produced her glittering smile. "Now that our *local expert* has joined us, perhaps we could discuss the operation."

Gwen spread her hands wide. "By all means. Perhaps you can tell me what exactly you're doing on my patch and how I can be of assistance."

"Well, major," said Xi, as she took a seat and leaned back languorously, "the floor is yours." She flicked her wrist in the commander's direction.

Taylor didn't react to the gesture, just stood as though this were any other briefing and brought up the holo display on the table. "Our target is the Coire Ansic's private car on the Burns Expanse Limited."

Gwen gave a low whistle. "Roche Flores's money train? That's definitely no milk run."

The commander nodded. "We're operating somewhat in the dark here. Gwen, can you tell us anything about what to expect?"

Tapping a finger against her lips, Gwen looked over the

schematic. "They keep security arrangements tight, but from what I've heard, the money will be stored in a car towards the rear with a coach full of Coire Ansic muscle between it and the rest of the passenger section. I'd expect half a dozen security at least." Her eyes went to Taylor. "Armed, too."

"Figures," muttered Tapper. "Something tells me it won't be as easy for *us* to get weapons onboard."

Addy glanced at Xi. *No way our* host *is going to allow us to have weapons.* But the syndicate boss didn't voice an objection, just sat back and continued watching.

"Gear is a priority anyway," said Taylor. "If we do this right, we won't have to fire a single shot. We're going to need some specific equipment for what I've got in mind. Perhaps our local contact can be of assistance?"

Gwen nodded. "Give me a list and I'll make some calls –" She put her hands up to forestall an objection from Xi. "Discreetly, of course."

"Good," said Taylor. "I pulled what information I could about the train and the surrounding area while we were en route to Caledonia. An air interdiction is out, thanks to the frequent and unpredictable sandstorms in the region. Similarly, trying to conceal ourselves in the train's baggage car and bypass the Coire Ansic security is impractical given our time constraints and lack of access.

"I believe the easiest approach will be to board the train as passengers – in small groups, so as not to attract any undue attention." The train diagram rippled into view, with several of the cars highlighted. "First priority will be tagging any of Flores's security that aren't in the private car. If possible, we avoid them; if any have to be neutralized, we do it – *quietly*. I don't want any flags being raised too early.

"Meanwhile, I'll tap into the onboard systems. According to the train schematics I acquired, the onboard climate systems rely on recirculating air for heating and cooling, which means carbon dioxide scrubbers. If I can disable the ones in the Coire Ansic car, that should make them drowsy enough for us to bypass or incapacitate them without too much trouble.

"A quarter of an hour before the train reaches the spur for Fort Mull –" The map zoomed out to show the abandoned mining town and the line running through it, " – we rendezvous at the private car and make our move. Once we've secured the money, we detach that car and the ones behind it from the rest of the train. The safeties ought to kick in at that point, shifting the rear cars into coasting mode. But," Nat said, raising a finger, "we also need to activate the track switch to move us onto the dormant spur line." She pointed at a second line branching off from the first; it glowed yellow. "This will require precise timing. If we detach the cars too early, we won't have enough residual momentum to get us to the Fort Mull depot. And we can't activate the track switch before the front cars have passed the branch, otherwise we send the entire train onto the spur line, which we definitely don't want."

Frowning, Tapper peered closer at the schematic. "How are we going to trigger the track switch?"

Nat nodded. "Good question. Normally the train would send a signal ahead of reaching the switch. I should be able to spoof that, but as I said, the timing will have to be exact." At another tap of her finger, the holoscreen showed the train cars approaching a wireframe model of a building. "Madam Xi will be waiting at the Fort Mull depot with ground transport, at which point we'll offload the money, and then drive our way out.

"The *Cavalier* will be in a high-altitude holding pattern and will rendezvous with the truck here." The map zoomed in on a rocky set of mesas to the east, just outside the Burns Expanse. "We'll transfer the money to the ship and make our way to orbit, where we'll dock with one of Madam Xi's other ships, which I believe is already inbound." She looked at the syndicate boss, who tipped her head with a slight smile. "At that point, we'll go our separate ways, all debts cleared." Taylor sat back quietly, like a lecturer awaiting questions from the class about the material.

Despite the impressive nature of the commander's plan, seemingly thrown together at a moment's notice, Addy's jaw had gotten tighter and tighter during the presentation. *So many ways for Xi to fuck us over.* She was sure that Taylor was trying to prepare for all the possibilities, but without the ability for them to coordinate, how were they going to avoid it?

"Elegant," said Xi at last, tapping a finger against her blood red lips. "But I want to be on that train."

Taylor's eyebrows went up. "I don't think that's a good idea. I can't guarantee your safety."

"I don't need you to guarantee anything, major," said Xi, amused. "But I will be there to show Roche Flores – and his *associate* – exactly what happens when you fuck with me. I want him to know it was me who presided over his humiliation."

Egotistical maniac. Though Addy couldn't say she was surprised. Taylor looked like she wanted to object, but Addy had spent enough time with Xi to know she wouldn't be talked out of something when her mind was set on it. As much as her chest tightened at the thought, she knew there was only one way to handle this. "I'll go with her."

It was hard to tell who was more surprised: Xi or Taylor. The commander did the better job of concealing it; her sharp look lasted a split second before melting back into her usual stoic demeanor. Xi, on the other hand, looked more pleasantly surprised – though it was tinged with an edge of suspicion.

"Fine," said Taylor. "That does mean someone else will have to assist with the truck." She fixed Xi with a hard look. "And my team is all needed on the train. Unless you think you can do it without us?" The message was implicit: time was short, and Xi's armed thugs were no substitute for a team of trained special operatives. That was, after all, why Xi had decided to use them in the first place.

"Yancy can go," said Xi, waving a hand carelessly in the direction of the woman. "She's more than capable."

That should even the odds a bit. Not that Xi wasn't a formidable opponent in her own right, but Addy felt more comfortable having eyes on her anyway.

"And our pilot?"

The syndicate leader projected an air of calm, but Addy had spent enough time with her to see she was annoyed. "He will be aboard your ship, as promised. My own people will accompany him just to make sure there are no… complications."

Addy's hackles went up. The idea of armed goons watching over Brody left her feeling ill; the only people she trusted less than Xi's people was Xi herself, whom Addy was convinced – no matter how pleasant she was pretending to be – would have no compunction about dispatching them all the moment they ceased to be useful.

If Taylor had any such misgivings, she kept them close to her chest. "Fair enough."

"Very well," said Xi. "Meeting concluded, then." The syndicate leader gestured at her employees to join her in one corner of the room, where they held a hushed conversation.

Oh good. I'm sure that's fine.

Addy spared a glance at Taylor, but the commander seemed unconcerned, consulting her tablet and chewing on her lip thoughtfully. Tapper, never one to turn down free food, was busy refilling his plate from the spread. Unsure of exactly what she was supposed to be doing, Addy settled on scowling vaguely in Xi's direction.

Apparently also at loose ends, Gwen drifted over and took a seat next to Addy, tracking the path of her glare sympathetically. "You're worried about him, aren't you?"

Addy flushed, not having to ask for clarification about who "him" was in this particular situation. *Is it that obvious?*

The redhead smiled, and reached down to clasp Addy's hands. "Don't worry. Brody's got a knack for getting himself out of scrapes like this. But I'm sure he'd be glad to hear you're concerned for him."

And with that, Gwen let go of her hands with a wink, and sauntered off to do her own final checks.

Addy kept her hands together for a moment, feeling the small slip of flimsy that the other woman had pressed into her palm. She didn't know what it was, but clearly Gwen didn't want Xi and her goons to see it, which made it all the more important. Her pulse quickened as she tucked it into her sleeve.

Let's just hope it's the advantage we need. For all our sakes.

CHAPTER 30

Much as Kovalic would have liked to claim the buzzing of his sleeve woke him from a deep and restful slumber, he'd been staring at the ceiling of the safe house's living room since he'd woken almost an hour earlier.

Lifting his arm, he wasn't surprised about the caller, but he still sighed and swung his legs off the couch. He'd left his earbud on the coffee table last night and he popped it in before accepting the connection.

"Were you going to tell me?" said Veronica Fayerweather.

"Morning to you, too, inspector. I assume you saw the news."

"God *damn* it, Kaplan. Kovalic. Whatever the hell your name is. What the fuck is going on? *Treason*?"

Kovalic tried, unsuccessfully, to stop his sharp inhalation – the treason charges hadn't been on the news report he'd seen, much less his real name – but Fayerweather caught his indrawn breath anyway. "Yeah, I called Rashad after I saw it, and he gave me the broad strokes. Something *you* should have done before dragging me into this."

Not the best news, but not without a silver lining either.

"And yet I can't help but notice I'm still here. No heavily armed Bureau agents knocked down my door last night. Hell, you called *me*."

"You still made me an accomplice! To treason!"

Kovalic raised an eyebrow, even knowing she couldn't see him. "Which you're now compounding by reaching out instead of handing this number over to your partner. Or did you call just to vent some spleen?"

"No. I just…" She sighed heavily. "It bothers me."

"What?"

"All of it! The treason allegation… you, a fugitive… your mole theory."

Kovalic stood and walked over to the kitchenette. The interruption to last night's shopping trip had come before he'd thought to buy real, fresh coffee, but a quick search of the cabinets did turn up some single-serving pods that were only a few weeks past their expiration dates. He popped one into the machine and put a chipped but clean mug beneath the dispenser; the contraption burbled away happily.

"So you believe me," he said. "About the mole."

"I didn't say that. All I said was it bothers me."

The machine finished with a last spurt and Kovalic picked up the mug and gave it an experimental sniff. Vanilla. Not his thing, usually, but any spaceport in an ion storm. "Enough to do something about it? How much poking around did you do, Ronnie?"

"Don't call me that," she snapped. "It's still Inspector Fayerweather to you."

"Sorry, inspector."

"And I did a *medium* amount of poking around."

Kovalic carried his mug towards the sliding patio door that let out onto the safe house's tiny balcony. It was early enough that Rance, Yevgeniy, and the general were still asleep, and he didn't want to wake them.

Out on the balcony, there was still a chill in the air as the Novan sun crawled upward from the horizon. "And what did this poking around find?"

"Nothing."

Kovalic stopped, staring out at the city, painted orange by the sunrise. "I'm sorry – nothing?"

Frustration seeped into Fayerweather's voice. "Nothing at all. There's no record of any counterintelligence report with the details you gave me. Nothing about couriers for Nova Front, Bayern bank accounts, any of it. And I'm not talking about just within the Bureau – there's nothing from any of the partner agencies within the Commonwealth. I even checked allied systems that occasionally share data with us: Haran, Jericho Station, even Bayern itself. But none of them had flagged any suspicious activity with those parameters. You're sure this thing is real?"

Kovalic sipped the coffee absently, grimacing at the overly sweet flavor. "Depends on your definition of 'real'. But, yes, I have reason to believe it exists." Kester had the information; it had to have come from somewhere.

Or, at least, Kovalic *thought* Kester had it – could he have been mistaken? Could there be some entirely different shoe about to drop on their heads? Either way, Kovalic knew the data was out there: Aaron Page had found it. More to the point, Isabella had *wanted* it found. Was it possible nobody beside Page had done so? His head spun.

"There's a possibility that this information could be classified beyond my clearance levels," said Fayerweather. "Maybe even retroactively, if this operation was deemed sensitive enough."

"I sense a 'but'."

"*But*," Fayerweather obliged, "I've seen that before and I know what it looks like: missing references, files that can't be accessed. This doesn't look like that. It looks like it was never here in the first place." She paused. "I assume this is somehow related to these treason allegations."

Kovalic rubbed a hand over his mouth. Fayerweather was sharp as they came, even running on no sleep. Denying wouldn't help him. "I have reason to believe Aidan Kester is in possession of this information."

"Hm," said Fayerweather. "I'll admit, it's enough to get me curious."

"You didn't happen to share your *curiosity* with Inspector Laurent, did you?"

"Not yet." Fayerweather's response was clipped, suggesting that she wasn't at all comfortable with that decision. "There's enough credence to your mole theory that I took to heart what you said about no suspects being eliminated. If Rashad had the evidence, he could have provided it to Kester – even if my gut is telling me that he would never do it."

Kovalic replayed his conversation with Laurent from the previous evening, specifically the inspector's attempt to get him to turn in the general in exchange for the rest of the team's freedom. Was that just another part of Isabella's ploy? Or was the inspector simply doing his job?

"For the moment, I'd like to keep it that way, if you don't mind."

There was silence on the other end of the connection for a moment, then Fayerweather blew out a long breath. "Fine. For now. But I can't hold onto this for more than twenty-four hours. So whatever you're planning on doing, it's time to get it in gear."

"Hold on to what? You literally found nothing."

"Ha ha. This is an active investigation; even not finding something is significant, you know that. I may be on leave, but I still have a duty to report what I know."

"Fair enough. And inspector?"

"Yes?"

"Thank you."

Somewhere in the background of Fayerweather's call a baby started wailing, and the woman issued a long sigh. "Don't thank me yet. This is going to get a lot worse before it gets better."

She cut the connection and Kovalic was left standing on the balcony, sipping his too-vanilla coffee and waiting for the sun to climb above the buildings.

So, assuming that Kester's evidence was in fact the Bayern report, it clearly hadn't gone through official channels. Which left two possibilities, to Kovalic's mind: either Kester was the mole, and the information had been passed to him by Isabella directly, or he was being used and some source had passed it to him off the books – maybe an asset he'd cultivated at some point. Kovalic spun back through what he knew of Kester's dossier: despite coming up in operations, the acting director had spent most of his time at CID headquarters, with the exception of a brief stint as deputy station chief on Hamza, the capital world of the Hanif. But the Hanif government had stayed out of the conflict between Commonwealth and

Imperium, which didn't exactly gibe with them monitoring financial couriers out of Bayern.

He wasn't sure if the coffee was growing on him, or his tastebuds were just being systematically assassinated, but the fourth sip was less offensive than the previous. Standing out here as he worked through possibilities, it was almost enough to make him forget his current predicament.

Almost.

Scratching the stubble that had begun to sprout on his chin – being on the run was not exactly conducive to getting a good shave – he slid the patio door open and stepped back into the apartment.

In the time his conversation with the inspector had taken, the other occupants had risen. Rance sat in one corner, feet curled under her as she studied a tablet; Yevgeniy was poking with curiosity at the coffee maker, attempting to figure out what incantations were required to produce a cup; and the general was just settling himself at the table with a cup of tea.

"Good morning, Simon," said the older man, tilting his head. "How does the day look?"

"Busy," said Kovalic. He laid out the information – or lack thereof – that Fayerweather had passed on.

Taking a musing sip, the general made a face, casting a dubious eye at the teabag string hanging over the rim. "Wretched stuff," he muttered, before clearing his throat. "If I may suggest, I think it is time for us to change tactics."

Kovalic dropped onto a stool at the bar. "What did you have in mind?"

The general's long, spindly fingers combed through his beard like a spider looking for prey. "We've been behind every step of the way, chasing after something that's already happened in a vain attempt to catch up. Perhaps it's time for us to go on offense."

"Traditionally, it's difficult to go on offense when you don't have possession of the ball," said Yevgeniy, who had conceded to the coffee maker and simply poured himself a glass of tap water. "Not to mention we don't even have a target."

"Not so," said the general, raising a finger. "There is exactly one person whom we know is involved in the charges against us." His ice-blue gaze landed on Kovalic's, unwavering.

"Kester," said Kovalic. "You want to go after Kester."

The silence held over them like a curtain had been dropped, then Yevgeniy gave a long exhale. "It's a big risk."

"No plan is without risk," said the general, shooting a glare at his old subordinate. "But sometimes you have to make an audacious move in order to gain some ground."

"'Go big or go home' only works when you have a home to go back to," said Yevgeniy pointedly.

"Well then," said the general, "let's just pack it all in and find a lovely little town in which to open a tea shop."

"It's harder than it looks."

"It would have to be, wouldn't it?"

Kovalic pressed a hand to his forehead. "OK, settle down, you two." There was merit to the general's plan. After all their digging and probing, Kester remained the only lead they had. If they wanted to make some headway, they'd need to confront him – otherwise they might as well just be spinning their wheels. He glanced at Yevgeniy and Rance. "Can we make it happen?"

Yevgeniy grimaced. "Our surveillance suggests it's a tall order. He rarely goes anywhere without his personal security detail."

Rance, who had been listening quietly, took this opportunity to pipe up. "That's not entirely true. We do know one place that he doesn't take his security. And we know how to get him back there, too."

Kovalic raised his eyebrows as he took up Rance's thread, but something out of the corner of his eyes caught his attention. The general's gaze had sharpened as they landed on the yeoman, as though he was seeing her with fresh eyes.

"Indeed," said the older man, thoughtfully. "An astute observation. Simon?"

Taking a last sip of his coffee, Kovalic put down the mug. "All right, then. Let's have another chat with Aidan Kester. On our terms this time."

CHAPTER 31

Eli was woken from a pleasant dream in which he was sitting by a pool, dappled sun shining through waving trees as a breeze ruffled his hair. And someone was delivering a cocktail right to him on a silver tray, one that smelled like summer and freshness and…

Then he was looking up into Andres's impassive face. "Time to go."

"Don't go into the wake-up call business," grumbled Eli, pressing the heels of his hands to his eyes, still gummy from sleep.

He'd slept on the couch in the tiny apartment, a fact that his neck made known as he levered himself into a sitting position. Under the guise of scratching his ear he made sure he hadn't lost the earbud Gwen had given him.

Prentiss was already up, drinking coffee while leaning against the counter. She didn't look particularly happy to be awake either. Or maybe that was directed at Eli. Or the world. Hard to tell.

"Can I get a cup of that?" he asked.

"Go fuck yourself," she said.

"So, that's not a 'no', then." His knee popped as he stood up. *Used to be I could roll out of a shipboard bunk and double-*

time it to a hangar bay in two minutes. But those days were long gone and he'd put on a lot of mileage since. He ambled over to the kitchenette, where Prentiss grudgingly slid aside and let him pour a half cup of the dregs. "Cheers," he said, raising it in her direction.

It was awful, but at least it was lukewarm. *On second thought, that doesn't make it better.*

Andres might as well have been an impatient parent, tapping his foot and checking his wrist for the time, but they were all out the door and piled into the hovercar within five minutes, retracing the path they'd taken from the spaceport.

Eli resisted the urge to tap the earbud and make sure it was still working. Neither Andres nor Prentiss seemed to be paying him any mind, but who knew what sort of monitoring they had in place.

At the spaceport, Andres parked the hovercar but didn't return it to the rental agency. *They're planning on coming back here.* Eli filed that away, just in case.

They passed quickly through the security checkpoints – nobody pulled him aside this time, which was a mixed blessing – and within ten minutes were out on the tarmac, walking towards a familiar shape on a landing pad.

The flat, squat sight of the *Cavalier* washed over Eli like a soothing balm. He found himself straightening up almost unconsciously, his muscles relaxing. *You have no idea how good it is to see you.* He ran his hand over the undercarriage, half-expecting to see dings or dents incurred in his absence, but nothing seemed obviously out of place.

"Open 'er up," grunted Andres.

Eli gave him a sour look. *Some people have no appreciation for the bond between a pilot and their ship.* But he tapped his entry code on the access panel, and the ramp lowered to the ground with a whine of hydraulics.

Their footsteps echoed eerily throughout the hold as they climbed onboard. Eli had been on the ship by himself plenty of times in the past nine months, checking this or that system, tweaking performance, or even occasionally taking the odd nap. But this felt different – not just empty, but vacant. Like a part of the ship was missing.

As outside, nothing was obviously missing or out of place, though if anything, it was a bit too clean. Usually there was a fraction more clutter or mess about the place – the detritus of a space that was not just their workplace but, more often than not, their home. It didn't look like any of the secret compartments where they'd cached their money and equipment had been disturbed, so Xi and her goons hadn't done a stem-to-stern search or anything.

Which was just as well, because the one thought burning a hole in Eli's brain at this very moment was the pistol that Tapper had secured beneath the pilot console. His pulse quickened at the thought. *Even if it's still there, then what?*

All too cognizant of Andres and Prentiss trailing impatiently behind him, Eli made his way into the cockpit and was about to plop down in the worn comfort of his seat – and maybe do a surreptitious check beneath for the hidden sidearm – when a meaty hand descended on his shoulder. He nearly jumped out of his skin, convinced that Xi's goons knew exactly what he was thinking. *Even I don't know what I'm thinking half the time!*

"Not there," said Andres. "Just get it started up. She'll handle the rest." He jerked his head at Prentiss, who had come in behind them, and was surveying the cockpit with a look of distaste.

"This is all non-standard," she said, scowling. "What the hell did you do to this thing?"

Eli moved to the co-pilot seat, forcing himself to swallow the lump in his throat, and started bringing the *Cav*'s systems online. "Started out as a standard *Kestrel*-class light transport, but we made some special modifications," he said, trying to sound casual as he flipped the engine ignition switches and felt the thrum reverberate through the deckplates like a heartbeat. "You sure you can handle it?"

The look she gave him could have vaporized steel. "A ship's a ship."

He opened his mouth to protest, then just shrugged. *Her funeral. Well, potentially all our funerals, I guess.*

"OK, systems coming up," said Eli, leaning back in the co-pilot chair and crossing his arms. "We'll be ready for liftoff in two minutes."

Prentiss sat down in Eli's own seat, grimaced, and then started yanking levers to tweak the height and distance from the controls. It took every bit of self-control for him not to lunge at her. Taking their ship was one thing, but *adjusting his seat*? No jury would convict him.

Andres disappeared into the cargo hold. Eli watched the gauges and readouts as the *Cav* finished its boot-up sequence, but whenever he leaned forward to so much as peer at a display, he earned a warning look from Prentiss. "Don't touch *anything*."

Eli put his hands up. "I was just going to tell you that the intermix runs a little hot, but clearly you know what you're doing."

She glowered at him, but her eyes did dart to the relevant monitor.

A minute later, the board showed green and Prentiss took the yoke for liftoff. The moment the ship floated upward on its repulsors, Eli realized he was gripping the edges of his seat like they were doing barrel rolls. *They say doctors make the worst patients – I wonder if there's a corollary for pilots.*

The ship bobbed, sliding to one side as Prentiss tried to correct for the slightly weaker output on the portside repulsor; Eli had long ago internalized that, among the *Cav*'s many quirks. *This flight is going to be interminable.*

And then they were off and away, the ground disappearing beneath them at a rapid rate as they climbed, and Eli was pressed back against his seat.

"Shit, what kind of thrust ratio does this thing have?" said Prentiss as she eased back on the throttle.

"We're usually in a hurry," said Eli.

There was a weird disconnect for Eli as the ship maneuvered through the atmosphere: the sounds, the motions, everything around him was as familiar as his own body, and yet it was somehow *wrong*, like remembering a dream while waking.

Or a nightmare.

After a few excruciating minutes, they reached cruising altitude, and settled into what Eli recognized as a holding pattern. He glanced down at the navigation readouts, or at least what he could see without reaching out to touch the controls.

The Burns Expanse.

Every kid born on Caledonia knew it: the huge desert that dominated the planet's southern continent, barren and inhospitable. Gwen hadn't been in touch to brief him on Xi's plan, and Andres and Prentiss certainly weren't the sharing type. He racked his brain for what else he could remember from his primary school geography lessons, but it wasn't much. There was something though, that he vaguely recalled–

An alarm blared and he shot forward, hands instinctively reaching for the co-pilot yoke.

"I've got it," said Prentiss sharply, banking the ship against the crosswind that had threatened to push them out of pattern.

"What the fuck was th…" The words died in Eli's mouth as he peered out the canopy and saw the whirling wall of brown to their port side.

Oh, right. That was the other thing. "Sandstorm."

They weren't exclusive to the Burns Expanse by any means; much of Caledonia, or at least the regions where settlers had ended up, was rocky and arid, without a lot of vegetation to keep the soil rooted.

But the ones here were a little more… intense.

"That must be hundreds of klicks across," he muttered, shaking his head. *What the hell is the rest of the team doing down there in* that? His hand drifted towards his ear again, but the earbud was still there, just silent.

Sticking his twitching fingers in his armpits, he forced himself back in the chair. Part of him wondered if he wouldn't be better off leaving the cockpit altogether, but every time he tried to get up and go, he felt rooted to the seat. *I can't help them from back there.* If something was going to happen, he'd need to be here.

Not that he could do much with Prentiss and Andres floating around. He needed to even the odds somehow.

A crowd of voices piled into his head, offering suggestions.

"Take the fight to them," said one, that sounded suspiciously like Addy.

"Watch and wait," advised another in Commander Taylor's even tones.

"When all you've got is a hammer, break the shit out of some stuff." No need to wonder who that was.

"You've got this, Brody. Use your head."

Kovalic. It had only been a couple days since Eli had last seen the major, but he missed the man's quiet confidence. He'd always been a steady presence, someone Eli could rely on, which he privately thought was because Kovalic believed himself responsible for getting Eli into this whole life. Which, to be fair, was true, but Eli had chosen to stay in it and, much as he'd struggled to adjust, he'd come to the conclusion that he enjoyed it. There were terrifying moments, to be sure, and if he never got kidnapped again it would be too soon, but overall he felt like he was doing something important. Making a difference.

And into this meditative moment came the reminder that not only was there a gun underneath the piloting console, but more important – *much* more important – this was *his* ship. His home-field advantage. All he had to do was just pick the right moment to act.

Thanks, team.

As if on cue, Prentiss cocked her head to one side, listening to something that Eli couldn't hear, then reached over to the comm panel and flipped on the loudspeaker. A voice crackled through, instantly recognizable as Commander Taylor's. "All stations green?"

"Green," came Gwen's lilt.

"As grass," said Tapper.

"Ready," said Addy, and Eli felt his heart skip a beat at her voice. *They're OK. They're all OK.*

Eli's mouth twitched, threatening a smile. The team was still here, even if they weren't *here*, and that was all he needed to know.

Prentiss toggled to a separate channel before transmitting back, Eli noted. "This is overwatch. Confirming we are in holding position and waiting for your mark."

That makes two of us.

CHAPTER 32

The gravtrain station wasn't exactly busy at 0630, which made blending into the background a challenge, but to Nat's mind they at least still had the element of surprise on their side. If Roche Flores was anything like other crime lords of her acquaintance, his chief weakness would be his overconfidence. She gave a sidelong glance at Ofeibia Xi, who was striding across the inlaid tile floor like she owned the place; Addy Sayers flanked the woman on the other side, eyeing her like a raptor waiting for its prey to slip up.

As they crossed towards the platform, Nat's earbud – Xi had provided them all with comms equipment, though locked to a single channel – crackled to life.

"Eyes on Flores," came Gwen's lilting Caledonian accent. "Ten o'clock."

It was a sign of the Coire Ansic boss's paranoia that he himself always accompanied the train to Tralee, then took an express sub-orbital hopper back to Stranraer. Not exactly a cost-efficient way of getting around, but when you had the money, you spent it.

"Copy that," Nat murmured, letting her gaze drift naturally in the direction indicated.

There was no mistaking the man. Half a dozen figures in dark suits strode alongside him, eyes looking outward in every direction for threats. Cocooned amidst them, talking with the loud tones of someone yelling down a comm connection, was Roche Flores himself: short, balding, and slight of build, but younger than Xi's reconnaissance photo had made him look. His bodyguards towered over him like castle walls.

The group approached the security checkpoint, but rather than stepping through the scanners they were quickly ushered off to one side and let through a swinging gate with absolutely no further checks.

Xi gave a sharp snort. "Nothing subtle about that." She cocked her head at Nat. "We could have done the same, you know. I don't know what Flores is paying them, but I assure you it would have been well within my means."

"We could have," said Nat. "But if the security guards are already on his payroll, they're not going to jeopardize that relationship. Or, worse, they'd take your money, then turn around and let Flores know that somebody else had bought their way aboard, putting the entire Coire Ansic on high alert – if they didn't just decide to completely scratch this run."

"You don't disappoint, major," said Xi. "I can see why you replaced Kovalic."

Nat didn't rise to the bait; the syndicate boss was always needling, probing around the edges, looking for a wedge to get any of them to give up information that they didn't mean to. She let the comment wash over her, relaxing the shoulder muscles that had tensed up at the mention of Simon. Hopefully he was safe, wherever he was. They'd be headed back to Nova soon enough. Maybe even with some intel that could help clear his name.

"All stations green?" Nat murmured over the comms.

"Green," said Gwen.

"As grass," came Tapper's voice.

"Ready," said Addy.

"Good," said Nat. "Keep comm usage to a minimum until checkpoint Echo. Good luck."

There were a series of double-click acknowledgments over the comms, which then went quiet. Even Gwen hadn't been able to suss out all the details of Flores's security arrangements, and it was all too possible that his people would be scanning for off-band transmissions. Everything should be on a clock from here on out anyway, assuming it went smoothly.

Though when did things ever go smoothly?

They stepped onto the platform, the gleaming tube of the gravtrain humming quietly on its repulsor fields as it snaked several hundred meters long through the station. The three women made their way towards their car near the front of the train. Tapper and Stack would board towards the rear, Gwen and Xi's other goon, Deng, in the middle. That would give them plenty of coverage, just in case the Coire Ansic had sprinkled more security throughout – and again, given how paranoid Flores seemed to be, they couldn't discount any possibilities.

Nat was about to climb aboard when Xi suddenly looped an arm through hers, as though they were two girlfriends on their way to a lunch date. The syndicate boss smiled at her, even as her nails pinched Nat's forearm. "Just to remind you, major: play this straight and everybody gets what they want."

As many times as Nat had cautioned Addy Sayers about

losing her temper and decking someone for the slightest provocation, she felt her own cool straining at the seams. How hard would it be to take Xi's own forearm, flip the woman over her hip, and leave her wheezing on the platform? Not hard. But all the consequences of those actions followed quickly in her mind's eye: Brody's life might as well be forfeit, and they'd have to spend the foreseeable future looking over their shoulders with no doubt an even higher bounty on their heads.

So instead she just gave Xi a curt nod as they climbed the steps into the train.

Most of the gravtrains Nat had ridden in her journeys across the known galaxy – on her home planet of Centauri, independent worlds like Haran, or even Illyrica's own surprisingly efficient public transit system – were designed for commuters: rows of seats, a few with tables for people to do work, maybe a rudimentary café car offering snacks and coffees.

The operators of the Burns Expanse Limited had clearly realized that nobody was riding this on a daily basis, and that those who had decided to undertake a journey that could more easily be accomplished by other more efficient means were here because they wanted to enjoy the experience.

So, instead of the usual rows of seats there were a series of private compartments, accessible via a narrow corridor. Nat had seen similar designs on old vids from pre-galactic Earth. It had a distinctly old-timey nostalgic feel, made all the more indulgent by the sumptuousness of the fixtures: from a thick, lush carpet beneath their feet, to the soft warm light from the wall sconces, to the richly varnished imitation wood of the compartment doors.

If nothing else, the compartment ensured they would have a secure base of operations, with nobody snooping on them.

Nat located their berth about halfway down the car and waved her sleeve at the door panel. It whispered open, letting them into a small room with an expansive window that covered the entire outer wall, two facing benches upholstered in plush faux velvet, and luggage racks overhead. Xi and Sayers followed them in; the glass in the door immediately frosted into privacy mode as it slid shut.

"Well," said Sayers, looking around, "this is cozy."

Xi sniffed, running her fingers over the bench's fabric. "Chintzy imitation. The appearance of luxury, perhaps, but nothing more than that." She sat down in the middle of the seat, arms stretched out along the back, effectively claiming that side for herself. Nat tried not to roll her eyes as she unpacked the bag she'd brought onboard: Gwen's discreet contacts had come through with all the equipment she'd asked for – or close enough – and they'd prepared specialized kits for each of them, according to their needs.

"Flores's car is towards the rear of the train," Nat said, as she laid out her gear, "and it requires an authorized sleeve to access. But it doesn't have dining facilities, so they'll have to venture out to the café car for refreshments. That's our best opportunity to surveil them and get a sense of what we're up against."

"Sounds easy enough," said Sayers, taking a seat opposite Xi. "I should be able to get close enough to clone one of their sleeves."

"You're certainly adept at worming your way into someone's good graces," said Xi with a silky tone that didn't quite obscure the snideness in her voice.

Sayers ignored the jibe, though Nat could see the muscles in her jaw twitch. Putting these two in close quarters had not been her first choice – Nat had read the reports from the *Queen Amina* job. They hadn't told the whole story, but Nat knew enough to read between the lines: Xi had gotten under Sayers's skin, played on her insecurities, her desires. Had it been genuine, or just a ploy? In the end, it didn't really matter.

Except Adelaide Sayers had taken it personally. She'd come a long way from the hotheaded young woman that Simon had recruited, but she still had a tendency to act first and think later. In the kind of high-risk scenarios the SPT all too often found itself, that could be an asset – but in a situation like this, with a player like Xi, one misstep could quickly be fatal.

There was a gentle chime over the loudspeakers and a pleasant automated voice announced a last boarding call before the train got underway. Nat checked her sleeve – right on schedule, as expected. Though the Burns Expanse Limited did have human operators to oversee matters, the system itself was largely automated. She spared a last glance out at the platform, which was now empty aside from a couple latecomers dashing to get onboard in time.

Once the train started moving, there was no turning back; the plan would be in motion, and everything depended on their execution. But the train wasn't the only moving part in this operation and there was a lot that could go wrong. Glancing over at Xi, Nat raised an eyebrow. "What's the status of our other teams?"

Xi tilted her head to one side. "Yancy's convoy was already en route this morning. They'll be in position on time."

"And our overwatch?"

The syndicate boss's eyelids lowered halfway. "Oh, your pilot is just fine, major. Maintaining the holding pattern, as discussed."

Sayers lifted one of the cases and slammed it into the luggage rack with somewhat more force than required, a fact that didn't go unnoticed by either Nat or Xi, though the latter seemed to derive somewhat more entertainment from it.

"Everything is right on schedule," said Xi, with her customary broad smile that hovered between charm and threat. "And I have the utmost faith in your plan."

Something about the way she said it did not inspire the same confidence in Nat. That the syndicate boss would try to double-cross them, well, that seemed obvious – the question was when. If Xi could have taken Flores's money without their help she would have done so, which meant that their situation was secure up until the moment Flores's money was in the crime lord's hands.

Then it was anybody's game.

Another chime and Nat felt the subtle shift as the gravtrain slid into motion, the platform slowly sliding by outside, then more rapidly as they picked up speed. After a moment, they plunged into the darkness of a tunnel before exiting into the blinding intensity of the Caledonian afternoon. The windows tinted automatically in response as the low buildings of Stranraer whizzed past, the desert of the Burns Expanse beyond.

Showtime.

CHAPTER 33

Less than ten minutes after the gravtrain got under way, Addy already thought she'd seen enough desert to last her a lifetime. *This planet could use a little color for damn sure. I think I'm getting why Brody left.*

With a shake of her head, she rose and retrieved her bag, where she and Taylor had put together the gear she'd be needing for her part of the job. Slinging it over her shoulder, she reached down and briefly clasped Taylor's hand, earning her a somewhat bemused expression from the other woman, which morphed into understanding. Taylor patted her hand awkwardly before releasing it.

"I'd wish you luck, Adelaide," said Xi, still leaning against the bench and watching Addy like a cat toying with a mouse, "but something tells me you don't believe in it."

Addy bit back a retort about exactly where Xi could put her best wishes, anatomically speaking, and saw Taylor visibly relax at her restraint. *I guess I'm making progress.*

Instead, Addy returned a saccharine sweet smile of her own. "You're welcome to join me, but I know how you prefer others getting their hands dirty for you."

She had just enough time to see a crack run through the syndicate leader's facade before she opened the door to the compartment and stepped out into the corridor, effectively throwing down the gauntlet. If Xi was going to do anything about it, this was her opportunity.

The door slid closed behind her, leaving Addy in the silence of the corridor; for the first time since Juarez 7A, she felt like she could hear her own thoughts. Leaning back against the wall, she heaved a sigh, some of the long-held tension draining out of her.

"Just a reminder," said Xi's voice over comms, "I still have your pilot. I'm granting you the leeway to do the job, but don't try anything too clever, or the only thing you'll be getting back will be a corpse."

So much for getting all the tension out. Addy's neck muscles had once again bunched up like a too-small sweater. "Copy that," she managed through gritted teeth, then stabbed the mute button on her sleeve like she was going for Xi's eyes. *I thought we were keeping comm traffic to a minimum.*

At least she'd managed to pass Gwen's note on to Taylor. She'd glanced at the slip of flimsy in a brief private moment in the refresher before the team had headed to the station, and despite her temptation to hold onto it as tightly as possible, she'd realized it would be more useful in the commander's hands than her own.

Still, the worry for Brody felt like a hundred-pound weight on her chest, and she remained less than thrilled about taking orders from the person who'd kidnapped him. But the only chance they had of getting him back was to do the job, so she deadlifted the concern up and off and got down to work.

The train cars in between their own and the café were largely identical: a small corridor running down one side, with a row of windows looking out at the bleak scenery of the Burns Expanse. Opposite the windows were the series of doors to the compartments, ten to a car.

There were a few other passengers about and the corridor was narrow enough that they had to step to the side to let each other pass. Addy offered each a tight smile and a curt nod of greeting, which most returned in kind. The clientele for the train was varied: old and young, those dressed in expensive clothes and those wearing casual attire. She gave a surreptitious once-over to each, but if any of them were additional security for the Coire Ansic, it wasn't obvious; based on what they'd seen at the train station, there wasn't any indication that Flores's organization was aiming for subtlety.

After making her way through more than half a dozen cars, she stepped through the gangway connector and into the café car, and her breath caught. The compartment doubled as a sort of observation car, with a transparent roof that seamlessly cascaded down the sides to give the illusion that they were riding in open air. Tables, adorned with white tablecloths, lined one side, while the other featured benches that faced the windows, where you could enjoy a drink while watching the scenery speed by.

Even just a quarter hour into their journey, the place was hopping. There were a couple dozen people in the car, some seated at the tables, sipping cups of coffee. Others waited for their drinks at the counter in the far corner, or had parked themselves there on the row of stools. Elsewhere, a few more people milled around in the center of the car, gawking through the transparent roof and walls.

And the view was impressive: dunes undulated by them at speed, a sinuous snake. The desert had a stark, desolate beauty to it, devoid of any sign of life – at least from the vantage point of 500 kilometers per hour. Perhaps most impressive were the shifting colors; one who had never seen the desert might think it drab and monochrome, but the light playing off the sands cast it shades of red, orange, yellow, like being immersed in a sunset.

All of that washed over Addy, seen and forgotten in a moment as one small knot of people towards the rear of the car seized her attention.

There were five of them, and it wasn't that they were dressed the same – no matching black suits here – but that there was something of a sameness about them: the way they held themselves, the perfect creases of their shirts, their pants. The word that came to Addy's mind was "regimented."

Ex-military? Feels like it.

She made her way to the counter, behind which stood a server in an iridescent purple waistcoat and matching bowtie.

They inclined their head as Addy stepped up. "What can I get you?"

Tempted as she was to put in an order for a neat whisky – her internal clock was way out of whack after their recent travels – it was probably best that she kept her wits about her. Her eyes alit upon a gleaming silver machine behind the bar.

"Espresso, please." She'd developed a taste for the strong brew at a local café in Salaam, although it sometimes left her buzzing. Still, a little extra jolt wouldn't go amiss in her current situation.

"Of course." The attendant turned and busied themselves with the ritual of preparing the coffee, punctuated by a symphony of grinding, thumping, and hissing. It gave her an opportunity to turn her back to the bar and study the small group more closely.

Three men, two women. None obviously armed, though at least two wore jackets that could conceal a small weapon with ease. They were talking in quiet voices, too low for Addy to make out, but she could see they were carefully positioned to have eyes on every angle of the room.

Gotta be the Coire Ansic. Unless there's another security team onboard for some reason. It'd be just their luck if someone else had decided that this, of all trips, was the time to make a play for Flores's money.

The next problem was getting close enough to clone one of their sleeves for access. She'd need to be within a few inches for probably about thirty seconds, which was going to require a heck of an excuse.

"Your espresso," said the server from behind Addy and she thanked them, swiping her sleeve over the terminal to pay – along with a generous tip. "What's that, bachelor party?" she asked the server, nodding at the cluster.

The server raised their pencil-thin eyebrows, their gaze flicking to the payment terminal, then back to Addy. Their mouth quirked in amusement as they produced a towel from the rack in front of them and began industriously wiping out a glass. "Regulars," they said. "From the private car in back. Don't know their business, but they come in once a month." They held the glass up to the light, inspecting it for streaks. "They order a lot of Turkish coffee."

"Good to know," said Addy. *I guess that means they're even more caffeinated than I am.* She eyed them again as she took a sip of the espresso, which was pleasantly hot and surprisingly good: acidic without any sharp tang of bitterness. The server knew their business, that was for sure.

The taller of the group's two woman, who had short dark hair that came to her ears, held the most obvious aura of authority amongst the group. In their murmured conversations, she seemed to be issuing orders to the other four; that made her the best target for cloning the sleeve, since she was most likely to have the access that Addy needed, but also potentially the hardest to peel off from the rest of the group.

An idea struck her, and she turned back to the counter. "Actually, can I get a Turkish coffee?"

The server blinked, violet eyes shifting from the still mostly full espresso in front of Addy to the cluster of five, then shrugged. "Sure. How much sugar?"

"Uh…" Addy nodded at the group. "However they took it."

"Coming right up."

A minute later, a second cup of coffee joined the first in front of Addy. The rich aroma, earthy and just a bit sweet, drifted out of the delicate porcelain cup to her nose and her mouth started watering of its own volition. Almost a shame she wasn't going to have a chance to drink it.

Getting to her feet, she took the coffee in both hands – the better to seem less threatening – and crossed towards the group, donning what she hoped was her most guile-free smile.

"Excuse me," she said, pitching her voice up an octave to bestow a degree of innocence. It grated to her own ears, but she wasn't the intended audience. "They gave me the wrong coffee at the counter, but the server mentioned you'd ordered the same thing, and I hate for it to go to waste." She locked eyes with the tall woman, who looked about as suspicious as Addy would if a stranger appeared, offering her a drink.

"Thanks," said the woman, her expression flat. "But we're good."

"Oh, are you sure?" said Addy hopefully.

"Come on, Bala," said one of the men, a blond crewcut whose shirt was too tight for his broad shoulders. "Let's help the lady out." His look at Addy was only shy of a leer on a technicality. He started to reach for the cup, but the woman cut him off sharply.

"We're on duty, Harmon. Just in case you've forgotten."

"It's *coffee*."

The woman, Bala, didn't say anything, just kept her glare leveled at the other man until he deflated and stepped back. At a flick from her fingers, the other four dispersed around the room, leaving her alone with Addy.

For her part, Addy kept the smile plastered on her face. She'd felt the telltale haptic from her sleeve rippling against her forearm – it hadn't been enough time to clone Harmon's credentials.

"Sorry," said Bala, her eyes still scanning the rest of the room even as she talked to Addy. "Nothing personal. We're working, and it's against our policy to accept gifts."

"Oh," said Addy. "I completely understand. Must be important work, though. What do you do?"

The searching look Bala gave her was thorough. "Security," was all she said. "Now, I'm afraid you'll have to excuse me; I need to get back to it."

"Oh, of course," said Addy, ducking her head. "I'll just get out of your way." And she started to step aside, then realized that she was stepping to the same side as Bala, tried to go the other way, and ended up doing an awkward little dance as Bala moved in that direction too. "Whoops, sorry!"

Turning to one side, Addy gestured with one hand for Bala to walk by, but as she did, she trailed that hand along Bala's arm. "I don't suppose I might... see you around? Perhaps a drink when you're off-duty?"

Bala glanced down at the hand and her cheeks flushed. "Uh, I'm afraid I'm working for the duration of the trip." Delicately, she reached over and removed Addy's hand from her own, though perhaps it did linger for a moment longer than even Bala expected.

As it did, Addy caught sight of a small tattoo on the inside of the woman's wrist, and her breath caught in her throat. *Oh shit.* Quickly recovering, she blinked her eyes at Bala as though recovering from their touch and allowed her hand to be returned. "A pity," said Addy, a tad breathlessly. "Perhaps we'll meet again."

Bala drew herself up, clearing her throat. "Maybe we will." She ducked her head and moved off in the same direction that her compatriots had taken earlier, leaving Addy alone with her coffee. Absently, she took a sip. The strong, hot brew left a scorching path all the way down her throat and into her stomach, but she was hardly even aware of the taste.

With a covert glance over her shoulder, Addy just saw Bala disappearing out the connecting gangway to the next rearward car, so she turned the other way, raising her coffee in salute to the baffled server behind the counter, and headed in the opposite direction.

The connecting space between cars was empty; Addy pressed herself out of the way, near the entrance to the refresher, and checked her sleeve. The haptic had confirmed she'd been able to clone Bala's credentials, but that was now a secondary concern. She patted the hairs on her arms, which were still standing on end.

"*Fuck.*" For a second she didn't even realize she'd said it out loud, but fortunately she was still alone in the compartment. Drawing a deep breath, she toggled her comm on.

"Uh, we may have a problem. I just ran into what I'm pretty sure is a security detail for the Coire Ansic and they're not your average rent-a-goons." She'd recognized the image in the tattoo on Bala's wrist: a stylized hawk emblem, bisected by a key. "They're Imperial Fleet Security."

CHAPTER 34

The door chime of M. Habib's shop made the authentic tinkle of an antique bell, albeit digitally synthesized. It was, like much of the rest of the store – the wood paneling and elegant floor-to-ceiling mirrors – a bit of intentionally charming anachronism, perfectly suited to the kind of establishment that dealt in custom-tailored clothing.

Not that Aidan Kester spent too much time dwelling on these details. He bustled in impatiently, checking his sleeve's chronometer and talking stridently over his earbud, in defiance of the "Please, no comms" sign sitting on the counter.

"…don't care who you have to cajole, coax, or threaten, Lawson," he said. "I'm briefing the Commonwealth Executive in two hours, and I need the latest details about the cordons. Don't bother calling me back until you have it for me."

The man who greeted him was expansive, in every sense of the word. He smiled broadly at the acting director, spreading his arms in a welcoming gesture. "Good morning, sir. How may I help you today?"

Kester barely spared him a glance at first, consumed as he was by tapping away on his sleeve. "I'm here to pick up a suit that was being altered." But he looked again at the unfamiliar man, eyes taking on a suspicious cast. "Where's Monsieur Habib? He usually handles all my business personally."

"Ah, yes. I regret that he has been called away on an urgent personal matter. I'm his cousin, Mordecai." He raised a finger in the air, as if recalling something. "But he did leave me instructions specifically for you. Mr Kester, is it not?"

"Yes, that's right." The edge of annoyance hadn't totally vanished from Kester's tone, but he stifled it well enough. "I got a call – I assume my suit is ready?"

Mordecai stepped smoothly over to the counter and brought up a holoscreen. "Of course, sir. He did note that he'd made the changes you requested, though he was a little unsure about some of them, and advised you try it on before you left the shop, just to make sure you were happy with them."

Kester flicked his fingers dismissively. "I don't have the time; if I need something altered, I'll just bring it back."

Mordecai's mouth drew up in a sad frown. "I'm sorry to say that my cousin may be away for quite some time. An illness in the family. I'm not sure when he might have the time for further adjustments. In fact, I'll be joining him shortly – I stayed behind as a favor, because he expressed how important your business was. If you'd care to try it on now, I can make any final adjustments as needed." He waved a hand towards the back of the room, where several stalls of dark wood waited.

Glancing over his shoulder at the front door, Kester worried his bottom lip with his teeth, then gave a sigh of resignation. "Fine. But let's make it quick."

Mordecai gave a shallow bow, hand still outstretched. "Of course. Right this way."

With one eye on his sleeve, Kester followed the big man towards the back of the shop. Mordecai opened the middle stall door. "I've put it in here for you. Do you need any help?"

"I think I can dress myself."

"Naturally," said Mordecai, ushering him in with a hand on his back. "I'll leave you to it, then."

Kester grumbled, stepping into the stall; the door closed behind him. He was already loosening his tie before he realized he wasn't alone.

"The fu –" was all he got out before his eyes widened in recognition. "*You.*"

Kovalic sat on the bench in front of the mirror, one leg crossed over the other. "Afternoon, acting director."

Whirling, Kester pushed against the door to the stall, but it refused to budge, as though perhaps a very large man was leaning against the other side. He turned back, his expression of surprise morphing into a more habitual superciliousness. "You've made a huge mistake, Kovalic. My security detail is right outside." Raising his wrist, he spoke into his sleeve. "Typhoon Three, repeat, Typhoon Three…"

But the only sound out of the sleeve was a garbled bleat, followed by static.

Esterhaus's voice came through Kovalic's earpiece. "Clock's running. You have only a few minutes. Perhaps ten. I'll monitor the situation outside."

Even if Kester couldn't reach his security detail directly, it wouldn't be long before they started to wonder where their boss was. Best Kovalic made the most of it.

"Very short range comm jammer," said Kovalic, holding up a small fob on which a red light blinked. "It's really only good within about ten feet, but…" He looked around at the small confines of the stall.

The color had begun to drain from Aidan Kester's face and he put his back against the door, trying to inject a note of bravado. "What do you want?"

"Believe it or not, I just want to talk."

Kester sniffed. "I don't have anything to say to a *traitor*."

One of Kovalic's eyebrows rose. "You seem awfully convinced of our guilt. I'd like to know why."

"I've seen the evidence."

"So you've said. What I'd like to know is where that evidence came from."

"You can't seriously expect me to tell you."

Kovalic shrugged. "You said it would all come out at the trial anyway. What's the harm of a sneak peek?"

"I… you… that is, it's simply… *not done*," he sputtered.

"Oh, please," said Kovalic. His patience with the man was wearing thin. "Let's not pretend you haven't bent – or even broken – the rules when it was convenient for you. You turned one of my own team into your spy. You maneuvered your way into that office you're sitting in now by blackmail and extortion."

Kester jabbed a finger in Kovalic's direction, his fear momentarily overridden by something even more deeply ingrained – pride. "I will not stand here and be insulted by someone who betrayed his own government."

"By all means, then, let's step outside," said Kovalic. "I'm happy to continue this conversation with another party present. Inspector Laurent, perhaps. I'm sure he'd be interested to know how you used information provided by the Illyrican Empire to build your so-called case against us."

A sudden bewilderment overtook the acting director. "What the hell are you talking about?"

Kovalic pressed his thumb and forefinger to his temples. "I really can't decide, Aidan. Are you an extremely competent double agent, or just a useful idiot blinded by your ambition?"

Kester opened his mouth to protest, and then seemed to sense the lack of good options. After a moment, he settled on obstinacy as a response, crossing his arms over his chest. "You're just turning your own guilt back on me."

Letting out his sharply indrawn breath in a deep sigh, Kovalic rubbed his forehead. "We're going round and round here – and maybe that's exactly what the Illyricans want. Look, cards on the table. I assume the evidence you have is a series of bank transactions from General Adaj's accounts on Bayern to a shell corporation, which then turned around and paid that money out to the Novan Liberation Front?"

Kester's eyes narrowed. "You're just incriminating yourself further, Kovalic. That information was highly confidential, and far beyond any clearances you might have – I ensured that myself. This just confirms you were in on it."

"No," said Kovalic patiently. "I know because the same evidence was provided to *me*, with the intent of calling the general's loyalty into question. And I have reason to believe that those transactions were concocted by the Imperial Intelligence Service for that explicit purpose."

"An IIS plot? Really?" said Kester, his voice shot through with skepticism. "That's the best you can do?"

"Think about it," said Kovalic. "You're spending all your time and energy chasing us. And to what end? If you catch us, we get court-martialed. Even if your evidence isn't good enough to merit conviction, it's going to be hard for us to erase the blemish of suspicion. The general will certainly not maintain his position, and I will be *lucky* if I get shipped off to a desk job to serve out the rest of my career."

"I don't see the problem."

Kovalic rolled his eyes. "Look beyond your own petty power games, Kester. Whatever problems you might have with the general or me, the Special Projects Team has been a valuable operational asset. You've seen the reports, you know what we've managed to accomplish. These accusations have effectively neutralized it. Ask yourself: who stands to benefit most from that?" He left it unsaid, but he could see the point strike its mark.

"Moreover," Kovalic continued, gaining steam, "the general has proved his worth when it comes to understanding and countering the Imperium. You can't deny that there are those on the other side who would be all too happy to see him lose any influence he might have."

For the first time, there was a crack running through the other man's cocksure facade. "So your contention is, what, that all of this is an IIS disinformation campaign, targeting you and Adaj?"

Kovalic spread his hands, as if presenting facts in evidence.

"Security is getting restless," said Esterhaus over the comm. "Wrap it up."

"Fine," said Kester, after a moment. "Let's say there's a chance that you're telling the truth here. The right thing for you to do is still to turn yourself in. Running just makes you look guilty."

And so they came to the crux of the matter. Kovalic's lips thinned. Kester wasn't totally wrong; this problem was far more difficult to solve from outside.

But Kovalic found himself suddenly thinking of Alys Costa, the leader of the Novan Liberation Front – and a former Commonwealth operative herself. It had been just a few days since Kovalic had been making this very argument to her. And what had Costa said when Kovalic urged her to turn herself in?

"Are you really that naive? You think they'd let me get that far? That I'd even survive to a trial? Or, even if I did, that anything *would change?"*

In the moment, it had seemed like paranoid raving, an attempt to justify the actions that Costa had already intended to carry out.

And yet, here they were.

"I can't," said Kovalic, shaking his head. "Not without knowing where your evidence came from. I believe the Illyricans planted it, knowing it would cross your desk. But that means there's a mole somewhere in the Commonwealth intelligence community."

To Kester's credit, he didn't immediately reject the idea; Kovalic could see him following the logic. Not for the first time, Kovalic reminded himself that Kester really wasn't stupid; in the space of just a few years the man had risen to chief of the Commonwealth's largest intelligence agency. His methods might differ from Kovalic's, but that was all the more reason not to underestimate him – if anything, it made him more dangerous.

"I don't remember the full details," said Kester finally. "I review dozens of reports every day. But…" And here he sucked in his breath as though about to dive underwater. "I can pull it and find out."

"Fair enough," said Kovalic. "Look, I'm not going to ask if we can trust each other – I know the answer to that. But," he raised a hand to forestall Kester's own snort, "I do trust that neither one of us wants to let the Imperium dictate the rules of the game. Get the report and we'll look at it together. Two o'clock, Udo Park, by the Rings."

"Fine," said Kester, his tone grudging. He jabbed a finger in Kovalic's direction. "But if you're wrong about this, you – and Adaj – need to turn yourself in."

Esterhaus's voice returned in Kovalic's ear. "His security's on its way in. Time's up."

Kovalic gave Kester a grim nod. Part of him hoped he was wrong; a mole with that kind of access could have already caused more damage than they even knew about. But his gut told him he wasn't. "Reasonable enough."

"I can't call off the Bureau – Laurent would get suspicious," said Kester. He gave a reluctant sigh, as if the weight of the world were pressing down on him. "But I suppose I don't have to mention this conversation, either."

"Can't ask for more than that." Kovalic grabbed a garment bag from the hook behind him and tossed it to Kester in one smooth motion.

Startled, the acting director caught it, stumbling back against the door, even as Kovalic dropped and swung himself under the partition wall that didn't quite reach the floor.

He pushed his way out through the neighboring stall's door, catching the eye of Yevgeniy Esterhaus, who was still leaning against the door to the other dressing room. The ex-IIS agent raised an eyebrow. "Get what you need?"

"Close enough," said Kovalic. "Let's go."

Without looking back, the two of them walked through the shop's rear door, into the back room.

Rance was sitting across a workbench from a small man with a neat gray beard wearing a sweater vest over a button-down shirt. A small, untouched cup of coffee sat on the table in front of him. He was kneading his thighs, bunching the fabric of his trousers and then releasing it in what seemed to be an unconscious gesture.

"Thank you for the use of your store, Monsieur Habib," said Kovalic. "I'm sorry about the circumstances."

"Uh, it was... no trouble at all," said the man, clearly lying through his teeth, but happy enough to see them go.

"Trust me when I say you're better off not mentioning this. It's just going to raise a lot of questions you don't want to answer." Kovalic jerked his head at Rance and the three of them made their way to the shop's back door, which led out into an alley behind the building. They kept walking towards the other side of the block, putting as much distance between them and the tailor's as possible.

"So," Rance asked. "What did Kester say?"

"Meet's set. He'll bring the original report."

"And what if *he* is the mole?"

If he was, then they had played directly into his hands, and Kovalic would give him a standing ovation even as the knife plunged into his back. But did it matter? The Commonwealth was already spending a lot of time and energy trying to track them down – if Kester was the mole, his best play would be to just keep Kovalic spinning his wheels. Isabella's whole plan could very well be about nothing more than keeping the Commonwealth distracted with her left hand while her right hand was busy with her real goal.

But Kovalic hadn't gotten this far in this line of work without being able to trust his gut, and his gut said that Kester – slippery as he was – wasn't an Illyrican operative. No, for that, you'd want somebody you didn't suspect, somebody you trusted without question, but who wouldn't raise an eyebrow. Kester would be just too damn convenient.

Or so he hoped. If not… he took a deep breath. "If Kester is the mole, then we'll deal with him. One way or another."

CHAPTER 35

Sayers's words echoed in Nat's head, but they hadn't quite sunk in. "Say again?"

"Imperial Fleet Security," the specialist repeated. "I don't know if they're ex-military or moonlighting or what, but I recognized the tattoo on one of their wrists."

Nat found herself shooting a surprised look at the only other person in the compartment but, to her credit, Ofeibia Xi looked equally nonplussed.

"Did you know about this?" Nat asked.

Xi tapped one slender finger thoughtfully against her lips. "No, though it does fill in some gaps. Apparently Flores's connection to the princess came with some perks. Illyrican backing would definitely help explain the speed of his rise."

Nat's mind spun through the logic, but it checked out. From what Xi had said, Flores had capitalized on the collapse of the Black Watch, slipping into the vacuum left behind. But the Watch were Caledonian nationalists, dedicated to shaking off the Illyrican rule of their homeworld.

The Coire Ansic, it seemed, had taken a more... flexible approach.

The real question, then, was what the Imperium was getting out of this arrangement. Why lend armed security to a criminal organization that already had its own surfeit of muscle? Illyrican Fleet Security wasn't even technically under IIS's purview. Had the princess called in some favors? Or did she, as not only head of the Imperium's intelligence apparatus but also a member of its royal family, have even more clout than Nat – or most of the Commonwealth – realized?

Suddenly, getting ahold of all the surveillance Xi had on Isabella was quickly becoming the highest priority.

"This does explain some things," Gwen said slowly over the comms. "I've wondered why local law enforcement hasn't been able to make any significant inroads into the Coire Ansic. If the crims are feeding them information, that would make sense."

Xi reached up and touched her own earpiece. "This is all *most* interesting, but you're here to take Roche Flores's money. I don't really care who his security is."

To a certain extent, Xi was right: security was security, whether they were private goons or Imperial soldiers. Granted, they were a higher caliber of protection than expected, but the fundamentals of the plan were still solid.

Not that Nat liked it. But the sooner this job was over, the sooner she wouldn't have to worry about Ofeibia Xi again. Her lips pressed into a thin line. "We proceed as planned," she said over comms. "Marking Checkpoint Alpha."

A chorus of double-click acknowledgements flitted over the channel, and then radio silence.

"If anything, this ought to make it all the more satisfying for you, major," said Xi, leaning back against the bench, her arms draped across the top. A smile tugged at her mouth. "Getting one over on the Illyricans would be a nice bonus."

That wasn't worth a response and Nat didn't deign to give it one. Instead, she reached up to the luggage rack and pulled down the bag containing the gear Gwen had acquired for her. Out came a portable terminal and interface cable.

She headed for the compartment's door, feeling Xi's gaze dog her every step. But the syndicate boss didn't say anything as Nat slipped out of the compartment.

In the corridor, with the door closed firmly behind her, she couldn't stop her sigh of relief from escaping. Having Xi looking over their shoulders every step of the way had proved not just complicated but downright irritating. She hadn't even had a second to look at the slip of paper from Sayers's brush pass; she plucked it from the inside of the collar of her shirt, where she'd hidden it.

It was a short note, but her eyebrows went up as she read it, and a smile threatened to break out despite all her frustrations. However Sayers had pulled this one off, it might be exactly what they needed.

Bringing up the train schedule on her sleeve, she watched the blinking dot that represented their progress along the route; still about an hour to go before they hit their target, which meant she had plenty of time for her next part in this job.

When she slipped into the third car forward from their position, though, she spotted a pair of people lounging near the far end, apparently engaged in a perfectly normal conversation. But the way both of their eyes tracked her as she entered, not to mention the set of their shoulders and their feet, told her everything she needed to know.

More security.

Nat didn't slow her pace, continuing forward as any average passengers would. She saw one of them spare a curious glance at the terminal she carried under one arm, but neither of them made an immediate move to intercept her. Still, she'd have to pass by them to get to the next car.

No conflict. Not yet. That would tip her hand and potentially jeopardize the whole operation. So instead, she'd just keep the polite smile on her face and walk on by without any problems whatsoever.

That was the plan, anyway.

When she reached them, she murmured "excuse me" as she squeezed by and felt their eyes rake her, looking for anything suspicious or out of the ordinary. But neither made a move to stop her, and she was almost through the passageway into the next car when one of their voices called out from behind her.

"Hey, wait…"

She forced herself not to freeze, not to hesitate, just to glance back over her shoulder with a quizzical look on her face.

One of them – a slender man with a hawk nose and heavy brows – was holding out a hand in which was coiled the interface cable Nat had been holding. "I think you dropped this."

Nat's heart thumped in her chest, but there was nothing to do but smile and hold out her hand. "Oh! Thanks," she said, trying to inject a note of brightness, even with her dead certainty that she hadn't been clumsy enough to drop a piece of her equipment. Had they made her? Her mind flicked through anything that might have given her away but came up empty.

The man grinned. "No problem," he said. "But if you'd like to thank me, I'd take a cup of coffee from the café car."

Oh good, he thought he was cute. Her smile was frozen in place, much as she'd have preferred to give him an earful.

His partner, the one who'd seemed curious about the terminal in the first place, rolled their eyes, and nudged them. "On duty," they muttered.

"Can't hurt to ask!" protested the first.

Just what she needed: a come-on from Flores's security. "Sorry," she said, dangling the cable from one hand. "Work calls! Maybe another time." Any hopes she'd had of remaining inconspicuous had just gone out the window, so her only remaining option was to make herself scarce.

The man's partner took him by the shoulder and dragged him away, casting Nat an apologetic look, but she didn't stick around; she was down the corridor and into the next car, not relaxing until the connecting door slid closed behind her.

Too close.

There was no security – no passengers, even – in the corridors of the next two cars, which brought her to the locked door leading to the train's operations center.

Not a lot of cover, she noted, looking around. Fortunately, the door was slightly obscured because the corridor jogged to the right here, around the row of compartments. Her best defense was that nobody else was likely to come this way.

Pressing herself out of the line of sight for any passengers coming and going from the compartments, she pulled out the multitool she'd brought, then ran her hands around the doorframe until she found the access panel. It only took a few moments to unscrew it and locate the interface port for the door. Jacking in her terminal, she fired up the bypass program she'd retrieved from one of her dead drops on the nets and, after a few seconds, the door seal released.

The operations car beyond was cold and dark, illuminated only by a few blinking lights on control panels in standby mode. Equipment hummed around her, and she flipped on the lantern feature of her sleeve, holding up her hand to peer around.

A handful of consoles lined the walls of the windowless car, monitoring a variety of the train's onboard systems: propulsion, climate controls, repulsors, communications, and so on. At the far end was another door that led to the operator compartment at the front of the train. While the vehicle itself was automated, a person could take manual control from the cockpit, if necessary.

Granted, if that happened, it was generally because something had gone *very* wrong.

Nat stepped up to the climate control console and plugged in the interface cable for her terminal. Her cracking programs made short work of the authentication, and the console blinked to life, showing off the current heating, cooling, air purification, water, and other relevant systems as lines of blue and red pulsing along a schematic of the train.

She activated the comm channel. "Passing Checkpoint Bravo."

Once again, there were double-clicks of acknowledgement from the rest of the team.

Isolating the Coire Ansic's car was simple enough; she tapped on its representation on the screen and selected the environmental controls. From there, it ought to be a simple enough matter to disable the carbon dioxide scrubbing, making for some very sleepy Coire Ansic goons.

ACCESS DENIED blinked in large red letters across the screen.

Frowning, Nat's fingers danced over the keyboard, circumventing the authorization request, but even once she bypassed it, there was still an error being thrown. "Environmental controls unavailable?" she muttered aloud. "Why the – oh, shit." She toggled her comm. "We've got a problem: there's no remote access to the Coire Ansic's car from the control center."

"I believe you said *everything* would be accessible from there," came Ofeibia Xi's voice, lined with something dangerous.

Nat gritted her teeth. Given that the syndicate boss had coopted them at gunpoint, it was hard to imagine she could get more irritated with the woman, but here they were.

"I hate to disabuse you of the notion that I'm infallible," said Nat. "But it looks like they've physically disconnected it from central control, along with most of the other critical systems." Xi had said that Flores was paranoid, but it was only now sinking in just *how* cautious the man was. He must have paid a pretty penny in bribes to have his car cut off from the train's systems – no doubt it violated any number of safety regulations.

Or perhaps that was where his Illyrican contacts had come in handy? The gravtrain was nominally under the authority of the local government, but no doubt a high-level Imperial could throw some influence around. Especially if they had some sort of vested interest.

"So now what?" said Sayers.

Nat's fingers drummed on the console. "We're shifting to contingencies. Sergeant, Gwen, head to the Coire Ansic's car immediately. I still need to establish the remote uplink to trigger the track switch. I'll join you once I'm done."

There were muted acknowledgements from Tapper and Gwen, but to Nat's surprise, the only objection to the plan came from an unexpected source.

"That puts almost the entire train between us," Sayers pointed out. "And who knows how much security. We can't leave you up there alone. We've already left *one person* on their own." The emphasis made it clear who she meant, but there was something else beneath it – almost like an injunction sent in Nat's direction.

"Your priority is to get the job done, Adelaide," said Xi. "Do what the major says."

"I appreciate the concern, specialist," said Nat more gently. "But I'll be fine."

Sayers grumbled to herself, and Nat thought she caught the word "stubborn" through the comm static, but elected to ignore it. There were far bigger problems to deal with.

For example, this next bit, which the specialist was *really* not going to like.

She took a deep breath. "Sayers, I need you to get eyes on the money. It's the priority objective. The next checkpoint's coming up and at least one of us needs to be back there to uncouple the cars. We miss that window, and this whole job goes up in smoke." There wasn't a sound from Xi but Nat could picture her listening, waiting like a coiled serpent to strike. As long as they got the money, the syndicate boss would be happy. The rest of them could always regroup once the train reached Stranraer.

Assuming Xi didn't use the opportunity to deal with them once and for all. But Nat couldn't worry about that right now. She drove the point home. "That's an order, specialist. There's an overhead hatch in the connecting compartment between the café car and the Coire Ansic; I'm unlocking it from here." Nat brought up the car schematic again and tapped a sequence of controls.

There was silence for a moment, then Sayers came back on the line. "I'm not going to lie: I was *really* hoping it wasn't going to come to this. You sure I can't just sweet talk my way through all those goons in between?"

Nat assumed that by "sweet talk" Sayers meant "beat the crap out of", but she didn't give the other woman time to elaborate. "Your kit should have all the gear you'll need."

"Yeah? I hope it has a defibrillator, because I'm going to have a fucking heart attack."

This was exactly the kind of plan that Nat, as the team's executive officer, would normally be trying to poke holes in, to make sure that they'd thought it all through. But now she was the one in charge, they were running out of time, and there wasn't anybody else to fill that role. So what seemed like it might be lunacy was actually pretty plausible.

Maybe that ought to have worried her more.

"Get moving. And Sayers?"

"Yeah?

"See you on the other side."

CHAPTER 36

Addy stared, dubiously, at her bag. *Everything you need,* Taylor had said. Somehow she doubted that, unless it also had a few concussion grenades and a full suit of body armor.

As if it were a dangerous animal she was attempting to pet, Addy opened the bag and surveyed the contents. Ballistic safety goggles, a breather mask, a pair of heavy gloves, and a cowl of abrasion-resistant fabric with a small control patch.

Peeling off her jacket left her in the snug dark purple jumpsuit she'd worn underneath, tight against her skin, and made from the same material as the cowl. *Can't have clothing flapping around at several hundred kilometers per hour.* She grabbed the small pocket breather mask from her bag and sealed it to her nose and mouth. It would filter out most of the dust and sand swirling around, even if its filters weren't really rated for long-term use.

Not like I want to hang out up top anyway.

With the cowl affixed onto the seals at the collar of her jumpsuit, breathing mask on, and the goggles and gloves in place, not a square millimeter of her would be exposed to the elements. *Which is good because I don't particularly want my skin to be sandblasted clean off.* Her breath came loud in her own head, and she could feel the sweat starting to bead on her forehead.

She slapped the control patch on the back of her forearm and then touched the activation control.

The fine hairs on her body tingled as the electrostatic current ran through the material of the jumpsuit and cowl and what had up until a moment ago been a flexible, pliable material, now hardened into an armored shell that would withstand anything short of a shotgun blast at point-blank range.

I don't know how the hell Gwen found this – especially in my size – but I owe her a drink. Actually, make that a whole bottle.

Embedded in the wall, a series of grooves formed an access ladder. At the top was a heavy door with a locking wheel and an electronic pad which, as she watched, blinked from red to green. Across the hatch, in large red stenciled letters, a sign admonished EMERGENCY USE ONLY.

I'm really going to do this, huh. She swallowed and wished she could wipe her sweaty palms against her trousers, but she'd already slid them into the gloves. As best she could with the bulky hand wear, she climbed upward. The train car was only maybe three meters tall, so it wasn't like it was an arduous ascent. There was a vertically mounted grab bar near the ladder's top which she gripped with one hand while turning the locking lever with the other.

It gave slowly, hissing as the seal was broken. With the lock undone, she reached over and hit the open control on the access panel.

Air roared in through the opening as the hatch lowered and retracted out of the way, and a cloud of sand and dust whipped in at speeds that nearly yanked Addy from her perch on the ladder. She clung to the grab bar with both hands, trying to grip the ladder's slots with her toes. The sound was deafening, so she reached over to her sleeve and activated her earbud's noise-canceling capabilities. A curtain of silence descended, though she could still feel the air buffeting her.

With a deep lungful of air enabled by the breather, she climbed up towards the access hatch and poked her head out.

The force of the wind nearly lifted her out of the train car, and she felt her neck wrench to compensate. The scenery sped by at a tremendous rate and particulates ricocheted off her goggles and the suit like being peppered with gunfire from tiny elves.

This is insane. This is an insane plan. But the good news about insane plans, as Brody was fond of pointing out, was that nobody ever saw them coming.

There was no safety harness up top, because nobody was supposed to be going out there while the train was in motion.

But the team had planned for this contingency, and having the right gear was the better part of valor. Technically, the gloves Addy had donned were designed for use in the vacuum of space, not on top of a moving train, but oh well, close enough.

Most importantly they may just keep me from killing myself.

Carefully, she maneuvered herself out of the hatch, pressing her chest flat to the car's roof and crawling like a baby. The wind shook her like a piece of flimsy, and she felt it start to tug her towards the vortex created by the train's speed. Even through her earbuds' sound dampening, a persistent whir buzzed in her ears as the train screamed through the landscape.

Raising her right hand, she tapped her middle finger and thumb together twice in rapid succession and a sudden warmth rushed through the glove; with a snap, it adhered to the train's roof like it had been glued. A series of lights on the back winked green, indicating that the gravglove's inverse repulsors were online; as she watched, the leftmost turned amber, reflecting the remaining charge. Without the massive battery pack of a spacesuit behind it, the repulsors would burn through their onboard power in a hurry.

So I better get moving. She powered up the second glove and began her long crawl along the top of the train car.

Even calling it a crawl was being generous: she'd seen babies move faster. Wind whipped around her, trying to shove her from behind, but she kept her attention on the train beneath her, making each movement slow and steady while fighting the urge to get the hell off this thing as fast as possible.

That's a quick way to end up part of the landscape. Her breathing came hot and heavy in her mask and she wondered whether, in that eventuality, anybody would even find her body amongst the vast scrub and sands of the desert wastes. Swallowing down her fear, she forced herself to focus on the train car in front of her.

The swirling sand and dust played havoc with her comms; she spared her sleeve a glance at one point and saw the red slashed circle indicating a lack of signal. If Taylor or any of the rest of the team was trying to reach her, she'd have no idea. Not that there was anything she could do about it from up here anyway. Her job was getting down into the next car – everything else was window-dressing.

The muscles in her arms and legs started to strain from the exertion as she continued working her way across, and she tried to concentrate on breathing slowly and regularly, even as her heart pounded against the metal of the train's roof. A few times she had to navigate around bumps and bulges of machinery, and each time it took more than a minute for her to navigate the turns, making sure that she wasn't going to slip off.

The bank caught her by surprise. It was gradual at first, the train starting to lean to one side as it took a long curve; she felt herself start to slide toward the right edge, and for a moment thought she'd just been caught by a particularly strong crosswind.

Then, suddenly, the whole train keeled over maybe ten degrees, and her feet scrabbled against the top of a car that was no longer parallel with the ground. Her legs swung towards the inside edge of the turn and then were violently sucked over by the winds, flailing towards the rear of the train; her arms, anchored by the gravgloves, screamed in protest, the only things keeping her from being sucked into the train's vortex.

Shit!

The indicator lights on the gloves blinked furiously amber as the repulsors ramped up to maximum adhesion. Addy desperately worked her core muscles, trying to bring her legs back to the train, but the wind flapped them around like fish on the line.

And then the tilt was over, almost as fast as it had begun, and her legs swung down and smacked into the side of the car; her stomach hit the edge, knocking the wind out of her, and she wheezed into the breath mask as she clutched desperately to the roof. Kicking her feet, she braced them against the side of the train and scrambled back up.

The whooshing sound of Addy's breath rang in her ears. It took her a solid thirty seconds to quiet her heartbeat from "force itself right out of her chest" back down to "just crawling across a speeding train like it's a normal day".

The indicators on her gloves had stopped blinking, but half of them were solidly glowing amber now; the added strain had depleted the power far faster than she'd hoped.

Christ, I hope nobody was looking out the window. Any of the Coire Ansic goons below who'd chosen that moment to glance outside would probably have seen Addy's feet kicking wildly from above. Though none of them would probably be in a hurry to volunteer going topside.

Still, it meant she might have trouble waiting for her when she came back through the access hatch. *What's the alternative? Do I live up here now?*

The second half of the trip was, at least, uneventful by comparison, without any further turns to risk throwing her off balance. She was so intent on not falling off that she almost went right by the access hatch.

This one was secured only with a keypad lock and it already blazed green, indicating that Taylor had released it remotely.

Addy hesitated before touching the control. There was a non-zero chance that she'd be welcomed with open arms bearing an assortment of weaponry. *I guess I'll deal with that shitshow when I come to it.*

Taking a breath, she reached out and popped the hatch.

But the compartment beneath proved, to her relief, empty. Addy dropped down into the blissfully less windy space and slapped the control to close the hatch behind her.

The blessed silence was deafening after the roar outside and she peeled off her breath mask, sucking in a lungful of fresh – by comparison anyway – air. Both the mask and her goggles were streaked with dirt and sand, and when she lifted a hand to wipe the sweat from her brow, it came away a dark, gritty brown.

The compartment was essentially identical to the one from which she'd gone topside. Addy glanced back at the door leading into the Coire Ansic's private coach. This connecting space was still technically part of that car, so she'd have to head further to the rear to find the uncoupling controls. On the opposite side of the compartment, another door led to the storage car that had sent them on this whole job to begin with.

Addy toggled her comm. "Checkpoint Charlie."

There was a double-click of acknowledgment. A moment later, the panel next to the car door flickered green as Taylor worked her magic and the door slid aside.

The storage car was dark, but rows of lights flicked on as Addy stepped in, illuminating several pallets stacked high with rugged cases of black plastic.

Addy let out a low whistle. *Are all those full of cash?* Whatever business the Coire Ansic was engaged in, it had clearly proved extremely profitable. No wonder Xi wanted to take them down a peg – if they were raking this in just from doing business on a single planet, there was no doubt they could mount a decent opposition for Xi's organization if they decided to expand.

Or, in other words, this galaxy isn't big enough for the both of them.

She crossed to one of the pallets and flipped up the latches on the top box. Best to verify everything before calling it in; it'd be pretty embarrassing if this turned out to just be some sort of decoy car.

Lifting the lid, her breath caught as she saw rows of carefully slotted-in currency chips. And that was just the top tray – she lifted it up and did a quick appraisal. There was room in the case for a half dozen of these, easy.

She pulled one out to check the denomination and did an instant double take. *What the fuck?* Just to make sure she wasn't seeing things, she set the top tray aside and picked a couple more chips at random. Then she arbitrarily chose another case and checked it too.

Swallowing, she toggled her comm. "We've hit jackpot," she said slowly.

"Copy," came back Taylor's clipped tones. "Let's move to –"

"There's just one thing," said Addy, her mouth dry. "It's not Illyrican marks."

There was a pause on the line, and then Taylor's voice returned, more sharply. "What are you saying?"

Addy looked at the credit chip in her hand, stamped with a tiny seal showing a series of intersecting ovals around a four-pointed star. "There must be a half a billion in here... and it's all in Commonwealth credits."

CHAPTER 37

The general was sitting out on the safe house's balcony when Kovalic, Rance, and Yevgeniy returned. He beckoned to Kovalic with one gnarled hand as the others dispersed to their own corners: Rance to the kitchen bar to consult her tablet, and Yevgeniy to the couch where he sat down heavily muttering something about being too old for fieldwork.

The noontime Novan sun beat down on the balcony, but it had been mitigated by an automated awning that had deployed, leaving them with only a cool breeze. Below, Kovalic could hear the whir of traffic, interrupted by the occasional chirping of birds. Drones zipped by overhead, delivering packages or capturing footage for news reports. All in all, a normal day on Nova for everybody who hadn't been accused of treason. Strange that everything else out there could just proceed as usual while Kovalic's world had ground to a stop like an old clock needing to be wound.

"How did it go?" asked the general.

"Well enough," said Kovalic. "Meet's set for two o'clock. At that point...well, we won't be in suspense anymore."

Stroking his beard, the general nodded in thought. "I would hope so." After a moment, he let out a sigh. "Simon, I don't believe I had the presence of mind to say it before, but..." his blue eyes, paler than the sky, fixed on Kovalic, "...I want to apologize. For everything that led to this." One hand waved to encompass their surroundings. "I offer no excuse other than to say that hubris got the best of me. I only wish it hadn't dragged you all down with it. However this plays out, I wanted to be sure that I had a chance to express that before... the next part."

Kovalic stiffened. He wasn't ready to have this conversation – not now, while they were still in the middle of everything. There were too many things to say, too many thoughts for him to process and organize, too many questions bubbling to the surface: LOOKING GLASS, the codename Page had first mentioned nine months ago on Bayern, still lingered in his brain. What was it? Why was the general attached to a military R&D project? To what end?

He swallowed the question down, but the general's overture wasn't the type of sentiment that one could leave hanging. "Thank you, sir," was the best he could manage.

The general nodded to himself, as though considering the matter settled, and Kovalic shoved everything he was feeling down into a strongbox and locked it shut. Healthy? Probably not. But it was something that operators got good at. Ignore and override. There'd be time down the road to reconcile all debts.

Right now, though, there were bigger matters to attend to.

"Regardless of whether or not Kester is the mole," said Kovalic, "I don't expect him to play fair with this meet. I'll need Rance on the perimeter looking for Bureau agents and snipers. Best case scenario, he'll try to take us in. Worst case, he'll just be looking to take us out – especially if it's covering his own ass."

The general raised an eyebrow. "And even with all of that, you still want to go ahead with it?"

"We need to see that report if we're going to have any chance of figuring out where it came from – and if we're going to clear our own names. It's the only evidence we can trace back to the mole. If there's any chance Kester's on the level, we need to take it."

"Still, it's risky," said the general.

"Yevgeniy's scouted a location from which he can monitor the meet," said Kovalic. "Full video and audio. It should provide some insurance – assuming we can trust him." Kovalic hadn't missed that Yevgeniy's perch also offered easy means to slip away should things go south.

The general let out a rueful chuckle. "If we can't, then we're the proverbial lobsters in the pot. We're already dead, we just don't know it yet." He cast a wistful eye through the window, back into the apartment. "I do probably owe him an apology before this is all over. I have not always treated him as one should treat their… friends." The last word didn't come easily, Kovalic could tell; to be fair, there weren't very many people left in the old man's life who fit the definition.

All the more reason not to squander the ones he had left.

Clearing his throat, the general focused back on Kovalic and gave a tight smile, banishing that topic for another place and time. "You have escape routes mapped out?"

"Four prepped," said Kovalic. "I chose Udo Park for a reason: it's public, and too wide open to lock down effectively. And at the height of the day we'll have excellent visibility."

"That cuts both ways," said the general. "It also leaves you exposed with nowhere to hide."

Kovalic gave a wan smile. "Let's hope that by the time this is all over, none of us need to hide."

With a thoughtful *hm*, the general's gaze drifted across the glass patio doors behind them, taking in the interior of the safe house. "I've been wondering," he said, after a moment, "if we've been coming at this from the wrong direction."

"How so?"

"We've been so focused on Kester that I worry we haven't done our due diligence on alternative possibilities."

"Oh?" said Kovalic. He followed the general's eyes through the windows to where Rance was still studying her tablet. "What are you getting at?"

"I just keep turning over in my head who would have access to operational details of SPT missions. Kester, certainly, but also the Commonwealth Executive, a few high ranking civil servants, and, in my office, Rance. If it were me, looking to place a mole in the Commonwealth – something that I definitely spent time considering in the past – then, yes, someone as high ranking as Kester would be a coup. But it's also very risky. There are options that would be... less exposed but would still get access to much of the same material."

Kovalic cocked his head to one side.

"I've been thinking, more broadly speaking about Isabella's strategy. She has a number of tools in her drawer," the general continued, his gaze unwavering, "but I think we can both agree that her weapons of choice are subtlety and misdirection. The fine art of making us look one way when we should be looking somewhere else entirely. It's worked to her advantage so far, but perhaps we can turn her own tactics back upon her." His eyes finally slid back to Kovalic, the skin around them crinkling into fine lines. "All of this is to say, I have a plan, and it *starts* with flushing out Isabella's mole. But it is… somewhat involved, and I'll need your help to put it into play. The timing is most critical."

Not for the first time, Kovalic found himself wondering what exactly went on behind those icy eyes. The general's mind worked unlike any other he'd encountered in his life; from the outside, it seemed like a terrifying funhouse of paranoia and obtuse angles in which Kovalic had no desire to spend more time than necessary.

But sometimes – especially in the life that they lived – it was exactly the kind of tool one needed to get the job done. He took a deep breath. "What exactly did you have in mind?"

The smile that crossed the general's face had an ironic sadness to it. "I'm afraid I must ask you to do something very difficult, given everything we've been through in the last few days.

"I'm going to need you to trust me."

Kovalic slid the patio door closed behind him, cutting off the noise from the city as sharply as though he'd switched it off. He was so lost in thought that he missed the first inquiry from Rance.

"Sorry, what?"

The yeoman smiled at him, tilting her chestnut head to one side. "Just asking if everything's all right."

"I think so," said Kovalic slowly. "Just working through some things." He had to admit, the general's idea had merits, and the more he turned it over in his mind, the more things seemed to click into place. But trust... trust was still in short supply.

"I guess I'd better go check on him," said Rance, getting to her feet. "I'm not sure he had any breakfast, and honestly, he'll forget to eat unless there's a giant holoscreen floating in front of his face reminding him."

"Actually, he asked to speak to Yevgeniy." Kovalic nodded to the former Illyrican spy, who appeared to have gone from sitting on the couch to napping on the couch.

Or perhaps not. The man's eye cracked open and he let out a sigh. "What does the old coot want to harangue me about now?" He levered himself up, an exercise accompanied by a score of grunts and popping joints, and shuffled over to the balcony door.

Rance's brow furrowed in thought as she watched him go, but she shrugged. "I guess breakfast can wait." She cocked her head as Kovalic made for the apartment's door. "Where are you headed?"

"I just need to step out for a moment. A personal matter to take care of."

"Got it," said Rance. She glanced down at her sleeve. "I'm going to head out shortly. The meet's in two hours and I'd like to start my recon sweep early, just to set a baseline."

Kovalic nodded. "Agreed. I'll see you there."

"Hopefully not," said Rance. "Because if you can see me, so can Kester's people."

With a snort, Kovalic conceded the point. "Fair enough."

He opened the door to the apartment and then paused, looking back at Rance. "Keep your head on a swivel, yeoman."

She tipped him an informal salute. "Best of luck, major."

"Yeah, I think we'd like luck on our side today." And with that, he shut the door behind him and took the stairs down and exited into the same alley that he'd used last night.

With the door propped open behind him so it wouldn't lock, Kovalic leaned against a wall and pressed his hands against his face. He was about to violate several operational protocols on the basis of a hunch. Then again, not the first time he'd prioritized a feeling over cold, hard facts.

Might be the last, though.

Letting out a breath, he raised his sleeve and initiated the same connection as the previous evening, waiting as his call was routed through the catalog of proxies and encrypted connections.

After a moment, the familiar deep voice answered. "Laurent."

"Afternoon, inspector."

There was the briefest of pauses and Kovalic imagined him once again starting the trace. By all rights, he should have made the call somewhere else – using the same location twice only made the job easier for the Bureau's boffins. But at least this conversation should be short.

"Twice in as many days," said Laurent easily, as though there had been no hesitation whatsoever. "To what do I own the pleasure, Kovalic?"

"I'm calling to offer you a deal."

"Really? Maybe I should hit the casino after work, because I guess it's my lucky day. What are you offering?"

"I'm offering you the collar of a lifetime. There's an Illyrican mole embedded in the Commonwealth's intelligence community."

Another pause, but this time Kovalic could hear the gears grinding in the inspector's head.

"Is there?" Laurent said finally. His voice was carefully neutral. "And you have proof of this?"

"No."

"Of course not." He sighed. "Kovalic, I don't deal in conspiracy theories."

"I've got something better. I've got the mole."

Laurent's voice sharpened. "You've what?"

"Call Kester's office and let him know that I can deliver the mole." He glanced at his sleeve did some quick math. The timing was going to be tight, but he could make it work. "Udo Park, three o'clock. The Rings."

"Wait, I –"

But Kovalic didn't let him finish, terminating the connection and then peeling off the sleeve and ripping the smart fabric in half. He tossed it in the building's trash receptacle and let out another breath, staring up at a white cloud drifting lazily across the narrow gap between all the buildings rising above him.

He couldn't deny a sense of relief washing over him, alien as it might seem. He was done waiting around: they were going dynamic now. The time for strategy was over; now it was purely about tactics – and tactics was where he lived. This he knew how to handle.

And, no matter what, in a few hours all of this would be over.

CHAPTER 38

"Commonwealth credits?" Nat repeated blankly. It didn't compute somehow, like Sayers had said that the boxes were full of containers of peanut butter. That a criminal organization – even one on an Illyrican-occupied world – might deal in Commonwealth credits was no surprise; the Illyrican mark had become increasingly shaky in recent years. But *half a billion*? Where the hell would they even get that much hard currency?

Nat pressed her hands to her temples. None of this made any sense. What should have been a simple snatch-and-grab was starting to feel like they'd pulled the thread of an extremely complicated carpet that was now unraveling beneath them.

She was supposed to be the analyst, the one who took in all the information and found the pattern, the signal amongst the noise. But weighed against every other consideration buffeting her – the safety of her team, Simon's fate – it *all* just felt like noise.

One clear note cut through that cacophony, like a bell tolling midnight. Illyrican marks were one thing: to be mercenary, if the Coire Ansic wanted to mess around on Imperium worlds, that was the Illyricans' problem.

But half a billion in Commonwealth credits sure felt like it justified Xi's fears that Flores was trying to expand to other worlds. Even if Nat's own footing with the Commonwealth was shaky at present, that was something she couldn't just stand by and watch. Half a billion could cause a lot of trouble in the Commonwealth; they couldn't afford to let Roche Flores hold onto that much hard currency.

And the same went double for Ofeibia Xi. Flores might be trouble for Caledonia, but Xi was already the head of one of the most powerful criminal organizations in the galaxy. The White Star Syndicate already had their fingers in smuggling, extortion, and arms dealing – an infusion of this much cash could make them unstoppable.

But with Xi and her people on their comms, there was no way for Nat to communicate that sentiment to the rest of the team.

She could change the plan unilaterally. It was an option. All they had to do was not detach the storage car and they'd keep barreling their way into Stranraer, avoiding the welcoming committee Xi had waiting for them in Fort Mull. It wouldn't be the first time her team had to adjust to a fluid situation; Nat trusted them to adapt.

But what then? They'd still be trapped with not just the Coire Ansic, but Xi and her goons, who would be all too aware that the plan was not going according to, well, plan. They'd be lucky to make it to Stranraer. And she might as well be shooting Brody herself.

No, they needed another way off this train – with the money.

"Boss?" came Tapper's voice over the comm. "What's the play?" Nat blinked – for as long as she could remember, he'd reserved the term of address for Simon. But the sergeant knew when to light a fire; she could practically hear him cracking his knuckles over the connection.

The chronometer on Nat's wrist was still counting down. Thirty minutes. Not a lot of time, especially with the number of pieces in play. Normally she'd be considering all the angles, waiting until the perfect moment, but they just didn't have that kind of time. She took a breath; this was going to be tricky.

"We continue as planned," said Nat. "I know we were trying to soften up the Coire Ansic's muscle instead of taking them head-on, but that ship has sailed, and we need to regroup with Sayers before we detach the cars. Sergeant, can you find something to even the odds a bit?"

"You're playing my song," said Tapper, his grin practically audible. "Any requests?"

Nat turned a chuckle into a cough. "Surprise me, sergeant."

"Copy that. Gwen, care to join me?"

"It'd be my pleasure, old man. Got some scores of my own to settle there."

"I'll meet you in a few minutes," said Nat. "Hold off on breaching until I arrive."

With that, she disconnected her terminal from the train's console and spun to find the communications station. In a normal environment, passengers would be able to rely on their sleeves' connection to the global network, but the sandstorm raging outside would play havoc with any external comm connections.

Still, you couldn't just send an entire gravtrain through the uninhabited wilderness without some way

DAN MOREN   327

of contacting the outside world. So some clever engineer had come up with a method that functionally turned the entire length of the train itself into an antenna, using it to boost the signal and cut through the sandstorm's interference. That wasn't without its own downsides – it drained a lot of power that the train needed for other systems like life support and, well, propulsion. Which meant that it couldn't just act as a passthrough for all onboard communications requests, lest the train end up stranded in the Burns Expanse, so access to the array was strictly limited to essential needs only.

Fortunately, it was all managed from inside the control center.

Nat jacked her terminal into the comm system and tapped a few keys, then pulled out the slip of flimsy Sayers had handed her and punched in the series of numbers printed on it.

Here went nothing.

"Lieutenant, I hope you're copying this, because we're going to need a pickup in about... fifteen minutes. I'm going to leave this data channel open and updating with our coordinates. Hope you can make it, because if you can't, we're all going to be in a lot of trouble."

She held her breath, waiting for any acknowledgement. The note from Sayers had been terse: EB 3720.80. A comm frequency; EB had to be Eli Brody. Nat wasn't sure where Addy had gotten it or how Brody had comms, but she had an inkling that Gwen must have been involved somehow.

Still there were plenty of other what ifs to account for: What if Xi had been bluffing and Brody was already dead?

Or what if he wasn't actually on the *Cavalier*? What if he was under armed guard? Too many variables, and she couldn't account for all of them. This was high-level algebra at its worst.

Time to take another page from the Simon Kovalic playbook and trust in her team.

After a minute with no response, she gave up and slid the terminal underneath the comm panel, hopefully out of sight. Then she set off with determination towards the rear of the train.

As before, the first car behind the control center was empty, but the moment she set foot in the next car, her heart sank. The same two security officers she'd seen on the way in were still lounging around, doing a fairly bad job of looking inconspicuous. She'd really hoped they'd have found somewhere else to be.

The one who'd asked her for coffee lit up when he spotted her, and she thought she detected his partner rolling their eyes at the same time. Her would-be admirer straightened up, donning what he clearly thought was a charming grin.

"Well, hello again," he said, as she closed the distance. "Reconsidering my offer?"

The idea of smiling back at him didn't appeal to Nat, but she also knew it would be the easiest and safest way out of this conversation. Even as she was starting to open her mouth to issue a polite demurral, the other security officer once again gave his partner a hard look.

"You're still on duty." His gaze shifted to her, then sharpened suddenly. "Hey... didn't you have a terminal before?"

Shit.

"Oh," she said, her mind scrambling as she tried to maintain her calm demeanor. "I left it in my compartment."

"I thought you were going to do work." His voice had taken on a suspicious tone, even as one hand drifted towards the inside of his jacket.

"Go easy," muttered the first officer, his befuddled look darting back and forth between the two of them. "It's just a terminal."

"Oh shut up, Garrett, you idiot," said the other man, exasperated. "If you don't stop trying to hit on every pretty face…"

His attention had shifted to his partner for a moment, hand still hovering near the opening of his jacket; Nat wasn't sure she wanted to wait to find out what was in there.

So she moved.

The corridor in the train car was narrow, which worked to her advantage. She darted forward at the suspicious security officer, pinning his arm against his own chest and making it impossible for him to get his weapon clear.

At the same time, she shifted her weight and stomped down hard on Garrett's foot. Probably not hard enough to break his toes, but enough to hurt like hell. And when he doubled over in pain, she bounced her knee directly up into his startled face.

That *might* have broken his nose.

The first man was so distracted with struggling to get his weapon hand free that it took him a moment to remember he had a second, unencumbered arm. He brought it around to take a swing at Nat, but it was clearly his non-dominant arm, so she ducked the clumsy hook and drove her own right hand into the man's solar plexus, knocking the wind out of him with a gasp.

She kept her momentum going, trying to slam him against the nearest wall, but even in his stunned state he was considerably heavier than she was; it was like trying to move a tree. She rebounded off him, widening the gap between the two of them to a couple feet.

The man stumbled backwards but held his ground even as he tried to catch his breath. He had just enough presence of mind to realize that she was far enough away that he could get to his weapon.

But his hand was shaky and even as he brought out the knockout gun, Nat was sliding sideways past him, careful to stay on the outside of his arm, away from the weapon's business end. She used all her weight to shove him sideways into the corridor's wall, then seized his weapon arm with both hands and wrestled his aim towards his partner, who was still doubled over, wheezing like he'd just run the hundred meter dash after a year of sitting on the couch.

"Goddamnit it," grunted the man, "let *go*." He tried to physically shake her off, but Nat held tight, wrapping one arm around the man's wrist while using her other hand to reach for the finger that was already on the trigger.

Garrett looked up, eyes crossing at the sight of a KO gun pointed in his direction, and tried to half-slide, half-fall out of the way. Nat stuck her own finger inside the trigger guard and used it to yank the security officer's finger back, firing the weapon.

The ripple of the stun field caught Garrett point blank and he crumpled to the ground with the sigh of air escaping a balloon.

With a growl, his partner shoved Nat, sending her sprawling to the floor. To her surprise, instead of shooting her, he raised his free hand to his ear, tapping it. "Status Falcon. Repeat, we are status Falcon," he said in a rasp, not quite recovered from the blow to his sternum. "Collapse on the cargo." Only then did he start raising the weapon toward her.

Nat wasn't about to look a gift opportunity in the mouth; from the floor, she lashed out in a snap kick at his ankles, even as she tried to roll out of the line of fire.

It mostly worked. His aim wavered as he pulled the trigger and she felt the edge of the stun field catch her in one side – head-on it would have immediately rendered her unconscious, but instead it just doused her right arm, leg, and that side of her torso in the unpleasant pins-and-needles sensation of having been slept on.

Not good.

Nat levered herself up on her good arm, just in time to see the man swinging the weapon back in her direction. This time he couldn't miss, and there was nowhere for her to run – her mind gave a bitter laugh, pointing out that with a numb leg, it wasn't as if she could run anyway.

"I don't know who the fuck you are," the man said, "but you've made a big mistake."

Behind Nat, the door to the next train car whispered open suddenly, and the man's eyes darted upward, widening in surprise.

"She's not the only one," said a mellifluous voice, followed by the soft *thwip* of a flechette pistol's three-round burst. The man looked down in bewildered shock as a perfect trio of red spots bloomed on his chest. With a tottering wheeze, he took a step forward, then face-planted into the carpet.

Rolling over, Nat found herself looking up at Ofeibia Xi. The crime lord's purple gaze was hard, and for a moment Nat wondered if she was about to suffer the same fate as the security officer. But it wasn't the flechette pistol that got extended in her direction; it was the other woman's free hand, helping her to her feet.

"I see everything's going according to plan," said Xi, her voice paper dry.

Nat stumbled to her feet, her right side still an uncomfortable mass of tingling and numbness. "No battle plan survives contact with the enemy. What are you doing here?"

Xi cocked her head to one side. "I couldn't raise Deng or Stack on comms. And I don't trust any of the rest of you. Which is why I disregarded your advice about bribing train security to look the other way about my... industrial equipment." She hefted the flechette pistol, this time pointed loosely in Nat's direction, making the implicit threat clear. "But I still need this job done."

An armed Xi hadn't been on Nat's bingo card, but there was nothing to do about it now. "Fair enough. In which case, we should get moving, because they know we're here. Which reminds me..." She toggled her comms. "Sayers, heads up. You're probably about to have company."

CHAPTER 39

The only thing more boring than waiting for action behind the controls of a ship was waiting for action and *not* being behind the controls of a ship.

Chin perched upon hand, Eli gave a glum sigh and leaned his elbows on the *Cavalier*'s console, staring out the cockpit canopy at the swirling morass of sand and dirt.

"Hey," said Prentiss, glaring at him. "Off the controls."

Man, she's a lot of fun. Eli put his hands up and leaned back in the co-pilot chair. Andres might not be a one-man party, but he preferred the big man's stoic nature to his compatriot's needling.

I never thought I'd miss being down in the fray, getting shot at. But being up here, while the rest of the team was in the midst of an operation, was making him anxious. He pressed his palms against his thighs. *This really sucks.*

And all the while, the memory of the gun that Tapper had stashed beneath the console ate away at him, like a bird pecking at seed. Was it still there? Had Xi's people found it and removed it? It wasn't as if they were going to advertise that fact to him, and checking too soon risked blowing any advantage he had.

Not that he was even sure about using it. He hadn't

fired a weapon since basic training; there wasn't a lot of call for sidearm usage amongst starfighter pilots. The idea of pointing a weapon at someone still made his hands twitch, transporting him to the debacle that had been the Battle of Sabaea – his last engagement as an Illyrican fighter pilot, and the only time he'd ever taken a life. Just the thought sent his stomach into free fall.

You don't have to use *it. They just have to think you will.* The thought rang hollow in his own head.

Anyway, this wasn't the moment. Not yet.

Andres's bulk filled the cockpit hatch. "Anything?" he rumbled.

Prentiss answered a short shake of her head. "Still out of contact. The interference is blocking most communications. We'll have to trust they're still on the timetable." She pushed back from the controls, stretching her arms over her head. "I gotta hit the head. Keep an eye on… things?" Her eyes on Eli left no room for interpretation about what she meant.

"Sure," said Andres, as she disappeared into the corridor and he took her place.

The seat creaked a little under his bulk, looking like a doll's chair beneath him. At least he didn't spend all his time giving Eli dirty looks; the man seemed strangely at home in his stillness. Despite everything – and maybe it was the Stockholm Syndrome talking – Eli had found himself kind of liking the big, quiet man. He seemed… transparent, for lack of a better word. What you saw was what you got.

"I have to ask," Eli said suddenly, leaning back as far as the co-pilot chair would allow. "How'd you end up working for Xi anyway?"

Andres didn't answer immediately, his eyes still on the sandstorm outside. For a few moments, Eli figured he might just say nothing at all, but finally a few words escaped, as though pried loose with a crowbar. "Needed a job."

"Well, sure, I mean, we all have to eat," Eli pressed him. "But why *her*?"

He shrugged. "She was hiring."

"I see you're really the introspective sort."

For the first time, Andres's eyes – blue flecked with gray – turned towards Eli, studying him as though he were an unfamiliar insect species. "It was that or prison."

Now we're getting somewhere. Eli opened his mouth, a barrage of questions ready to rain down on the man, when a voice crackled in his forgotten earbud, so loud and screeching that he visibly winced.

"...hope you're copying... pickup in about... –fteen minutes... leave ... channel open... hope you can make it... lot of trouble."

Andres eyed him, only the faintest hint of suspicion in his eyes. "What's wrong with you?"

Eli pressed a hand to his cheek. "Uhhh, bit my tongue." But his mind was already off and racing: Taylor's message was heavily broken up, but she'd found a way to get through, and between the fact that she'd chosen this moment and that ominous bit about trouble, things looked like they were hitting the proverbial fan.

His pulse ramped up suddenly, and he felt the old fighter pilot awareness kick in as his vision widened, looking for threats. Prentiss was still out of the room, leaving only Andres to watch him. Not exactly a fair fight, but if Tapper's gun was still there, it would lend him an edge.

If there was a time to act, it was now. But he was only going to get one shot at this. *Maybe literally.*

Eli rolled his neck, as if working out a kink, and hoped that Andres wasn't picking up his quicker breathing or the sweat beading on his forehead. *Maybe I should profess my love for him. That would explain it* and *probably throw him off for a second.*

The bigger problem was that Tapper had put the gun near the pilot's seat, figuring that it would be in reach if Eli had needed it, but they hadn't counted on someone the size of a small horse being in the way. Which meant Eli either had to get him to move, or – much less plausibly – go through him. And something told him that Andres wasn't going to fall for the old "look over there" trick.

OK, Brody. Think. You may not be a combat badass like Kovalic, but you're still in a cockpit. There was an array of controls that could cause all sorts of distractions, but most of them would take too long. He needed something quick, simple, and decisive...

Eli had, in the past, conjectured that being a good pilot came down to there being a subsystem in one's brain that directly connected impulse to reflex, bypassing any conscious thought. So he was as surprised as Andres when he suddenly grabbed the co-pilot yoke, slamming it forward and putting the ship into a dive.

For the first time in their brief acquaintance, Andres's stoic demeanor cracked. His eyes widened as the acceleration pressed him backwards, the compensators taking a moment to react to the sudden change. He struggled forward against the force, making a grab for the pilot's yoke.

That was all the opportunity Eli needed; he'd braced himself for the maneuver and, as Andres reached for the controls, he darted towards the pilot's seat, hand scrambling underneath until it closed on the weight of the object secured there.

The big man managed to level the ship out, but by the time he did, Eli was already back in the co-pilot's seat, a safe distance out of the big man's reach, pistol pointed directly at him. Despite the sweat from Eli's palms, he kept the weapon steady.

Andres spared a glance in the direction, looking if anything less concerned about this change in events than Eli's madcap maneuver of a moment ago. He gave a noncommittal grunt that, in another circumstance, Eli might have described as impressed.

"Sorry," said Eli. "I'd say it's not personal, but, well, it kind of is? Your boss did blackmail me and all of my friends into committing a crime for her. Wait, why am I explaining this to you?"

"What the fuck is going on?" echoed a voice from down the corridor.

Shit, Prentiss. Part of Eli had hoped that the sudden dive might have taken the woman unaware, maybe even knocked her out, but that was apparently asking too much of the universe. He could see the calculation in Andres's eyes: in a moment, Eli was going to have to choose who to shoot first, and whatever he did – or didn't do – was going to be telling.

But there's another option.

Keeping the gun trained on Andres, he reached over and slapped the cockpit hatch control. There was just enough time to see Prentiss rounding the corner, her anger transmuting into shock, as the door slid closed between them. Eli hit the lock button and keyed in his security override, careful to keep one eye on Andres. An alert flashed on screen, indicating that the door was sealed.

For what felt like the first time in the minutes since he'd gotten Taylor's message, he let out a breath and felt himself relax.

"You're not going to shoot me," said Andres. His eyes had narrowed in thought.

So much for relaxing. "Yeah, you think?"

"You could have, right then. Shot me. Shot Prentiss. But you didn't." He nodded at the console, where the door lock indicator still showed. "Took the coward's way out."

Eli flushed at the word, but tamped down the flare of anger. "You're probably right," he said, forcing his voice into a casual tone. "But this?" He lifted the weapon. "It doesn't make you brave."

"You haven't thought this through," said Andres, shifting in the chair and giving the impression of a coiled snake about to strike.

Eli grinned. "Yeah, I don't think we've really met." And with that, he swung back to the controls and hit the *Cav*'s throttle.

The ship jumped forward and Andres hesitated. That was all the opportunity Eli needed; he tossed the gun to a surprised Andres and grabbed the yoke with both hands, pointing the ship's nose directly into the sandstorm.

"What the hell are you doing?" Andres fumbled with the gun, then managed to level it at Eli. But his eyes kept shifting to one side to look out the canopy at the encroaching mass of sand and dirt.

Eli felt the yoke start to buck in his hands as they reached the outer edge of the whirlwind, and the ship danced from side to side. He spared a glance at Andres, then slowly took his hands off the controls, which started jerking around of their own accord, and folded his arms over his chest. "Go ahead, shoot me. But I hope you can fly this thing on your own."

The big man's eyes were bouncing back and forth like ping pong balls. "Prentiss," he grunted.

"That hatch is sealed with my personal security code. Maybe you could override it, but you don't really have that kind of time."

The ship sheared sideways suddenly, throwing them both off balance. Andres windmilled his arms, trying to stay in his seat. Eli barely managed to hold on.

Andres looked at him, then out the canopy at the brown mass and, with a muted growl, slapped the gun down on the console, where its magnetic holster stuck with a snap. "Fly the damn ship."

"Don't mind if I do," said Eli. "I'll just be needing that chair, if you don't mind."

"Can't you do it from there?"

"Do you really want to argue right now?"

The ship yawed crazily to one side, then the aft dipped and they both bounced up and down. There was a thump from out in the hallway with a muted curse that sounded like someone might have just rebounded off a bulkhead.

"Fine," said Andres, lurching to his feet and grabbing the back of the seat to keep himself steady.

Eli flung himself into the pilot seat, shrugging into the safety harness. "I wouldn't just stand there," he advised. "You're going to want to buckle up."

With a stifled sound that might have been a moan, the big man stumbled to the co-pilot's seat and got himself strapped in as Eli seized the yoke and started flipping switches on the control panel. He settled into the seat, readjusting the settings Prentiss had messed with and feeling the familiar long-worn grooves and indentations, the one spring that poked you right in the underside of your left thigh.

"Don't worry," said Eli, reaching out to pat the console reassuringly. "I'm back." He glanced over at Andres, hands white-knuckled on the chest straps, and grinned. "Hey, don't worry. I grew up here. My Aunt Brigid was a pilot – showed me the ropes when I was barely taller than her knee, and sandstorms were the first thing she taught me to deal with."

Andres seemed to relax a bit. "Yeah? How?"

"Easy: just avoid them at all costs." And with that Eli turned the *Cavalier*'s nose directly into the storm and accelerated.

CHAPTER 40

"Sayers, heads up. You're probably about to have company." Taylor's voice had no sooner faded in Addy's ears than she heard the clomping of footsteps outside the cargo car.

Well, shit. It was fight or hide time, and until she had a better idea of how many partygoers might be attending this particular shindig she was going with the latter.

Hiding behind the pallets might work, but if they took anything more than a cursory look around then it was going to be quicker than a game of hide-and-go-seek in a one-tree field.

Leaving wasn't an option either: the door to the next baggage car was still locked; Taylor had only opened the one at the front.

Can't go forward, can't go back. What about... up? The ceiling was low, but the lighting strips ran along the top edge of the walls, leaving the rounded roof in shadow.

Then the door at the far end of the car was sliding open, and she didn't have time to think further. Climbing up on the nearest pallet, she jumped and braced her hands against one wall and her feet against the opposite.

Three people entered, all dressed in dark suits; she

recognized all of them from her encounter in the café car: the Imperial Fleet Security team. All had weapons drawn and were peering around the car carefully, looking for intruders in every corner.

Addy's arms and legs, which had spent the first thirty seconds or so feeling fine, had now started to burn from the effort of keeping her up. *Weirdly enough, they never made us do this move in training.*

One thing was clear, she realized, as the security team continued their slow sweep of the car: she wasn't going to be able to hide up here forever. Which meant she had to pick her moment. And, more to the point, her muscles needed to hold out until then.

Her left arm twitched and threatened to give way a few moments before the lead of the team – the woman they'd called Bala, whose sleeve she'd cloned – stepped directly beneath her, but she managed to press it more firmly into the wall, her teeth clenched as she ignored the fire creeping up towards her shoulders.

Come on, Addy. You can do this.

All four of her limbs were shaking now, but it didn't matter, because the middle security was right below her and it was time to let go.

The man – she had just enough time to recall his name was Harmon – glanced up at what seemed like the last possible second, his eyes widening.

He gave a strangled cry as she came down on him like a Novan drop bear, except without the slavering teeth and nasty claws. The two of them collapsed in a heap, Addy grabbing for the pistol that had been knocked loose from his grasp.

"The *fuck*?" Bala had whirled, pointing her own pistol in their direction, but her aim wavered as Addy and Harmon's limbs were tangled amongst each other, blocking any clear shot.

Addy got one hand around the pistol and started to bring it up towards Bala, but the third member of the security team darted up from behind, kicking her wrist and sending the gun spinning away into the far reaches of the compartment.

Grunting in pain – her wrist was severely bruised, but hopefully not broken – Addy rolled to her side and attempted to scissor kick the standing man's legs out from underneath him. But with her own legs still burning from the exertion of keeping her suspended overhead, she couldn't quite summon enough force, and her feet bounced off his shins. He didn't fall over, but he didn't look happy about it either.

Great. This really wasn't going as well as she'd hoped.

There was a deafening bang in the confined space and a red hot round left a hole in the deck plating not a foot from Addy's head.

"Don't move or the next one's through your head," said Bala, her pistol aimed steadily at Addy.

In all the tussling and jockeying for the gun, she'd gotten too far from Harmon, who had scuttled away, leaving Addy exposed. The other officer – the one she'd kicked – was mirroring Bala's stance from the opposite side, and between the two of them, they had Addy dead to rights.

But at least not dead. Addy raised her hands slowly and, as she looked up, she caught the flash of recognition on Bala's face. "You. What the fuck are you doing in here? Who are you?"

Addy's mind whirled. The team hadn't discussed a cover – the plan hadn't needed one, if it had gone as intended – and the last thing she wanted to do was to blow the mission, but she needed to give Bala something if she wanted to keep breathing.

Kovalic's advice rung in her mind: stick as closely as possible to the truth. Or, at least, parts of it.

"My name's not important," said Addy. "I'm just an independent contractor."

Bala raised an eyebrow but didn't seem surprised. "Who hired you?"

"One of your boss's rivals." Addy nodded at the strongboxes. "You're carrying a lot of cash and let's just say it made an attractive target."

"I bet. Harmon, check the cargo. Make sure nothing's missing."

The officer Addy had landed on scrambled upward, scooping up his dropped weapon. He walked over to the container Addy had opened, noting the broken seal, and checked it. "Everything looks OK here."

"Check the seals on the rest," said Bala, not taking her eyes off Addy. "Just in case." She waved her pistol at Addy. "Meanwhile, you and I are going to take a little walk."

Addy climbed to her feet very slowly, making sure to keep her hands visible at all times. The only thing worse than getting caught mid-operation would be getting killed for doing something stupid like slipping as she got up.

Harmon and the other security officer were peering at all the boxes but Bala didn't let her stick around to see the end result, motioning her to walk back towards the front of the car. The woman kept a professional distance; not so close that Addy could wrest her weapon away, not so far as to let her easily move out of the line of fire.

Fleet Security isn't someone you want to fuck around with. She'd heard that from any number of folks who had dealt with them. They had a reputation for being well-trained and extremely diligent in their work.

Which once again raised the question of what the hell they were doing here, working as muscle for a criminal organization. That Isabella had loaned them to Flores seemed a lock, but why? What did the director of Imperial Intelligence get out of propping up a criminal organization? And where had the Commonwealth credits come from? Addy couldn't help but feel she was missing a piece of the puzzle.

A memory of her old friend Boyland, the Novan cop who'd been the closest thing she'd ever had to a family, swam to the surface of her mind. He'd been working on some case or other; Addy had found him sitting on a park bench, staring up at the sky in thought.

"Cui bono, Addy," he'd said at last. *"That's the key when you're thinking about motive: who stands to benefit?"*

Bala herded her through the connecting compartment and into the Coire Ansic's private car. Unlike the rest of the train, this car wasn't divided into smaller private compartments, but set up like a lounge, with one large open space dotted with tables, comfortable chairs, and even a bar in one corner. Wide, panoramic windows showed off the landscape outside – or probably did, at least, when there wasn't a sandstorm raging. *It definitely looks nicer from inside than it did from outside.*

There were half a dozen people present, besides her and Bala: three who had the look of security, with the same dark suits and hard looks, and then a pair that seemed more like flunkies: their clothes were better cut and they held drinks as they bent their heads together quietly.

The last person present needed no introduction; Addy recognized him from the pictures Xi had shown them before the mission.

Roche Flores.

He sat in a plush armchair at one of the low tables, cutting a more imposing figure in person than in the images; something about the way he held himself, with the kind of overly relaxed posture of someone working too hard to conceal the tension within. He might not have the seductive and magnetic presence of Ofeibia Xi, but he gave the impression of someone who clung tight to everything he'd gotten in life. At the same time, there was an air of discomfort about him, like he was wearing someone else's clothes.

Pale hazel eyes, almost watery, gave Addy an up and down as Bala approached, and Addy sensed the other woman tensing. "Caught her in with the cargo," said Bala. "No sign of her accomplices."

"Maybe you should go find them, then," said Flores. His voice was nasal and unpleasant. "It's not exactly a big train."

"I'll post security with the shipment for the remainder of the trip." An aggrieved edge had slipped into Bala's voice.

Flores waved a hand at her in a sharp dismissive motion. "Yeah, yeah." But he hadn't taken his attention from Addy, leaning forward in what was probably intended to be a threatening fashion. "And who are you working for, sweetheart?"

Anger flared in Addy's chest, and only the reminder that Bala stood a couple feet away with a lethal weapon kept her from leaping across the table. If this had been Ofeibia Xi, Addy would have said the dismissive tone was an attempt to throw her off balance, force her into making a mistake. But there was something in Flores's gaze – cruel and dumb – that suggested this was no sophisticated ploy: Roche Flores was a bully, plain and simple.

She smiled, showing her teeth, determined not to give him any satisfaction. "I wouldn't get very far in this business if I betrayed my employers' trust. Unless, of course," she added, raising an eyebrow, "you're tendering a counteroffer."

The suggestion seemed to strike a nerve in Flores, and his dark eyebrows knit. "I don't pay for information." He glanced over her shoulder at Bala. "Kill her and throw her off the train."

Bala stared at him, and Addy swore she could hear her holding back a long-suffering sigh. "What about the rest of her crew?"

"What, do I have to think of *everything*?" Flores snapped. "Security is your job. You *deal* with them."

"Yes, sir," said Bala, through gritted teeth. She reached out and grabbed Addy by the upper arm, wrenching her back towards the door through which they'd just entered. "Let's go."

Damn it, stall.

"This is a big mistake, Flores," Addy called over her shoulder. "You're going to regret it, trust me."

Flores didn't even bother to respond; he'd turned back

to his two flunkies. *OK, threats aren't going to do it.* Her mind spun as she tried to come up with some other wedge, something she could use against the man.

But Bala just shoved Addy forward, putting space between them once again, and forced Addy to keep walking towards the car's rear, closer to an unfortunate fate. *This is how it ends, huh?* Her mouth had gone dry even as she scanned the compartment for options. Dive over that chair? She'd get shot before she made it a foot. Jostle Bala in the connecting door and make a play for the gun? The odds seemed bad, but she wasn't going to go out without a fight.

She was still a few steps from the door, steeling herself for a move, when a familiar gruff voice spoke in her earbud, and relief flooded in along with it.

"I'd hit the deck, if were you," said Tapper. "It's about to get pretty toasty in there."

CHAPTER 41

Nat and Xi made their way through the rest of the train to the Coire Ansic car, where they found Gwen and Tapper waiting outside, looking antsy.

They also, notably, were missing their babysitters. If Nat had to guess, Deng and Stack were incapacitated inside an empty compartment somewhere.

Xi cast a gimlet eye upon the two, seeming annoyed but not particularly surprised that her people were missing, but neither the sergeant nor their local expert appeared remotely embarrassed. Despite being the only one amongst them carrying a lethal weapon, the syndicate leader elected not to comment on the situation.

"Major," said Tapper, giving a sidelong glance at Xi. "Good. Sayers is on her own in there, and I think it's only fair we even the odds a bit." He held up a canister as thick around as her thigh, to the top of which had been affixed – with a prodigious amount of duct tape – a small box.

"Do I want to know what that's going to do?" said Nat, raising an eyebrow. The sergeant's knack for locating – or, in a pinch, devising – a wide range of explosives, even while in the most straitened circumstances, was legendary.

"You did say to surprise you."

She'd been wondering if she was going to regret that, and here was the universe providing an answer. "Well, we're not going to help her sitting out here." She glanced at her sleeve. "We've got five minutes before we hit our window. Let's get moving."

As Nat was about to step over to the access panel next to the door, Gwen produced a pair of KO guns from the back of her waistband and held one out to her, grip first.

"I've a feeling this might come in handy," said the redhead with a mischievous smile.

Nat could feel Xi's eyes boring into the spot between her shoulder blades; the weapons were clearly the same make and model that the syndicate leader's security had been using. She was all too aware that Xi was still carrying a lethal weapon, and if there was one thing Nat was sure of it was that the crime lord would turn it on them without a second's hesitation. They'd have to deal with her eventually, but for the moment, they were still – much as it might bemuse all present – on the same side.

At least there weren't flechettes in her back – not yet, anyway.

"Thanks," said Nat, checking the charge on the weapon before stowing it. "Now, let's get this done." Prying open the access panel, she seized the hefty manual override handle, pulled it down, and twisted it to the unlocked position.

There was a quiet click, barely audible over the background noise of the train, and the access pad next to the door flickered from red to green. Gwen took up position by the door, gripping the handle with both hands.

"Major?" asked Tapper.

Nat drew the KO gun again and gave him a sharp nod. "Execute."

The smile on Tapper's face might have been that of a schoolboy told to go ahead and jump in a mud puddle. He reached up and triggered his comm. "I'd hit the deck, if were you. It's about to get pretty toasty in there."

Gwen heaved the door open, then pressed herself against the bulkhead, out of the line of fire.

Raising his makeshift device with both hands, Tapper planted a dramatic kiss on it, then heaved it through the doorway. Distantly, Nat heard a clank as it hit the ground and rolled.

From within the car came a sudden pop and hiss, followed by a chorus of shouts.

As one, Nat, Gwen, and Xi's eyes all slid to the sergeant, who gave a modest shrug under the three women's gazes. "I think I surprised them, too."

The four of them pushed through the door and into what had been, until moments ago, a large and no doubt expensively outfitted private car, with decorative sconces, plush upholstery, and fine brass fittings.

Or at least Nat had to assume, because all of it was now entirely coated in a thick layer of fire suppression foam.

No less than four armed security personnel were staring at each other with shellshocked expressions, soapy gobs of white bubbles hanging off them from the tops of their heads all the way down to a thick carpet around their ankles. Another unarmed trio were wiping at their faces, though they were mostly just getting more foam everywhere.

A laugh bubbled up in Nat's throat, but she pushed it down as the befoamed goons spotted them and started to raise their weapons.

From behind Nat came the rapid stutter of Xi's flechette pistol, and one of the security personnel went down, the foam on their chest rapidly turning pink.

One fired back, but the slipperiness of the foam on their grips sent their shot wide, pinging into the bulkhead behind Nat. Two more were still trying to clean off their weapons while, at the very back of the car, a dark-haired woman was carefully lining up her own shot.

Before Nat had a chance to react, a figure rose from the floor, covered in a thick layer of foam, and tackled the dark-haired woman, great gouts of white suds splashing upwards as they both hit the deck.

A stun field rippled outwards from Nat's left, and another of the security officers went down, their eyes rolling backwards in their head as they toppled into the foam, felled by Gwen's knockout gun.

Tapper, meanwhile, had charged the last armed guard, hitting him firmly in the mid-section and plowing him directly backwards into what proved to be an armchair. There was an *oof* from the man as the wind was knocked out of him, and he didn't recover it before Tapper landed a solid right hook to his jaw, laying him out cold.

Xi stalked through the foam, her face painted with the distaste of one who'd ordered a fine steak only to be presented with chuck roast. She held the pistol outstretched before her, aiming at the man in the center of the three unarmed figures, who was still busy wiping foam from his eyes.

DAN MOREN   353

"Hello, Flores," said Xi. "Such a pleasure to finally meet you face to face."

Behind them, on the other side of the car, Sayers and her adversary were still tussling in the foam. A symphony of grunts and yelps issued forth as they wrestled for control of the one weapon between them, but it kept slipping out of their hands like a bar of soap.

Flores flicked foam from his fingers and squinted at Xi blearily. "Who the fuck are you?"

Of all the things one could say to Ofeibia Xi, that might have been the deepest cut, but the syndicate leader's expression didn't flicker; she just lowered the flechette gun and shot Flores in the leg.

"I'm the woman whose business you don't fuck with," she said calmly over his howls.

Flores had fallen back into one of the chairs, clutching his thigh, where blood streamed from several small wounds; from Nat's quick glance, it seemed to have at least missed any critical arteries, which was either extremely good aim on Xi's part or dumb luck – she wasn't sure the crime lord cared either way.

"I don't know who you are *or* what you're talking about," said Flores, through gritted teeth. Tears streamed down his face, cutting twin paths through the foam like streaked makeup. "I'm just doing what I was told!"

That got Nat's attention.

Xi's too. Her brown darkened. "Explain."

From the back of the car came the deep wet *thwack* of a punch, and Nat glanced over in time to see a grinning Sayers, covered in foam, standing over her limp adversary.

Flores, still holding his leg, glanced around at his retinue, but his security contingent was now all incapacitated and his other two compatriots were looking around blankly as if they couldn't explain how they'd ended up here. The only way they could have looked more disingenuous was if they had actually twiddled their thumbs and whistled innocently.

"Don't look at them; I'm the one with the gun pointed at you. Who told you to do what?"

Flores jerked his head at the downed security team. "Look, a little more than a year ago I'm just a mid-level enforcer for a second-rate organization. Did I have aspirations? Sure, I wanted a bigger house and nicer clothes and the good life. So when these people came along and said they could make it happen, I didn't ask questions."

"The Illyricans," said Nat, her mind spinning. Beside her, she felt Gwen go still. No surprise there; the Caledonians' relationship with their occupiers was complicated, to say the least.

"Yeah," said Flores, wincing as he tried to adjust his leg to a more comfortable position. "I didn't know they were crims until later. I would have never taken them up on it if I had." The protest rang hollow to Nat's ears; Roche Flores was not proving himself to be a man with a strong moral compass.

"Just over a year ago," said Gwen, her foot squishing in the foam as she tapped it. "That'd be right around the time that the Black Watch collapsed."

"Convenient," Nat agreed. "The Illyricans get to pick exactly who fills the power vacuum in Caledonia's criminal underworld."

Xi stepped forward and put her foot up on Flores's chair, directly between his legs. She put her elbow on her knee and her chin in her palm, favoring him with a smile that was anything but pleasant. The flechette pistol dangled from her hand. "And what did they ask for in return?"

Flores hesitated and Xi pivoted her heel so her toes were resting on his wounded leg. "I hate repeating myself."

"OK, OK," he moaned. "The Coire Ansic, we run the business: protection, drugs, gambling… but the crims, they provided the startup investment. So they take a cut of everything. A big one. And we do them favors. Money comes in, money goes out – but not the same money, if you know what I'm saying."

Nat rocked back on her heels. No wonder Fleet Security was on hand to protect the investment – this operation was worth a fortune. Not only was it a whole additional revenue stream for the Imperium, but it let them launder money into untraceable cash.

More specifically…

"Your containers back there are full of Commonwealth credits," Nat said, nodding towards the rear of the car. "Not easy to find on an Illyrican colony, especially in those quantities. Where'd you get them?"

"The crims hooked me up with a contact," muttered Flores. He was starting to look a bit ashen; no doubt shock was kicking in. Even if Xi hadn't hit an artery, he'd lost a not insignificant amount of blood. "I only met him the one time. Weaselly blond kid in a cheap suit. Not from around here. He drops off the currency in Stranraer, we run it up to Tralee and pass it on. Where it goes from there, I got no idea."

"Why credits?" Nat was pretty sure she knew exactly what the answer would be; it had already clicked into place as the details had filtered through her mind and she assembled the larger puzzle picture. But she wanted to hear confirmation from Flores.

"Nobody wants to do business in marks right now. Credits are solid."

Nat shook her head. Something still didn't add up here, but she was struggling to put her finger on it. Black markets dictated the currency they did business in, and it didn't entirely shock her to hear that even the ones inside the Imperium preferred Commonwealth credits.

"What about the princess?" Xi asked darkly. "What's her part in all of this?"

Flores looked as befuddled as if he'd already passed out. "Princess? What princess?"

"Your Illyrican contact," said Nat, pressing closer. "You met her on Earth."

"On Earth?" Flores looked puzzled. "The only person I met there was some old bald guy – he's the one who set this all up."

The description didn't ring any bells, and Nat's lips pressed together. Isabella had been smart enough to keep her real job under wraps, of course she wasn't about to have a face-to-face with a two-bit hood like Flores; she'd use a cutout for something like that, someone deniable.

Xi, for her part, had taken a new look at her supposed rival, and was shaking her head in disappointment. "You're nothing more than a stooge. Not even worth my time." She considered the flechette gun. "Or the ammunition."

"Very worth the attempted murder charge, though," said Gwen, raising the KO gun she held and leveling it at the crime lord. "You're both under arrest."

Xi cocked her head to one side. "How interesting. I was sure you had some secret tucked away there, Ms Collins, but... law enforcement? Really?"

"That's Special Agent Gwendolyn Rhys, Caledonian Security Agency."

Nat's eyebrows went up. With Xi around, Tapper hadn't had the opportunity to fill the rest of them in on Gwen's background. But it clicked a few things into place: her concern about the Coire Ansic evading the authorities, her knowledge of the local crime scene, even her willingness to take on this job.

"Gotta be *kiddin'* me." Flores's moan was slurred with pain as he clutched his leg.

"Very disappointing," said Xi, shaking her head. She spared a glance at Nat. "That goes for you, too, Major Vinson. I offered you a chance to clear your debt to me in good faith, but you decided not to trust me."

Nat stepped to one side, making sure she was out of the line of Gwen's fire. She waved Tapper towards the back of the car, where Sayers still stood, holding the weapon she'd wrested from the downed security officer. "You'll have to forgive me if the word of a criminal was less than reassuring. My priority is getting my team out safely."

"A shame, then, that your pilot will be the one to suffer the consequences."

A lump rose in Nat's throat, but she pushed it back down. Xi didn't have an easy way to contact her people with the sandstorm in full force, so Nat had to hope that her own transmission had gotten through to Brody. And that the pilot had done what he did best: pull a rabbit out of a hat.

Xi looked at her, eyes narrowing, as if peering into her thoughts. "Hm. I can see you may need additional convincing." She raised the flechette, pointing it in Sayers's direction. "Perhaps Adelaide would make for a more compelling target."

There were a pair of whines as Gwen and Tapper both readied knockout guns in Xi's direction, but the crime lord didn't so much as spare them a glance, keeping her aim on Sayers. "It seems we have an impasse."

"No we fucking do *not*," Gwen growled. "You don't need to be conscious for me to take you in." She squeezed the trigger on the KO gun.

But no stun field rippled forth; instead, there was just an electronic *blatt*, and the indicator lights on the weapon blinked red.

"Come now," said Xi, raising an eyebrow. "You took those weapons off my own people – you don't think I'd have a way to disable them?" She raised her free arm and shook her bangles, one of which blinked a matching red. "Now, if you'll all kindly drop your guns and make your way to the next car, we can conclude our business."

CHAPTER 42

"Initial perimeter sweep clear." Rance's voice came across the comm. In most of Kovalic's interactions with the general's aide, she'd displayed an aura of supreme confidence, but suddenly there was a sliver of trepidation threaded within, like a thin ribbon of frosting between two layers of cake. "Working inward, but there's only so much ground I can cover on my own."

Kovalic shaded his eyes against the bright, mid-day sun hanging in Nova's blue sky. He had to smile; espionage aficionados would scoff at holding a clandestine meeting on a sunlit afternoon. They were supposed to happen on foggy nights, with two trench-coated figures on a park bench in the illumination of a single lamppost.

But here he was, strolling through a busy section of Udo Park, Salaam's biggest open green space. Kids ran back and forth, yelling and kicking balls or throwing discs to each other; people walked dogs and strollers down paved paths, chatting away on their sleeves; somewhere, in the distance, Kovalic could even faintly hear the calliope of the park's carousel.

Intelligence operations were about managing risk. And keeping a lot of plates spinning at the same time. Right now, he felt like he had an entire dinner service going. Even just keeping track of them was proving a challenge. Laurent, Kester, Isabella... even the general was a rapidly rotating saucer hovering precipitously over his head, ready to smash down as soon as he took his eye off it for the briefest of moments.

As if summoned by Kovalic's thoughts, the old man added his own voice to the comm channel. "I would still feel better if you'd allowed me to accompany you."

"Oh yes," said Yevgeniy over the comms, his voice paper dry. "You definitely should have let the old man with the sword come along. That surely would have evened the odds." But his mocking tone was decidedly gentler than it had been. Kovalic wasn't sure if the general had ended up apologizing to his old friend or if Yevgeniy had just decided that the mood called for a little less hostility.

"Can't put all our eggs in one basket," said Kovalic, eyes scanning left to right as he walked. "If Kester decides to take me in, then at least the three of you are still out there. Find Nat and the rest of the team; make sure they're safe." The thought of his people out there still ate at him, like a riverbank eroding chunk by chunk. It was only the reminder that they were still depending on him to make sure they had a home to come back to that had kept him from taking the next flight out of Nova and tracking them down. So this meet had to go well – it was the only chance any of them had.

"Yevgeniy, everything in place?" Kovalic glanced at his sleeve. They still had twenty minutes before the appointed time; Rance had been here for a couple hours, slowly walking a circuit of the park to tag any security personnel. So far there'd been nothing at all, which meant either Kester had kept to his word...or the people he'd put in place were better than they were. Not something Kovalic would have banked on normally, but they were under-equipped, shorthanded, and low on sleep.

"Transmitter is operating nominally," said the old Illyrican spy. "I have eyes and ears on you, including redundant backups, just in case. We're as ready as we can be." He'd set up a position on one of the tall buildings surrounding the park, high up enough for a clear line of sight on the meet location, but at a significant distance. If they were compromised, he should have little trouble avoiding the authorities.

Kovalic wondered idly what the man would do in such a scenario – probably just go back to his tea shop. This wasn't his fight, and the only reason he was here at all was clearly some vestige of loyalty to his former boss and, yes, friend. Which one of those relationships exerted the stronger pull, Kovalic couldn't be sure, but his money was on the latter.

"Heading to the monument," said Kovalic. He turned down a curving path, the gravel crunching under his boots. It wasn't the most direct approach, for obvious reasons, but it would give him a clear view of the monument, just in case anybody was waiting for him.

Granted, it was hard to miss. The founding of the Commonwealth, roughly twenty years earlier, may have been largely in response to the Illyrican Empire's invasion of Earth, Centauri, and Caledonia but, even as a reactionary move, its formation had been a matter of pride. A few years afterwards, a monument commemorating the founding had been built in a prominent plaza in Udo Park.

It had a formal name, something like "Birth of the Commonwealth", but everybody just called it "The Rings".

A three-dimensional homage to the Commonwealth's insignia, three enormous brass rings on opposing biases wobbled around a central object: a four-pointed star held in mid-air by repulsor fields. The entire contraption hung over an infinity reflecting pool, the constantly flowing water intended to represent the continual path to the future.

And around it, lining the edge of the plaza, rose six dark walls, each twenty feet high. From this far away, they seemed to shimmer as though reflecting the water below the monument, but when you got closer, it became clear that they weren't just static surfaces but stone with holoscreens projected on them, across which rippled tiny text: a cosmos of names. All those who had perished during the Illyrican invasion, the deaths that had helped make the Commonwealth possible. Tens of millions of lives had been lost across the colony worlds; many of them military personnel, but no shortage of civilians either.

Each wall represented a world whose citizens had fought the Imperium: Earth, Centauri, Caledonia, Nova, and Trinity. The sixth was reserved for a mixture of those from independent worlds, as well as the Commonwealth's newest provisional member, Sabaea. Even the stones weren't the complete record of the lives the invasion had cost – simply the ones who still had people to remember them. Somewhere in there, Kovalic was sure, were the names of people he had known: childhood friends, distant family members, those he had served with. But he'd never brought himself to go looking, because, deep down, a tiny part of him knew that if he started he would never stop. He'd drown in the sorrow, as surely as if he threw himself into the reflecting pool.

Even more than the sadness was the cold fury the memorial brought to the surface. It was always there, he knew, carefully frozen beneath a thick insulating layer. Twenty years ago he'd left Earth, watched it fade to a pale blue dot out the window of a medical frigate.

He hadn't been back since.

Not for lack of opportunities. Earth was fertile ground for Commonwealth intelligence operations, and there had been any number of times the SPT could have deployed there.

Except for the promise Kovalic had made to himself: that the next time he set foot on his homeworld, he wouldn't leave until it had been freed from the Imperium, once and for all. The idea of being forced from his home *again* was too much to bear.

He walked between the Caledonia and Nova walls of remembrance and slowly began a circuit around the sculpture. Taking his time and, under the guise of admiring the rotating rings, Kovalic eyed the other people he passed. Most paid little attention to the sculpture itself, instead standing in front of the walls, strolling by the infinity pool, or just passing through on their way to another portion of the park. To many, especially the younger generation, it was just a monument that had always been there – part of the scenery.

So he paused a moment when he saw a small boy, maybe five years old, squinting up at the rotating rings as though he could see through them all the way back to the founding of the Commonwealth itself. He was wobbling his head left and right in time with the rings, synchronizing with them.

Watching him, Kovalic couldn't help but smile.

"You've got incoming," said Yevgeniy's voice in his ear suddenly, breaking him from his reverie. "On your seven o'clock."

Forcing himself to keep his pace, Kovalic continued around the fountain, looking carefully for tails or other surveillance. Any of the people here might be CID or Bureau agents, of course – that elderly man sitting on the edge of the infinity pool, the woman walking the dog, or even the parents of the little boy. But nothing tickled that innate part of his brain, the one that sensed danger even when he couldn't see it.

"Sound off," he murmured.

"Perimeter clear," said Rance.

"Immediate surrounds also clear," said Yevgeniy. "You've got the green light whenever you're ready."

Kovalic glanced down at his sleeve. They were still early, but that was just fine by him. Promptness meant a readiness to deal.

He hadn't specified an exact place for the meet, which meant he got to pick on the fly. Wending his way around the monument a final time, he chose to exit between the black walls for Trinity and Centauri, and then continued on to a bench up on a little knoll that overlooked the Rings.

Taking a seat, Kovalic crossed his legs and looked out at the sculpture as though he were appreciating its artistic qualities: the way the light gleamed off the rings as they rotated, or how its reflection hung suspended in the infinity pool. He waited patiently for his quarry.

The man approached slowly, clutching the strap of a bag slung over his shoulder. Looking around nervously, as though he were the fugitive on the run from the authorities, he crunched across the gravel path. But apparently satisfied with whatever he saw – or didn't see – he made his way to the bench and sat down at the opposite end.

After a moment, he seemed to realize that Kovalic wasn't going to make the first move, so he cleared his throat awkwardly. "Uh… I'm probably not who you were expecting, major."

Kovalic cocked his head to one side, as if inviting him to say more.

The man craned his neck, peering all around them, then pulled out a small black ovoid and moved to push a button atop it.

"Oh dear," said Yevgeniy over the comm. "Is that what I think –"

Kovalic's ears popped and the former Illyrican agent was cut off as the baffle's anti-eavesdropping field descended around them. Nobody outside of a ten-foot radius would be able to hear a word they said, and his comms were effectively dead.

"There," said the man, though he still seemed anxious, shifting his weight back and forth from one foot to the other. "Just us."

"To what do I owe the pleasure?" said Kovalic. He leaned back against the bench, trying to put the other man at ease.

"It's just… I thought you needed to see this." Reaching into the bag, the man pulled out a tablet and proffered it to Kovalic.

"What's this?"

"Proof." The man swallowed. "Proof that Aidan Kester is a mole for the Illyrican Empire and the one who framed you for treason."

CHAPTER 43

Eli Brody's life had seen its fair share of exhilarating piloting moments, but flying through a humongous sandstorm on his home planet might just have been the most impressive – even if it might be the last.

I can't decide what's worse: that I'll be remembered as a traitor twice over, or that I died doing something this stupid.

The *Cavalier* was tossed side to side by the crosswinds, buffeted up and down as it dropped through the various layers of whirling air, and peppered continuously by what felt like a hail of small arms fire from the particulates being blown about at hurricane-level speeds.

It took everything Eli had to maintain his hold on the yoke, which kept threatening to vibrate right out of his grip. Control was a laughable proposition. Even figuring out which direction to go was proving its own challenge: visibility out the canopy was zero, even with his heads-up display's enhancement systems.

Besides him, Andres was still clutching the sides of his seat in a grip that would have, in other circumstances, probably been around Eli's throat. The big man clearly couldn't decide whether it was better to have his eyes open or closed to face his impending doom and was going through an endless cycle of peeking through them, seeing the madness out the canopy, and then squeezing them shut again.

Not an option for me. Although would it really matter at this point?

A particularly violent crosswind sheared through the *Cav*, sending it spinning on its axis. Eli wrestled the yoke back into a modicum of steadiness.

Telemetry from Taylor's signal was intermittent and, given the speed of the train, every time Eli did get a reading, it was miles from where it had been a minute ago. But it was all he had to home in on. At least he could roughly use it to project the train's course; with a little luck he should be able to shadow its route and maybe even get ahead of it.

Well, maybe more than a little luck.

From out in the corridor came another muted thump. Eli had hoped that Prentiss would be smart enough to go buckle in; even though she hadn't been particularly friendly, he didn't feel great about his flying causing the woman serious injury.

There was a ping from the console as Taylor's signal surfaced once more, now ahead off the *Cavalier*'s port bow, and Eli did his best to adjust his heading to follow it, gaining altitude to try and catch an air pocket moving in the right direction.

"This is insane," Andres muttered, his eyes still shut. "You can't fly through a sandstorm."

"Fly, no," Eli agreed, eyes darting back and forth between the canopy and the few instruments that were providing useful information. "That *would* be crazy. You gotta ride it." And with that he pulled back on the yoke and hit the pocket, sending them sliding to port like a surfer catching a wave.

His stomach leapt into his throat as the ship bumped and tumbled through the air, but it was only partly from fear. He remembered this feeling, from his earliest days of piloting, when danger seemed to lurk at every turn and the only way through was to trust his instincts. But the more he'd done it, the more it had turned into a chore – a means to an end. First to get off Caledonia, then to make it through the Imperial Naval Academy, then just to survive. He missed the simple joy of alternately cooperating and contending with nature, the unexpected and the magical.

Even the pants-crappingly insane.

Another ping; was it his imagination or was Taylor's signal coming through stronger now? He glanced at the range and was surprised to see he was much closer than he'd expected to be. Reaching over to the comm panel, he patched his earbud into the ship's array.

"Major… uh…" he racked his brain, trying to remember the alias Taylor had been using back on Juarez 7A. "Vine? Vin… tage? Veni… Vidi… Vinson! Major Vinson, do you copy?"

No response. He kept one hand on the yoke while trying to peer out the canopy to the surface below, but the sand was still obscuring everything.

Lower. Need to get lower. He'd been trying to hold at ten thousand feet, plus or minus a few hundred, until he'd localized the signal, but that clearly wasn't going to work.

"Hold on," he said, more to himself than to Andres as he pushed the stick forward.

The *Cav* nosed down and started to slide like it had just crested the steepest rise of a roller coaster. On the console, the altimeter ticked down in a steady, if slow manner, as Eli let the sandstorm's currents do most of the work for him.

This is going surprisingly smoo–

Alarms blared as the ship jolted and the starboard side dipped precariously. Eli steered port to compensate, but something was wrong; the controls were sluggish, jerky. Even as he kept fighting with the stick, he checked the console and saw a large red warning light on the starboard engine cluster.

Offline.

"Oh, shit."

"What?" Andres slid one shaky eye open. "What is it?"

"Nothing, nothing. Just a flameout on the starboard engine. No problem!"

"We lost an engine? That sounds like a *big fucking* problem!"

"It's fine. We've still got two clusters port and stern. I just need to restart it!" Eli reached over and flipped the toggle for the starboard engine.

Nothing happened.

Huh. He peered as closely at the console as he could while still keeping an eye on the flight instruments. The starboard engine cluster was misfiring and not igniting – probably, in Eli's expert opinion, because it was full of sand.

Still, they could get by on two engines; he'd just have to adjust the output to compensate, and they'd lose a little stability.

"Soooo," he said, one hand flipping switches on the console as he kept the other on the controls, "this may get a little bumpy."

Andres's head slowly swiveled to face him, both eyes now open wide. "It may *get* a little bumpy? What the hell do you call this?"

"A pleasant thrill ride?"

"If we survive this, I am going to kill you."

"Optimism! That's the spirit." And with that Eli hauled the controls to port and down, pressing them both back into their seats.

The ship was definitely bucking even more under Eli's hands than a few minutes ago; he could feel the loss in stabilization. Nothing he couldn't handle, but the tolerance for further failures was going to be a lot lower. He wasn't sure how much longer the *Cav* could hold up in this storm. One thing he hadn't told Andres: he'd checked the readings on the other two engines, and they were rapidly clogging as well. Maybe fifty percent on the port, and thirty-five on the stern. That meant there was an upper time limit before they could bug out of here, and it probably wasn't more than about ten minutes. Possibly a lot less.

So if they were going to find the train, sooner was definitely preferable.

As if summoned by that particular worry, a repeated beeping issued from the comm panel, and he glanced over to see Taylor's signal coming through much more clearly. There were still occasional drop-outs, but cohesion was upwards of eighty percent.

He toggled the transmitter again. "*Cavalier* to Vinson. Do you copy? We are inbound on your position. ETA..." He looked back at the console, did some rough math and hoped that he'd remembered to divide instead of multiply, "...five minutes. Hope you've got all your luggage packed, because we are definitely not sticking around."

Only static came back.

Eli's jaw clenched and his hands tightened on the yoke. This was going to work. He was going to make it in time. Addy, Tapper, Taylor, Gwen – they all needed him.

He pushed the controls forward, diving further through the storm, winds and sand whipping at the canopy with so much force that he wondered if they were leaving permanent scratches on the transparent aluminum. The ship rocked beneath him, as though it were a boat awash on rough seas, but he anticipated the swells, leaning into the turns until it felt like he and the *Cavalier* had become one.

And then, with a sudden *thump*, there was a break, and they dropped below the storm's strongest layers and into skies that felt, by comparison, relatively clear. Windspeed dropped and some semblance of control returned. There was even a few miles of intermittent visibility and, through it, a long winding silver snake that Eli recognized, after a moment of trying to get his bearings, as gravtrain tracks.

He grinned. "Now we're in business."

Beside him, Andres slumped in his chair, releasing some of the tension he'd been holding, and even going so far as to crack his eyes open.

The ride still wasn't smooth and the ship continued to jostle and bump, but it was far from the maelstrom they'd just weathered.

Eli throttled up, one eye on the console, and followed the tracks. The signal from Taylor was coming through even more consistently now, and he had a bead on its direction and speed. They ought to close with the train in just a couple minutes, but this calm in the storm wouldn't last indefinitely. Atmospheric sensors suggested that he only had a few minutes before they were back in a bad patch.

"I don't know how you think you're getting out of this," said Andres, shaking his head. "You're a dead man."

"Not the first time I've heard it. And yet, here I am."

"She's going to hunt you down. You, your family, everyone you love."

Eli sighed. "You're a real cheery guy, anybody ever tell you that?"

Outside the canopy, Eli caught a glimmer of movement; he upped the magnification on the HUD to see the tail end of the gravtrain skimming through the barren expanse at what, from the perspective of a ship going probably half again its speed, seemed surprisingly slow. They'd be on top of it in just moments, and none too soon: on the horizon loomed another wall of sand, the end of this relatively peaceful stretch. If he didn't get them out before then, well, it was going to get a whole lot harder. And sandier.

Time for another approach. He tapped the comm panel again, adjusting the frequency; it was a long shot, but they might be close enough for a point-to-point transmission to punch through the interference. "Gwen, do you copy? *Cavalier* on approach. Pickup clock at five minutes and counting down."

No response; not even a double-click of acknowledgment. Eli felt a lump forming in the back of his throat. More than anything, he avoided looking in Andres's direction, sure that the other man would have a self-satisfied smile on his face.

It's not over, he repeated to himself, even as his eyes went to the imposing wall of sand and dirt just ahead of them. *It's not over* yet.

CHAPTER 44

I can make the shot.

That's what Addy's brain kept repeating as she stared down the sights of the knockout gun at Ofeibia Xi, who was in turn, staring down the sights of a flechette pistol at her.

It wouldn't even be difficult: Xi was maybe five meters away, there were no obstructions in the way, and unlike Gwen and Tapper, the weapon she'd picked up wasn't from the syndicate leader's goons.

Except for one pesky fact: fast as a stun field was, it wasn't faster than someone pulling a trigger. Sure, Addy might take Xi down, but there was a good chance she was going to end up with several metal darts in her, and that was going to be considerably less pleasant than being rendered unconscious. And that was *if* Xi wasn't wearing a disruption matrix to counter the stun field, as her people on the *Queen Amina* had. As bets went, it was a bad one.

She didn't dare let her eyes slide to Taylor, but her widened awareness took in the commander, and she felt like she saw a flicker of movement in her peripheral vision that, much as she wanted it to be a nod, looked distinctly like a shake of the head.

And the worst part was that she couldn't even contain her relief.

Who the hell are you? Addy of six months ago would have pulled the trigger and damn the consequences, but all of a sudden here she was *considering* consequences. Somewhere up there, she could hear old Boyland chuckling, maybe with a self-satisfied "I told you so".

Because she knew what had changed: she had something to keep living for. Her team – her family. Brody and his bacon, much as she hated to admit it.

Fight another day.

Without breaking eye contact with Xi's violet gaze, she lowered her arm and then tossed the KO gun onto the foam-sodden carpet, where it landed with a splash-thud.

"Thank you," said Xi. "I do appreciate your reasonableness. Now. Walk." She gestured with the gun towards the door leading to the baggage car.

This time Addy did find Taylor's eyes, and the commander lazily inclined her head. Addy hoped to hell the other woman had a backup plan, because they'd left the original far behind.

With a barely concealed grunt of frustration, Addy turned and started walking through the ankle-deep foam towards the door. She could hear the slosh of other footsteps behind her as the rest of the team fell into line.

Good, we're lined up, so Xi can just shoot through all of us at once. Glad we're helping her conserve ammo.

Addy's mind raced as she stepped into the connecting compartment. The temptation to press herself to the side, out of the line of fire, and try to ambush Xi was high, but the crime lord still had a clear view. She'd just be condemning the rest of her team. What they needed was something outside of the woman's control, some variable that Xi wouldn't expect.

Patience. The cautionary voice in her head still sounded a bit like Boyland, even all these years after his death. But the dead man was right; there was a time for violence of action, and it was in service of a plan.

"Don't be too hasty, Madam Xi," said Taylor as she stepped into the compartment with the rest of them. "This deal can still be mutually beneficial."

"I don't think your friend here would agree," said Xi, her voice all icy calm. "She's not about to walk away from this, are you, Special Agent Rhys?"

Gwen's gaze was locked to Xi. "I'm afraid I can't do that, no."

"See? That's the problem with law enforcement – the ones you can buy off prove they can't be trusted, but the trustworthy ones are so... inflexible. Alas."

Addy let out a sigh even as her pulse continued at double time. "Just kill us and get it over with. I'm good on monologuing, thanks."

"Oh, Adelaide," said Xi with a *tsk*. "Ever so impatient. I'm not going to kill you. We had a deal, and I intend to honor it to the letter." The door to the Coire Ansic's car slid closed behind her, leaving them all closeted in the connecting compartment. "Besides, I'll need your help unloading all my money." She waved her pistol at Taylor. "Now, Major Vinson, I believe we're approaching the branch line; if you'll kindly activate the remote switch while Adelaide decouples the cars, we can get on with it."

For a brief moment, Addy started to contemplate simply not doing what Xi asked, leaving the cars attached to the rest of the train as they barreled their way to Stranraer. But the end of that plan trailed off into a series of question marks. Xi would be pissed and, despite her protestations to the contrary, Addy had no belief that the woman would simply let them go. They'd all be stuck on the train together for the rest of the trip, and it would go a bit beyond awkward.

Stiffly, she marched over to the access panel and pulled it open, revealing a large red lever surrounded by warning signs in bold print, small print, and everything in between.

Out of her peripheral vision, she saw Gwen stiffen suddenly, her eyes unfocusing as though she were listening to something the rest of them couldn't hear. After a split second, she blinked, and her eyes went to Addy, sparkling with something that looked suspiciously like amusement, before turning to Xi.

"I have to say, Madam Xi, you're being awfully *cavalier* about all of this." The redhead raised her eyebrows significantly.

Addy froze, hand clutching the lever. Brody. He was alive – and on the *Cavalier*. A swell of relief broke over her. Despite all of Xi's posturing and threats, he'd squirmed his way out of yet another improbable situation through, what... force of will? Sheer dumb luck? She should take him to the casino if they got out of this.

Her heartbeat amped up as suddenly as if she were standing on the edge of a precipice, teetering.

"It's not my first time being threatened with arrest, Agent Rhys," said Xi calmly. "But nobody's ever managed to seal the deal. And I'm still the only one holding a weapon."

Tapper snorted. "Like none of us have ever been held at gunpoint before. Big fucking deal."

Clearing her throat, Taylor raised her arm. "If you're all finished, maybe we can proceed with this job and everybody can go home without getting shot?"

Xi inclined her head. "A most reasonable position, major. Please."

Locking eyes with Addy, Taylor nodded her head. "Sayers, go ahead. Hold on tight."

Turning back to the access panel, Addy drew a deep breath. Here went nothing. One hand flipped off the safety catch, the other, damp with sweat, gripped the lever.

She yanked it down.

The compartment's lights shifted to red, and she heard a click as the door to the Coire Ansic's car locked, followed by a deep *ka-chunk* as the coupling released somewhere beneath them. They all rocked backwards as the car started to lose its speed, going from being propelled forward to just coasting on its own momentum.

Taylor had her eyes locked to her sleeve, and Addy could see her mouth forming numbers as she counted down the seconds until the rest of the train was clear of the track branch. "Activating switch... now." She tapped something on her sleeve, and a moment later they all leaned to one side as the car veered off onto the spur track, headed for Fort Mull.

And Xi's welcoming committee.

"Excellent work, everyone," said Xi, looking around with a smile all the more fake for its broadness. "I knew we could do it if only we worked together. How long until we reach –"

The crime lord didn't get to finish her sentence. As soon as Xi had looked away from Taylor, she'd looped her arm through a railing and then tapped on her sleeve again.

Hold on, thought Addy in a panic, *she said to hold on*. She grabbed the decoupling lever with both hands, as though her life depended on it, just a split second before the car's brakes engaged.

The front of the car came to an abrupt stop, throwing them all violently forward, and Addy's arms were stretched to their limit as she held on to the lever. Tapper and Gwen careened towards Xi who, as the person closest to the front of the car, was slammed into the now locked door with tremendous force. The normally self-assured expression on the syndicate leader's face was wiped away with wide-eyed, visceral fear, and the gun she'd been holding a moment earlier spun from her hand as the breath wheezed out of her.

Tapper and Gwen each grunted as they hit the floor, but they both managed to tuck into a roll along with the momentum. Almost gracefully, they popped out of the rolls and threw themselves at Xi, each grabbing ahold of one of the woman's arms.

"Let *go*," she snarled, struggling to escape their grasp, but they'd pinned her to the floor.

Addy let go of the lever, her biceps feeling like limp noodles. *Between that and my little rock chimney exercise in the baggage car, I think I can skip arm day.* Stalking up to Xi, she looked the syndicate boss up and down as she struggled against Tapper and Gwen's grip, and saw for the first time what all the elegance was masking: rage and, yes, more than a little bit of fear.

"You know I will come for you," Xi said, looking around wildly. "All of you."

"Oh, shut *up*," said Addy, rolling her eyes. She hauled back and, even with her arm as sore as it was, socked Xi straight in the jaw. The crime lord's head bounced off the metal door and she collapsed into a heap of fashionable clothes.

Tapper let out a whistle as Addy massaged her sore fist. "Long time coming, huh?"

"Too damn long," Addy muttered.

Gwen produced a pair of quick cuffs from somewhere and looped them through a handhold and around Xi's wrists. "You all had better get going. Brody's on his way in. I can take Xi and Flores from here."

"What about the money?" asked Tapper, casting a glance to the rear of the car.

"Evidence, old man," said Gwen. She raised an eyebrow. "Unless you want me to take you in for theft too?"

"We need to know where it came from at least," said Taylor, crouching down by Xi. The crime lord was still down for the count, but the commander seemed less interested in her than her jewelry. Unclipping one of the woman's many bangles, she slipped it in her pocket, before sparing a glance for Gwen. "Sorry, Agent Rhys, but we've all got our priorities."

The agent put up her hands. "I just collared two of the biggest criminals in the galaxy; let's call it a fair trade. I'll patch you through to Brody's comms. Just do me a favor and, as soon as you get clear of the sandstorm, put in a call to my colleague Agent Liang and let her know I'm out here. Before I, you know, starve to death in the middle of the desert." She waved her arm in Taylor's direction, and the commander's sleeve pinged.

"Can do," said Taylor, with a businesslike nod. "Thanks for your help, Agent Rhys." Walking over to the overhead access hatch, she climbed up the ladder and keyed it open.

"Guess this is it," said Gwen, looking around.

"C'mere, lass," said Tapper. The weathered sergeant wrapped the woman in a bear hug. "I'll be in touch."

"You'd better be," said Gwen. "Maybe next time we can have a visit that doesn't involve a train robbery."

Tapper grinned. "What do you want to rob instead?" He gave her a wink, then followed Taylor up the ladder to the train car's roof.

Addy tipped the other woman a two-finger salute. "Pleasure working with you, Gwen."

"You too... and Addy?"

"Yeah?"

"Keep an eye on Brody. He's lucky to have you."

Addy flushed a red only slightly paler than Gwen's hair. "I'll do my best." And then she was up the ladder before she could say anything more embarrassing. *Jesus, does everybody know about us?*

On top of the train car, the wind was still whipping sand and dirt around them, and Addy raised a hand to shield her eyes. At least it was slightly calmer when you weren't also going five hundred klicks an hour.

There was a loud roar as the familiar shape of the *Cavalier* broke through the clouds and came to a slightly unsteady stop overhead, wavering back and forth on its repulsors like an ice cube skittering on a hot metal pan.

"Hey team," said Brody's voice, filtering over Addy's earbud and filling her with a wave of relief. "I think I've had my fill of sand. What do you say we get the hell out of here?"

CHAPTER 45

The ride out of the sandstorm was interesting, to say the least. Nat, Addy, and Tapper took a tow lift up onto the hovering *Cavalier*, where they found one of Xi's goons unconscious and a bit bruised in one of the ship's corridors, as well as a big man looking shaken in the co-pilot seat next to an in-his-element Eli Brody.

Getting the thugs off the ship and into Gwen's custody only took a few minutes, and the CalSec agent seemed a bit gleeful at the pile of bodies she'd amassed – in the end, she locked them all in the connecting compartment while she sat in the car full of money.

"Maintaining the chain of evidence," she said, before shooing them away with a promise that she'd heavily edit the official report.

Brody seemed his usual confident self as he waited for them to take their seats. "It'll be easier on the way out. I think I've basically figured out how to fly through this thing."

Tapper, who'd taken the lead on escorting the bigger of Xi's goons out the door, looked skeptical but buckled in behind Brody nonetheless. Addy, who'd stopped to give the pilot a firm squeeze of the shoulder, took the seat behind Nat.

"The band's back together again," said Brody, glancing behind him with a grin. "Everybody got all their belongings? Because we are definitely not coming back here."

At their vociferous assent he threw the throttle open and sent them rocketing back up into the maelstrom.

Calling the ride "bumpy" was an understatement. The *Cavalier* was tossed about like it was in an industrial mixer, and the onboard compensators did little to buffer them against the impact of the winds. Even Tapper, who as a marine had spent his fair share of time on drop ships, was starting to look a bit green around the collar by the time they finally broached the sandstorm back into Caledonia's pale blue sky.

The first order of business was to report Gwen's whereabouts. The agent had been very specific that they speak only to Agent Liang. Apparently previous attempts to take action against the Coire Ansic had resulted in CalSec's agents ending up dead or simply disappearing – a result they could now conjecture came from the organization's connections with the Illyricans. CalSec might have jurisdiction for local law enforcement, but they were still on an Imperium-controlled world, which meant a requirement to share all their information with Illyrican agencies. Including both Fleet Security and IIS.

Still, the whole imbroglio left Nat with at least one outstanding question: Where had the Coire Ansic gotten so many Commonwealth credits? Who was the connection Flores had mentioned?

At least she had an inkling of where to start looking. She turned to the console beside her and pulled out the bangle she'd appropriated from Ofeibia Xi. Connecting it to the

Cavalier prompted her for a password, so she set one of her cracking programs to the task and swiveled to face the rest of the team.

They'd done well, all things considered, and, more to the point, they were all still in one piece. She caught Tapper's eye and the old sergeant seemed to sense her thoughts, giving her a nod and something that might have passed for a wink.

"So," said Addy, unbuckling as the ship stabilized. "Where to now? We've stolen from spaceliners and trains... should we go find a boat or something?"

"Just, whatever we do, not back to Juarez 7A," said Tapper, pinching the bridge of his nose. "I just don't think I can take the rain."

Brody cleared his throat as he activated the *Cavalier*'s autopilot and spun around to face them, a rare look of uncertainty on his face. "Actually," he said, scratching his head awkwardly, "if we don't have any immediate plans, I'd like to make a stop up north. There's somebody I should go see while I'm here." His eyes darted to Addy, then away, as he looked somehow even more abashed. "And I wouldn't mind some company."

The small coastal village of Berwick didn't really have a spaceport, so Brody set the ship down in an open field a couple kilometers outside the town.

The pilot had explained en route that his sister lived in a home here with a caretaker; he didn't spell it out but it seemed clear that she'd been dealing with some challenges for a while now. Belatedly, the pilot extended an invitation to Nat and Tapper to join them, but it wasn't hard to tell it was halfhearted, so both demurred to let Brody and Addy have some time alone.

Nat, for her part, took the opportunity to dig through her network feeds. Caledonia was, at least, on the main relays, though being on an Illyrican colony world did make some Commonwealth sources harder to access.

But a news report about a trio of fugitives on Nova was still big enough to reach this side of the bottleneck, including grainy images of the three clearly captured from a security camera.

Her heart thumped at the picture of Simon, but there was no subsequent indication that any of them had been apprehended. So they were still at large, and still presumably in need of their help.

Tapper grunted, reading the news over her shoulder. "Gonna take more than some desk jockey like Kester to bring them in."

"You think they're still on Nova?"

"The boss doesn't like to leave a job unfinished. Yeah, I'd wager they're there somewhere, laying low." He gave a rueful smile. "Probably not so low, let's be honest."

Nat's fingers rippled across the console, tapping out a drumbeat.

"You want to go back," said Tapper.

"Is it that obvious?"

The older man shrugged. "I don't blame you. Getting clear of the mess was the right move at the time, but now it just feels like we're sitting around twiddling our thumbs while the action's back there."

"Going back is risky – for all of us."

"Yeah, sure, but risk is kind of our job. Sayers, even Brody, they'd volunteer in a heartbeat."

Nat ran a hand through her hair. It had gone stringy with sand and sweat; she could definitely use a shower, even if it was in the *Cav*'s often janky and frequently warm-water-at-best refresher unit. "Logistics wise, it seems like Maldonado's transponder system could get us back onto Nova undetected. And those identities we pulled should still be clean, even if they're a bit thin."

Tapper leaned back in his chair, interlacing his hands behind his head. "Seems like you've already thought it through. But I'd expect nothing less from you, commander."

Nat got up and stretched her arms, then gave an experimental sniff. Yeah, she could definitely use a shower. "I'm going to hit the refresher. When Brody and Sayers get back, we can get under way."

The *Cav*'s shower lived up to its reputation – icy cold with intermittent spurts of water – but Nat still felt better afterwards, especially after she pulled on one of the clean sets of spare clothes from her footlocker and tossed her bedraggled garments in the ship's onboard laundry processor.

Tapper was still sitting in the cockpit when she got back. He nodded to a light flashing on the communications console. "Two things: I think your decryption on Xi's whatchmacallit there finished. And we got a message from Gwen that you're going to want to see."

Nat leaned over and tapped a control; a holographic screen flickered to life, showing the CalSec agent sitting at a desk somewhere – not still on the gravtrain, thank goodness.

"Thanks for the assist again, old man. We've got Flores, Xi, and all their people in custody and I'm just waiting for the paperwork to come through on their charges. Here's hoping we'll have them locked down for a while to come.

"Flores wanted to cut a deal and turn on *everybody*, but given that he's near the top of the food chain, all he has is that vague description of the Illyrican that he dealt with." Gwen shook her head, her red curls bouncing. "The crims set him up perfectly. *But* he did have one thing to share that I thought might be of interest to you. The contact who supplied him with the credits? Flores says he heard the guy worked out of the Commonwealth embassy in Raleigh City." She raised her eyebrows significantly. "Figured that might help you track him down. Anyway, this report's going to be a bear, but it won't be the first time I've had to... *elide* some details." She coughed meaningfully, then her eyes darted offscreen. "I gotta run, but thanks again. And tell Brody he still owes me a dinner."

The screen vanished, leaving Nat and Tapper eyeing each other.

"We need to pull the list of embassy person –"

"Already done," said Tapper, fanning his hand to spread out a series of thumbnail images on a holoscreen. "I was just going through them. Flores said the guy was blond and – I'm using his words here – 'weasely', but so far I can't find anybody who fits even that broad description."

Nat chewed on her bottom lip, then checked Xi's bracelet. As Tapper had said, the decryption had finished, so she pulled up the images that the syndicate leader's surveillance had captured of the meet with Flores. "Him," she said, pointing to the blurry figure standing behind Flores. There was just

DAN MOREN   387

a smudge of light-colored hair, and from what she could tell about the man's build, it was on the slighter side. There were other images on the bracelet from the meet, and she cycled through them, but none provided a clearer picture of their target – he definitely hadn't been Xi's primary interest.

Tapper scanned through the images again and shook his head. "Double check me, but none of these look right."

Nat flipped through them as well, but the sergeant's assessment was correct. The Commonwealth's diplomatic presence on Caledonia wasn't huge – only about fifty people. A couple of the men did come close; she stopped on one with brown hair and freckles, but even from the blurry images, the shape of the face was wrong.

She pulled up the roster again. "Let's try a different approach. Who would have access to that much cash on hand?"

Tapper blew out his cheeks. "Only a few people. The ambassador, probably, and the deputy chief of mission. But it clearly isn't either of them. I checked their immediate staff too."

"What about the CID station chief?" said Nat. "They'd be able to move a lot of cash quietly."

"Yeah, but there isn't one right now," said Tapper slowly. "CID canned Walter Danzig after the Caledonian op we ran here, almost two years ago."

Nat raised her eyebrows. "What if Flores's contact *did* work at the embassy…"

"But doesn't anymore," Tapper finished her sentence, his hands already flying over the console. "Here's the records of embassy personnel who have left in the last two years." There were only ten or so, and the winner was

THE ARMAGEDDON PROTOCOL

easily apparent. Tapper brought up his personnel record image and it filled the holographic screen. The sergeant huffed out a slow breath, his eyes widening; Nat's breath caught in her own throat as well: the face, which had rang a slight bell at its thumbnail size, set off an entire clocktower at fullscreen.

"Fuck *me*," said Tapper. "I *knew* he looked familiar."

"Recall Brody and Sayers right the hell now," said Nat, moving to the co-pilot seat and starting the *Cavalier*'s pre-flight. "We need to get to Nova before it's too late." But the knot rising rapidly in her throat made her wonder if it already was.

CHAPTER 46

The baffle's sound-dampening bubble was bi-directional, which made it decidedly surreal for Kovalic sitting in the middle of a busy park – like watching reality on mute.

A young kid in a yellow shirt and purple shorts ran by, some twenty feet away, mouth wide in a wordless shriek of joy as he cavorted with a dog. Beyond, the massive rings oscillated, their eternal flow of water silent.

Admittedly, this complicated matters; he'd counted on having Yevgeniy's recording for evidence. But they'd passed the point of no return.

Kovalic raised an eyebrow as he took the tablet the man was holding out to him and skimmed the contents. "This is a report about General Adaj's finances. Transfers routed through Bayern to the Novan Liberation Front." The exact evidence he'd asked Kester to provide at this meet.

The other man nodded. "On the face of it, it seems legit enough, but if you start digging into the metadata, that's where things start getting weird. Normally a document like this would have a... provenance, for lack of a better word. Or maybe a chain of custody? Something that would show where the raw intelligence originated, which analyst had reviewed it, what agencies and departments it had been circulated to, and so on."

"But…?" said Kovalic.

The man nodded at the tablet. "May I?"

"Certainly," said Kovalic, holding it out to him.

With a few taps, another set of text scrolled up alongside the first. There was a variety of information about the document format, creation date, and so on. With one finger, the man indicated a blank heading. "That's where it *should* be. The only thing that it shows for the file origination is 'local' – meaning it was created on Acting Director Kester's own terminal."

"Hm," said Kovalic rubbing his chin. Not a surprise, exactly; that was more or less what he had expected, and why he'd wanted it to see the original report. "It's Lawson, isn't it? Kester's assistant?"

The man's pale skin flushed, as though he hadn't counted on being recognized. "Yes, sir."

"I don't have to ask how you came by this. But I am curious as to what made you suspicious about your boss."

Lawson scratched his head, looking embarrassed. "I don't know exactly. He's just been so single-minded about tracking you down, never willing to hear alternative theories or explain why he's so convinced that he's right. It just seemed odd, more than anything. And when Inspector Laurent called the office to relay the information about this meeting, I knew I had to bring this to you."

"That shows initiative," said Kovalic. "I assume you didn't tell your boss about this meet when Inspector Laurent called?"

If anything, the other man looked even more abashed, as though he'd violated some cardinal rule of being an assistant. "I did not."

Kovalic nodded. "Good work. Trusting your gut and taking action are both qualities of an excellent intelligence officer. How long have you been in CID?"

Flushing with the praise, Lawson ducked his head. "Four years."

"Four years and you're already aide to the director," said Kovalic. "Impressive. How long have you been with Kester?"

"About a year," said Lawson.

"And did anything else in that time raise your suspicions?"

Lawson's brow furrowed. "Now that you mention it... there were a few other missions that he took a special interest in while he was in charge of operations. I didn't notice at the time, but looking back, there may be a pattern." His face fell. "I should have caught it sooner."

"Not at all," Kovalic reassured him. "There's a reason they call them moles. Catching someone burrowed that deep is a tricky proposition. If my hypothesis is correct, this isn't some sudden change of loyalty; it was a long thought-out plan that's been gestating for years as the mole worked his way up through the ranks. It probably started back before even his last posting on Caledonia."

Lawson blinked, cocking his head. "Director Kester came up on the Hanif desk, major. I don't believe he was ever stationed on Caledonia."

Kovalic snapped his fingers, pointing off into the distance, and crooked his index finger. "Right, right." He leveled his gray gaze at Lawson. "But *you* were."

The other man's mouth opened and closed like a fish on the hook, but no noise came out.

"I admit, you fade into the background quite well," Kovalic continued. "I didn't even clock you while we had Kester under surveillance, but then the general pointed out something very astute – shouldn't be a surprise, I guess. The man's probably forgotten more about spycraft than either of us have ever known." Too bad the baffle's comm interference meant the general couldn't hear him; Kovalic wasn't one to lay on effusive praise.

"He noted that a high-ranking official's *assistant* is the perfect position for a mole. Access to sensitive materials, far less scrutiny, and more often than not the keeper of all of their boss's secrets. It would be relatively easy for them to, say, insert an intelligence report into the stack for a daily briefing. Even," continued Kovalic, raising the tablet, "use their boss's terminal to create said report."

Lawson shook his head. "You've got the wrong end of the stick here, Kovalic."

"Do I? It's just a coincidence, then, that you were assistant to Caledonia station chief Walter Danzig two years ago when a CID operative was killed there. And that, when Danzig's failures came to light, you managed to wrangle yourself a move to the desk of the up-and-coming deputy director of operations."

"What are you talking about?" Lawson blustered. "That's all just happenstance. It's not proof of anything. You're trying to pin all of this on me, when it's *Kester* you should be looking at!"

"I honestly can't blame you for trying," said Kovalic, ignoring the man's outburst. "I had my own sights far too fixed on Kester, in no small part because of my personal dislike of him. But *my* gut was telling me that no matter how much he might rub me the wrong way, that didn't make him a traitor."

Lawson had begun inching away from Kovalic under the onslaught of accusations, and at this, he got to his feet, hands worrying at each other. "I don't know what game you're playing, Kovalic, but I brought you information in... in good *faith*. And now you want to turn this frame around on *me*? Maybe *you're* the dirty one." Panic had crept into the man's eyes, roaming wild.

He was afraid, Kovalic realized. Something had convinced Henrik Lawson to betray his government. Some turned for greed, or for a bizarre sort of personal aggrandizement. Others out of bitterness and spite. Some were even true believers, harboring a secret ideology.

But Lawson was in yet another category: the ones who were trapped.

"It was on Caledonia that Eyes turned you, wasn't it?" asked Kovalic, injecting a note of sympathy into his voice. "Some small inconsequential thing, but like a piece of grit lodged in an oyster it grew, layer upon layer, until it was a pearl stuck in your craw." He locked his gaze on Lawson's, silently willing the other man to stay with him.

Lawson flinched, and started to look around, but Kovalic spread his hands slowly, keeping the other man's attention fixed on him. "Henrik, I can help. It's not too late."

"No..." said the blond man slowly. "I don't think you can, not really. You can't even help yourself." His voice had gone pitchy with stress. "I think I'll just be going." He started to back away from the bench in a most conspicuous manner.

"That would be a mistake," said Kovalic, but he didn't budge from his spot on the bench. "I'm just going to have to come after you."

"What are you going to do, tackle me in the middle of a public place in broad daylight?" He gestured at the silent tableau around them. "You might as well just turn yourself in." His breathing had turned shallow and rapid, eyes too bright.

"Funny, I was going to say the same thing to you. Espionage, treason – take it from someone who knows; these are serious crimes."

"You have no *proof*," Lawson scoffed. "It's all just circumstantial, and nobody's going to believe a fugitive."

"Maybe. If it were just my word against yours. But that's not quite true." With his right hand up, palm out, Kovalic slowly dipped his left into his jacket and produced a data chip. "A few hours ago, I received a high priority message from operatives in the field with evidence linking *you* to a Caledonian criminal named Roche Flores and, via him, Illyrican Intelligence."

Color drained out of Lawson's face at the name, and he looked like he'd just swallowed a rock. "Fake. You faked it." He didn't even sound like he believed what he was saying. One hand slowly reached into the bag he was clutching and seized something inside.

Kovalic didn't have to see it to know it was a weapon. He gave Lawson a tight, sympathetic smile. "Before you do something you regret, there are two more things you should know."

"I don't have to listen to you!"

"One," said Kovalic, ignoring the outburst while enumerating on his fingers. "Baffle fields extend about ten feet outward in every direction."

Lawson blinked, confused.

"And two: when I set the meeting with Inspector Laurent for three o'clock, that was because I already had an earlier engagement."

Even as realization dawned on Lawson, there came the hum-buzz of a stun field from behind him; his eyes rolled back into his head and he crumpled to the ground.

"Blast," said Aidan Kester, as he lowered the KO gun he was holding and brushed a rare errant strand of hair back into place. "I suppose I'm going to need a new assistant."

CHAPTER 47

There's something about non-fugitive air that just smells better. Standing in the open hangar door, Eli drew in another lungful.

OK, a military base might not be the perfect example, what with the crisp ozone tang of ship engines and the tarmac baking in the hot sun. Still, the point stood. Not worrying about whether or not someone was going to burst in and attempt to throw them into a cell had a certain freshness to it.

With a contented sigh, he turned and walked back into the hangar where the *Cavalier* perched in its usual spot. It looked a bit worse for wear from its trip through a Caledonian sandstorm, the hull pitted and abraded from the onslaught of sand and dirt. Cassie Engel, the team's mechanic, had given him a dead-eyed stare when she'd seen the condition of the ship, then told Eli in no uncertain terms that he would be fetching her coffee for the next month. He'd been so relieved to see her that he didn't even argue.

Getting back onworld had proved easier than expected; by the time they'd arrived, the Bureau had already arrested Henrik Lawson. The evidence Taylor had sent on ahead, of Lawson funneling money from the Commonwealth embassy on Caledonia to the Coire Ansic – and ultimately, to IIS – had made the case vacuum-tight. Kester had been uncharacteristically generous in sharing that Lawson had apparently used his boss's authorization to divert money from a black ops slush fund intended to bankroll CID operations on Caledonia.

Eli shook his head as he made his way to the team's small conference room in one corner of the hangar. As he passed the *Cav*, a figure traipsed down the entry ramp.

"Oh, Brody! Just finished the audit of the ship's systems. Somebody definitely tried to compromise the main computer, but they didn't get very far – my quarantine system actually worked!"

If Cary Maldonado had any lingering ill effects from their treatment at the hands of Commonwealth marines, it didn't show – nor did they seem to harbor any resentment. They'd bounced back with their usual resilience, diving straight into their work. When Eli had asked if they wanted to take some time off, the response had been a blank stare, and he'd quickly swallowed any follow-up questions. Privately, he thought the Commonwealth government owed Mal a lot more than a non-apology, but that was probably asking too much.

"Great, Mal, thanks," said Eli.

"Also," said the tech, scratching their head. "I was wondering if you could put in a good word for me with the major."

Eli raised his eyebrows. "What for?"

"Well, I'd just been thinking that instead of having to do all the maintenance with the ship's systems during downtime, maybe, it might kind of be useful for me to be, you know, *there* to provide tech support. In real time."

It took a moment for Eli to unravel Mal's circumlocutions, but then his jaw dropped. "You want to come *on a mission*?"

Mal shrugged, awkwardly bouncing from foot to foot. "Yeah, kinda? It's just... I think I could be helpful."

Eli had been literally blackmailed into his first operation with the team, and here Mal was just volunteering. He somehow doubted the tech knew what they were asking for, but he felt equally certain that he – and the rest of the team – owed them. "No promises, but yeah, I'll mention it."

Brightening, Mal nodded. "Thanks! That'd be a huge help." They cast a look over their shoulder. "That just reminded me, I noticed the lockout system had a potential loophole. I should get on patching that. Catch you at lunch." And with that, they ambled back up the ramp and disappeared into the ship, leaving Eli shaking his head.

He walked into the conference room to find two of his teammates already present. Addy sat at one end, legs up on the table, as she chatted with Tapper, who was leaning against one of the low cabinets.

"...just glad Owen's too young for me to have to explain why his grandfather was wanted for treason," Tapper was saying, rubbing his chin. "It can wait until he's older."

"Like pretty much every other story about his grandfather," said Addy dryly. She spared a smile for Eli as he dropped into a chair on the opposite side of the table. "Maybe just stick to the ones about you and your drinking buddies; they're probably the tamest."

The sergeant's nose wrinkled and he wobbled his head from side to side, a look that seemed to say "fair enough".

"So," said Eli, looking around, "anybody know what this meeting's about? We've only been back a day, I figured we'd get a little more leave before they put us to work again."

"A day of downtime?" said Tapper. "That's *luxurious.*"

Eli rolled his eyes and lowered his voice to a gravelly tone. "Back when we were on Mars, the only downtime we got was the ten minutes between being thrown out of a dropship and landing on the surface! And that's when we did all our paperwork!"

Tapper shot him a sour glare. "Pilots have it too easy."

Eli grinned. "Should have learned to fly, I guess."

At that moment, the door slid opened to admit Taylor and Kovalic. The relief when Eli had first seen the major had been surprisingly palpable. He hadn't realized until that moment how much he'd been worried about his boss's well-being without the rest of them there to back him up. But Kovalic had been at this a long time and, from what Eli had heard about the man's adventures, Rance, the general, and a mysterious third-party had made a reasonable substitute.

Even if they couldn't hold a candle to the real thing.

"Afternoon, everyone," said Kovalic, looking around. His smile reached up to his gray eyes as he took each of them in. "It's good to see you all in one place. And, more importantly, in one piece." Pulling out one of the empty chairs, he joined them at the table; Addy swung her legs down and straightened out, and Taylor took one of the other chairs.

"So," said Tapper, not bothering to leave his position leaning against the cabinet, "what's this about, boss? We getting spun up?"

Even the normally stoic Taylor looked exhausted at that prospect, but Kovalic shook his head. "No, I've made sure that you've all got at least two solid weeks of leave. Take a break, get out of the city. Enjoy yourselves." He spared a glance at Addy and Eli. "Try to find a way to think about anything that's not work. I know how hard that can be."

Personally, that sounded good to Eli. He'd had his eye on a vacation rental about an hour outside of Salaam. Nothing to do but sit on a patio and enjoy the warm air off the water. He hadn't broached the topic with Addy just yet, but he'd been planning on it right after this meeting. If she wasn't too busy repacking their go-bags.

"I also wanted to commend all of you on the past several days," Kovalic continued. "The circumstances were unforeseen, but I wanted to say that I was honored you all had my back. Really, it means the world to me. I couldn't ask for a better team. Or family."

Eli pushed down the lump in his throat. He'd taken Addy to visit his sister, who had improved a little bit since he'd seen her last. She seemed more cognizant of her surroundings, and actually recognized Eli – even smiled at him – but she still didn't talk much. Fortunately, Eli had never had a problem filling silences; the problem was stopping once he started going. But Addy had taken it all in stride, and Meghann had taken a shine to her when they went on a slow walk around the grounds.

His sister was all the family he had left, but guilty as it made him feel, it sometimes felt like she belonged to the life of another Eli Brody. One that had never left Caledonia, never joined the Illyrican Navy, never ended up with a team of Commonwealth special operators.

No, this Eli Brody had more family, and it was sitting around him now. And the idea that he wasn't the only one to see it that way made all the difference.

"I also appreciate all the work we did to take Isabella's mole off the board," said Kovalic. He'd filled the rest of them in on all the details of the princess's plan to discredit him and the general. "I'm hoping Lawson will be willing to cooperate, even if it won't reduce his sentence much, but I have to suspect that whatever Isabella's agenda was, anything he knows probably isn't going to put a significant dent in it."

There was a grunt from the sergeant. "She's a wily one, that's for sure. Always seemed so nice in those photos where she's feeding orphans or cutting giant ribbons or whatever."

"Gotta watch out for those ceremonial scissors," said Eli.

"So," said Tapper, "if this isn't about our next job, why'd you call us in? More debriefing? I don't know that we've got anything that isn't in the very long reports we all wrote." He wasn't kidding; Eli had spent a solid eight hours writing up everything that happened during their time offworld. It had been an eventful couple of days, that had been sure, and not one that he was eager to repeat. Though he couldn't stop thinking about that reuben on Juarez 7A. Sometimes he could still taste the dressing…

"This… is a tough one," said Kovalic, breaking into his thoughts. Slowly, his gaze landed on each of them in turn. "We've all been through so much together." His chest expanded as he drew in a deep breath, and Eli blinked. He could count on one finger the number of times he'd seen Kovalic nervous, and it was right now; that lump from his throat had worked its way up into his mouth, which was suddenly dryer than the Burns Expanse.

"I don't really feel it's within my rights to ask anything *more* of you," Kovalic continued. "But I also know I can't be in the position of keeping any more secrets. There's been too much of that already, and you all deserve better."

Eli's eyes slid across the rest of the team: it seemed pretty clear that Tapper and Addy had no idea what the major was talking about. Taylor, on the other hand... the commander always kept her cards close to her chest, but something in her bearing, even stiffer than usual, told Eli that she knew what shoe was about to hit the floor with a resounding thud.

"So," said Kovalic, "in the interest of maintaining full transparency, I want to tell you exactly what I'm about to do."

CHAPTER 48

The scene in the general's office was eerily familiar, both in terms of location and the cast of characters. Rance had reclaimed her desk in the outer room and, as Kovalic entered, she was straightening a stack of flimsies with a critical eye. The yeoman wasn't about to earn herself a medal for helping her boss evade the Commonwealth authorities, but Kovalic had heard that the general had lobbied hard for a significant paygrade increase as part of their return – and, having himself earned plenty of decorations over the years, Kovalic knew which he'd prefer.

Yevgeniy, for his part, had apparently declined the general's offer of contract surveillance work, opting instead to return to his tea shop where, as he put it, the only thing he had to keep an eye on was a pot of Assam. Still, the two had parted on thawed terms, with the general murmuring something about the incompatibility of old age and regret.

A sentiment Kovalic was starting to understand. He tugged at his too-tight collar.

Rance spared him a warm smile, which transmuted suddenly into a quizzical look at his appearance, then inclined her head towards the general's inner sanctum beyond.

Within, the general was already deep in conference with both Inspector Laurent and Aidan Kester, though rather than looming over him as they had just a few days ago, they sat comfortably in the pair of chairs opposite. Someone had removed the slagged terminal from the desk, leaving it unnaturally empty, though if anything its broad expanse made the general seem even more imposing.

"Mr Lawson has not been overly cooperative so far," Laurent was saying as Kovalic entered. The inspector glanced up at him and nodded, even as he continued. "But I feel confident that he'll realize it's in his best interests."

"That would be critical," the general said, running his fingers through his beard. "There's no telling how much sensitive information he had access to during his tenure." He carefully avoided looking at Kester.

The mark still hit home: the acting director's brow, already furrowed, only creased further at the mention of his former assistant. "CID's inspector general is already conducting a thorough audit of Lawson's files and possessions, as well as my own over the same period."

Kovalic suppressed a smile. Kester may have been a useful ally in the end, but he didn't mind seeing the man a little uncomfortable. It was good for you. Built character.

"I've already recommended to the Commonwealth Executive – which has graciously seen fit to restore me to the position of Strategic Intelligence Adviser – that such a review be conducted throughout the entirety of CID, just to be on the safe side," said the general. "The amount of money Lawson was funneling was a mere fraction of what the Imperium, in its cash-strapped state, needs. Which raises the question: how many other Lawsons are there that we *don't* know about?"

Kester's jaw was tighter than a rubber band, but somehow he'd found untapped reserves of diplomacy. "A housecleaning may be long overdue," he said, grudgingly.

"Indeed. As for my team," said the general, gesturing to Kovalic, "I assume their clearances and credentials will be reinstated with all due haste. It seems the Executive has plenty on their plate with Lawson's unmasking. They're content to write off Isabella's appropriation of funds as a... misjudgment on my part. More to the point, they agree that her attempt to sideline us only confirms our status as a threat – and nobody in the Commonwealth has more insight into her thinking than we do. I believe the word the secretary-general used was 'indispensable'." His white brows arched at that, a faint gleam of amusement in his eyes.

Laurent shifted in his seat as though it had suddenly sprouted spikes. "Of course. Although I'm afraid the images given to the press during the investigation can't be retracted."

Kovalic chewed his bottom lip. He'd known there was no coming back from that. The Bureau had reported an end to the search and clarified that the people it had been looking for had merely been sought for questioning and then released. Lawson's arrest had not yet been made public, though from what Kovalic had heard, that was merely a matter of timing by the prosecutor assigned to the case.

Either way, having his picture out there definitely would make his life harder. He shifted his weight from foot to foot.

"That is unfortunate," the general said. "Though not wholly unexpected." His pale blue eyes went to Kovalic, acknowledging him for the first time. "But you've never

been one to shy away from a challenge, have you, Simon?"
He blinked and cocked his head to one side as he noticed
Kovalic's attire.

It was a while since he'd last squeezed himself into his
uniform. The major's tabs on his collar still felt unfamiliar;
he found he still expected to see the captain's double bars
when he looked in the mirror. More to the point, it probably
needed a little tailoring here and there – he wondered if
Monsieur Habib did military uniforms. "No, sir."

"Well," said the general, looking back at the pair of
officials across from him. "I look forward to seeing further
reports on what information Mr Lawson has to offer as part
of our new and improved sharing agreement." The broad
smile that crossed his face was all too genuine, and only
widened at Kester's discomfort. "If there's nothing else, I
believe Major Kovalic and I have some matters to discuss."

Laurent and Kester moved to stand, but Kovalic cleared
his throat. This was his now-or-never moment, and he found
himself surprisingly nervous as the cliff loomed before him.
"Actually, this will just take a moment, gentlemen. Don't
leave on my account."

The two froze mid-rise, and Kovalic could see Laurent's
eyes shifting back and forth between him and the general,
as if trying to see the invisible strands connecting the two of
them. Kester, for his part, gave a surreptitious glance at his
sleeve, but it seemed like he didn't have the excuse of another
meeting to beg off to, much to his dismay. Slowly, they both
sank back into their chairs.

The general's white eyebrows had risen at Kovalic's
invitation, but he put out one hand in a gesture of invitation.
"By all means. What's on your mind, major?"

Unconsciously, Kovalic found himself adopting an at-ease position, hands clasped behind his back, eyes front. Now that the moment had arrived, his chest had tightened. But as the general had said, he'd never shied away from a challenge, and he wasn't about to start now.

Sometimes, as a crotchety old sergeant liked to say, the only way out was through.

"I'd like to tender my resignation from the Special Projects Team, sir."

In the silence that ensued, Kovalic thought he could hear electrons buzzing. Laurent stared fixedly at a spot in front of him, the only concession to the news his widened eyes; Kester, meanwhile, had done a double take, shooting a speculative glance in Kovalic's direction.

The general seemed to not react at all, beyond a slow blink. After a moment, he leaned back in his chair and steepled his fingers. "I see. May I ask why you're making this request?"

"Request" was a careful choice of words. Kovalic was technically on secondment to the general's staff from his official assignment at the Marine Intelligence Group, and, as such, it was ultimately up to his superior officers in the Commonwealth Marine Corps whether to recall him from his tenure here – or for the general himself to ask for his dismissal. Kovalic just went where the orders stated.

So it was well within the rights for the general to inquire and, ultimately, make the decision.

"Permission to speak freely, sir?"

"I've never known you to be less than frank, major."

Kovalic ducked his head. "I'm... tired."

The general raised an eyebrow. "Understandable, after everything we've been through: first the Novan Liberation Front, then this whole Lawson affair. I believe you have some leave due to you –"

"That's not it, sir. I'm tired of the whole…" Kovalic waved a hand, "…cat-and-mouse game. No sooner do we neutralize one threat than another rears its head. Like you said a moment ago: we found one mole, but how many others are lurking out there?" He shook his head. "It's not what I signed up for. I think I can ultimately be of more use to the Commonwealth by returning to my active duty post."

Genuine surprise crossed Laurent's face, while Kester seemed to be covering something that looked suspiciously like a smirk. In an ideal world, Kovalic wouldn't be doing this in front of them, but it was all too easy to walk back a decision made in private.

"That is most… disappointing," said the general at last, his voice carefully neutral. "Especially in the light of our recent progress. We've only just discovered Isabella's nature – her agenda remains a mystery to us. This move to take me off the board, Commander Taylor's report about the Illyricans buying up palladium… it all speaks to a larger stratagem. We're just starting to analyze the surveillance footage of Isabella's compound retrieved from Ofeibia Xi to see what else we can glean. There's more work to be done."

"There always is." Kovalic hesitated, then plowed forward. "But this isn't where I need to be right now."

The old man eyed him, blue gaze inscrutable as ever. "Then there's nothing I can say to make you reconsider?"

Kovalic straightened his back. "I've made my decision, general."

With a nod, the older man reached for a tablet and stylus. "Well, far be it from me to keep someone against their will. You hereby stand relieved of your position as commanding officer for the Special Projects Team, effective immediately. I'll contact General Wyman in personnel to have her process the order." He scribbled something on the tablet and passed it across the desk to Kovalic. "I'll also notify Commander Taylor that she will be acting as CO until further notice." The general cocked his head to one side. "Unless you've already informed her of this decision."

Kovalic's hands clutched each other more tightly behind his back. "I'll leave it to Commander Taylor to discuss the particulars with you, but it is my understanding that she is shortly being recalled for an opportunity in NICOM."

"Ah," said the general. "The role as Admiral Chatterjee's chief of staff, yes." Fingers drummed across the desk. "Am I also then to assume that Sergeant Tapper will be making a similar request, given your long association?"

"That's up to the sergeant, sir."

"I'll take that as a yes. Very well." He glanced at Kester, brandishing a self-deprecating smile. "It seems my team is much reduced. Lieutenant Brody and Specialist Sayers are both very adept, but two people severely limits our operational capacity." The general let out a pent-up sigh. "I'm afraid the Special Projects Team has reached the end of its present path. A fact you'll no doubt be delighted to hear, Aidan, given our contretemps over it."

The acting CID director straightened his tie. "I can't say I'm sorry, Adaj. Your people have always played fast and loose, working outside of the chain of command." Kester relented slightly. "But I agree that Major Kovalic and his team managed to accomplish a great deal in their tenure." He looked up at Kovalic and dipped his head. "I'm sure the Corps will be glad to have you back."

Kovalic returned the nod. "Thank you, director." Summoning his last ounce of wherewithal, he reached up and peeled the unit patch from his shoulder, then stepped forward and placed it on the general's uncluttered desk. "I appreciate everything we've accomplished together, sir. And I wish you the best of luck from here on out. Perhaps our paths will cross again."

The general made no move to pick up the patch, though Kovalic thought he saw a bolt of sadness cross the older man's face as his eyes landed upon it. "And to you, major," he said quietly. "I hope you find whatever it is you're looking for."

Kovalic straightened, if not unburdened then at least through the worst of it. "There's only one thing I'm looking for, general. And it's the same reason I first agreed to work with you. I've given more than two decades of my life to this service for a singular purpose, and I feel I've been drifting farther and farther from that goal."

Kester's head swiveled back and forth between the two; the only thing he was missing was a bucket of popcorn. As Kovalic's words hung in the air, he inserted himself into the silence. "And what's that, Major Kovalic?"

Fixing the director with a hard stare that made the well-dressed man shrink in his seat, Kovalic smiled. "Earth, Director Kester."

And with that, he executed a smooth turn on his heel and walked out of the general's office, leaving the three men gaping in his wake. The road ahead was full of twists and turns and he had no idea long it would take, but he found that if he squinted he could still see, just over the horizon, a slowly spinning globe of blue-and-green hanging in space, a world that he hadn't set foot on for more than twenty years, but one that he still saw every night in his dreams – that the merest smell could bring him back to, as surely as if he'd been teleported. He'd put it off far too long, and the last few days had made him realize that the opportunity would never be handed to him on a silver platter; he had to make the choice. The Illyricans had taken it away from him, but damn it, he was determined to do whatever was necessary to take it back.

Home. He was going home.

ACKNOWLEDGEMENTS

It's been a long time coming, but it appears we've reached the end... at least, of this particular chapter.

Even though the author's name is on the cover, every book is the work of more than just one person. Yes, it turns out that authors do not design their own covers, edit their own words, or lovingly print out each copy on their home inkjet. Who knew! So, allow me to extend my gratitude to the many key people involved in this book's production.

The folks at Angry Robot have been very supportive of this series since the earliest days, for which they have my deep appreciation: Eleanor Teasdale, Gemma Creffield, Simon Spanton, and Desola Coker all did their utmost with this book to help be the best it could be. Robin Triggs ably took over editorial duties, making sure that everything made sense, and copyeditor Andrew Hook had the unenviable task of adding all the words I occasionally forget to include. Karen Smith designed a (literally) kicking cover.

Almost a decade ago, my agent Joshua Bilmes took a chance on my first book starring Simon Kovalic and Eli Brody, and he has always been enthusiastic about their subsequent adventures. Thanks to him and the rest of the JABberwocky crew, especially James Farner, Susan Velazquez, and Valentina Sainato.

Even more so than some of my previous books, I owe a lot to my veteran beta reading crew on this one. Antony Johnston, Jason Snell, and Brian Lyngaas all offered insightful comments to help improve the story. As usual, in matters of science and physics, I turned to Gene Gordon, who pointed out the many ways that somebody crawling across a very, very fast train could go wrong. It should go without saying that any remaining errors all rest on my own shoulders, to which I can only say "Creative license!"

The world of the writer is a solitary one, so I continue to appreciate the online communities that keep me feeling connected (especially in the increasingly fractured social media environment). My pals at Relay FM, The Incomparable, the Fancy Cats, and all the listeners and readers at Clockwise, Six Colors, and The Rebound always make me feel at home. Special thanks to my many writer friends who put up with me and offered steadfast encouragement on those days where griping and handwringing gets the best of me: Helene Wecker, Adam Rakunas, Eric Scott Fischl, Auston Habershaw, and Zac Topping.

My parents, Harold Moren and Sally Beecher, have been my biggest cheerleaders throughout all the ups and downs of life; love to you both. And my extended Beecher/Kane/Moren clan are the best street team any writer could ask for.

Last, but very far from least, my wife Kat is the absolute

THE ARMAGEDDON PROTOCOL

best. I have literally no idea what I would do without her unflagging support. She pulls no punches in her critiques of my writing, and these books (and even these acknowledgements!) would not even be half as good without her input. This is also the first book I wrote since our son was born, and seeing his goofy grin every day was often all the moral support I needed. I love you both more than anything.

ABOUT THE AUTHOR

DAN MOREN is the author of the Galactic Cold War series of novels, as well as a freelance writer and prolific podcaster. A former senior editor at *Macworld*, his work has also appeared in the *Boston Globe*, *Popular Science*, *Fast Company*, and many others. He co-hosts tech podcasts Clockwise and The Rebound, writes and hosts nerdy quiz show Inconceivable!, and is a regular panelist on the award-winning podcast The Incomparable. Dan lives with his family in Somerville, Massachusetts, where he is never far from a set of polyhedral dice.